# I WILL FIND HER

# ALSO BY A.M. STRONG AND SONYA SARGENT

## THE PATTERSON BLAKE THRILLER SERIES

*Sister Where Are You* • *Is She Really Gone*
*All The Dead Girls* • *Never Let Her Go*
*Dark Road From Sunrise* • *I Will Find Her*

## PATTERSON BLAKE PREQUEL

*Never Lie to Me*

## STAND-ALONE PSYCHOLOGICAL THRILLERS

*The Last Girl Left* • *Gravewater Lake*

# I WILL FIND HER

### A PATTERSON BLAKE THRILLER

## A.M. STRONG
## SONYA SARGENT

**WEST STREET**

West Street Publishing

This is a work of fiction. Characters, names, places, and events are products of the author's imagination. Any similarity to events or places, or real persons, living or dead, is purely coincidental.

Copyright © 2024 by A. M. Strong & Sonya Sargent
All rights reserved.

No part of this book may be reproduced in any form or by any electronic or mechanical means, including information storage and retrieval systems, without written permission from the author, except for the use of brief quotations in a book review.

NO AI TRAINING: Without in any way limiting the author's [and publisher's] exclusive rights under copyright, any use of this publication to "train" generative artificial intelligence (AI) technologies to generate text is expressly prohibited. The author reserves all rights to license uses of this work for generative AI training and development of machine learning language models.

Cover art and interior design by Bad Dog Media, LLC.

ISBN: 978-1-942207-57-3

*For Izzie and Hayden*

# ONE

**ONE WEEK AGO**

CARL WATCHED the fly land on his mother's pallid, dead face and crawl inside her mouth, even as the stench that filled the kitchen assaulted his nostrils, making him gag.

A small TV on the wall near the breakfast nook provided a surreal backdrop of inane chatter—a trio of female morning show presenters going nuts over the latest celebrity engagement. A couple who were apparently doomed to failure given the film actor groom's roving ways. If Ma hadn't been lying on the kitchen floor with her housecoat open to reveal plump, sagging breasts, a swollen stomach, and flabby thighs, the skin of which had turned a purplish blue, she might have found the show fascinating. As it was, the microwave popcorn she had been preparing when death took her would remain forever uneaten, and the undignified display of postmortem nudity would forever be seared into Carl's brain.

He stared down at the corpse, watched another fly circle lazily around her head, even as his disbelief turned to grief. In the forty-two years the pair had shared the farmhouse, he had never contemplated this moment. Never even given it a thought.

Ma had always been there, and as far as he was concerned, she always would be. They were separated only when Carl was driving his big rig, taking pallets of TVs, boxes of cheap Chinese-made clothing, and even the occasional load of watermelons or beefsteak tomatoes to wherever his employer said they needed to go. But at the end of his trips, when he returned home hungry and tired, Ma had always been there with a hot cup of cocoa and one of her freshly made apple pies. And later, after Carl had taken a hot shower and climbed into bed, she would bring Angel to him, ready and willing to perform her nightly duties.

*Angel.*

The thought crashed through Carl's mind like a sledgehammer. He had been gone for eighteen days, crisscrossing the south, driving back and forth in his rig. And who knew how long Ma had been dead on that floor. Judging by the decomposition—even with the air conditioning running at the arctic levels she preferred—it had been a while.

Carl tore his gaze away from Ma's bloated corpse and raced to the back of the house. The door to her bedroom stood open. The same bedroom she had occupied since he had first laid eyes upon her sixteen years ago in Santa Fe. She truly had been an angel, bartending at a local watering hole called Amy's Roadhouse. That was back in the days when he still had a relationship with his father, who had walked out on his mother the previous year, leaving Carl, then in his early twenties, at the farmhouse and relocating to Santa Fe where he had taken a job with the railroad. At first, Carl had visited him often, driving his beater of a pickup truck five hours east. That was how he had come to be in the roadhouse that evening, downing beers with his old man and talking about nothing in particular. And there she was, his Angel, although back then she was going by the name of Stacy. He later learned that her real name was Julie Blake, and that she was using her friend's identity and driver's license because she wasn't yet twenty-one.

It was a Saturday night. He was supposed to head home the

next day ready for work on Monday morning. Instead, he decided to extend his trip and call in sick. He spent every evening of the next week visiting the roadhouse, staying until closing on the nights that Angel was working, and leaving after one drink on those nights that she wasn't. She was flirty. Vivacious. Gorgeous. The most beautiful creature he'd ever seen. She also had a boyfriend. A loser guitarist and singer who was doing his best to sound like Trent Rezner, possibly because they shared the same first name, and failing miserably. Even so, he slipped her his number one boozy night, scrawling it on a napkin and pushing it across the bar.

"If you get bored watching the sluts hit on your boyfriend, call me," he had said in a slurred voice. "I'll treat you better than he ever will."

It was a crass come-on fueled by one too many pints of Budweiser. He woke up on his father's couch the next morning with a headache and a healthy dose of embarrassment. He'd blown it with his Angel. Carl was so sure she wouldn't talk to him again that he didn't go to the bar that night. Instead, he decided to head back to the farm the following day. Then, out of the blue, came the midnight call, and in that moment, he knew she would be his forever.

Now, Carl stood in the doorway of the room where his Angel had lived for the past decade and a half and stared in horror at the empty space beyond. She was gone, and so was his daughter. All that remained to show that they had ever been there were a few meager scraps of clothing, a stuffed bear that Cherub had named Yogi after the old cartoons he sometimes let her watch, and an empty inhaler used to treat his daughter's asthma.

Carl's gaze lingered on the discarded inhaler as if it would somehow provide a clue regarding what had happened in the days that he had been away. But it didn't. Instead, it nailed home the fact that his family was gone. All of them.

Then another thought occurred to him. Angel wouldn't have left on foot. It would have been too challenging. Especially with the kid dragging her down. The interstate, where she might have been able to thumb a ride, was a good fifteen miles distant. The closest town was even further away. And she didn't know the area beyond the small world of her bedroom and the scrap of land visible through the farmhouse windows.

Carl ran back through the house, peered out of the living room window, and his worst nightmare was confirmed. His mother's old Sebring, the one she hadn't driven in ten years, was gone. He could see the spot where it should have been parked—where he had left it after he last drove the vehicle a couple of months before—as a barren patch of dirt surrounded by ankle-high weeds.

He stood in the window for a long minute, staring at the bald oblong of weed-free ground. His Angel had vanished. She had taken his daughter, stolen Ma's car, and driven away. He turned back to the kitchen and the slowly decomposing corpse within.

And in that moment, he knew.

This was all Angel's fault. After everything he had done for her, opened his home and treated her with love and kindness, fed her, clothed her, taken her to his bed and let her bear his offspring, she had killed his mother and ran away like the worthless, ungrateful bitch that she was. And by now, she could be anywhere. She might be telling the police any number of lies about him. Repeating those same lies to her whore of an FBI agent sister.

The fury came all at once.

It washed over him like a tsunami, fast and powerful. He turned to the 50" flat-screen TV on its stand in the living room, gripped it by the edges, and heaved it onto the floor with a crack of broken glass. He picked up a dirty mug from the coffee table, it's inside lined with a bloom of green mold, and hurled it against the wall. Then he tipped the coffee table over, spilling magazines from the grocery store checkout aisle, an ashtray full of cigarette butts from Ma's once daily morning nicotine fix, and a gaggle of half-empty pill bottles, across the carpet.

This went on for a further ten minutes.

He tore through the living room and into the kitchen, sweeping crockery onto the floor, ripping the smaller kitchen TV from the wall with a rage-filled scream and heaving it across the room where it shattered, ending the morning show hosts' ridiculous babbling. And in the abrupt silence that followed, he came to a halt; the anger subsiding almost as quickly as it had arrived. Rage would get him nowhere. He needed to assess the situation, see just how bad it really was. See if Angel even had the means to flee. To hide from him.

He turned and left the kitchen, went to his bedroom and checked the secret compartment under a floorboard near the closet where he kept a stash of fifty-dollar bills. Four thousand dollars rolled and secured by rubber bands. They were still there. She hadn't found his hiding place. Or at least, she hadn't found this one. There were four other such hidey-holes in the house, all of them filled with cash. Money earned through years of hauling goods across the country and squirreled away because Carl hated banks. Didn't trust them one little bit.

He checked every location in turn, his fear easing with each undiscovered stash, until there was only one left. A cashbox hidden under the insulation in the attic. When he climbed the attic stairs, found the small metal box right where he'd left it, he breathed a sigh of relief. Wherever Angel had gone, she hadn't taken any money. That would make finding her easier.

Except that when he opened the box, it was empty. Thousands of dollars, enough money for her to get far away from this place and disappear. But worse, so was the gun he'd hidden there. A pistol his father had left behind when he walked out all those years ago.

Angel wasn't just flush with cash and driving a stolen car, she was also armed, and that was bad. Like, really bad.

# TWO

CARL SAT in the shattered mess of his living room and stared at the empty spot his TV had recently occupied. He stayed that way for over an hour in an almost trancelike state, a thousand thoughts swirling through his mind. Memories of his mother and Angel. Of the years they had shared and the ones to come that had been stolen from him by what had occurred in the days he had been gone. And of his current situation. Angel was out there somewhere, running hard and fast. Where she would go and what she would do was anyone's guess. He half expected a SWAT team to kick in his door at any moment, or a clutch of FBI agents to surround the house, yelling for his surrender.

But none of that happened. The home lay under a blanket of unusual quietude, the sound of talk shows and reality TV that had been a constant backdrop while his mother was alive forever silenced by her passing, and Carl's destructive, if brief, swell of rage.

Angel hadn't gone to the police. That much was obvious. Because, thinking about it, he wouldn't be sitting here if she had. They would have been waiting for him the moment he returned home and arrested him before he even discovered that she was gone and his mother was dead.

And he probably had the threats to thank for that. He had told her over and over again that if she ever ran, went to the cops with those lies about being abducted, or tried to contact her family, that federal agent sister of hers, he would kill them all. And even though he wasn't sure the capacity lay within him for such deadly violence, Angel didn't know that. And it was for her own good. She was his and always would be. He knew what was best for her. Loved and nurtured her. Gave her a life she couldn't find anywhere else.

What did she do in return? She betrayed him. Killed his mother and ran away with his daughter. And try as he might, Carl could not think of where to look. Except for one place. A small, nondescript home in a suburb of Queens. A place she had talked about often during those early years, when she begged him to take her there and cried herself to sleep. He knew the home well. Had been there several times over the last decade and a half when his travels had taken him to New York. He'd been there even more times on the internet, stalking her father, mother, and sister. Her parents had split up, but she wouldn't know that. Her sister had become an FBI agent, but she wouldn't know that, either. All she would know was her home in Queens.

It was a long shot given his threat to kill her family, but it was all that he had. Besides, he couldn't stay at the farmhouse. Not now. It was a ticking time bomb. Even if Angel hadn't yet gotten up the courage to spread her lies, he couldn't guarantee that she wouldn't do so in the future. Then there really would be a SWAT team at his door. No, he had to get the hell out of there. Vanish, just as his Angel had.

But first, there was something else that he needed to do. A task the very thought of which turned his stomach. But it had to be done. He couldn't leave his mother on the kitchen floor. He also couldn't report her death and give her the sendoff that she so richly deserved. Much as it pained him, there would be no funeral for his mother. No one coming back to the house to drink beer and commiserate on his loss. Not that he knew anyone well enough to invite them to a wake. He hadn't dared let a soul inside the house since Angel had come to live with them. His friends, the few he'd made in high school, had grown distant over the years. He knew a few people in passing from his employment but kept them at arm's length. He had a reputation as a loner and liked it that way. It was one of the things that had attracted him to driving big rigs in the first place. There was no one to pry into his business. It was just him, his truck, the open road, and solitude.

Carl rose to his feet, steeled himself for what he had to do next. Even if he couldn't put Ma in a shady plot next to his grandparents in Greenacre Cemetery, he could at least find a place where she would be happy to rest for eternity. And he knew just the spot. He stepped outside and went to the barn, found a shovel, then walked to the back of the house and across the junk strewn yard to a patch of ground upon which sat a westward facing bench with a view of the distant Agassiz Peak, the second-highest mountain in Arizona. It was one of his mother's favorite places on the property. She would often step outside on a summer's night and watch the sun drop behind the mountains in a fiery display that never ceased to take her breath away.

It was a perfect place to bury her.

He'd never dug a grave before, but how hard could it be?

He soon found out.

The ground was hard and difficult to cut into with the shovel. After the better part of two hours, he was barely three feet down in a hole nowhere near wide enough to contain his mother's girth and probably not long enough, either. Even worse, the ground was full of rocks, at least one of which was too big to move on his own. There was no way he was going to reach the commonly accepted depth of six feet under. He could also feel the pressure of time weighing upon him. His risk increased with every passing minute he stayed at the farmhouse. His chance of finding Angel before she did something stupid diminished in tandem. Like it or not, he would have to settle for a shallow grave. Which meant turning his attention to the task he had been dreading more than anything. Moving his mother from the kitchen to her final resting place.

This, like digging the grave, turned out to be harder than he expected. The old woman was a literal dead weight. Worse, despite closing her robe, it fell back open the moment he tried to move her, revealing even more purple, lifeless flesh than before. Her tongue, swollen in her mouth, poked from between her lips as if she were making a final commentary on her son's undignified handling of the situation. Carl could barely stand to look down as he dragged the body out from behind the kitchen island, through the house, and toward the back door.

Thirty minutes later, covered in sweat and gasping for breath, he finally deposited her in the barely adequate grave he had prepared. Half an hour after that, about ready to faint from exhaustion, Carl threw the last shovelful of dirt atop the grave and sank down onto the bench, staring at his handiwork.

It was hardly perfect. With Ma in the hole, the dirt rose above the surrounding ground like a miniature hill. The grave would be obvious to anyone who stepped into the yard, but there was nothing he could do about that. He certainly wasn't going to dig another grave, exhume his mother moments after burying her, and move the body. And even if he had possessed the energy to do such a thing, it wouldn't have made any difference. The ground would be just as impossible to dig through, regardless of the spot he chose. It was enough that she had been given a burial, and certainly more dignified than slowly rotting naked on the kitchen floor, save for a flimsy housecoat that wouldn't stay closed. He briefly thought about marking the grave with a cross, but swiftly dispelled the notion. It wasn't like he had one lying around, and he wasn't about to waste the time to make one.

He had better things to do. Like get out of there before someone with a badge showed up asking questions. And he knew exactly where he needed to go...

# THREE

**NOW**

PATTERSON BLAKE SAT in her camper parked in front of Amy's Roadhouse in Santa Fe, in an almost comatose state of shock.

"There's another one. A postcard," her father had said when he had called her less than an hour before. "It's from Julie. Your sister is alive."

The words still echoed in Patterson's mind, playing in a loop as if they were a stuck record. After all the years wondering if her sister was alive or dead, grieving her in absentia, following her trail across the country hoping at least she would find a body and be able to put her sister to rest, a postcard. Just like that, out of the blue. At first, Patterson hadn't believed it. She had questioned her father relentlessly. Was it Julie's handwriting? Did the postcard look old? Where was it from? What was the date on the postmark?

He had answered each of her queries with weary determination. Yes, it was Julie's handwriting. No, the postcard didn't look old. It was from San Diego and was postmarked four days prior. He had even photographed the postcard with his phone and sent it to her.

When she saw it, Patterson knew the postcard was real. There was no mistaking the way that her sister had signed it, with the swooping, Curly J at the beginning of her nickname, and the equally flamboyant way she finished the Y. She had spent so long looking at her sister's other postcards that Patterson would have recognized the handwriting anywhere. She had forced back a sob, wiped tears from her eyes, even as her mind spun. Other than the postmark, there was nothing to indicate where Julie was right now. But there were ways that she could find out.

The FBI had a field office in San Diego, and she was sure they would be more than willing to make inquiries, especially if the request came from her boyfriend Jonathan Grant, Assistant Special Agent in Charge and next in line for SAC at the New York field office. Maybe, if she was lucky, someone would remember speaking to her sister, or seeing her mail the postcard. It was a long shot, but it was all that she had, at least until she could get there, which would take the better part of the day, and start searching for herself.

She didn't want to wait that long, because she knew all too well that in cases like this, every second counted. Julie had mailed the postcard many days before, giving her sister plenty of time to leave the area, but even if her sister hadn't left the city, it was still a vast area to search. The odds of finding her in such a densely packed metropolis, especially when she could be using another name, were a million to one. The sooner they started, the better.

Which was why she had placed a call to Grant immediately after hanging up with her father. When she told him about the postcard, and what she needed, he was more than happy to help and agreed to contact the San Diego field office the minute they were done talking. He also volunteered to send an agent to her father's house later that day to collect the postcard so the forensics lab could examine it. He wasn't sure what they would find, if anything, but he wanted to leave nothing to chance.

Before ending the call, he had left her with a sobering piece of advice. "Don't get your hopes up, even in the face of what appears to be overwhelming evidence. Until we find her, until you stand face-to-face with your sister and know for sure that she is alive, nothing has changed. Handwriting can be faked. This could be someone trying to throw you off the trail. Send you searching for ghosts."

Patterson knew Grant was only trying to protect her, but she also knew that the handwriting was not fake. Her sister really had sent that card. She was sure of it.

Now, she sat staring at her screen, reading the words on the oblong slip of cardboard over and over again, almost as if they would impart some hidden meaning—provide some extra nugget of information—if only she studied it enough.

*Mom, Dad, Sis,*

*I know it's been a long time, and I'm sorry for all the heartache my disappearance must have caused. I can't tell you where I've been all these years or where I am now. It's too dangerous. There is a bad man. He said that he would hurt you if I ever left him, and I'm afraid that he might mean it, which is why you all need to be careful.*

*When it's safe to come home, I will. Promise.*

*In the meantime, please know that I am safe, and that I love and miss you all.*

*Jelly*

Eventually, Patterson put the phone down and pulled herself together. She wiped the tears from her eyes, grabbed a protein shake from the camper's small fridge in lieu of breakfast, and called her father back to tell him that someone would be around later for the postcard. Then, with a heart full of hope and a head full of questions, she slipped into the driver's seat and started the engine. A few minutes later, she pulled out onto the highway and left Amy's Roadhouse in her rearview mirror. Fifteen minutes after that, she was on the interstate and speeding west toward San Diego, and what she hoped would be the last stop on her quest to find Julie.

# FOUR

IT HAD TAKEN Carl the better part of four days to drive from the family homestead fifty miles north of Flagstaff in Arizona, to the New York borough of Queens. Since Angel had stolen his mother's car, the only vehicle available to him had been his pickup truck, which he wasn't entirely sure would make it all the way to the East Coast given its age and the number of miles the vehicle had racked up over the last twenty-three years. But that was not why he had taken it slow, driving at or below the speed limit the entire way, even on the lonely stretches of highway where he could have put his foot down and flew.

It wasn't that he wanted to delay his arrival in Queens. Far from it. He was anxious to reach the former home of Julie Blake, which was the only place he could think that she might have gone. And even if she hadn't shown up there, she could very well have contacted her family despite his threats of violence against them hanging over her head. But he could not afford to get pulled over or otherwise run afoul of the law. Although he found it unlikely, he still didn't know for sure that Angel—he refused to think of her as Julie even now that she was gone—had not contacted law enforcement. At best, a traffic stop would show that he was driving east toward Queens and the Blake family home. At worst, he might show up as a person of interest in a sixteen-year kidnapping case when they ran his license.

It was a risk he couldn't take, so he had stuck to the speed limit, ignored his urges to drive faster, and stopped every night at a motel that took cash, figuring the less of a trail he left, the better.

He had arrived at his destination the night before and checked into yet another squalid dump of a motel, paying for two nights of accommodation up front, again with cold hard cash. The room was filthy and outdated, with a faint odor of mold hanging in the air. It was not worth the nightly rate, but it was also the sort of place where he would go unnoticed. Where no one would ask questions.

After a restless night during which he could think of nothing but Angel, he had risen at dawn and driven to the house where she had grown up and where her father still lived. After that, he sat in his truck and watched.

Now, four hours later, he was still there. So was the old station wagon that he assumed belonged to Angel's father. It was sitting in the driveway all morning and into the early afternoon without moving, even as the old man came and went a couple of times, walking from his front door to the detached garage and back with a toolbox in his hand. He still worked for the MTA, New York's transportation authority, but hadn't gone to work, which probably meant that it was his day off. Of Angel, he had seen no sign, which didn't surprise him. If she had been there, then undoubtedly cops would have been there too, milling around in a frenzy. Not to mention the FBI. Her sister, Patterson, was a fed, and would surely have been involved.

Carl relaxed a little. Angel had not run home. But that didn't mean she hadn't contacted her family at some point during the days she had been missing. Her father had never changed his phone number, never sold the home and moved, presumably because he hoped that one day, against all odds, his daughter would get in touch.

Carl had to know.

The question was, how? He couldn't exactly walk up to the front door, knock on it, and introduce himself to her father as the man who had kept his daughter locked up against her will for the last sixteen years. There was only one way that conversation ended. But there was another way, and it involved Angel's sister.

He had been keeping tabs on Patterson Blake even before she joined the FBI. His interest had only grown more intense once she became a federal law enforcement officer. It hadn't been easy. The younger Blake sister shied away from social media, maintained no online presence save for a single Yelp account.

Patterson liked to post restaurant reviews.

That had given him all he needed to track her movements. Imagine his surprise when, a few weeks before, he had noticed that she was reviewing restaurants in cities associated with Angel's movements the summer that he had met her. There was a review for Portillo's in Chicago, the city where her sister had attended college and had also been the starting point for her ill-fated road trip. There was another in St. Louis. By this time, Carl's suspicions had been aroused. He placed a call to the FBI's New York field office—using a burner phone and withholding his name, of course—and asked to speak with her on an urgent matter. They had told him she was on leave and tried to put him through to another agent, at which point he had hung up and ditched the phone. But it told him all he needed to know.

Patterson Blake was on her sister's trail.

The question was, how much did she know?

There was only one way to find out. He would have to watch her. Observe her movements. But he couldn't do that from afar. Luckily, his job as a long-distance trucker gave him a freedom of movement most other occupations lacked. Like many long-distance truckers, he was employed on a subcontract basis, which gave him the opportunity to pick his jobs. It hadn't taken long to locate a load destined for Oklahoma City—the next obvious stop on Patterson Blake's cross-country investigation—and get it assigned to him.

Leaving Angel in the care of his mother, Carl had driven the cargo to its destination, dropped it off, then checked into the same hotel that Angel and her friend had stayed at all those years before, figuring that Patterson would probably do the same. And she did. After that, it was easy to watch her. He'd even struck up a conversation at one point while he was sitting in the hotel bar. The place had become his favorite spot to watch her come and go from the hotel, and late one night, when she returned from an evening out, she veered from the lobby and approached him as he sat on a barstool sipping a pint.

For a brief moment, he thought that she was on to him, but it soon became apparent that she just wanted a drink. By the time she left, his heart was racing. After that, he was more careful. He trailed her to Dallas, and then on to Amarillo. By that time, it had become obvious that she didn't have a clue where her sister was. He had picked up another load, this time heading west, and left Patterson Blake to her own devices. A short time later, he had arrived home to find his mother dead and Angel missing.

Which was what had brought him to the Blake sisters' family home. Now, he sat in his old pickup truck and contemplated the plan he had been mulling over. It was a risk, but far outweighed by the rewards. And it would be possible thanks to his relentless stalking of Patterson Blake. Taking a deep breath, Carl exited the truck. He looked down at himself, at the black cargo pants and white polo shirt that he was wearing. The clothes wouldn't have been his first choice of outfit for what he was about to do, but they would suffice.

Running a hand through his hair to pat it down, he crossed the road, walked up the path of Angel's old house to her front door, and rang the bell.

The man who answered looked like the weight of the world was on his shoulders. His face was lined, giving him the appearance of a person much older than his years. His salt and pepper hair was thinning. A haunting sorrow glimmered in his eyes.

"Can I help you?" He asked.

Carl swallowed. He forced his arms to his sides even though he wanted to fold them, because he'd read an article on body language in one of his mother's old magazines which said that this posture instilled trust and confidence. Finally, he managed to put on a thin smile. "I certainly hope so, Mr. Blake. My name is Special Agent Daniel Brent. I work with your daughter at the Bureau, and I have some questions about her sister."

# FIVE

AFTER CALLING HIS YOUNGER DAUGHTER, Franklin Blake spent the rest of the morning and into the early afternoon going between pacing his living room and obsessively looking down at the postcard from Julie, which he had placed message side up on the coffee table.

It almost seemed impossible that after so many years, a decade and a half, his missing child should reappear in such a startling way. He had almost given up hope of ever finding her alive, had all but accepted that she had met a terrible fate somewhere on that lonely road trip not long after he had lost touch with her all those years ago. Some of that was thanks to Patterson, who had done her best to prepare him for the worst. As an FBI agent, she knew the stats regarding missing persons, especially young attractive women, better than most. But the passing of time had taken its toll, too. With each year that went by, his resolve had faded, just a little more.

Yet even in his darkest moments, when Franklin had imagined the worst, there was always that slight glimmer of optimism, barely more than a faint pulsing light in the blackness of his despair. Until someone told him she was dead, until they found a body, the door was not closed.

Now that glimmer had blossomed into full-fledged brilliance. Against all the odds, Julie had reached out and let him know she was safe. Or at least, that she was alive. Because the content and tone of that postcard told a story that turned Franklin's blood cold, and two lines in particular.

*There is a bad man. He said that he would hurt you if I ever left him…*

The words echoed in Franklin's mind, conjuring up a scenario too awful to contemplate. That someone had snatched his daughter during her road trip, had kept her captive all these years. And he could only imagine the abuse she had endured. One only had to watch the true crime shows on television to know what happened in such circumstances. And even though Franklin had tried not to watch those shows, had done his best to avoid them, a certain morbid curiosity—or was it self-torture—had sometimes gotten the better of him.

Franklin read the postcard for the twentieth time since talking to Patterson, standing with his arms folded and staring down at it.

By now, his younger daughter would surely be on her way to San Diego. It was ironic that he had tried to talk her out of chasing Julie's ghost. Had tried to stop her from taking the same trip that his missing daughter had made, although years ago. But Patterson had been adamant. Always strong-willed, she had grasped the challenge of finding out what happened to Julie with both hands. Yet at every turn, Julie had slipped further away, until Patterson had arrived in Santa Fe, and run up against a brick wall. The trail had gone cold. The last person to have seen her alive, a teenaged girl she had met at the hostel where she and her musician boyfriend were staying, had claimed that Julie had caught her boyfriend kissing another girl at the bar where he was playing a gig, returned to the hostel, then climbed into the truck of an unknown man and driven off somewhere around midnight. That was the last time anyone saw of her, and since the pickup truck driver was unidentified—what Patterson called an unsub, or unknown subject—there was nowhere else to look. And then came the postcard, that in an almost unbelievable turn of events had provided not only a place to look for Julie, but renewed hope.

And there was more. Jonathan Grant was sending an agent to pick up the postcard so that the forensics lab at the New York field office could examine it. And even though Patterson had warned her father not to get his hopes up, that the lab might find nothing of relevance, he couldn't help but feel excited. Which was why, when his doorbell rang a little after one in the afternoon, he hurried to answer.

The man standing on his stoop quickly identified himself as Special Agent Daniel Brent. Franklin wasted no time inviting him inside and led him straight to the postcard.

"My daughter told me to put it down and refrain from handling it," he said, even as the special agent looked down at the postcard, his eyebrows raised. "I hope your forensics lab can do something with it."

The special agent was silent for a moment, then he nodded. "I'm sure that they can." He reached down, picked up the postcard and slipped it into the back pocket of his trousers.

Franklin was momentarily taken aback. "Shouldn't you put that into an evidence bag or something?"

Special Agent Brent nodded. "I have one in the car."

"Oh. Of course." Franklin's gaze dropped to the empty spot on the coffee table where the postcard had previously sat. "You'll return it to me once you're done, right?"

"Absolutely." The special agent looked around the room before he stepped toward the fireplace and reached for a framed photograph sitting on the mantle. A photo of Julie standing in front of a car sculpture outside of Amarillo. It had been taken not long before she vanished and had come from a pack of photos

Patterson had given to her dad after retrieving the negatives from a witness she had interviewed. Someone who had briefly known Julie back then. A friend of the man she had been dating. The same man who had cheated on her and sent his daughter running into the arms of a stranger with a pickup truck who had driven her off into the unknown. Of all the photographs in the pack, this was his favorite. Julie was standing in front of the car, which was standing half buried in the earth by its front-end, just like the other cars in sculpture. It had become a tradition to graffiti the cars with spray paint, leaving messages behind for those who came after. The message Julie had left was dear to his heart. It simply read, *for you, dad*, because she had known he always wanted to visit the strange sculpture, which he had read about years before in a magazine.

The special agent lifted the framed photograph from the shelf and looked at it for a moment before uttering a single word under his breath. "Angel."

"I'm sorry?" Franklin wondered if he had misheard the agent.

"Your daughter," the man replied quickly, placing the photograph back on the mantle. "She was so pretty. An angel."

"Yes, she was." Franklin swallowed the lump that rose in his throat. His eyes dropped to the man's trouser pocket. "Please take good care of the postcard."

"Naturally." Special Agent Brent tapped his pocket before turning toward the living room door. "I should get this back to the office right away."

"Of course." Franklin led the man out of the living room and through the hallway to the front door. He watched him descend the steps and hurry down the front path before turning away and closing the door.

He retreated into the living room and sank onto the sofa. With the postcard gone, the house felt empty, as if the small piece of carboard had carried with it a piece of his daughter.

Now that the FBI agent had taken it, she was once again lost, and Franklin was alone.

He sat there for what seemed like forever, but was probably no more than thirty minutes, before the doorbell rang again. Surprised, Franklin rose to his feet and answered, wondering if the FBI agent had returned for some reason. But instead, he found another man standing there. This one was wearing a black suit over a pressed white shirt. His black tie was impeccably knotted. A pair of dark sunglasses hid his eyes. The man's scrupulously neat attire, posture, and clean-shaven face reminded Franklin of every fed he had ever met in the years that Patterson had been with the Bureau.

"Can I help you?" Franklin asked, even as a twinge of apprehension rattled through his mind. This visitor was so neatly groomed and official looking that he couldn't help but realize how *unofficial* his last house guest's attire and body language had been. Something he hadn't noticed at the time.

"Special Agent Lance Driscoll," the man replied, slipping a hand into his pocket and withdrawing a credentials wallet that looked just like the one Patterson carried. He flipped it open to display his badge and ID. "I'm here for the postcard."

# SIX

CARL DROVE STRAIGHT BACK to the motel after leaving the home of Angel's father. He parked the truck in front of his room and hurried inside, closing and locking the door. The bed was still unmade and the towel he had used to shower the evening before was on the bathroom floor, thanks to the DO NOT DISTURB sign he had hung on the outside door handle prior to leaving earlier that morning. The last thing he wanted was some nosy maid in his room.

Stepping away from the door, he went to the window and inched the closed curtains open a crack to look back out. He was sure that no one had followed him from the small suburban house in Queens—there was no reason why they would since the old man had clearly bought his story about being an FBI agent—but it never hurt to be cautious.

He reached into his back pocket and withdrew the postcard, now crumpled because he had been sitting on it all the way back to his accommodation. He sat down at the small table in front of the window and studied it. The card was definitely from Angel. He recognized the handwriting.

He could hardly believe his luck. He had gone to the house

intending to ask the father about his daughter, and if she had been in touch. But before he could say anything, the old man had led him into the living room and showed him this postcard. Not only that, but he had acted as if he was waiting for an FBI agent to show up and take it. That presented an opportunity too good to pass up. There was no way Carl was leaving the card with the old man after that, so he played along. But at the back of his mind was a nagging unease. If the father was waiting for an FBI agent, then they might show up at any moment and blow his cover story. The best thing to do was get out of there quickly, but not so fast that it would raise suspicion. Which was why he had forced himself to stand there, even though the thought of coming face-to-face with the real FBI agent sent a prickle of fear up his spine.

At least until he saw the photo of Angel sitting on the mantle. It took his breath away. She looked just like when he had first met her in Santa Fe. In fact, the photo was taken at a well-known sculpture a day's drive down the road in Amarillo. A row of rusting cars standing half buried in the dusty earth and covered with graffiti. The photograph must have been taken not long before Angel arrived in Santa Fe and took a job bartending at Amy's Roadhouse. He had picked it up to get a closer look, stared at that heavenly face, radiant and full of joy. And before he knew it, the name slipped past his lips.

Angel.

He had covered the gaffe, then quickly placed the photograph back on the mantle and made his exit. But now, thinking back on it, he was worried. Because it wasn't just that he had said Angel's name out loud, and let the old man hear it, but he had also picked up the photograph with his bare hands. One stupid mistake compounded by an even dumber one. After being so careful until that point, and touching nothing but the postcard, he had let himself become distracted and left his fingerprints on the frame.

He cursed under his breath, felt a familiar rage rising from somewhere deep within. But then he took a deep breath and forced it back into the dark pit of his subconscious, where he kept it buried most of the time. It really wasn't so bad, he reminded himself. It was unlikely that the old man would even remember him picking up the photograph under the circumstances. He was clearly more focused on his missing daughter than anything else, and it was such a brief interaction. Besides, the visit had been a resounding success in every other way. Angel's father had accepted him as an FBI agent without even asking for ID, which was lucky because it hadn't occurred to Carl that he might have been asked to prove his identity. It was only later, when he was driving back to the motel and going over the encounter in his mind's eye, that he realized his plan could have fallen apart right there on the doorstep.

And then there was the postcard, which confirmed that Julie hadn't run back to her family home after she escaped, even if she *had* gotten in touch despite his threats. Warned them about him. But even that wasn't as bad as it looked, because it told Carl where she was. Or at least, where she had been five days ago. San Diego, California. A city he knew well because he had driven his truck there many times over the years to pick up cargo. The city had a deep-water dock, and as such, was a preferred port for container ships. He had even satisfied his urges a few times across the border in Tijuana, where a man like him could do things that would be frowned upon in the good old US of A. Might even land him in jail.

Now, it looked like he would be heading there again. The only frustrating thing was that he had driven his ageing pickup truck all the way to the East Coast—a journey that had taken four days—only to discover that his Angel had been less than a half day's drive from the farm in the other direction. Of course, he hadn't known that at the time.

Carl picked up the postcard, touched a finger to the name written at the bottom. Jelly. He had no idea why she had signed the postcard like that. It made no sense. All he could think was that it was some childhood nickname she had acquired because it rhymed with Julie. Not that it mattered. Soon, he would find her and his daughter, bring them both back to the farmhouse, and after that, he would never let Angel out of his sight again. Assuming that he let her live, that was.

# SEVEN

PATTERSON HAD BEEN DRIVING for six hours, following I-40 west, then taking Arizona route 77 toward Phoenix, when her phone rang. It was her father. She knew that even before she answered thanks to the ring tone that she had assigned him. Hotel California by the Eagles. One of his favorite songs.

"Hey, dad," she said with the phone on hands-free, the call routed through the shiny new sound system the Dallas PD had installed after Marcus Bauer convinced them to renovate the old van, turning it into a luxurious bedroom workspace combination on wheels. "What's up?"

"Nothing, I hope." There was hesitation in her father's voice. "That agent your boyfriend sent over here to pick up the postcard…"

"What about him?"

"He showed up twice. The first time it was a guy in a polo shirt and slacks. Then, not long after, another FBI agent showed up. This one was wearing a suit. Gotta say he looked a lot more official than the first guy."

"What?" None of the special agents that Patterson had ever worked with wore a polo shirt while they were on duty. Suit and tie were the accepted norm, at least for male agents, and they didn't deviate from that.

"It might be nothing, but I can't help feeling that something isn't right."

"Hang on." Patterson spied a turnoff up ahead. A dusty road that ran toward a distant ridge of mountains in front of which she could make out the hazy sprawl of a remote town. Pulling over and coming to a halt, she turned her attention back to the call. "Okay. Tell me what happened."

Her father cleared his throat. "There really isn't much to tell. This FBI agent showed up on the doorstep and took the postcard. Then, not long after, another agent came to the door. He showed me his credentials and introduced himself as Special Agent Lance Driscoll."

"I know Lance," Patterson said. "He's a good guy. What about the other agent? Did he show you any credentials?"

"No," her father replied sheepishly. "I didn't even ask. I was expecting someone to come for the postcard, and well..."

"It's okay. Did the man tell you his name?"

"U-huh." There was a brief pause. "It was Briggs. No, wait. Brent. That's it. Special Agent Daniel Brent."

Patterson thought for a moment. "I don't know anyone by that name who works at the New York field office. Are you sure it was Daniel Brent?"

"Yes. I'm sure," her father said, then added hopefully, "Maybe he's new."

"FBI agents don't call on people wearing polo shirts and forgetting to present their credentials, dad. He's not new."

"I was afraid you'd say that." Her father huffed, clearly annoyed with himself. "I'm so stupid. I should have asked for his credentials. I don't know what I was thinking. My own daughter is an FBI agent, for heaven's sake."

"It's fine," Patterson said. "Don't beat yourself up over it."

"Easy for you to say. You didn't let a strange man into the

house," her father growled. "He took the postcard. I just handed it over, let him walk right out the door with it."

"What's done is done." Patterson's mind was going a mile a minute. "What did Driscoll say?"

"Not much. When I told him another agent had already picked up the postcard, he thanked me and left. He looked a bit confused, but I mean, what else was he going to do?"

"Right." Patterson made a mental note to call Grant just as soon as she finished with her father. She was sure that Daniel Brent had nothing to do with the New York field office, which begged the question, who was he and why had he shown up on her father's doorstep with such unerring timing? "What did he do when he was inside the house?"

"I told you already. He just took the postcard and left."

"That's it? He didn't do anything unusual?"

"No. Well, maybe. He took the card and put it in his back pocket. No evidence bag. Nothing. Just handled it with his bare hands, which I thought was mighty odd. I mean, don't you always put things like that in an evidence bag? Even on TV, they use evidence bags."

"He should've bagged it," Patterson agreed.

"That's what I thought. And here's the thing. When I queried it, he said he had an evidence bag in his car." The elder Blake tutted. "I should've seen through him right there and then. Should never have let him take that postcard."

"You did the right thing," Patterson said. "If he wasn't from the FBI, and I'm pretty certain that he wasn't, then he could have turned violent if you confronted him."

"I never thought of that."

Patterson thought for a moment. "You said he took the postcard with his bare hands?"

"Yes."

"So just to be clear, he was not wearing gloves of any kind?"

"No."

"Okay. This next question is very important, so think hard.

Did he touch anything other than the postcard while he was in the house? Like maybe the front doorknob?"

"He didn't touch the front door. I opened it to let him in and out, then closed it after him when he left."

"I see. So he touched nothing at all?"

"I don't think he... Wait. There was the picture frame," her father exclaimed with a note of excitement. "That picture of Julie that you gave me. The one where she was standing in front of the car sculpture outside of Amarillo. It's on my mantle in a silver frame. He went over and looked at it."

"He picked it up?"

"Yes. I'm certain of it. He took it down from the mantle to look at it. Told me she was beautiful. An angel. Thinking back, the way he said it was... well, kind of creepy."

Patterson drew a sharp breath. "Have you touched the frame since?"

"No. Why would I?"

"Good. Don't." Patterson could hardly believe her luck. The man who had visited her father was clearly not with the Bureau. Grant wouldn't have sent two different agents to pick up the postcard. Hell, he wasn't even dressed like an FBI agent. But he had made a crucial mistake in touching the picture frame with his bare hands. He had left behind fingerprints. With any luck, he would be in the system. "I'm going to call Grant right now. Have Driscoll come back over and collect that picture frame so that forensics can take a look at it."

"Oh, okay."

"And in the meantime, don't answer the door to anyone else. Don't let anyone inside. Not even if they claim to be with the Bureau. Only Special Agent Driscoll, who you've already met. Is that understood?"

"There's no need to talk down to me," her father said, obviously irritated. "I screwed up, but I'm sure as hell not going to make the same mistake twice. You tell that agent friend of yours to come get the picture frame. Then maybe we can find out who stole Julie's postcard, and why."

"That's the plan," Patterson said. She said goodbye to her father and hung up, then placed another call. This time to Jonathan Grant. Twenty minutes later, after filling him in on what her father had told her, she rejoined the highway, keeping her fingers crossed that they would find a usable fingerprint on that picture frame, and match it to a name. Because a scenario was forming in Patterson's mind. Julie had sent the postcard not only to let her family know that she was still alive, but also as a warning. There was a bad man out there somewhere. A man who had kept her sister prisoner all these years. Now Julie was free, and her captor was on the hunt. Worse, he had visited her father. The thought of that man standing in her family home filled her with anger. A rage that burned white hot. But at the same time, she realized something else. If it really was Julie's captor who took the postcard, then he would have seen the postmark and be on his way to San Diego, just like she was.

Which meant that Patterson was now in a race against time to find her sister. Because if the man who had introduced himself as Special Agent Daniel Brent found her first, then Julie would vanish all over again. And this time, it might be forever.

# EIGHT

CARL WAS on the road and heading back west.

It had been less than two hours since he had left the Blake residence. After returning to the motel, he had packed up his meager possessions, throwing his dirty clothes into a backpack he had brought with him, not bothering to separate them from the clean clothes already in the bag. Then he grabbed his toiletries and stuffed those on top. Finally, he had slipped the small laptop that he always carried with him when he was away from home into the backpack's front pocket and zipped it closed.

After looking around the room to make sure he hadn't left anything behind, Carl had headed to his pickup truck and dumped the bag into the seat well on the passenger side before returning his room keys to the lobby and checking out. Thankfully, he had possessed the good sense to pay for the room in cash and use a false name, slipping the clerk—a skinny kid in his early twenties with greasy, limp brown hair, and a face so full of acne that Carl could barely stand to look at him—an extra twenty-five bucks not to bother with his ID. He already had a cover story ready to explain why he couldn't provide identification—that his wallet had been stolen, which was why he had no identification or credit cards. It was the same story he had used at the other hotels on his drive to the East Coast. But it had turned out to be unnecessary. When he had told the kid that he didn't have his driver's license, and slid the extra cash across the counter, Acne Face had merely shrugged, pocketed the bribe, and handed him a set of keys, saying only, "Room 106. No smoking and no loud music. Oh, and the ice machine is broken."

Carl was satisfied that he had left behind no evidence that he was ever there. Except for one thing. The fingerprints he might have deposited on the picture frame. Despite his best efforts to convince himself that it was fine, that the old man probably wouldn't even remember him touching the frame, let alone have the wherewithal to tell anyone about it, he couldn't quell a nagging unease, mostly because of an incident that had occurred two-and-a-half decades earlier when he was still a teenager and too full of hormones to control his urges.

Never a popular kid in school, he had endured more than his fair share of humiliation at the hands of his peers. And most humiliating of all was how the girls looked at him whenever he had asked one of them out. A rare event usually preceded by smoking a joint behind the bleachers. It was the only way he could muster enough courage to approach a member of fairer sex and engage them in conversation. Not that it ever worked. He usually ended up red-faced and stammering when the object of his affections burst out laughing, or worse, ridiculed him. On the day that he was arrested, Carl had snapped. Sure, he had aimed a little above his station. A gorgeous blonde by the name of Leslie Peterson who was not only on the cheerleading squad but had also done a little modeling after a talent scout discovered her at a local beauty pageant. Or at least, that was what she had told anyone who would listen.

What she told Carl on that day had nothing to do with modeling. The word *creep* had crept past her perfect, pouty red lips, along with *pervert*. This was swiftly followed by a rebuke—handed down in front of all her friends on the cheerleading squad—that had left his ears ringing and his cheeks burning.

Carl had snapped.

One minute he was watching her turn away from him with a snicker, the next, she was on the ground and screaming blue murder. The strange thing was, he didn't even remember pushing her. To this day, the interval between Leslie Peterson turning her back on him and ending up horizontal with scuffed knees and a twisted ankle that would subsequently prevent her from cheerleading for the rest of the football season, was a blank.

But it hadn't mattered.

Everyone else had seen it, and they were only too willing to rat him out. Carl had ended up arrested and charged with assault. But because he was a juvenile with no previous marks against him, he had gotten off with a slap on the wrist—three weeks of community service—and a promise from the judge that the record of his misdemeanor would be sealed so long as he did not re-offend. But still, he worried that his old arrest, which had included his being fingerprinted, would come back to haunt him. After all, he wasn't dealing with dimwitted local cops like the ones he'd encountered during his years of cross-country trucking. Cops who couldn't solve a crossword puzzle, let alone a crime. These were the feds. Angel's own sister had become an FBI agent, for Pete's sake. And when her colleague—the *real* FBI agent—showed up at her father's door for the postcard that was now tucked into Carl's backpack, it would become obvious that something was amiss.

Shit! Carl pounded the steering wheel, overcome by a sudden anger both at his stupidity back when he was a teenager, and a couple of hours earlier in the house. If only he hadn't pushed that girl. If only he hadn't picked up the picture frame, unable to help himself at the sight of his Angel smiling back from the mantelpiece.

If only, if only, if only.

Well, it was no good dwelling on his mistake now. It was done and in the past. And chances were that the record of his juvenile indiscretion had been sealed, preventing anyone from finding it, just like the judge said. Besides, after so much time had passed, the record probably didn't even exist anymore.

That made Carl feel better. Everything was going to be okay. Soon he would arrive in San Diego. The GPS on his phone told him that it was a forty-three-hour trip, assuming there were no holdups along the way, which he deemed wholly unrealistic. Since he couldn't drive straight through—twelve hours was about as long as he dared stay behind the wheel before pulling off the road and recharging his metaphorical batteries—he figured it would take the better part of four days, and maybe even five, to reach his destination. With any luck, Angel was still there. And somehow, deep down, Carl believed that she was, even though he couldn't explain how he had come to that conclusion. Maybe it was the bond that they shared. A connection so deep that not even thousands of miles could sever it. Or maybe he just knew Angel better than she knew herself. Either way, thought Carl as he left New York City behind and crossed the border into Pennsylvania, he was coming for her, whether she liked it or not.

# NINE

PATTERSON ARRIVED in San Diego at ten o'clock in the evening and headed straight for the camping area she had found on the internet during a brief stop for food on the outskirts of Phoenix, Arizona. She already had a reservation for three nights with the option of extending if necessary, and it didn't take her long to settle in. She was happy to be out of the driver's seat and wasted no time in freshening up before changing into her PJs and climbing into the camper's queen-sized bed, eager to start her search for Julie the next morning.

It didn't take her long to fall asleep. A disturbed slumber filled with dreams of Julie, running from a faceless man who stalked her with relentless precision. Fleeing through darkened streets, banging on doors, and screaming in futile desperation for someone, anyone, to help her.

Patterson awoke at 6 AM, drenched in sweat and with her heart thumping against her rib cage. She sat bolt upright, sucking in a trembling breath to steady her jangled nerves. After a minute, she sank back down, pulling the covers up to her chin and watching the sun's first rays creep into the camper's small but well-appointed cabin and push away the shadows.

She lay there for a while, letting the bad dream disperse like the gossamer threads of a spider's web caught in a breeze.

That was when her phone rang.

She rolled over and scooped it up from its charger on a small shelf next to the bed. She answered to Jonathan Grant's familiar voice.

"Hey. The lab got back to me on that picture frame. We pulled three sets of prints."

Three sets. Patterson sat up, propping a pillow behind her back. She was eager to hear what he had to say. "I bet one of them is mine."

"It is. The second set belongs to your father. We took his fingerprints yesterday to eliminate them."

"And the third set?"

"That's where it gets interesting. We lifted two partials and a full that were not left by either you or your father. The partials were on the back. The full, probably a thumbprint, was on the silver part of the frame on the front. We ran it through AFIS, and we got a hit. But here's the incredible part. It's old. Like two decades old. And it wasn't in relation to crime."

"A background check?" Patterson asked. AFUIS stood for the Automated Fingerprint Identification System. A database that the FBI had maintained since 1999. But it wasn't just used by local, state, and federal law enforcement agencies. It was also used by private companies to run background checks on their prospective employees. And once that background check had been run, the prints remained in the system.

"That's right. The prints belong to a man named Carl Edward Bonneville. Forty-two years old and a lifelong resident of Arizona. In fact, he's lived at the same address all of his life. An old cattle ranch north of Flagstaff. There's one other occupant listed at the address. Lori Bonneville, his seventy-three-year-old mother."

"Then how did he get into the database?"

"He's a long-distance trucker. Works on a subcontract basis

for a Phoenix-based company called Bolton Transportation. Been with them for twenty years."

"A trucker." Patterson was already developing a mental picture of the man she now suspected had taken her sister. He had never moved out of the family home, still lived with his mother. He was employed in a favorite occupation of serial killers and other predators thanks to its transient lifestyle and the ability to commit crimes in multiple states that local authorities might never connect. It also allowed the perpetrator to transport victims hundreds or even thousands of miles from the location of their abduction. The chances were that he was a loner and socially awkward.

"Right. He probably didn't even realize that an employment background check could land him in a national fingerprint identification system. Most people assume that if they haven't ever been arrested, then they aren't identifiable to the authorities."

"He doesn't have a criminal record?" Patterson asked. If Carl Edward Bonneville really was the man who had taken Julie, then his crimes had not started with abduction. Individuals who took young women and kept them captive for their own sick pleasure, or even murdered them, often worked up to it, starting with smaller acts that may or may not be legal, and gathering courage as they got away with them. Of course, a lot depended on their nature. If Bonneville was a psychopath, then he would be a meticulous planner. A man who could pass as normal and put on the charm even as he remained emotionally dead inside. If he was a sociopath, on the other hand, he would act on impulse, and would probably be quick to anger.

"No. There is no criminal record. At least, not at first glance."

"What does that mean?" Patterson asked.

"He was arrested for assault when he was seventeen. Attacked a girl who rejected his advances. Because it was his first offense, and he was a juvenile, the judge sealed his record. It wouldn't have shown up in employment background checks, or even to local police."

"But it would show up to the FBI."

"Correct. Sealing a record doesn't make it go away completely. Bonneville, assuming that he's our man, has probably convinced himself that it doesn't matter if we pull his prints. That his only arrest has been buried so deep that no one would ever find it. And I'm sure he's never even given a thought to a background check from two decades ago."

"Then I guess it's our lucky day," Patterson said. She was already calculating how much time she would lose in driving to that cattle ranch outside of Flagstaff. "Do we have enough to raid the farm?"

"Already on it. There's a search warrant in progress. I should hear back from the judge within the next hour or two. And I've reached out to the locals in Arizona. Flagstaff only has a Resident Agency—a single agent—but there's a field office in Phoenix. When we get the go-ahead, they'll have a tactical team ready to roll. If Carl Edward Bonneville took your sister, we'll know soon enough."

"You realize that he probably won't be there, right?" Bonneville had been in her father's house less than twenty-four-hours before—a fact that filled Patterson with rage. If Julie had escaped his clutches, then he was surely looking for her, and poking around the most obvious place that she would go. He couldn't have known about the postcard, which meant that his timing was purely coincidental. Bad luck for them, and a stroke of good fortune for him. She doubted he had flown from Arizona to New York because he wouldn't have wanted to leave such an obvious trail, so he had probably driven. In that case, there was no way he could have gotten back to the farmhouse so quickly, even if he still perceived it as a safe haven. But there was another reason she didn't think he would be there. Bonneville had the postcard, which meant he knew Julie had been in San Diego less than a week before. The same thought occurred to her now that had crossed her mind the previous day when she learned of the fake FBI agent and the missing postcard. Bonneville would be racing to reach San Diego and find Julie before anyone else did.

"I know," Grant said. "But his mother will be, and I have a lot of questions."

"I need to be there," Patterson said, even though she didn't want to leave San Diego and give up her advantage in finding Julie. "I know this case better than anyone. If Julie was at that farmhouse—"

"I figured you'd say that, and I respectfully disagree. You need to be in San Diego. You need to find her before Bonneville does, because there's no way that he isn't on his way there right now," Grant said, revealing that his own deductive reasoning had led him to the same conclusion as Patterson. "But I agree that we need a pair of experienced eyes on the team. Someone familiar with the intricacies of Julie's case. And I know just where to find them…"

# TEN

MARCUS BAUER WAS GETTING FED up with desk duty. Apart from his brief, unofficial sojourn to rescue Patterson Blake from spending the rest of her life in prison for a murder she didn't commit, it felt like he'd been sidelined forever. The gunshot wound he had sustained putting a vicious killer named Duane Snyder behind bars several weeks earlier had pretty much healed, but Walter Harris, Special Agent in Charge of the Dallas field office, had decided to extend his desk duty anyway, probably as punishment for the off-the-books activities he and Phoebe Cutler had recently engaged in. Now, he sat with a pile of paperwork in front of him and wondered if he was ever again going to see sunlight.

"Hey, you," a familiar voice said to his rear.

He swiveled in his chair to see Phoebe standing behind him. As usual, she took his breath away, even dressed in the modest black knee-length skirt, white blouse, and flat shoes she wore to the office nine times out of ten. "What brings you down from the hallowed halls of power?"

"SAC Harris wants to see you, pronto." Phoebe was the SAC's assistant, which had done nothing to keep either of them out of trouble.

Bauer groaned. "What have I done now?"

"That's a good question," Phoebe shot back. "Patterson Blake isn't around to lead you astray, so it can't be that bad."

"You were just as eager to help clear her name as I was," Bauer reminded his girlfriend. "But you're right. A summons to the SAC's office usually has something to do with Patterson. I just don't seem to be as good at getting into trouble without her around."

Phoebe laughed. "Don't be too hard on yourself. I'm sure you can get into plenty of mischief all on your own." She glanced toward the elevators. "Now, get a move on. SAC Harris is not a patient man, and I don't want any part of whatever he's about to scream at you for now."

"Which is why you walked all the way down here instead of just calling me, which would have been quicker?"

"The SAC sent me down to drop off a package at reception. Figured I'd kill two birds with one stone and collect you on the way back up. Besides, any excuse to spend time with you."

"Aw, shucks." Bauer feigned embarrassment. "She loves me."

"Hey. Enough of that." Phoebe swatted at him. "Now hurry up."

"Yes, ma'am." Bauer tried to suppress a grin and failed. He rose to his feet and pushed his chair under the desk, his eyes settling briefly on the stack of paperwork that seemed to grow every day despite the Bureau's commitment to going digital. "Maybe Harris wants to commend me for my fine work clearing this backlog of reports."

Phoebe laughed again, even as she turned and started toward the elevators. "You keep telling yourself that."

"Oh, I will." Bauer picked up his phone and followed Phoebe to the elevator, where they were whisked up to the fourth floor. A few minutes after that, he was standing outside the SAC's office door while Phoebe resumed her position behind her desk and picked up her phone to let Harris know that he was there.

After a brief conversation, she looked up at Bauer. "You can go in."

"What, no last meal for the condemned?" Bauer asked, his hand resting on the doorknob.

"I have a bag of jellybeans in my desk drawer," Phoebe replied. "Do those count?"

"You got any of the red ones left?"

"Nope. But I have a lot of the licorice-flavored ones."

"Gross. You can keep them." Bauer turned the knob and stepped into the SAC's office.

Walter Harris sat behind his desk, which was considerably larger and more imposing than the one Bauer had been assigned. His attention was focused on his laptop screen.

He didn't look up at the special agent's entrance.

"Sir?" Bauer took a step toward the closest chair, wondering if the visit would be lengthy enough to warrant getting comfortable.

Harris answered his question without diverting his attention from the laptop. "Take a seat, Special Agent Bauer."

Bauer's worst fears were confirmed. This wasn't going to be a flying visit. He sat down and watched his boss peck at the laptop's keyboard for a minute before Harris finally looked up.

"You look uneasy, Marcus."

Great. They were in first name territory, at least on one side of the conversation. Bauer had no intention of referring to his boss as Walter. Not if he wanted to still have a job at the end of the day. Right now, he wasn't so sure. A return to the LAPD, his home prior to joining the FBI, was becoming more appealing with each new pile of paperwork that appeared on his desk. He pushed the thought aside and replied with a curt, "I'm fine."

"Pleased to hear it." Harris cleared his throat and sat with one hand resting on the desk. "You're probably wondering why I called you up here."

"Yes, sir."

Harris studied him for a moment, perhaps relishing the

junior agent's discomfort, before speaking again. "In a word, Patterson Blake."

*That's two words*, Bauer thought to himself, even as his gut clenched at the mere mention of her name. How on earth could she have embroiled him in yet more trouble from all the way up in Santa Fe, over six hundred miles away in another state? "I don't understand, sir."

"You're familiar with her missing sister's case, are you not?"

"Yes. Julie Blake. She disappeared sixteen years ago after taking a road trip with a college friend. Special Agent Blake recently uncovered new information and has been searching for her."

"That's correct. And you've been helping her."

"I was assigned to help with the case while Special Agent Blake was in Dallas, yes," Bauer replied, hoping that his boss wasn't going to once again bring up his and Phoebe's involvement in clearing Patterson's name weeks before when she became the target of Texas senator Bill Newport's ire and ended up on the run, accused of murder.

Harris did not bring it up. "Would it be fair to say that apart from Special Agent Blake, you possess the most knowledge of Julie's case, and the recent developments that have brought it back to the fore?"

"I suppose, yes." Bauer wondered where this was going.

"Excellent." Harris turned back to his laptop. "I'm emailing you a file outlining a break in the case that occurred only yesterday. Please give it your full attention. I'll assign someone else to your current tasks."

"Yes, sir." Bauer's curiosity was piqued even as his heart leaped at his release from drudgery. "Might I ask what this break is?"

"Everything is in the file that I'm sending to you. However, I can give you the condensed version now. A suspect has been identified in Julie's disappearance. One Carl Edward Bonneville. A long-distance trucker who lives outside of Flagstaff. The

Phoenix office is putting together a task force to raid his property at the request of Jonathan Grant from the New York FO. Given your knowledge of the case, ASAC Grant has also requested your presence since Special Agent Blake is otherwise engaged."

"Oh." Marcus was speechless. Not only was he released from the hell of sifting through old paperwork, but he was apparently being put back into the field. And on the very case that had gotten him into trouble so many times before. But one thing nagged at him. "Time will be of the essence. The task force won't want to wait, and Flagstaff is more than a day's drive from Dallas."

"Which is why you aren't driving, Special Agent Bauer. You're booked on a flight to Phoenix out of DFW that departs in ninety minutes. You'll be briefed at the Phoenix field office before heading out with the task force. There's a car waiting to take you to the airport, so I suggest you get a move on."

"Yes, sir." Bauer stood up and turned toward the door.

But SAC Harris wasn't done yet. "Special Agent Bauer?"

"Yes?" Bauer looked back over his shoulder.

"You'll be speaking to Special Agent Blake in short order, no doubt," the SAC said. "Please let her know that I send my regards. With any luck she'll nail the bastard who took her sister and put him away for a very long time."

"I'll pass your message along, sir," Bauer said, surprised at the emotion in the SAC's voice. Then he turned and left the office, closing the door behind him.

# ELEVEN

THE CAMPING AREA that Patterson had booked was on the outskirts of San Diego, not far from I-8. Even with the camper's AC running, she could hear the steady thrum of vehicles, a distant rumble that never let up regardless of the hour. But she didn't mind. Having grown up in Queens, she was used to traffic noise. In fact, she found the unending silence of remote locations almost worse.

Now, she sat at the small table in the back of the van with her laptop open, browsing the web for any information she could find on Carl Edward Bonneville, the man who had visited her father the day before and whom she was sure had also abducted Julie all those years ago. With any luck, the impending raid on his farmhouse outside of Flagstaff would provide concrete evidence of her hypothesis. She was only sorry that it would take place without her. It didn't make sense for Patterson to leave San Diego now that she was in possession of the first lead on Julie's current whereabouts since starting to search. Her sister was close by. She could feel it, even if she had no idea where to start looking. Maybe the raid would turn something up to help her in that regard, too. San Diego was a sprawling city with close to 1.4 million residents, and its proximity to the Mexican border meant it was also home to a large undocumented population. In short, it was the perfect place to disappear.

Patterson looked away from the screen and rubbed her temples. She hadn't moved since Grant had called almost three hours before, even though the web search had been a pointless endeavor. All she had found on Bonneville was his photo on a page from an old high school yearbook that someone had scanned and uploaded to social media. Most of the students staring back at her from the page had been tagged and linked back to their profiles, but not Bonneville. He was mentioned only in the comments, and even then, it was in passing. A brief mention by another former student who remembered him as 'a bit odd'.

Beyond that, Bonneville might as well have been a ghost. Which made sense, given the impromptu profile she had worked up for him in her head based on what little knowledge she possessed. Bonneville was probably antisocial. A loner who had trouble forming meaningful relationships, especially with the opposite sex. She doubted he had any close friends. His job as a long-distance truck driver meant spending hours, days, or even weeks with no company except his own, which further confirmed her theory. The one close relationship he might have was probably with his mother, whom he still lived with when he wasn't working, and that was hardly going to be a heathy one.

Except for Julie.

Patterson had tried not to dwell on what her sister must have gone through, kept captive all those years by such a man. She had told herself over and over again since Grant's call to avoid jumping to conclusions. Until something surfaced that definitively tied Julie to that farmhouse, and Bonneville, all she had was circumstantial evidence and speculation. And she knew better than to let herself get trapped in a rabbit warren of false assumptions and half-truths.

But waiting was torture.

The Phoenix field office was moving quickly, but they still

had to wait for the search warrant, assemble a task force, and then drive over two hours north to Bonneville's abode. It reminded her of an old adage: Hurry up and wait. But at least there would be a friendly face on the team when they made their move. A person that Patterson trusted more than anyone else to act as her surrogate. Her old partner, Marcus Bauer. It seemed that the two were inextricably linked. No matter how far from Dallas she traveled, they always ended up in each other's orbit, one way or another.

Which probably didn't please Phoebe, who, while viewing Patterson as a friend, surely also thought that trouble followed whenever the pair worked together. And she was right. But this time, the association would be remote. Bauer had been sequestered to take part in a raid hundreds of miles away from Patterson's current location. A raid that should go off without a hitch, given that the only person they expected to encounter there was an old woman.

Patterson closed the laptop and leaned back. She had spoken to Bauer on the phone during his ride to the airport. He had promised to call her back as soon as the raid was over. That would be several more hours, she was sure. Which meant that she had nothing but time to kill.

She rose and went to the fridge. It was early afternoon. Her stomach was rumbling, reminding her she needed to eat. Patterson had a habit of skipping meals, especially when she had other things on her mind. Grant had chastised her about the habit on occasion. She could almost hear his voice echoing in her head. *You need fuel to keep your strength up.* That was why she had turned recently to protein shakes. They were quick and easy. But she couldn't make them her only source of sustenance. Which was why she grabbed a carton of eggs, intending to whip up a quick omelet on the camper's small propane stove. But at that moment, she heard a crunch of tires, followed not long after by a light knock on the camper's door.

She answered to find a fresh-faced young man in a dark suit

standing on the other side. It didn't take a genius to figure out that he was an FBI agent even before he flashed his credentials, and a junior one, at that. But she wasn't surprised to see him. In fact, she had been expecting the visit. One of the first things that she had done that morning after she spoke to Grant, was to place another call, this time to the San Diego field office. And not just as a courtesy to let them know she had arrived in the area and would be conducting inquiries. She had a much more mundane reason to reach out. The camper van, while small compared to many RVs, was still big enough to make driving around a city like San Diego a chore. Parking spaces were tight, and traffic would be heavy. Better to leave the camper parked in its space and procure a more sensible mode of transportation. Which is where the man standing in front of her came in.

"Special Agent Blake?" He asked, squinting up at her against the bright sunlight that slanted through the trees and down over the camper's roof. He held up a set of keys. "I have a pool car for you."

Patterson glanced past the man toward a dark colored Ford sedan parked on the gravel roadway that looped around the campground. Behind it, idling gently, was a second equally bland vehicle with a silhouetted figure behind the wheel. This was, no doubt, the junior agent's ride back into the city.

She took the keys and thanked him.

The man hesitated a moment, taking in Patterson's casual dress. A faded black T-shirt and a pair of comfortable yoga pants. He looked down at her bare feet before his gaze strayed to the camper, which he probably thought was the strangest federal vehicle he had ever laid eyes upon. Eventually, his attention drifted back to Patterson.

"Um... my supervisor told me I'm to be your liaison while you're in town." The junior agent, who was probably only a couple of years younger than Patterson, shuffled from one foot to the other. "He said that you have the full backing of the San

Diego field office. If you need anything at all, all you have to do is reach out and I'll do my best to make it happen."

"Thank you, Special Agent...?"

"Holmes," replied the man, even as a slight blush touched his cheeks. "And yes, I've heard all the jokes. I don't carry a magnifying glass. Nor do I play the violin."

"I had no intention of cracking a joke at your expense," Patterson said, even as she suppressed a smirk. "I'm sure that your choice of profession as an investigator was purely coincidental to the obvious association with your surname."

"Yes, it was." Special Agent Holmes reached into his pocket and pulled out a business card, which he handed to her. "My work cell and email address."

Patterson took the card. "I'm good right now, but if I need anything going forward, I'll let you know."

Holmes nodded, then turned stiffly and made his way back toward the waiting car.

Patterson watched until he climbed in, and the car drove off, its wheels crunching on the gravel as it went. Then she closed the camper door and went back to making her lunch. But even as she sat down to eat, her thoughts turned yet again to that farmhouse outside of Flagstaff, and what might be waiting there.

# TWELVE

MARCUS BAUER ARRIVED IN PHOENIX, Arizona, two and a half hours after his flight took off from Dallas. When he exited the terminal, a car was waiting that whisked him straight to the FBI's field office in the northwest quarter of the city. An hour later, after a hurried briefing, he was once again on the move, driving north toward Flagstaff with the task force in a convoy of four identical vehicles.

It was midafternoon already, which meant that they wouldn't arrive at the farmhouse that Carl Edward Bonneville shared with his mother until early evening. Bauer used that time to reacquaint himself with Julie's case and go over the file SAC Harris had emailed to him earlier in the day. By the time they arrived in Flagstaff, he was up to speed and eager to make his mark.

After passing through the city, the task force continued north for another thirty minutes, stopping at a preordained location a mile south of the property. Here, they regrouped and went over the plan of action one more time, studying satellite photographs of the farm and surrounding area on iPads, acquainting themselves with all possible exit points, and making sure everyone knew their role. Finally, they donned tactical body armor, checked their weapons, and make sure that their radios worked. That done, the four black sedans continued down the road and turned onto the dusty trail that led to the remote homestead.

The plan was simple. The sixteen federal agents that made up the task force would fan out across the property, approaching the house from both the front and rear, while simultaneously checking the farm's dilapidated barns. Bauer was assigned to the team entering through the front.

As soon as the cars came to a halt they were on the move, exiting the vehicles and rushing toward the buildings, guns drawn and senses on high alert. They weren't expecting trouble, but that didn't mean there would be none. After all, this was the home of a suspected kidnapper believed to have held a woman captive for over a decade and a half. Even though Bonneville was likely not there given his recent movements, anything was possible.

As Bauer approached the front door of the farmhouse, flanked by a pair of agents on each side, he felt the familiar rush of adrenaline mixed with a healthy dose of apprehension that always came upon him in such situations. The blood rushed in his ears. One of the other agents stepped forward and pounded his fist upon the front door, announcing their presence in a firm voice as the rest of the team took up tactical positions to the left and right of the entry point.

Silence was their only answer.

The lead agent tried one more time. When he again received no response, he reached out, tried the doorknob and found it locked. With an easy entry barred, he silently motioned his intention to breach the door in a coordinated assault with the team, who had circled around to the back. Then he put the plan into action with three short words quickly spoken into his radio.

"Go, go, go."

The agent behind Bauer stepped from his position beside the door. In his hand was a heavy tube made of metal with a pair of handholds on top. A one-person battering ram that was quicker and safer than trying to kick the door in. He wasted no time in positioning himself as the lead agent stepped aside, then delivered a well-placed blow to the door directly beneath the lock.

With a splinter of wood, the door flew open.

Bauer pivoted from his position of safety, gun raised, and stepped over the threshold with the other agents in lockstep at his rear. From the far side of the house came another splintering thump as the other tactical assault team entered and started through the building, going room to room in search of occupants and working toward them.

It took less than ten minutes to search the house and confirm that they were alone. A brief conversation with the remaining team members on other parts of the property yielded a similar result. Not only was Carl Edward Bonneville absent, but there was no sign of his mother, either.

But that didn't mean the raid was a bust. It didn't take long before a shout went up from one of the agents sweeping the bedrooms at the rear of the property. When Bauer entered the room, any doubt regarding Bonneville's role in Julie's disappearance melted away.

It was less of a bedroom than a prison cell. And one that someone had clearly broken out of. The door stood ajar; its frame destroyed where a pair of deadbolts—installed one above the other with the levers on the outside so that the door could be locked from the corridor—had once kept it secured. Nearby was a heavy floor lamp with an iron base. No doubt the instrument of the occupant's escape.

But that wasn't all that he saw.

The room's only window had been bricked up with concrete blocks, miring the small space in a Stygian blackness that was pushed back only by the crisscrossing beams from the powerful flashlights they had been carrying on their utility belts. At least until someone snapped on a light.

It was only then that Bauer realized the full horror of his surroundings. A metal framed bed with a thin mattress was pushed up against one wall. A large plastic bucket occupied a closet in the opposite corner, from which the doors had been removed. Its intended use was obvious, thanks to the odor of stale urine that hung in the air, and the clutch of flies that circled lazily above it.

Bauer swallowed his shock and continued examining the room. There were two small piles of clothes in the corner. A jumble of garments so mismatched that he found it hard to believe they had come from anywhere but a thrift store. Yet it wasn't the lack of style that caught his attention. While one pile clearly belonged to an adult woman, the other was clearly for a small girl. He picked up one of the pieces of child's clothing, looked at the label and saw it was for a girl between the ages of four and six. He checked another one. It was the same.

Bauer stared at the clothes, trying to make sense of what he was looking at. And then it hit him all at once. Julie had not been alone in this horror show of a bedroom. She had shared it with the child. And there was only one reason Bauer could think of why she would do so. She had borne a daughter at the hands of her abductor.

He took a step back, wondering what on earth he was going to tell Patterson, when his gaze alighted on something else laying on the floor near the bed. A small blue inhaler of the type used to treat asthma. After pulling on a set of nitrile gloves, he walked over and picked it up. He was about to drop it into an evidence bag when another shout went up, this time from somewhere outside at the back of the property.

There was a sound of running feet, and one of the other agents poked his head into the room.

"We've got something out here," he said breathlessly to Bauer. "Something you'll want to see."

Bauer dropped the item into the evidence bag and sealed it, then followed the agent outside and across a dusty yard filled with junk. There, at the edge of the property under the shade of an alligator juniper, a tree named for the rough bark on its trunk that had the appearance of scales, was a low mound of earth that one of the other agents had cleared at one end with a shovel to reveal a grizzly sight.

A bloated and partially decomposed face that looked back at him with an almost accusatory stare, as if the corpse was annoyed at the indignity of its hasty burial.

Bauer looked down at the makeshift grave and cursed under his breath. There was only one person it could be. Carl Edward Bonneville's mother. Which meant that he probably wouldn't be returning to the farmhouse anytime soon.

# THIRTEEN

AFTER THE SAN DIEGO field office had dropped off her loaner vehicle, Patterson headed out to get the lay of the land. She had never been to San Diego before and had no idea where she was going or even what she was looking for as she drove toward the city. But it was better than sitting in the camper and waiting for news of the raid in Flagstaff. News that might not come for many hours.

She spent the rest of the afternoon and into the evening cruising neighborhoods with names like Chula Vista, San Ysidro, and Otay Mesa. She knew the city was a hotspot for illegal border crossings, both where the City of San Diego met Tijuana, and also many miles to the east where migrants entered the country through a boulder strewn desert that was almost impossible to secure. But what she hadn't expected was the level of homelessness. She saw several encampments where those with nowhere else to go had set up tents along the sides of major thoroughfares at the edge of the city's downtown area. They crowded sidewalks and patches of public land. A small army of lost souls that had fallen through the cracks of society.

The inhumanity of their plight broke Patterson's heart. But more than that, she couldn't help but wonder if Julie was hiding somewhere among the forgotten. If so, Patterson wondered how she would ever find her. With every street she traversed, her hope faded, just a little more. What had felt like a challenge only a few hours before, now felt like an impossible task. There was only one silver lining. If Patterson, a trained federal agent, couldn't easily locate her sister, then neither could Carl Edward Bonneville.

Yet even as Patterson drove back out of the city toward the comfort of her camper for the night, she couldn't help but slow down constantly to study the faces of every shuffling vagrant she passed who was pushing a shopping cart loaded with meager possessions collected from dumpsters and thrift store donation bins or sitting at the entrance to a tent and staring out with eyes that had lost their capacity for hope. But at no point did she see anyone who looked even remotely like her sister, which simultaneously filled her with relief and frustration.

When she arrived back at the camper a little after 9 PM, she grabbed a towel and her toiletries bag, then made her way to the campsite's shower block where she found a stall and stood under the piping hot water for almost half an hour, washing away not only the sweat of a sweltering California day but also a prickly sense of griminess that had followed her back from those homeless encampments. Afterward, she returned to the camper and was about to rustle up a light supper when her phone rang. It was the call she had been waiting for all day long.

When she answered, Marcus Bauer wasted no time on pleasantries. "Bonneville's mother is dead. We found her in a shallow grave at the back of the property."

Patterson took a moment to absorb this statement, then asked, "Did he kill her?"

"No. Doesn't look like it. We'll know more once the ME has conducted a full autopsy, but she probably died of natural causes. Heart attack, most likely." Bauer fell silent for a few seconds. "There's more. We found a bedroom at the property that had been converted into a cell. The window was bricked up and there was a bucket that had been used as a makeshift toilet in the closet. There were also locks on the outside of the door, like someone had been held captive inside. Looks like whoever was in there busted their way out using the base of a floor lamp."

Patterson fought back a wave of lightheadedness. "Julie?"

"Hard to say. We conducted a thorough search of the property and found nothing that would positively identify whoever was being held in that room as your sister. But given what we already know, I'd put money on it." Bauer cleared his throat. "We worked up a theory regarding the sequence of events, although bear in mind that it's purely speculative."

"Go on."

"There was a bag of uneaten microwave popcorn in the kitchen, and some stains on the linoleum indicative of a body lying there for several days. The living room was trashed and a TV that had been mounted on the kitchen wall was smashed. We know that Carl Bonneville worked as a long-distance trucker and was away from the family home for days or even weeks at a time. We checked with the company that he worked for, and he had recently completed a twelve-day stint driving from the east to the west coast and back. My best guess is that he left his mother in charge of Julie when he was working. On this particular occasion, she happened to have a heart attack and died, apparently while making a nice healthy snack of microwave popcorn drenched in butter. That left your sister with no recourse but to break out of her room, something she probably would not have had the nerve to do otherwise. Upon finding one of her captors dead, and the other absent, she fled."

"And apparently ended up in San Diego," Patterson said.

"Exactly. There are three vehicles registered to Bonneville and his mother. The tractor-trailer that Bonneville uses for his work, which was parked in a barn, a pickup truck owned by Carl, and an old Chrysler Sebring that belonged to his mother. We didn't find either the pickup or the Sebring on the property."

"Julie must have taken one of them when she escaped."

"Right. And Bonneville took the other to go looking for her. He probably came home and found his mother dead and Julie missing, then flew into a rage, judging by the destruction in the living room and the broken TV. At some point after that, he pulled himself together and did the only thing that he could think of."

"He went to New York and visited my father, hoping to find some clue regarding Julie's whereabouts."

"Exactly. And having taken the postcard, he's now on his way to San Diego."

"Where I'll be waiting for him," Patterson said through gritted teeth. "Thanks for the information, Marcus."

"Don't thank me yet. There's more." Bauer took a deep breath. "Bonneville wasn't holding one person captive in that bedroom. There were two."

"What?" Patterson could hardly believe what she was hearing. "He abducted another woman?"

"Not quite. This person was considerably younger. No more than six years old." Bauer paused, as if preparing himself for what he was about to say next. "Under the circumstances, there's only one logical conclusion. Whoever was in that room had a daughter. And given how long your sister has been missing, Bonneville must be the father."

An icy dread enveloped Patterson. "You're saying that Carl Edward Bonneville held my sister captive in a filthy bedroom for a decade and a half, with only a bucket for toilet, abused and raped her, got her pregnant against her will, then locked their child up right alongside her."

"Yes," Bauer replied, his voice dropping to a level barely above a whisper. "That's what I'm saying."

# FOURTEEN

PATTERSON REELED with the horror of what Bauer had told her. During the years that Julie had been gone, all manner of scenarios had played through her mind, from her sister simply wanting to vanish and start a new life, to darker situations, such as the one that now presented itself. She had imagined Julie dying at the hands of a serial killer or being abducted by some depraved individual to satisfy his sick urges. She had wondered if her sister was out there somewhere, waiting to be found. And through it all, Patterson had remained steadfast, believing that when she finally discovered the truth, no matter how awful, it would come as a relief.

Now, she realized just how wrong she had been.

It was one thing to speculate and wonder, to hope for the best while imagining the worst, but something else entirely to know for certain. It was, she thought to herself, horrific, even as Bauer continued speaking, his words nothing but a faint buzz in her ear.

"Patterson." Bauer's voice cut through her fugue.

"What?" She shook off the dire thoughts and focused once again on the here and now.

"You zoned out there for a while." There was concern in Bauer's voice. "Did you even hear what I was saying?"

"Yes. I mean, no." Patterson stumbled over her words. "Well, some of it."

"Then I'll tell you again. We didn't just find children's clothes in that room. There was something else, too. I need to ask you a question, and I want you to think hard before you answer."

"Okay."

"Did Julie ever suffer from asthma?" Bauer asked. "Did she have any allergies that caused breathing problems, like from pet dander or pollen or anything else like that?"

"No," Patterson answered quickly. "None of that stuff. In fact, just the opposite. She was always the athletic while growing up. Could run rings around me even though I was younger. She even played lacrosse for a while at college. At least, until…"

"Right."

"Why are you asking about asthma?" Patterson was confused. She couldn't see how his line of questioning was relevant.

"Because I found an inhaler in the room where she and her daughter were being kept. If it doesn't belong to Julie, then…"

"It must be for her daughter."

"Exactly."

"Which means we have a place to start looking." Patterson's despair at locating Julie in a metropolis as large as San Diego shifted a little toward hope. "She'll have a prescription, need refills. We can check pharmacies, see if anyone recognizes Julie."

"Not so fast," Bauer cautioned her. "The inhaler might not have come from a pharmacy. At least, not one close to home. I did some research. The medicine is sold in the USA, but not under this particular brand name. It's mostly distributed in Asian countries and Australia. There's no way an American pharmacy would have filled a prescription for it."

"Then what are you saying?" Patterson was confused.

"I'm saying that it was probably purchased online, from some shady internet pharmacy. There are lots of them in places like India that have no problem sending medication of all shapes and sizes through the mail with nothing but a promise from the purchaser that they need it. No doctor required."

"That has to be illegal."

"It is, but it's also almost impossible to crack down on. And the FDA has better things to do than try to intercept packages traveling through the mail that might or might not contain illicitly obtained prescription meds, especially since most of them are for things like diabetes, underactive thyroid, or weight loss."

"And asthma inhalers."

"Right."

"In other words, low priority stuff when hard drugs like fentanyl and crack cocaine are pouring into the country practically unabated."

"Something like that."

Patterson was disappointed, but not surprised. "It makes sense that Bonneville would use an online pharmacy. If he really did have a daughter with Julie than he would want to keep it a secret, given how she was conceived."

"My thoughts exactly. She probably gave birth right there in the farmhouse and I bet the child doesn't have a birth certificate or a Social Security number."

"Because he wouldn't want to draw attention to her. Registering the birth would raise questions, like who the mother was. She probably isn't going to school, either," Patterson said. "If what you said about online pharmacies is true, then we're not much better off than we were before. There won't be any valid prescription for the medication, which means that Julie won't be able to obtain it from a genuine pharmacy when her daughter runs out of whatever medication she took with her when they fled."

"That's true," Bauer replied. "But she probably won't know how to get the medication online, either. If Bonneville kept Julie locked up in that bedroom for sixteen years, he wouldn't have let her use a computer or browse the internet, and he certainly wouldn't have let her anywhere near a cell phone. As far as she's concerned, technology stopped advancing a decade and a half ago."

"Unless someone is helping her."

"It's a possibility. Julie could have met a sympathetic individual since escaping the farmhouse. Someone willing to offer their assistance, even if they don't know the truth behind her past. But I still don't think she would risk using an online pharmacy. It would require providing a name and delivery address. She would also need a credit card to pay for the medication, and there's no way Julie has one of those under the circumstances. Chances are that whoever might be helping her doesn't have one, either. San Diego is home to a large population of both illegals and the homeless."

"I know," Patterson said. "I saw it firsthand this evening when I drove into the city."

"Those would be the most likely communities for her to hide within. She won't have any ID, nothing to prove who she is, and wouldn't want to use her true identity, anyway. It would make her too easy to locate, and I'll wager that she's terrified of Bonneville and what he might do if he finds her."

"The postcard indicated as much," Patterson said, thinking back to her sister's warning of a bad man.

"She won't be completely out of options, though. There are clinics in San Diego that treat both the homeless and undocumented immigrants. Many of them are low cost, or free. They don't ask questions or require ID. Perfect for someone like Julie, who wants to stay hidden. That's where you should start."

"I'll get on it first thing in the morning," Patterson said. But then a thought occurred to her. The only way that she was going to make any progress was if someone recognized her sister, and that presented a problem. "I only have old pictures of Julie from sixteen years ago or longer. She must've changed a lot since then. Especially with all that she's gone through since."

"You never had an age progression done?"

"No. I should have asked forensics to do one when I started following Julie's trail, but..." Patterson was mad at herself for overlooking something so basic. "Even if I get Jonathan involved, ask the lab to make it a priority, it could take days or even weeks."

"Then don't go through the FBI."

"What do you mean?"

"Artificial intelligence. There are all sorts of apps out there these days. Some of them are even free. Upload an old photo of your sister, and you can age it to whatever parameters you enter."

"Really?"

"Really. Of course, the results might not be as good as the FBI lab, but the tradeoff is that you'll have a photo tomorrow instead of three weeks from now."

"That just might work." Patterson wished she could reach out through the phone and hug Bauer. "Thank you."

"You're welcome." Bauer yawned. "I'm exhausted, and you must be, too. Get some rest, Patterson Blake. We can touch base again tomorrow."

"Sure." Patterson said goodbye and ended the call. But she didn't go to bed. Not right away. Instead, she opened her phone's app store and found one of the apps Bauer had told her about. When it finished downloading, she brought up a photo of Julie—the one of her sister standing in front of the car sculpture—and cropped it to display only Julie's head and shoulders. Then she sat and stared at her screen as the software transformed her sister from a college student in her late teens to the woman Julie would have grown into if she hadn't vanished.

And the results were stunning.

For the first time since she was a child, Patterson found herself looking at her sister in real time. A face that was familiar, and also a stranger. A face that reminded Patterson of how much her family had lost, and what it would mean to bring her back.

# FIFTEEN

A DAY and a half after leaving Queens, Carl was closer to San Diego than he had expected. He had figured that twelve hours behind the wheel at a time would be about as much as he could push himself without succumbing to exhaustion. He rarely allowed himself to drive longer than that when he was thundering down the highway in his tractor-trailer with 50,000 pounds of freight at his rear. Doze off in such a situation, and it was lights out. But Carl wasn't working now, and every hour that he wasted sleeping was an hour that Angel and Cherub slipped further away from him.

He had left New York in the early afternoon and driven for the rest of the day and into the early hours of the next morning, only stopping for bathroom breaks and living on candy bars and bags of chips purchased from rest area vending machines. He had notched twelve and a half hours beneath his wheels before pulling off the highway sometime around four in the morning and stopping in the trash strewn parking lot of a restaurant that looked like it had been closed for years.

There was a faded For Sale sign at the edge of the property, although it had clearly received no takers, probably because of its remote location along a lonely stretch of highway mostly devoid of human habitation. The building had begun to deteriorate, with broken windows, loose siding, and a patch of roof that had lost its shingles. Only a single lamppost remained, illuminating the structure's gradual slide into decrepitude. Carl had parked as far away from the light as he could, nudging his car into the shadows close to the building, turning off the engine, and finally closing his eyes.

When he woke up several hours later, bright sunlight was streaming in through his windshield. He blinked against the glare, waiting for his eyes to adjust, then climbed out of the car and went behind the building to relieve himself. After a quick breakfast of half a Mounds bar and a couple squares of dark chocolate washed down by a bottle of water, he resumed his journey.

Now, fourteen hours later, he was once again driving through the darkness and struggling to stay awake. He was more than halfway through his journey, and approaching Oklahoma City, which he had last visited while keeping tabs on Angel's FBI agent sister, Patterson Blake, weeks before.

He didn't want to stop, considered pushing on through his exhaustion, but he knew better than to try. When he came upon the lights of a 24-hour diner shining through the darkness on the outskirts of the city, he left the interstate behind and stopped, figuring that some real food and a couple mugs of hot coffee might give him the stamina to keep going for a couple more hours before finding a place to lay his head.

The diner was mostly empty. A couple of tractor-trailers sat across several spaces in the parking lot. The weary-looking drivers sat at the counter, digging into plates of steak and eggs, sipping coffee, and holding a stilted conversation. They wouldn't stay long, Carl knew. Time was money. They would want to reach their destinations as quickly as possible to deliver their cargo, pick up another load, and retrace their route back in the other direction.

A sign at the entrance told patrons to seat themselves. Carl ignored the two truckers and made his way to a booth at the front of the restaurant with a view of the parking lot, passing a few other occupied booths along the way.

After settling in and ordering the Midnight Special—three eggs over easy, corned beef hash, two sausage links, and a half stack of buttermilk pancakes—he sipped a mug of coffee and stared out at the parking lot while tapping his fingers on the table to the gravelly voice of the Man in Black playing over the diner's speakers as he sang about Folsom Prison.

And that was when he saw the car pull off the road and come to a halt in the darkness at the edge of the parking lot, where the light from the sodium vapor lamps didn't reach.

An old, dark colored Sebring.

Carl sat up straight, suddenly alert.

The driver's side door opened, and a woman climbed out. Carl put his hand to the window glass, his heart pounding, and squinted to get a better look. She was wearing a pair of blue jeans and a black T-shirt that all but blended with the night pressing in around her. But it wasn't the woman's attire that caught Carl's eye. It was her hair, straight and blonde, cropped short to just above the shoulder in a style that he knew only too well. And when she turned around, her face briefly illuminated by the headlamps of a passing vehicle out on the road, he drew in a sharp breath. She looked just like...

"Angel." He spoke her name under his breath, hardly daring to believe his eyes. Of all the places that she would stop... Pulling off the highway and into the same restaurant in the middle of the night. But was it really so much of a coincidence? Maybe she had decided not to stay in San Diego, risk returning home to Queens, and the house that she had grown up in. He couldn't believe his luck. An hour either way and they would have passed each other on the highway without ever realizing how close they had come.

Carl scooted out of the booth and walked toward the door, keeping his emotions in check, making sure not to run like a mad person and draw unwanted attention. As he reached the door, a voice called out from behind him.

"Hey, mister, your food's ready."

He glanced over his shoulder to see the server, an older woman with wiry gray hair and a face lined like cracked ice, watching him with the Midnight Special in one hand, and a half-empty pot of coffee in the other.

"I'll be back," he mumbled, pulling clumsily on the door. "Just going to my car. Forgot my wallet."

"U-huh." The server didn't look like she believed him.

Carl didn't care. He got the door open and stepped out into the balmy Oklahoma night. Angel was still over by the Sebring. She had gone to the trunk. When he looked back over his shoulder, the server hadn't moved. She was looking out of the window, no doubt waiting for him to climb into his car and drive off without paying for the coffee or the uneaten meal.

Shit.

He changed course, walking toward his own vehicle even as he kept an eye on the woman and the Sebring across the parking lot. He reached into his pocket, fumbled for his keys, finally got them out and opened the door. Then he reached inside and made a show of looking around before slipping his wallet from his pocket. He slammed the door and held the wallet high, waving it in the air, and started slowly back toward the restaurant.

The server watched him for a moment longer, then, apparently satisfied that he wasn't a dine-and-dash looking for a free coffee, put his food on the table and sauntered off.

No sooner had the server turned her back on him than Carl changed course. He veered to the left and picked up the pace.

Angel was still at the car, her head inside the trunk as she rummaged around, looking for something. This was perfect. She hadn't even noticed his approach.

A tingle of anticipation surged through Carl. The closer he got, the less chance she had of escaping, screaming for help, or trying to get back into the car and flee. And once he reached her… then he noticed something. The car door was still open, and he could see no one else inside the vehicle.

Where was his daughter?

Angel would never have left Cherub behind in San Diego, or anywhere else, for that matter. Despite everything, she loved the girl. At least, so he had assumed. A sudden stab of fear tightened in Carl's chest. Had something happened to his daughter? What had Angel done to her? Then the answer came to him. Cherub must be curled up asleep on the backseat. Yes, that must be it. Carl breathed a sigh of relief even as he closed the last few feet to the Sebring.

Now Angel noticed him.

She looked up from the trunk, startled. Her eyes flew wide even as she took a step back, a scream building on her lips.

And in that moment, Carl realized his mistake.

She wasn't Angel.

Although the woman bore a passing resemblance to her, he could see it now. Her haircut wasn't quite the same, her face was rounder, and she was at least six inches taller. She was also a good ten years younger. The kind of girl Carl might have considered taking for his own and starting over with if he hadn't been so hell-bent on getting Angel back.

"Whoa. Easy." He lifted his hands, palms flattened. He thought fast, realizing he only had a few seconds to defuse the situation. "Didn't mean to scare you, sweetie. Just coming over to offer my assistance. Looked like you might need some help there."

The young woman studied him with suspicious eyes. "I'm fine, thank you."

"Okay, then. If you're sure." Carl was more than happy to back away. The last thing he needed was to get himself into trouble over a misunderstanding. "Guess I'll just head on back into the restaurant, then."

"Yeah. You do that." The young woman's hand was inside the trunk. Was she holding a tire iron, ready to swing at him?

Carl didn't care. She wasn't Angel, and that was all that mattered. With another mumbled apology, he turned and walked away. He stepped back into the diner and went to his booth, where he ate quickly, gulped down a second cup of strong black coffee, then dropped enough cash to cover the bill and a decent tip on the table, and got the hell out of there. Fifteen minutes later, temporarily refreshed but shaken from his run-in with the girl who wasn't Angel, he was back on the highway and barreling westward once more.

# SIXTEEN

JULIE BLAKE and her daughter had spent the last seventeen days since their arrival in San Diego, living in The Del Ray Inn, a squalid motel in a rough area of town. The accommodation was cheap, at least by West Coast standards, but it was still eating through the cash she had taken from Carl's farmhouse. Between the bus tickets to get them there, the hotel accommodation, and their living expenses, she had already blown through half of the five grand that Carl had kept hidden in his attic.

In hindsight, she should have spent more time searching the house. There must have been more money stashed in other places. Carl was about as paranoid as a person could get and was convinced that the government used banks to keep the population in line and track their movements. How the financial institutions managed this was anyone's guess, but it didn't stop him turning his paychecks into cold, hard cash.

Not that it mattered now. In another couple of weeks, the well would run dry, leaving her and Cherub penniless. Which meant that Julie needed to find work, and quickly. How she would accomplish that while living under a false name and possessing no ID was also anyone's guess. She had abandoned

Angel, the moniker Carl had given her, within a few days of arriving in the city. After so long living under that name, it was hard to stop thinking of herself as Angel, but she also hated the name. It was a reminder of everything the man had done to her. But she couldn't use her real name, either. That would be too obvious. Which was why she had checked into the Del Ray under a name borrowed from the author of Black Beauty, her favorite book when she was a kid.

Anna Sewell.

It was easy to remember, and obscure enough not to raise eyebrows. But even that would be no help in securing gainful employment. She couldn't prove her identity as Anna Sewell any more than she could as Angel or Julie Blake. But all was not lost. There were plenty of employers in San Diego willing to look the other way when it came to such things. Employers who liked the low wages and lack of employment taxes that undocumented immigrants made possible. At least, according to Gloria, the woman who occupied the room next door to her. And Julie might as well be undocumented, even though she hadn't grown up in Mexico, or some other hardscrabble place that made the USA seem like a shining beacon of freedom and opportunity.

But even if she understood those jobs existed, she didn't have a clue where to find one, or what to do with her daughter during work hours if she did. Again, Gloria had come to the rescue.

"I know a man," she had said one afternoon a few days before, when she and Julie were sitting in a pair of lawn chairs outside their rooms on the Del Ray's second-floor balcony. "He finds work for people like us. Ways to make quick money. All cash and no deductions. I can introduce you, if you like?"

Julie's gut twisted. She was far from naïve. She knew the kind of work a man like that might force upon a vulnerable woman with nowhere else to turn and a fear of the authorities. After spending sixteen years succumbing to Carl's every whim, no matter how debased, she had no intention of doing the same again just for a few dollars.

"I don't think so," she had replied quickly. "I really don't want to do things like that."

"Things like—" A look of horror passed across Gloria's face. "Oh, honey, I didn't mean *that* kind of work. Whatever do you take me for? I was talking about cleaning hotel rooms and washing dishes. Mopping floors. That sort of thing."

"Oh." Julie hadn't known what to say next. She hoped Gloria wasn't offended. Then her thoughts turned to Cherub, who was sleeping in the hotel room behind them at that moment. "Thanks for the offer, but I'm not sure how that would work. I can't leave my daughter alone for hours on end."

"You wouldn't need to." Gloria placed a reassuring hand on Julie's knee. "I mostly work evenings down at the bar, prefer it that way. Too much time alone at night, and… well, let's just say that it's easy for the old demons to rear their heads. Addictive personality."

"Tending bar doesn't tempt you?" Julie asked, surprised. "All that liquor around?"

"Nah. Booze was never really my bag. But, a good line of coke, well…" Gloria sniffed, as if to prove her point, then seemed to shake the thought off. "Anyway, the offer's there. So long as you can find work during the day, I can keep an eye on your daughter."

"Really? You would do that for me?" Julie gushed, overcome with relief that at least one part of her problem was solved, even if she didn't know that much about the woman. But she seemed nice enough, and it wasn't like Julie had much of a choice. "It's a lot to ask."

"Yes, it is." Gloria tapped Julie's leg. "Which is why you'll be making it up to me with half of whatever you earn."

"Half?" Julie hadn't even met Gloria's contact yet, had no idea how much he paid women in her situation, but she knew it wasn't going to be top dollar. It might not even reach the threshold of minimum wage under the law. It would be hard enough to survive on a pittance like that without having to split it with Gloria. "Thanks for the offer, but I don't think I can afford it."

Gloria had merely shrugged. "Whatever. Good luck finding work on your own. Especially work that will let you bring the kid in with you. It's a tough world out there, honey. You're going to need all the help you can get. You'll see, soon enough."

And with that, Gloria had risen from her chair, picked up the packet of cigarettes sitting on the arm, and ambled back into her room, closing the door.

Now, after spending the last couple of days thinking about Gloria's information, and her offer, Julie was no closer to figuring out what she was going to do for money in the future than she was before. She couldn't leave Cherub with her neighbor while she hunted for work, that much was obvious. Gloria's previous helpfulness, watching Cherub while she had gone to the post office and mailed that postcard back home, had been nothing but a free sample. If Julie wanted more babysitting, it would come at a price. Half her paycheck, apparently. And without Gloria's friend, who she claimed could find discreet work for people unable get a job through regular channels, she was screwed. Julie lay back on the lumpy bed in her dingy hotel room and slid her arm around Cherub, who was curled up next to her, sleeping. Maybe next week, or the week after, she would be forced to do what Gloria wanted. But until then, she still had some money. And who knew, maybe something would come up in the meantime. An opportunity that didn't involve Gloria. And if not, well, she would figure something out, because the alternative was too dreadful to contemplate.

Not for the first time, she wished she could go home to Queens, to her parents and sister and the comforting embrace of family. But it wasn't possible, because Carl was out there somewhere. If she went back, they would be in danger, and she knew first-hand just how violent and dangerous he could be. No, it was better this way. She and her daughter would find a way to make a life for themselves, and she would do everything possible to keep herself, her daughter, and her family back in Queens safe from that monster.

## SEVENTEEN

THERE WERE a lot of walk-in clinics in San Diego. Dozens of them, if not hundreds. That was the first thing that Patterson learned the morning after Bauer and the task force had raided Carl Bonneville's farmhouse outside of Flagstaff. What had felt like a break in her search for Julie only hours before now felt like a hopeless endeavor, even with the digitally aged photograph on her phone.

But it wasn't just the magnitude of the search that weighed upon Patterson. It was also the new information that Marcus Bauer had provided after the raid. Her sister had borne a daughter to her captor. After ending the call with Bauer the night before, Patterson had laid awake in the darkness, overcome by the implications of his discovery. Julie must have gone through hell these past sixteen years, locked up and forced to satisfy the sick urges of her captor. Impregnated by him and forced to have his child. And worse, Bonneville's mother must have been involved. The pair lived together, after all. There was no way that he could have hidden Julie from her. Especially since Bonneville worked as a long-distance truck driver and would have spent long periods away from home. The thought of that disgusted Patterson almost as much as what Bonneville himself had done to her sister.

As she sat in her car, parked next to the fifteenth clinic she had visited that morning, Patterson buried her head in her hands. After finally giving up on sleep and rising at dawn, she had sat at the small table in the camper and used her laptop to identify the most likely areas where Julie might be hiding. Her sister would have no identification, and probably be low on funds, which narrowed the search to the less salubrious areas of the city. But Julie would also want to keep a low profile and avoid using her real name, knowing that Bonneville would surely come after her. That made the task of locating her ten times harder, even with the reduced search area.

Then Patterson had discovered just how many walk-in medical centers and clinics there were, and it was impossible to know which of them catered to undocumented immigrants without visiting each one in turn. It was exhausting. It was also apparent that she was getting nowhere fast. Not only were the clinics reluctant to cooperate, citing patient confidentiality even after she flashed her creds, but some of them, especially those that treated immigrants, didn't even require patients to give their names or provide an address. This was, no doubt, a way of protecting themselves if ICE—short for U.S. Immigration and Customs Enforcement—showed up on their doorstep, even though the agency avoided what they termed as sensitive locations. A humanitarian policy meant to allow anyone, regardless of immigration status, access to necessary care without fear of arrest. The staff who worked in such places apparently didn't see much difference between Homeland Security and the FBI. Even when Patterson explained her situation, they were suspicious. Every visit took longer than it should have. She needed help, and there was only one place she could get it.

The FBI's San Diego field office.

# EIGHTEEN

FOUR DAYS SITTING in the Clark County Jail, not far from the garish lights of downtown Las Vegas and Fremont Street, had given Corbin Pope plenty of time to think. And most of those thoughts had centered on revenge for the people that he perceived as putting him there. Notably, the FBI agent bitch, Patterson Blake, and the man who had hired him to kill her, Senator Bill Newport. In fairness to the Texas politician, Newport had not played a role in getting Pope arrested beyond hiring him to make the FBI agent go away permanently. The betrayal had come after that, as the hitman—who was so careful that he had never even had so much as a traffic ticket—was sitting in the county jail waiting to discover his fate. During Pope's first hours in custody, he had undergone the humiliating ordeal of being fingerprinted, having mug shots taken, and being put into a large holding cell with several other prisoners awaiting arraignment. Then, a day later, had come his appearance before a judge, who swiftly denied bail and ordered him to be held pending trial. That meant a move into the jail's general population, which was where the good senator's betrayal took place. He had orchestrated an attempt on Pope's life in an attack so clichéd that it might as well have been a scene in a low-budget prison movie. An attack motivated, no doubt, by the senator's fear of what the hitman might say to investigators.

Pope had been in the showers a couple of days after his arrest. At first, there was nothing out of the ordinary, but after a few minutes, he noticed that the other inmates had cleared out, leaving him alone. At least until a pair of men, one burly enough to be a TV wrestler and the other skinny enough that he almost looked malnourished, made their entrance. Both men were naked. The first was bald, while the other sported a military style buzz cut. That was where the similarities ended. They both bore tattoos covering their arms, chest, neck, and even their foreheads. Tattoos that were just as clichéd as their mode of attack. Lightning bolts, barbed wire, and a heart speared by a knife, among others.

Pope knew very well what the tats symbolized. Hatred and division. The men were white supremacists. They were also there to do him harm, judging by the shivs they both carried. And if he was in any doubt regarding the individual who had arranged the attack, it was quickly dispelled by the larger of the two men.

"Senator Newport sends his regards," he said in a gravelly voice, before advancing with narrowed eyes.

Pope had no time to think, but he didn't need it. His reflexes were honed by years of navigating violent confrontations on the fly. Likewise, his ability to sum up a situation and make a snap decision. He also suspected that he was a more proficient killer than either of these hired goons.

He didn't move, didn't attempt to flee. Instead, he allowed the closer of the men to approach him with the patience of a spider waiting for a fly to stray into its web. It wasn't until TV Wrestler made his move with the shiv that Pope sprang into action. He sidestepped the assault with deft precision and grabbed his assailant's wrist even as the makeshift knife found empty air. Then he wrapped his free arm around the other man's elbow and swiftly applied downward pressure to the man's wrist, using the arm as a fulcrum, until he heard a gratifying crack that elicited a cry of pain from his would-be murderer.

The knife fell from the man's hand.

Pope pushed him away, while simultaneously delivering a deadly blow with the side of his hand to the man's neck under his chin, crushing his windpipe and sending him to his knees, sputtering. Then, in a fluid move so fast that Skinny Guy—advancing a step behind his companion—barely had time to register, he scooped up the shiv, and drove it up and into the man's solar plexus, before twisting the knife and slicing his abdominal aorta.

By the time he pulled the knife out, the man was already on his way to the floor of the shower room, where he would live out the last brief minutes of his life.

Pope turned his attention to the first man, who was now lying motionless, dead eyes staring at the ceiling. Satisfied, he rinsed the knife under the shower jet, removing any fingerprints, then dropped it close to the body and sauntered casually from the room. There were no cameras in the showers to record either the attack, or Pope's deadly reaction to it, and the jailhouse guards would have little incentive to investigate beyond a cursory examination of the scene, where they would soon conclude that the pair of tatted gang members had turned upon each other in a violent confrontation that cost both of them their lives.

Now, two days later, Pope's thoughts were consumed with pay back. In the days since the shower attack, there had been no further attempts on his life, although he wasn't naïve enough to think that it would remain that way. Newport had failed once, but he would try again, and this time, he might not send a pair of amateurs. Which led Pope to an undeniable conclusion. He had to get out of there, and fast.

Luckily, he had long ago put in place a contingency plan for an event just such as this. While Pope had always relied upon his skill as a professional assassin to avoid even the most innocuous of confrontations with the law, he was not stupid enough to believe the sky would never fall. And all it would take was one phone call to put his plan into effect. A phone call he had made the previous day, and which would, by now, have set in place the sequence of events necessary for his liberation.

All he had to do was wait.

He didn't have to wait very long.

At noon on Pope's fifth day in custody, a pair of guards entered his cell. The closer of the two instructed him to stand up and turn around with his hands behind his back, then promptly snapped a pair of handcuffs on his wrists.

"What's going on?" Pope asked.

"It's our lucky day," the guard said in a voice laced with venom. "We'll soon have one less scumbag to deal with around here."

For a moment, Pope's heart leaped into his throat. Was this the follow-up attack he had been expecting? If so, he was at a disadvantage, having allowed the guard to cuff him with such ease. He wondered how it would go down. Would it be as crude as a knife between the ribs, or would he be found hanging from the rafters of his cell, a looped bed sheet cutting into his neck? Either way, it amounted to the same thing.

Pope was screwed.

At least, until he wasn't. Because instead of closing the cell door and perpetrating violence, the guards spun him around and marched Pope out onto the catwalk and through the jail, to a small holding cell of which he was the only occupant. Fifteen minutes after that, two more men entered, who identified themselves as U.S. marshals and informed Pope that he was being transferred to a federal facility out-of-state by order of the FBI.

After that, they waited patiently while the same guard who had originally cuffed him placed a belly chain around his waist before securing the handcuffs to it. Next came a pair of leg irons, which would allow him to walk at a normal pace but would preclude breaking free and running. Finally, the guard attached a chain from Pope's wrists to his ankles, preventing him from lifting his arms. This was known in prison terms as full restraints.

The feds were taking no chances.

They watched as Pope was shackled. Then, once they were satisfied of his inability to do them harm, he was led out of the jail building, and across a parking area surrounded by barbed wire fence, to a black sedan with federal law enforcement emblems on the doors. Minutes later, he was being driven out of the jail and through downtown toward I-11. After that, they picked up I-15, upon which they drove for a little under two hours, leaving Nevada behind, crossing into Arizona, and continuing until they drew close to the Utah border.

During the ride, neither of the marshals said a word to Pope. They chatted among themselves while playing a country station on the radio that faded into static so frequently that Pope wondered why they even bothered. Eventually, the car pulled over behind another vehicle, waiting on a desolate stretch of highway surrounded by dusty scrubland baking under the brutal afternoon sun. An older model Ford Taurus so bland it wouldn't elicit a second look.

One of the marshals turned to look at Pope. He held up a set of keys and waved them back and forth. Then he said, "You ready to vanish?"

# NINETEEN

CARL HAD DRIVEN for another three hours after stopping at the diner, flying down the interstate as fast as he dared. Then, with his eyelids drooping and fearing that he might fall asleep behind the wheel and drive off the road, he had taken the next exit he came to and booked a room at the cheapest roadside hotel he could find. He had crawled into bed, happy to be out of the car, and fell asleep instantly. The alarm on his phone woke him again five hours later at 8 AM. He grabbed a quick breakfast at the hotel's meagre buffet, which was mostly composed of bagels, muffins, and various individual sized packages of cereal, then climbed back behind the wheel and continued his journey.

He still had fifteen hours to go, a drive that would take him through the Texas Panhandle, New Mexico, and Arizona, before reaching California. His encounter with the girl he had mistaken for Angel the night before was fresh in his mind. If he hadn't been so tired, he might not have thought it was her, but it raised a possibility that he hadn't considered previously. With so much time to think, Angel might have decided to risk going back to New York despite the threats against her family that he had made so often over the years. Which was why he kept his eyes peeled and studied every car driving in the other direction that looked even remotely like his mother's Sebring. It soon turned into a kind of game that kept him alert, which was good, because he had no intention of stopping again for anything more than a bathroom break or a bite to eat despite the daunting amount of road that still lay ahead of him. When he pulled off the highway to fill up with gas, he also purchased a supply of energy drinks, which he figured would keep him awake as day turned back to night and the miles took their toll.

And as he drove, he thought about Angel, and how she had rewarded him for his love by leaving his mother dead on the kitchen floor and stealing her car. Not that he had reported the car theft any more than he had alerted anyone of his mother's untimely demise. That would lead to questions that he couldn't answer. At least, not if he wanted to stay a free man.

Then his thoughts turned to the farmhouse, and Ma in that shallow grave out back. One of the options presented to him by his phone's GPS went through Flagstaff, and he had selected that route, perhaps subconsciously steering himself close enough to pay her a visit. Now, he considered the wisdom of taking a small detour.

He had no idea if Angel's father had remembered him touching the picture frame, but if so, it would now be in the hands of the FBI, especially since his deception would have become obvious the moment a real FBI agent showed up on Franklin Blake's doorstep. And if they somehow managed to match his fingerprints, then the farmhouse was no longer safe.

That left him in a quandary, because he would love to stop and see his mother one more time, visit her grave and tell her everything that had happened since he had left her alone in that shallow hole in the ground many days before. And, he realized, there might never be another opportunity to pay his respects. If the FBI had learned of his identity, then they would surely visit the property, and his mother was not well enough buried to go undiscovered. They would remove her, take her to some cold, clinical lab where they would violate her corpse and cut her up to see how she had died.

That thought was too much. Maybe he should go to the farmhouse, and not just to see Ma, but to find out if the FBI had been there. It was, he reasoned, a no loss scenario. If the authorities hadn't been there, then he could breathe easy. That snafu with the picture frame would not have cost him anything, and he could go to his mother's grave and pay his respects before continuing on toward San Diego. If the FBI had been there, then he would know for certain. That knowledge would be priceless later, when he was searching for Angel. Which was why, in that moment, he made up his mind. First the farmhouse, and then on to San Diego.

# TWENTY

SENATOR BILL NEWPORT was not a happy man. Not only had Corbin Pope failed to deal with the FBI agent who had ruined his plans for the contaminated plot of land outside of Amarillo, and almost sunk his senatorial career in the worst way possible, but he had gotten himself caught in the process. A turn of events Newport would never have expected, given the assassin's meticulous craftsmanship and attention to detail, that had made him something of a legend in certain circles. Or maybe a myth would be a better description, since few people were privy to the truth of his existence, and even fewer had met him in person. Corbin Pope, who had been dubbed the *Angel of Death* by conspiracy theorists and murder junkies who populated the darker corners of the internet, had made a career out of showing up, doing his job, then fading back into the shadows like a ghost without anyone ever knowing he had been there. Most of that was due to his unique method of execution, making every death look like an accident.

Even Newport, who was about as close to Pope as anyone ever could be thanks to the number of times he had utilized the assassin's services, didn't even know the number of hits the man had notched. It might be a hundred, or a thousand. He certainly came to mind every time some inconveniently moral politician who thought they could change the system flipped a motorboat and drowned while on vacation in Aruba, or a climate change activist with a big mouth and too many social media followers ended up lost for days in the very wilderness they were trying to save and succumbed to the elements. Pope was, in short, a genius when it came to the art of murder.

Except for this time.

The FBI agent had gotten the better of him, anticipating his attack and turning the tables. It would have been better if she had put a bullet in his head, but instead Pope had ended up in a jail cell, and no doubt wondering how he could use his knowledge of the many clients he had served, including Newport, to his best advantage. Which required swift action.

But Pope had not only survived the attempt on his life, orchestrated by Newport through his clandestine association with certain extremist right-wing organizations, but he had made short work of killing the two gang members—both of them serving life terms thanks to their proclivity for violence—tasked with the job. And then, as if that wasn't enough, Newport had just received word that Corbin Pope had escaped custody after a pair of men posing as U.S. marshals, and carrying false transfer paperwork, had sauntered into the Clark County Jail in downtown Las Vegas, and walked out the front door with him in a jailbreak ballsy enough that it might be the plot of a Hollywood action movie if it hadn't been true. Hell, it probably would be a movie soon enough when some sleazy producer heard about it and purchased the rights.

Newport cursed under his breath.

He should have known that Pope, a man who left nothing to chance, had devised an exit strategy for this very scenario. But what bothered Newport far more than the ease with which the assassin had dispatched the men sent to kill him, or his escape from custody, was what he would do next.

Pope surely knew that the pair of gangbangers were sent at

the senator's behest, if only because Newport had given them a message to deliver. He had wanted Pope to know exactly who was responsible for his impending demise.

A stupid thing to do, in hindsight. All he had managed was to put a target on his own back. Not that Pope wouldn't have realized who was behind the attempt on his life, anyway. It didn't take a genius to figure out that the senator had a lot to lose if the hitman opened his mouth to investigators, told them exactly who had hired him to off the FBI agent, and why.

Newport rose from his desk and crossed his office, located in the Texas State Capitol building in downtown Austin. He opened the door a few inches and peered nervously out into the corridor beyond, even though there was no way that Pope could have made it all the way from Las Vegas to Austin in the brief amount of time since his unorthodox liberation. But that didn't mean that he wasn't coming, which meant that Newport needed to think fast.

The State Capitol was a practical fortress, with its own police force dedicated to keeping the lawmakers within safe. There was round-the-clock security, too. Like surveillance cameras that covered just about every inch of the exterior, and much of the interior, metal detectors, and retractable bollards made of carbon steel at every gate, designed to block unauthorized vehicles from gaining access to the grounds. Newport was safer inside the capitol building than anywhere else on earth, other than perhaps the Pentagon or the Capitol in Washington, DC.

Yet he didn't *feel* safe, and he couldn't stay in his office forever. At some point, he would have to leave and go back to either the apartment he owned in Austin or to his home in Dallas, which itself was fortified, although nowhere near to the level of the Capitol. And unlike ex-presidents, he didn't get a full-time security detail made up of Secret Service agents who would leap in front of a bullet to save him. The only way he was going to get any help from that quarter was if he could prove that there was a credible threat to his life. But telling the Secret

Service that a hitman he had hired to murder an FBI agent was pissed at him and out for revenge wouldn't exactly help his situation. In fact, it would amount to a confession that might save his life but put him behind bars at the same time.

He wished that his pet cop, Detective Sergeant Ortega, was still around. The man might not have possessed Corbin Pope's cunning or deadly skills, but he had a dedication to violence and a willingness to kill that would have put Senator Newport's mind at ease, at least a little. If only the detective wasn't currently being held without bail pending trial for his part in a deadly scheme to frame Patterson Blake for murder. Which left Newport with no choice but to fend for himself.

Turning away from the door, he crossed to a closet on the far wall within which hung an exquisitely tailored Italian blouson made of cashmere with leather detailing. It was a coat that he would never have purchased for himself. The staggering price tag, more money than many of his constituents spent on their family car, was an extravagance that he indulged, like many of the other fine items he possessed, because they were a token of thanks from one of the many wealthy donors for whom he had done a favor, like pushing business friendly legislation through or relaxing regulations on a particular industry. But it wasn't the coat that interested him right now. He pushed it aside to reveal a hidden wall safe within which was a Desert Eagle semi-automatic pistol. A firearm renowned for its power. He removed the gun and closed the safe, then retreated to his desk and slipped the pistol into the top drawer. There was nothing he could do to stop Pope from coming after him, but at least now it would be a fair fight. Or at least, as fair a fight as it ever could be against a man who meted out death with the same precision that a virtuoso violinist played a fine Stradivarius.

# TWENTY-ONE

IT TOOK another ten hours for Carl to reach Flagstaff. He had hoped to make it there in less than nine, but that didn't account for traffic and stopping at rest areas to answer the call of nature. Now, as he took a detour from his planned route and headed north toward the farmhouse, he was filled with a mixture of anticipation and apprehension.

He also found himself overcome by a powerful sense of familiarity. He had driven this road so many times over the years in the cab of his truck, returning from a long stretch hauling cargo, weary from hours of driving, and excited to spend time with his family. If he tried hard enough, if he pushed recent events to the back of his mind, he could almost imagine that Ma's death and Angel's escape were nothing but a bad dream and everything was just fine, and that he would arrive at the farmhouse to find them waiting for him. Then, after a hot meal and an even hotter shower, he would retreat to the bedroom, where Angel would keep him company, her warm body pressed against his, for the rest of the night.

He had to keep reminding himself that none of that was true. Not anymore. Angel was gone and his mother was dead. Worse, the FBI might know who he was and what he had done.

Everything that had happened since he returned to the farmhouse days before wasn't just a dream. It was a nightmare. How much of a nightmare remained to be seen, but he would find out soon enough when he arrived home.

Carl gripped the steering wheel tight and hunched forward, scanning the road ahead as he drove because he was concerned that if the authorities had discovered his identity, they would be looking for him, possibly even expecting him to return to the farm. Traffic was light, but even so, he studied every vehicle that he encountered, wondering if it was an unmarked police car or FBI vehicle. At one point, when he was still ten miles from the farmhouse, he spotted the familiar black and white paint job of a Flagstaff Police Department interceptor heading toward him.

For a moment, he panicked, almost swung the wheel, pulled a one-eighty, and tore off in the other direction as fast as he could. But that was a foolhardy thing to do. He had no idea if the cop was even aware of him. Still, he didn't want to just keep going until they were close enough that his options for escape dwindled to zero. Which was why, when he saw the semicircular driveway to a house up ahead, he slowed and pulled in, as if that had been his destination all along. And since the driveway curved around to a second entrance, he wasn't trapping himself. Thankfully, it appeared no one was home. The driveway was empty of other vehicles and there were no lights on in the house, even though it was dusk. Carl came to a stop and waited, praying that the cop wouldn't turn in behind him.

But that didn't happen. The interceptor breezed on by and kept going, much to Carl's relief. Even so, he sat there for a minute, just to make sure. Then, when he thought it was safe, he pulled back out onto the road and drove the last miles to the farmhouse. Or at least, to the dirt road that led there. Because he went no further.

The first thing Carl noticed as he approached the turnoff was the amount of dirt that had been kicked up from the unpaved road and onto the blacktop. Dirt that clearly showed the impression of tires from several vehicles as they turned in and out of the narrow access road.

Carl slowed and pulled over onto the thin strip of grass that bordered the road. He glanced around, checking the road ahead and in his rearview mirror to make sure that he was still alone, before climbing out of the car and approaching the turnoff on foot. There were more tire impressions on the dirt road. Lots of them. It looked like an entire fleet of vehicles had been going back-and-forth. There was only one reason Carl could think of for that. The FBI had figured out who he was and where he lived. And if he needed any further proof, it came a few seconds later when he saw a strip of torn yellow plastic caught on the wire fence that bordered the narrow trail and flapping in the breeze. A short ribbon with eight bold black letters upon it that had him backing away in fear even though the phrase they spelled out was cut off mid word.

CRIME SCE...

Shit.

Carl looked around again, expecting to be swarmed at any moment by FBI agents pointing guns and screaming at him to get down on the ground. But he was still alone. At least, for now. Carl had no intention of sticking around to find out if the farmhouse was under surveillance. He all but ran back to the truck, jumped behind the wheel, pulled a fast U-turn, and sped back toward Flagstaff and the highway just as fast as he dared. And as he went, he realized what those tire tracks and that scrap of yellow plastic meant. He was now a wanted man.

# TWENTY-TWO

AFTER SPENDING MOST of the day going from one walk-in clinic to another, Patterson was no closer to finding Julie than she had been before. They either didn't recognize her sister from the digitally aged photograph, or wouldn't say either way, citing privacy concerns. Finally, after realizing that she could never visit every clinic in the city on her own, she had taken the local field office up on their offer of help.

Special Agent Holmes, who had visited her only that morning when he dropped off her loaner car, wasted no time in rounding up a couple more agents with the SAC's approval, and together they headed out into the city to make inquiries. Nothing had come of their efforts, but Holmes had promised that they would hit the streets first thing the next morning and keep searching. If Julie was in San Diego, Holmes had assured her, and if she had gone to one of those clinics to secure medicine for either herself or her daughter, they would find out eventually.

And that was the big unknown. Julie had been in the city almost a week before—Patterson knew that much—but she might not have stayed there. What if her sister was merely passing through on her way to some other destination? There was no way to answer that question, but she had a hunch. A feeling that Julie secretly wanted to be found, that she had sent the postcard not only to warn them about Carl Edward Bonneville but also as a subconscious cry for help. Granted, it was unlikely she would have known that Patterson had become a federal agent—even though Bonneville clearly did given how he had shown up at the house back in Queens—but Julie would certainly have been aware that her family would not rest until they found her. The postcard was a pin on the map, begging *I'm here, come get me.*

And Patterson had every intention of doing exactly that.

But not right now. It was late, almost ten o'clock, and she was exhausted. As the sun had slipped below the horizon, and the day gave way to night, the search had come to a halt until morning. That was when Holmes and his team had extended to her the hospitality of the San Diego field office by inviting her out for pizza and beer. At first, she had declined. Patterson was hardly in the mood, but they had insisted.

"What would we look like," Holmes had said to her, "if we let a fellow agent sit all alone in her camper eating a frozen dinner when she could be enjoying the best pizza on the West Coast?"

"I wasn't going to eat a frozen dinner," Patterson had replied. And it was true. She would probably have ended up with a protein shake, her go-to of late. "And I'd hardly be the best company."

But Holmes and his colleagues had insisted, and she knew better than to snub them, especially since she needed their help. Which was how she had ended up back at the camper with a belly full of pizza and a box full of leftovers—an easy meal for another day. She was putting them in the fridge, rearranging items in the tiny space to make the box fit, when her phone rang.

It was Jonathan Grant, which surprised her, because it was 1 AM on the East Coast.

"Hey," she said, after picking up. "You calling to whisper sweet nothings in my ear before I climb into the sack?"

"Hardly." There was a tone to Grant's voice that told her that his call had nothing to do with their relationship. "There's been a development."

"In Julie's case?"

"No. It concerns the hitman Senator Newport sent to kill you in Vegas—"

"I think the good senator would object to that accusation," Patterson said dryly.

"I'm sure that he would. But it doesn't alter the fact that we all know he was behind it."

"True." Patterson didn't like where the conversation was going. "What About him?"

There was a moment of hesitation on the other end of the line, then, "He escaped custody this afternoon."

"What? How?"

"Couple of U.S. Marshalls walked him right out of there. Said he was being transferred to a federal facility at our request. It was bullshit, of course. Transfer papers were fake… good ones, but fake. It was hours before anyone realized anything was wrong. By that time, he was in the wind and those bogus U.S. Marshalls had vanished back under whatever rock they crawled out of. State Police found the car they were driving dumped near Salt Lake City, but the killer probably parted ways with his accomplices way before that. By now, he could be anywhere."

"And the car?" Patterson asked. "Forensics should be able to get something from that."

"Torched. Nothing but a blackened shell."

"Crap." Patterson stared out of the camper window at a woman walking a small dog that looked like a Jack Russell back and forth on a patch of grass under a tree in the next lot over, clearly hoping it would pee. If only she knew the dangers that lurked in the night, Patterson mused—the thought popping into her head unbidden—the woman might not be so bold in venturing out into the darkness like that.

"You need to be careful, Patterson," Grant said, breaking her train of thought.

"I'm always careful," Patterson shot back, still watching the woman as she made her way back inside the monster RV—big as a city bus—that barely fit on the plot of ground they had rented for the night.

If Grant thought otherwise, which she suspected he did, he didn't say as much. Instead, he offered a stark warning. "Until we catch this guy and put him back behind bars, you're a target. I'm sure you won't want to hear this, but I think you should come back to New York. Let us put you in a safe house... just until this all blows over."

"No way. Absolutely not." Patterson's ire rose so fast that it surprised even her. "I'm not abandoning the search now. Not when I'm so close to finding Julie."

"I could order you back."

"But you won't. Not if you ever want to see me again outside of work. Besides, SAC Khan has—"

"The SAC agrees with me. I already briefed her on the situation. This obsession with finding Julie isn't worth losing your life over." Grant let that sink in before continuing. "And there's no need to pull the relationship card. This isn't personal."

"Then that's it!" Patterson said. "I'm done, just like that."

"I never said—"

"You realize this might be my only chance of finding Julie, right? She's in San Diego. I know it. But she might not be here by the time I return if you force me to sit around in a safe house staring at the walls for weeks on end."

"I know that. Which is—"

"The man who took her is probably on his way to San Diego right now. If he gets to her before me, then—"

"Patterson." Grant barked, cutting her off. "For the love of God, will you let me get a word in, just for once?"

"What?" Patterson replied sullenly.

"I'm well aware that your current investigation is time-sensitive. I'm also aware of the threat posed by Carl Edward Bonneville. Which is why I'm not recalling you to New York. Not yet at least."

"You're not?"

"No. But I'm also not willing to leave you out there on your own. Not while that hitman is on the loose. And honestly, it might take us a while to find him. We know nothing about the man. He might as well be a ghost. His fingerprints aren't in any database. Likewise, his face. He was carrying no ID beyond the driver's license he used to check into the hotel in Vegas, which we're sure is fake. All we have is an alias and there's no way he'll still be using that. If he's the professional we think he is, then he'll take on a new identity, might even already have done so."

"What are you trying to say?"

"I'm saying you need someone to watch your back while you're looking for Julie."

"You mean that rookie agent from the San Diego FO? Holmes?" Patterson wasn't impressed. The man was a couple of inches shorter than she was, and probably weighed a hundred and thirty wet. "Because nice as the guy is, I'm not sure he's bodyguard material."

"I would remind you that he graduated from Quantico, earned his badge, just like you did, Patterson. You shouldn't be so judgmental. But no, I'm not talking about Special Agent Holmes. I was thinking of someone more familiar with your propensity for trouble. I already cleared it with his SAC."

"I'm fine," Patterson said. "I can look after myself."

"Past events would indicate otherwise," Grant said. "And I'm not taking any chances with a vicious killer on the loose. Marcus Bauer will be there first thing in the morning."

# TWENTY-THREE

CORBIN POPE HAD LEFT Utah behind many hours before. He was speeding along the interstate and heading east toward Texas, feeling more relaxed than he had in almost a week. The contingency plan he had devised many years before, a scheme he had truly believed would never need to be put into action, had worked flawlessly, even if the circumstances that predicated its implementation had been a humbling lesson in hubris. The two men who had walked him out of the Clark County Jail right under the noses of the very guards whose job it was to make sure he didn't escape, were not genuine U.S. marshals, of course. They were, rather, operatives for a certain clandestine intelligence agency who looked out for America's interests overseas. He had done a number of jobs for the CIA in locales across the globe, and even one particularly daring hit deep within Russia, assassinating a soviet era general who had transitioned to a new, if equally corrupt, life in the federation that rose from its rubble. The man had met his maker on the steps of the Kremlin, and no one, not even the SFB—Russia's federal security service—suspected that his death was anything but a tragic accident. In doing so, he had earned the gratitude of some powerful men. Which was his intention all along, even if he had hoped never to cash in.

Now, as he drove through the remaining hours of daylight and into the night, he was thankful for his foresight, and that his Agency associates had come through. He was also looking forward to what would come next. Taking care of the man who had tried to kill him only a few days before. And what a joy it would be to see the light fade from Newport's eyes, even if Pope hadn't yet decided exactly how the senator was going to make his grand exit. And after that, there was the FBI agent. The instrument of his only failure. He would enjoy killing her even more.

# TWENTY-FOUR

AFTER HER CALL with Jonathan Grant was over, Patterson sat on her bed at the back of the camper van, lost in thought. The weeks leading up to her arrival in San Diego had been a whirlwind of conflicting emotions and dashed hopes, but now, against the odds, she was at the end of her journey, one way or the other.

Reaching down, she pulled the plastic tub containing all the information she had gathered about Julie from under the bed. She placed it in front of her and lifted the lid, then removed items one by one and studied them. There were the original postcards that Julie had sent over the weeks of her road trip many years before. When she held her phone up, compared them side-by-side with the photograph of the most recent postcard, which had arrived at her father's house in Queens only a few days ago, there was no doubt about its author.

This was in sharp contrast to the postcards that had prompted her search for Julie—the ones that had been sent weeks after the last postcard that she believed was genuine, and which her father had hidden from her for years. Those postcards had been signed Julie, instead of Jelly, and although they looked like her sister's handwriting, the messages did not sound like her sister at all. Now, looking at them with fresh eyes and with the benefit of new information, she wondered if Carl Edward Bonneville had forced her sister to write the postcards so that no one would come looking for her. He had probably dictated what he wanted her to say, no doubt with the threat of violence if she refused.

But Julie had been smart. She knew something that Bonneville didn't. She had signed the postcards with her given name rather than the nickname that she had adopted as a child and had used on every other communication, whether it was the letters she wrote her sister from college, or the previous postcards. It was an obvious cry for help that her father had picked up upon, but that the police back then had dismissed. Not that it would have made any difference. No matter how much they had searched, the LAPD would never have found Julie, because by then she was locked in a bedroom hundreds of miles away from Los Angeles on a farm north of Flagstaff. In fact, Julie had never even made it to LA. Bonneville had snatched her late one night in Santa Fe after an argument with her boyfriend. It pained Patterson to think that Julie's fate was sealed in that moment for the next sixteen years. No matter how many coded messages she had sent, no matter what she did, there was no hope of rescue.

Patterson laid the old postcards back in the tub and picked up a package of photographs. Prints made from negatives supplied by Mark Davis, a member of the band Sunrise that Julie had traveled with for a while prior to her disappearance.

She opened the package and took the photographs out, going through them and studying her sister's face in each. Brief snatches of her sister's last days of freedom frozen forever. Sad reminders of the sunshine before the darkness. Some pictures were taken at TexFest, the music festival where the band had played, and which Julie had attended. The later photos had been taken at the car sculpture outside of Amarillo. She wondered what her sister had been thinking at the very moment the photos were taken. She looked happy, and Patterson was glad for that, because it wouldn't be long before her life became a living hell.

Patterson continued through the prints, stopping at one particular photo, a copy of which was sitting on her father's mantle in a silver frame. A photo that had given her the name of Julie's abductor and led them to the farmhouse where she had been held captive for so long. If Bonneville had not let himself become distracted by that photo, had resisted picking it up, he might be as much a ghost now as he had been for the past decade and a half. And Julie was to thank for that. She could not have known it at the time, but posing for that snapshot, spraying that message to her father on the rusting half-buried car in a field outside of Amarillo, would one day become the clue that might free her of Bonneville forever.

Patterson slipped the photographs back into their pouch and wiped a tear from her eye. She reached down and touched the folded road map that Julie's friend Stacy had given her back in Chicago when Patterson was at the start of her search. It bore silent witness to a journey never completed. Maybe someday, when she and her sister were finally reunited and the horrors of the past sixteen years were nothing but a bad memory, she and Julie would complete that trip together, finally ending a chapter in their lives that had begun so long ago.

Or maybe not.

Sometimes it was better to let the past stay right where it was and focus on a happier future.

A faint smile crossed Patterson's lips despite the aching sadness that had been her constant companion for so long. She put the lid back on the tub and slid the container back under her bed. There was only one thing that mattered now. Finding Julie and bringing her back home safe and sound while putting the man who took her behind bars. And that was exactly what Patterson intended to do. Carl Edward Bonneville might not realize it yet, but his arrival in San Diego would be akin to an insect flying into a spider's web. All she had to do was wait, and the bastard who caused her family so much pain would come to her. There was only one problem. Bonneville wasn't the only one who might show up in San Diego. There was also the hitman that Senator Newport had sent after her. Somehow, against the odds, he had escaped custody. And now he would want to exact his revenge, which meant that her life had just gotten a whole lot more complicated… and dangerous.

# TWENTY-FIVE

CARL HAD GIVEN a lot of thought to his future over the past few hours since discovering that the FBI knew who he was and what he had done, and had come to an inescapable conclusion. He would have to vanish just as surely as Julie Blake had vanished all those years ago. Disappear as if he had never existed. That would mean a new identity, something he had no idea how to go about securing. At least, not yet. It might also mean leaving the country and getting as far away from the FBI, and Angel's sister, as was humanly possible. Patterson Blake would never stop looking for her sister, which meant that the case would never grow cold.

Luckily, he knew the perfect place to go. Tijuana—a town he was intimately familiar with thanks to his more basic urges—was just across the border from San Diego. It was a wild place run by gangs who trafficked drugs and women. A dangerous place where an American could end up dead in a heartbeat. But it was also a place where a person could drop out of sight. Even better, it was a gateway to the rest of Mexico, and a host of countries beyond, like Ecuador, Bolivia, and Venezuela, that either hadn't signed an extradition treaty with the United States or made extradition difficult. Once he found Angel, it would be easy to slip across the border and start a new life, especially since he had possessed the foresight to gather all the cash he'd hidden around his home over the years and bring it with him. Almost $40,000 that now resided behind the passenger seat of his truck inside a zipped-up duffel bag. Not enough for him, Angel, and their daughter to live on for the rest of their lives, but an amount that would make life easy until he found a fresh source of income south of the border. His only regret was that Ma wouldn't be there with them.

A lump formed in Carl's throat when he thought of that, swiftly followed by a stab of anger. He gripped the steering wheel tightly and waited for the rage to subside, only to be replaced by a bitter sense of self-pity.

If he hadn't gone on that last road trip, none of this would have happened. Even if Angel wasn't responsible for his mother's death, she had done nothing to stop it. Ma had lived the last moments of her life alone and afraid on the kitchen floor while one of her stupid chat shows babbled in the background. It never occurred to him that Angel would have been unable to come to his mother's aid even if she had wanted to, since she would have been locked in the bedroom at the back of the house. And in that moment, he wondered if Angel would make it to Tijuana, even if found her. Maybe it would be better for all involved if he just dispensed with her entirely, took his daughter, and found a new love in a place where an American with money was appreciated, even one who was on the run, and a woman knew better than to ask too many questions.

The more he thought about it, the more Carl came around to that idea. Because, after all he had done for her, Angel had betrayed him. Taken his daughter and ran without so much as a thought for what it would do to him. And even if he found her, she would never stop looking for a way to escape all over again. It pained him to think it, but she was a liability, and as such, could not be trusted. But, as the old saying went, *dead folk tell no tales*. With Angel gone, and Cherub—too young to cause trouble

—in his grasp, Carl would be free to pursue a new life south of the border. It wasn't ideal, but it was better than the alternative. But he didn't want to go there alone. That would be torture. And now that he thought about it, a Mexican woman might not be his best choice of partner. Sure, the women who hung around the flop houses and cheap hotels in Tijuana were good for a night's entertainment, but long term? Not so much. He didn't speak the language—it didn't occur to Carl that being able to converse in the local lingo might be useful for other things—and didn't much care for the temperament. What he wanted was Angel, or at least, a new version of her who would be more pliable. Submissive. Maybe, once he had taken care of business in San Diego, he would find himself the perfect replacement before heading south. And this time he would keep her close. There would be no escape. No, not for his new and improved Angel.

# TWENTY-SIX

CHERUB WAS SLEEPING CURLED up on the bed. It was late. Almost midnight. Julie was sitting next to her with the TV on, playing a documentary about sharks, but she was hardly paying attention. Her mind was on other things. Like the fact that she would be out of money within a couple of weeks at the rate she was spending it. Flat broke. And most of that was because of the hotel. It was one of those places that offered weekly and monthly rentals, making their money from people with nowhere better to live, rather than tourists or business travelers looking for a place to lay their heads while they visited the city. But it still wasn't cheap, and the weekly rate was practically no discount off paying by the night.

She could have saved a little more by paying for an entire month upfront, but Julie balked at putting down that much money in one go, which would have left her with barely any cash to live on. But that wasn't the only reason to pay by the week. She felt safe enough at the Del Ray Inn right now, but that could change at any moment. It wasn't in the best area of town, and there was still Carl to consider. She wasn't naïve enough to think that he would just let her walk away. You didn't keep someone captive for sixteen years, abuse and humiliate them, and then shrug your shoulders and move on when they escaped. He was out there looking for her and Cherub. She was sure of that. And even if Julie didn't think he would know where to look, she wasn't taking any chances.

But that wasn't her most immediate problem. It didn't matter whether Carl came poking around the hotel if she couldn't afford to stay there. And she had no desire to live on the streets, eking out a miserable existence with her daughter in a tent that did nothing to keep out the stifling heat, or anything else, for that matter.

Which was why Julie had reluctantly decided that there was only one option. She would have to take Gloria up on her offer, at least until she knew enough to find work on her own. And time was of the essence. She didn't know how long it would take to get set up and earn her first paycheck, but the sooner she started, the quicker she would earn some money.

It was Thursday night, which meant Gloria would be slinging beers at The Barrel Room, a dive bar a block down the street from the hotel. That was a shame, because now that Julie had made up her mind, she wanted to set the wheels in motion before she had second thoughts, and Gloria always slept in on the mornings after she pulled a shift at the bar. She might not rear her head until the next evening. That was too long to wait.

Next to her, Cherub was snoring lightly. Julie watched her for a minute. The girl was a deep sleeper, always had been, which Julie had been thankful for back at the farmhouse when Carl had summoned her for what he called her *nightly duties*. The only thing worse than what he did to her in that bed had been the thought of her daughter hearing it from the next room. Now, her daughter's heavy slumber might serve a different purpose. The bar, open until 2 AM, was only a five-minute walk down the street. She could slip out, tell Gloria to get in touch with her man —the one she claimed could find work for people like them— and be back in the room before her daughter ever knew she had left. Fifteen minutes, twenty at most.

Her mind made up, Julie rose from the bed, being careful not to disturb Cherub, and tiptoed to the door. With a quick glance back over her shoulder to make sure that her daughter had not stirred, she pulled it quietly open and slipped outside, then closed it softly behind her after making sure that the key was tucked into the back pocket of her jean shorts. One of many items of clothing she had picked up at a local Goodwill after arriving in the city.

She descended the stairs to the ground floor and hurried across the hotel parking lot to the road, then turned right. She could see the bar down the street, its red neon sign glowing in the darkness like a beacon. It was late, and there was no one around. Julie almost changed her mind and scurried back to the hotel room but resisted the urge. A few minutes on a dark and lonely street right now was better than spending entire nights outside living in a tent on the sidewalk. Steeling herself, she pressed on, walking at a brisk pace with her eyes fixed on the sign.

She was halfway there when the sound of an engine caught her attention. A car was coming along the street behind her, the twin beams of its headlights piercing the darkness. An older model muscle car with a large air scoop on the hood and twin white stripes running up and over the roof. She watched it approach, slowing a little as it cruised by her. The windows were heavily tinted, and she couldn't see within, but felt the weight of the occupant's stare, nonetheless.

She folded her arms, suddenly aware of how she looked in the cutoff jeans and white tank top. For a moment, she thought the car would come to a halt, that the window would roll down, and the man inside—because she was sure the driver was male —would proposition her, thinking she was walking the streets so late at night for an entirely different reason. But soon, the car rolled past, and Julie relaxed.

She watched as it continued down the street, then slow again and turn right into the small parking lot next to the bar. For the second time in as many minutes, she hesitated, wondering if she should turn back. The car had given her the creeps, which was probably more to do with her current surroundings than anything else, but she was still uneasy.

*Don't be ridiculous,* she thought to herself. *There's nothing to worry about. It's just some guy looking to quench his thirst with a cold beer.*

But the feeling persisted, even as she forced herself to keep going. By the time she reached the bar, her unease had grown to a prickly fear that she couldn't explain.

The main entrance to the bar was on the side of the building in the parking lot. There was another entrance at the front, between a pair of blacked out bay windows, but it was locked with a handwritten notice directing patrons to use the other door. The sidewalk was drenched in red light from the neon sign above.

*Nothing to worry about,* she repeated to herself, picking up the pace and hurrying around the corner and into the parking lot. There were only a few vehicles parked there, including the muscle car, which occupied a spot near the bar entrance. She went to step around it, but at that moment, the driver-side door opened, and a muscular man climbed out. He had short brown hair, faded black jeans, and a dark colored T-shirt with the word CHAOS written across the front. He closed the door and looked at her, a leering smile breaking across his face.

She heard the passenger side door open, looked around to see a second man climb out of the car. He was thinner and taller than his companion, with stubble darkening his chin, and slicked back hair that glistened with grease.

"Aren't you a cutie?" said the driver, licking his lips at the same time, as if he were about to enjoy a succulent steak dinner. "Buy you a drink?"

"I don't think so," Julie said quickly. "I'm here to see a friend."

"I'll be your friend," said the other man, taking a step toward her, his eyes roaming the length of her body.

Julie recoiled and cast a futile glance at the entrance to the bar, which was now blocked, deliberately or otherwise, by the muscle car's driver. "Please, just let me pass. I don't want a drink, and I don't want to be your friend."

"Well now, that's not very nice," the taller man said, his face creasing into a scowl. He took a quick step toward her, reaching out to grab her arm at the same time.

Julie stumbled backwards, a swell of panic tightening her throat and stopping her rising scream. She turned, looking for an avenue of escape, and found the muscle car's driver closer than before. So close, in fact, that she could smell the sweat that glistened on his skin.

Then he lunged forward, fast as lightning.

# TWENTY-SEVEN

CARL ENTERED California five hours after leaving Flagstaff, and the farmhouse that he would never see again, in his rearview mirror. Along the way, he had passed through Yuma, where he almost considered stopping for the night after seeing the lights of a motel on the outskirts of the city. He was finding it hard to keep his eyes open. Many days of driving, pushing himself to the limit, had drained him of the stamina he usually tapped into when behind the wheel of his big rig. He had exhausted his supply of energy drinks before he even reached the Arizona border and was now sipping on the dregs of an iced coffee—mostly melted ice at this point—that he had purchased when he last stopped for gas.

Now, as he drove the last miles to his destination, with the varied landscape of the Cleveland National Park spreading out around him in the darkness, his head drooped, his eyes fluttered closed, and for a moment, he was back in the farmhouse.

*Angel was in his bed, laying naked beneath him. Her pale white skin glowed with ethereal light. She gripped his shoulders, pushing back against his weight as he bore down upon her. From somewhere else in the house came an indistinct murmur of voices, broken by an occasional snatch of music. Ma was watching one of her shows, no doubt sitting on the couch with a large bucket of popcorn drenched in butter on her lap.*

*"Please don't stop," Angel said in a breathy voice, ignoring the sound of the TV.*

*Carl, caught in the moment, said nothing. He merely grunted.*

*"Please don't," Angel said again, her voice frantic now. "Stop!"*

*She bit her bottom lip, teeth digging into her silky soft skin. She closed her eyes, a solitary tear escaping and meandering down her cheek to her chin.*

*Carl shifted position, hips thrusting, and...*

A blaring cacophony of noise and brilliant white light shattered the illusion. His eyes snapped open in time to see a truck bearing down, thirty tons of steel and cargo blocking his path. The vehicle's headlights filled his windshield, dazzling him.

Carl spun his steering wheel hard to the right. Somehow, he had drifted clear across the median onto the other side of the highway and into the path of oncoming traffic.

Carl's front wheels bounced onto the ribbon of dirt separating the east-west lanes of the highway with a bone-jarring thud. The truck breezed past, horn honking, and barely missed him.

He slammed on his brakes, his wheels kicking up dust as the pickup truck bumped over the rough terrain and came to a screeching halt.

Carl's heart thudded against his rib cage. He must have fallen asleep at the wheel. Because it was so late at night, traffic on the interstate was light, which was the only reason he was still alive. If it had been earlier in the evening...

Carl pushed the thought away. He didn't want to think about that, so instead he focused on the dream so rudely interrupted by that 18-wheeler. He remembered that night as if it were yesterday. The evening Cherub was conceived. It was one of his favorite memories, and he dreamed of it often. But never before while he was zipping down the highway at eighty miles an hour. That was an experience he hoped never to repeat.

Carl sat in the median for a good fifteen minutes, engine idling, as cars and trucks flew past him on both sides. None of them slowed to look. No one pulled over to see if he was okay. They probably thought his vehicle had broken down and been left there, waiting for a tow. He picked up the iced coffee, was disappointed to see that nothing remained. Reaching behind the truck's passenger seat, he rummaged in his backpack until he found a Snickers bar he had purchased the previous day and was saving for an emergency. A trick he'd learned after so many years of driving the country's highways and byways. A sugar rush was as good as a caffeine fix, at least in the short term.

He tore the wrapper off, wolfed it down, and waited for the glucose to hit his system and provide the final jolt he needed to make it to San Diego, now less than an hour down the road.

Then, when he trusted himself not to doze off again, Carl pulled back onto the interstate, pressed his foot to the floor, and continued on his way. As he went, he dreamed of Angel, and all the things he would do when he found her. Only this time, he kept his eyes wide open.

# TWENTY-EIGHT

JULIE FINALLY FOUND HER VOICE. She let out an ear-piercing scream as the driver of the muscle car made a grab for her. She twisted from his grip, but it was only a momentary reprieve, because from her rear, she sensed his friend closing in. Julie had no idea exactly what their intentions were, but she had suffered at the hands of a man long enough to hazard a guess, and the thought filled her with terror.

From somewhere behind the trio, a door banged open.

"Hey. Leave her alone."

Julie recognized the voice. It was Gloria. She was standing at the entrance to the bar with a baseball bat clutched in her hands.

The muscle car driver spun around, surprised. When he saw Gloria, his eyes widened. "Who the fuck are you?"

"Never mind who I am." She swung the bat, slamming it into the wall next to the door with a resounding thud. "Step away from her, or the next time, it'll be your heads on the receiving end of this bat."

"Whoa. Easy there." The driver backed away from Julie. "We were just being friendly."

"I saw what you were being, and I don't much appreciate it." Gloria stepped out of the doorway and into the light of a lamp mounted on the wall above. She motioned to Julie. "Come on over here, hon."

Julie hurried around the two men and ran to the bar entrance. Gloria looked at the two men. "We all good here?"

The driver nodded. "Hey didn't mean nuthin'. Just having some fun."

"Next time, take your fun somewhere else."

"Sure. Whatever you say." The driver took a step toward the bar entrance with his buddy right behind.

"Where the hell do you think you're going?" Gloria steered Julie inside the bar and stood, blocking the entrance.

"We just want a beer." The driver stopped in his tracks. "We won't cause no more trouble."

"You should have thought about that before you accosted a woman in the parking lot of my bar."

"It ain't *your* bar."

"It is when I'm working, and you aren't stepping foot inside. Neither of you. Now scoot before I call the cops."

"Seriously?" The driver looked at his buddy, then turned toward the car. "Come on. Let's get out of here. This place is a shithole, anyway."

Gloria watched as they climbed into their vehicle. For a moment they didn't move, perhaps deciding if they really wanted to be humiliated by a woman, but then the car backed out of the parking space, pulled forward, and peeled out of the lot with a screech of tires.

Gloria turned to Julie. "You alright?"

"I will be." Julie was shaking. She regretted leaving the safety of the hotel at such a late hour. What had she been thinking?

"Come on inside," said Gloria, leading her into the tavern's dimly lit interior. A faint pall of cigarette smoke hung in the air even though it was illegal to smoke in bars. Neon signs hung on the walls, advertising beer brands. A pair of guys were shooting pool on a table near the back of the room, and a couple of booths were occupied, but otherwise the bar was empty.

Gloria motioned for Julie to take a seat at the bar, then stepped around the counter. She put the baseball bat under the bar, then pulled a liquor bottle from the well and poured a shot before pushing it across the counter. "Here, drink this. It'll steady your nerves."

"I don't drink," Julie said, staring at the amber liquid in the glass. The last time she had consumed alcohol was back when she was traveling with Trent Steiger and the band. After that, there had been no opportunity. Carl might have liked his beer, might even have downed a stiff one once in a while, but he sure as hell wasn't sharing any of it with her. "What is this, anyway?"

"Bourbon. Not the good stuff, but it'll get the job done." Gloria leaned on the bar. "Drink it. Don't think. Just slam it back."

Julie looked at the drink for a moment longer, then put the glass to her lips and chugged. Then she sputtered as the astringent alcohol hit the back of her throat. "Crap. That stuff is *nasty*. People really drink this?"

"Yeah. It's an acquired taste. Gets better if you persevere. Trust me."

Julie pushed the empty glass back across the bar. "I'll take your word for it."

A faint smile touched Gloria's lips. "Wanna tell me what you're doing out so late at night all on your own?"

"I was looking for you, actually. I've been thinking about your offer."

"And you want me to hook you up with my contact. Find you some work."

Julie nodded. "Yes."

"I think that can be arranged. Deal hasn't changed, though. You want the kid watched while you're working, then you gotta pay."

"I understand. But does it have to be 50 percent? I'm going to need all the money I can get."

Gloria observed her for a moment with narrowed eyes. "Tell

you what, I'll cut you a deal, since we're friends. How about 40 percent. Take it or leave it."

Julie didn't need to think about it. She had braved the night and almost ended up in a situation as bad as the one she had escaped to come here in search of Gloria. She responded with a quick, "I'll take it."

"Then we have a deal. I'll call my friend tomorrow. It might take a few days to set something up—he's a busy man—but he should be able to find you a job."

"Thank you." Julie slumped with relief, tempered by a sudden nervousness. She hadn't held a job in… well, practically ever. Except for a part-time gig back in college, but that was so long ago.

"Don't thank me yet. You might not like what you have to do."

"Honestly, I'll take anything." Julie might not have ever worked a real job, but it wasn't like she'd spent the last sixteen years lazing around doing nothing. Carl had made sure of that, along with Ma, whose aversion to cleaning was almost as strong as her aversion to exercise and healthy eating. While her son saw Julie as someone with which to share a bed, whether she liked it or not, his mother saw something else. A pair of hands to do everything she had no interest in. Julie had scrubbed the toilet, mopped the floors, and went down into the basement not just to do the laundry, but also to remove the carcasses of mice caught in the traps Carl was willing to set up and bait, but not to deal with when they did their job. She couldn't imagine any gainful employment that would be worse than Carl and Ma.

Gloria watched her for a moment. "You may not have much common sense, coming down here on your own at night wearing that outfit, but you have determination. I'll give you that." She picked up the empty glass. "Now, I think it's time that we got you back to the hotel."

The hotel. Crap. With all that had happened, Julie had momentarily forgotten about Cherub, who was all alone in the room. But she also didn't want to walk back on her own. What if those two guys were still cruising the neighborhood, looking for easy prey? If they saw her again, who knew what would happen?

Thankfully, Gloria came to the rescue once again. She reached behind her and flicked a switch on the back wall three times, flashing the lights to get the attention of the few patrons that still remained. "Bar's closed. Drink up and take it somewhere else."

One of the guys at the pool table looked up. "It's not even one yet. You can't close."

"Watch me." Gloria winked at Julie. "I'm doing you all a favor. Your wives and girlfriends will be glad to see you come home at such an early hour. They might even thank you in the bedroom."

"Fat chance," someone called out. "By now, my wife's gone through two bottles of cheap wine. She's probably passed out on the sofa."

"Not my problem." Gloria turned the lights up full.

Ten minutes later, once the last stragglers had left the bar, Gloria locked up. They walked back to the Del Ray together. Julie was nervous, her eyes scanning the empty street for the muscle car and the two men who had accosted her. She didn't relax until they reached their accommodation. On the second floor, Gloria bade her farewell for the night.

Julie entered her room… and that was when she saw Cherub. The little girl was sitting upright in the bed, eyes wide, gasping for breath. An asthma attack. She had suffered from them all her life, but until now, Carl had taken care of the situation, providing the medication that she so desperately needed.

Now it was up to Julie. She ran to the nightstand to fetch Cherub's inhaler. The same one she had brought with her from the farmhouse in those first few panicked hours after she discovered Ma dead on the floor in the kitchen. But when she handed her daughter the medicine, nothing happened.

The inhaler was empty.

# TWENTY-NINE

CHERUB'S FACE was twisted with exertion. Her breaths came in short, ragged gasps. Julie stared at the inhaler, horrified. How could she have been stupid enough not to check it was working before now? Cherub's attacks were infrequent these days—Carl had said she would probably grow out of them eventually—but they still happened. There must have been other inhalers at the farmhouse. Carl purchased them from some overseas pharmacy and always got a bunch at a time. If only she had stopped to think, took the time to look for them, then her daughter might not be suffering right now.

"It's okay," Julie said, trying to calm Cherub down. "Take long, deep breaths. In through your nose and out through your mouth. Try to relax."

"I woke... up and... you weren't... here," Cherub said in a gasping, stilted voice interspersed with wheezy breaths. "I got... scared."

"I'm here now." Julie rubbed her daughter's back. She didn't know if it was helping, but it was better than doing nothing.

"Where... did you go?" Cherub looked up at her, wide-eyed.

"I was talking to Gloria," Julie said, omitting the fact that her conversation was down the street at a bar. "There was nothing to worry about."

"I thought maybe... he'd found us." Cherub's breathing was coming easier now. Her shoulders didn't heave with each fresh inhalation.

"You're safe here. He won't find us." Julie felt terrible. She should never have left her daughter alone, not even for an instant. She knew that stress triggered Cherub's condition. More than once, she'd returned from Carl's room after performing her nightly duties to find her daughter gasping for air with tears streaming down her cheeks. Julie had never asked whether it was because Cherub had been left alone, or because she could hear what Carl was doing to her mother in the room next door, because she might not have liked the answer.

"I don't like this place," her daughter said, finally forming a complete sentence without gasping.

"Me either," Julie said. "But we don't have much choice right now."

"When are we going to leave?" Cherub asked. "It smells weird here, and the sheets make me itch."

"Soon," Julie replied, even though she had no idea how long they would be stuck in the hotel. But at least the conversation was calming her daughter down. Cherub was breathing better, and that was all that mattered. "How about tomorrow we take the bus down to the waterfront and get ice cream?"

Cherub nodded, a smile coming to her lips for the first time since Julie had returned to the hotel room. "Can we get strawberry?"

"Whatever you want." Carl had been picky about his flavors. His favorite was vanilla, probably because that was also the only kind Ma would eat, so that was what everyone else got, too. On the rare occasion that he brought home a different flavor, more because it was on sale and there was no vanilla left than because he wanted variety, Cherub would beam. If Carl noticed his daughter's happiness, he didn't show it. The next time he went shopping, there would be a tub of boring, bland vanilla, regardless of how much Cherub begged for something different.

"What about chocolate?" Cherub was almost back to normal now. "No. caramel."

Julie laughed at her daughter's sudden exuberance. "How about all three? I bet they'll do a scoop of each."

"I like mint, too."

"Okay. Now you're pushing it."

Cherub scrunched her nose.

"Tell you what. I'll get mint, and you can have a bite of mine."

"Really?"

"Really." Julie glanced toward the clock on the nightstand, which read 1 AM. She brushed a strand of hair from her daughter's forehead. "But not if you don't get some rest. It's way past the time that little girls should be sleeping."

"I was. But then I needed to go bathroom, and you weren't here."

A shadow passed across Cherub's face. "You're not going out again, are you? I don't like being here my own."

"No, honey. I'm not going anywhere. I'm never going to leave you alone again. Promise. Now lay back down and close your eyes."

Cherub considered this for a moment, then slid back down under the covers and laid her head on the pillow. She looked up at Julie, her blue eyes catching the light from the bedside lamp. "I'm sorry," she said in a small voice.

"What for?"

"Scaring you. I didn't want to get wheezy."

"I know that." Julie bent low and kissed her daughter's forehead. "It's not your fault."

"Okay." Cherub closed her eyes.

Julie Rose and went to the sink where she brushed her teeth. She undressed and pulled on a pair of flannel PJs, then returned to the bed and got in. She turned off the light then pressed close to her daughter, putting a protective arm around her.

"Mommy?" came a voice in the darkness.

"Yes?"

"I'm glad it's just you and me now. I don't like daddy. He scares me."

"Me, too," Julie said. A lump formed in her throat. It was one thing for Carl to abuse *her*, but quite another to terrify his daughter. Little girls shouldn't be afraid of their father, no matter how awful he was to everyone else.

A picture of Ma dead on the kitchen floor flashed through Julie's mind, and in that moment, she wished it wasn't just the old woman rotting away on the linoleum. She wished that Carl had been right there alongside her, because he deserved nothing better. When she had first found Ma, Julie had been afraid of Carl's reaction when he finally came home. But now, she took wicked delight in imagining what must have gone through his mind when he first saw her lying there in nothing but that awful housecoat she always wore, the garment open to expose her naked, dead flesh. A final indignity deserving of a lifetime's cruelty to everyone around her. And right there, Julie decided. If Carl found them, if she was the only thing standing between him and his daughter, then one of them wasn't going to survive the encounter, and Julie was determined that it would be Carl.

# THIRTY

WHEN PATTERSON WALKED through the doors of the FBI field office in San Diego at 9 AM, a familiar face was already there, waiting for her. Marcus Bauer had set up shop in a small office on the second floor. He sat reclined in a chair with his feet up on the desk and a laptop on his lap. When she entered, he dropped his legs and straightened up.

"We have to stop meeting like this," he said with a wide grin.

"Because you're worried about me getting you shot again, or because of what Phoebe might think?" Patterson asked, perching on the edge of the desk, arms folded.

"A little of both." Bauer placed the laptop on the desk and closed it. "I'd say it's good to see you again, but since your life is in danger..."

"Yeah. It's becoming a habit. Of course, none of this would be necessary if other people were doing their jobs right. How the hell does a professional hitman just walk out of jail and vanish?"

"He didn't exactly walk out on his own. He had help. And as for being a professional hitman... well, we really don't know what he is, because we know nothing about him. He's a phantom. No matches for his fingerprints. No hits on facial recognition. The only name we have is an alias—"

"That's my point. Amateurs aren't that skilled. You saw the tech he had in Vegas. He cloned room keys. Hacked into the reservation system of a major casino. Breached their firewall and accessed their servers. No easy task. And anyway, we know who sent him, and I have a feeling that the good senator doesn't hire neophytes to do his dirty work."

"Well, whatever he is, we'll be ready if he comes for you again," Bauer said.

"*When* he comes," replied Patterson, because she suspected that their hitman, whoever he might be, would abhor loose ends, and that was exactly what she was right now. And more than that, she was the person who had put him in jail. But right now, there were more pressing concerns.

As if reading her mind, Bauer said, "I've been doing some research on pharmacies and clinics that cater to undocumented immigrants. Places that Julie might go to get medicine for her daughter."

"When did you have time to do that?" Patterson asked, surprised.

"I've had plenty of time since the raid on Bonneville's farmhouse. Like the two hours I spent sitting in a departure language waiting to board a flight to San Diego, the hour and twenty minutes I was in the air, and the four hours that I've been sitting here, waiting for you."

"You've been in this office since 5 AM?"

Bauer shrugged. "The FBI, in their wisdom, booked me a room in San Diego starting from tonight. I can't check in until four. It was either come here or sit on a park bench."

"There are some very nice benches in San Diego," Patterson said, looking around at the stark, windowless office lit by fluorescent lamps set in the ceiling.

"So I've heard." Bauer cleared his throat. "Anyway, like I was saying, I did some research. First, I narrowed down the search to the most likely areas Julie would be hiding. For example, she probably didn't check into a hotel anywhere around Balboa

Park, the Gaslamp Quarter, or the harbor. Places where the tourists go. She'd want something cheaper and more anonymous. Those are the neighborhoods that I focused on, starting with the ones in the south of the city, near the border."

"I already did that. The SAC provided three agents, and we spent yesterday afternoon visiting every clinic and pharmacy we could find."

"I know. I saw the list of places that you went to. I put those aside and focused only on clinics you didn't visit, which was still a daunting task. I never knew there were so many of them."

"Me either," Patterson agreed.

"Which is why I needed to narrow it down even more, and the best way to do that was to consult an expert. I made a call to the San Diego Charitable Mission. They provide beds for the homeless, including the undocumented, with nowhere else to go. The woman who answered wasn't keen to talk at first, especially when she found out that I'm an FBI agent. But after I explained the situation, and that we weren't looking to cause trouble for any of their guests, she opened up. There are a couple of clinics that cover South San Diego and the San Ysidro area, where people go when they have no other option. Clinics known for their discretion and willingness to treat anyone who walks through the door, regardless of circumstance. Neither clinic was on the list of places you visited yesterday. She also told me about some other potential locations, but I think we should start with those."

"Agreed." Patterson could have reached across the desk and hugged Bauer, except that she suspected he would object. Still, she was grateful for his help. Back when they first met, when the SAC of the Dallas field office, Walter Harris, had ordered her to mentor the freshly minted agent only weeks out of Quantico, she had objected. In fact, she had made her feelings known in no uncertain terms. But now, she almost felt incomplete when he wasn't at her side. Nothing romantic, mind you—they had almost gone down that road at one point but slammed the brakes on just in time—but a bond had grown between them anyway. A mutual friendship born out of trust and understanding.

Bauer climbed to his feet, closed the laptop, and slipped it back into its case. He picked up his suit jacket from the back of the chair and put it on. "You ready, partner?"

"Ready as I'll ever be."

"Great." Bauer went to the door, stepped into the corridor, then held it open for her to follow. "Let's go and find Julie."

# THIRTY-ONE

JULIE HADN'T GOTTEN much sleep. She had laid awake most of the night worrying about Cherub. Unlike her mother, the little girl hadn't found it hard to fall asleep. No sooner had her head hit the pillow, than she was out, and remained that way for the rest of the night. Thankfully, she didn't have another asthma attack, but Julie didn't want to leave anything to chance.

She had no idea how or where to get a new inhaler. Carl had always taken care of that stuff. There was only one person she could think of to ask. Gloria. There was only one problem. Her friend in the room next door would be sleeping, having worked a long shift at the bar the previous night.

But this couldn't wait.

Taking her daughter by the hand, Julie stepped out onto the balcony and went to the room next door. She was about to knock but hesitated, loath to disturb Gloria. But then she reminded herself that the woman was happy to take 40 percent of her paycheck—theoretical as it might be right now—for watching Cherub while she worked. With that thought at the back of her mind, Julie banged three times on the door with her fist.

A few seconds later she heard movement from within the room, and a faint shout of, "Who's there?"

"It's me. Anna," Julie said, using the pseudonym she had adopted for herself.

"Go away. I'm sleeping."

"I know, and I'm sorry. But this can't wait. I have a question. It will only take a moment of your time, and then I'll let you go back to bed."

There was more movement from the other side of the door before it cracked open a couple of inches. Gloria peered out through the gap. "This better be good."

"I really am sorry. I wouldn't disturb you if it wasn't absolutely necessary."

"Yeah, yeah." Gloria yawned without bothering to cover her mouth. "Get to the point."

"I need medicine for my daughter. I don't know where to get it. She has asthma, and her inhaler ran out."

"That's all you're worried about?"

"Isn't it enough?"

"Look, there's a walk-in clinic over on Third. SD Health Partners. Everyone goes there. They don't ask questions and they won't rob you blind. They'll take care of your daughter."

"Thank you, so much." Julie almost fainted with relief. "You're a lifesaver."

"Yeah, so I've heard." Gloria went to shut the door. "I'm going back to bed."

"Wait." Julie put a hand on the door to stop it from closing. "How do I get there?"

Gloria let out an exasperated sigh. "Take the 704 bus to Third and Naples. It's in the plaza behind the McDonald's. You can't miss it."

"Thanks again." Julie pulled her hand away from the door.

"Anything else."

"No."

"Good." This time, Gloria closed the door.

Julie led her daughter back to their room. No sooner was she inside, than Cherub looked up at her with wide eyes.

"Mommy?"

"Yes, sweetie?"

"Are you going to leave me alone again?" There was a note of panic in Cherub's voice. "I don't like being here on my own."

"I'm not going to leave you alone again," Julie promised. She felt like a terrible mother because of what had happened the night before. How could she have even *thought* of leaving her daughter like that in a strange place, let alone walked blocks to a seedy bar in the middle of the night? Apart from anything else, it wasn't safe. What if those two men with the muscle car had gotten their way? How long would Cherub have ended up alone and frightened in the hotel room then? There was no excuse. She should have just waited until the next time she saw Gloria, because then her daughter wouldn't have panicked and had an attack. Of course, Julie also wouldn't have discovered that the inhaler was empty. And the next asthma attack might be worse. So maybe it had worked out for the best, after all. This circular reasoning should have made Julie feel better, but it didn't. The nagging sense that she was a terrible parent remained. Of course, she hadn't exactly been given the opportunity to be anything else. The sole extent of Julie's parenting skills amounted to keeping her daughter quiet when Carl and Ma didn't want to hear her and singing Cherub to sleep with the same lullaby that her own mother had sung to her when she was a child. Beyond that, her captors had taken care of all the important stuff. Like disciplining the little girl, both for real and imagined transgressions. Schooling her. Feeding and clothing her. And making sure that she didn't run out of medicine.

That last one stuck in Julie's mind. She might not have done a good job of looking after Cherub since they ran from the farmhouse—leaving her daughter alone in the middle of the night was hardly going to win her *parent of the year*—but now she could set things right. There was a bus stop one block from the hotel. She had seen it the previous evening on her way to the bar. She had no idea which buses stopped there, but she figured one of them must be the 704, or Gloria would have been more specific in her instructions.

She turned to her daughter, who was still wearing the fluffy pink PJs with pictures of dinosaurs that Carl had come home with several months earlier after a trip. They were one of the few articles of her daughter's clothing that Julie had taken when they left the farmhouse, gathering the PJs and whatever else she could lay her hands on quickly, and stuffing everything into a bag before they fled. "Get dressed. We're going on a little adventure."

"Where?"

"To see someone about your asthma," Julie replied, tussling her daughter's hair. "To make sure that what happened last night never happens again."

"Oh." Her daughter's gaze dropped to the floor. "You said we were going to have ice cream."

"We are," Julie said quickly. She had forgotten about her promise from the night before, and now felt even worse. "Strawberry, chocolate, and caramel, just like we agreed."

"And mint choc chip. Don't forget that."

"And mint, too. But only if you hurry and get dressed."

"Yay!" Cherub ran to the pile of clothes Julie had washed the day before in the hotel laundry and found an outfit. Ten minutes later, she was dressed and ready to go.

# THIRTY-TWO

CORBIN POPE WAS IN AUSTIN, Texas. It had been a long drive from Utah, and he was just about tuckered, but it was better than sitting in a jail cell in Las Vegas. Even better, he would soon reap his revenge on the man who had put him there—in a roundabout way—then tried to silence him permanently. And he knew exactly where to find Senator Bill Newport because he had placed a call to the Texas State Capitol's Public Information Office—using a prepaid phone he had purchased at a Walmart outside of Albuquerque—figuring that if anyone knew the senator's whereabouts, it would be them.

Posing as Harvey Bent, a journalist wanting to do a feature piece on the senator's charitable work—which was laughable given Newport's aversion to largesse—he had gotten put through to a member of the Media Relations team. A chirpy woman by the name of Sandra, who was only too eager to help a reporter from the West Texas Star-Tribune, a newspaper that didn't really exist, at least as far as Pope knew. He had made the name up on the spot and adlibbed from there.

"Well now, Sandra," Pope had crooned in his best Texas accent after the woman told him that Newport would be in residence at the capitol for at least the next week in a special session of the Texas Legislature that the governor had called to discuss a topic near and dear to the hearts of his constituents—gun control, or rather, the lack of it. "You've been mighty helpful. A real peach."

Sandra had tittered, apparently taken with the smooth-talking journalist from the Star-Tribune. If she had known that the man she was flirting with was actually a ruthless assassin who had put as many men and women—Pope was an equal opportunity killer—in their graves as most undertakers, she might not have been so eager.

Having confirmed that the senator was in Austin, Pope turned his attention to the next item on his agenda. Figuring out where Newport stayed when he was in town. This was important, because by the time Pope had hit the Texas border, he had a plan. During his long drive, he had considered many scenarios for the senator's grand exit, most of which he had discarded. Yet one in particular had appealed to his sense of poetic irony. But he needed somewhere private to end the senator's life. He could hardly stroll into the Capitol and take care of him right there in his office surrounded by his colleagues, gaggles of bored schoolchildren touring the building, and the Capitol Police. And while there were several ways of neatly dispatching the senator out in the open, like on a city street or in a park, that Pope had used before with resounding success, none of them would work in this instance. He wanted some time alone with the senator first, an hour or two in private, to extract the information he needed, because Newport wasn't his only target. There was also the FBI agent.

For the task of tracking down the senator's abode in Austin, Pope went to the library. Not because he thought the answer would be in a book, but rather because they offered free Wi-Fi and anonymity. People in libraries rarely paid attention to anyone else. They were too invested in browsing the shelves or sitting in a quiet corner and reading. They didn't want to be bothered and did their best to avoid bothering anyone else.

He carried a laptop with him. Not his laptop—the one with NSA level encryption and a host of tools installed that would make a career spy drool with envy. That machine was on a shelf in an evidence locker back in Vegas, and he had no way to get it back. It didn't matter. There was nothing incriminating on the laptop, nothing that would give investigators even the smallest clue to his real identity, and even if some whiz kid in a forensics lab managed to crack the encryption, the machine would handily wipe itself clean and fry its own hard drive without the 12-digit passcode that resided only in Pope's head. Rather, the laptop that Pope had brought with him to the library was a cheap off-the-shelf model purchased in the same Walmart where he had obtained the burner phone. But he didn't need to do anything fancy, because he suspected that Newport would not want to waste his money on hotel rooms since he spent so much time in the city. In short, he would own property. Something that would serve not only as a place to lay his head, but also as an investment. It might not be the grand mansion that he called home in Dallas, but it should be easy enough to find, even though he suspected that Newport wouldn't have put it in his own name.

And it was.

Even with his bare-bones laptop, it didn't take long for Pope to follow a paper trail on the Secretary of State's website and follow a string of business registrations, then hack into the database and obtain information not visible to the public. He started with companies that Pope knew the senator owned thanks to the pair's previous dealings. LLCs registered for no reason other than to distance himself from investments he didn't want his constituents, or the elections board, to find out about. After half an hour, he had compiled a list of entities, many of which did not appear to have any legitimate business associated with them, that Newport might have used to buy property.

Next, he found a back door into the local tax assessor's database, and bingo! The senator had used a shell company to purchase a condo in a luxury high-rise right there on Congress Avenue several years before. With the address in hand, Pope quickly found the old condo listing on a couple of different realtor websites from when the previous owner had put it up for sale. Newport had paid close to 1.3 million for his home away from home. Overpriced, even with a view of the Capitol Building thrown in for good measure. But Pope didn't care how deep the senator's pockets were. He cared about the interior layout of the property, and thanks to the photographs that were still online, he soon had the floor plan memorized.

His task complete, Pope left the library and drove across town to a hotel he had booked a couple of hours earlier, paying extra—with a credit card in a false name provided by the same people who had sprung him from jail—to secure a room many hours earlier than the normal check in time. He was exhausted, and he never worked a job when he was tired. That only led to mistakes, and he could not afford any more of those. But later, once he was rested, when his mind was sharp and his body operating at peak performance, he would put his plan into action and pay the senator a visit. And, thought Pope with a shiver of anticipation, it wasn't going to be pretty. No, not pretty at all!

# THIRTY-THREE

IT TOOK forty minutes to get from the hotel to the walk-in clinic. Gloria had been right. It was easy to find, located in a plaza right behind a McDonald's on the corner of Third and Naples. After they disembarked, Julie steered her daughter toward the clinic. But Cherub had other ideas. She was staring at the fast-food restaurant, and an advertisement in the window advertising two for $3 muffin breakfast sandwiches.

Her eyes grew wide. "Those look yummy."

They really do, thought Julie. She had stopped briefly at a McDonald's while they were on the road and before she had ditched Ma's car at the airport in Phoenix. They had purchased cheeseburgers and fries, wolfing them down in the parking lot before continuing on. But Julie hadn't eaten a breakfast sandwich since before Carl snatched her. It had been so long that she couldn't even recall what one tasted like, but some part of her subconscious must have remembered, because her mouth started watering. She looked down at her daughter, who was holding her hand and still looking at the advertisement for the breakfast sandwich. "I don't think it's ten-thirty yet. We still have time. You want one?"

"Really?" Cherub's eyes grew even wider, but then she frowned. "What about the ice cream?"

"We can still do that after we visit the clinic," Julie said, leading her daughter toward the restaurant. "Unless you'll be too full, that is."

"I won't be too full," Cherub replied in a determined voice. "It's ice cream."

Julie laughed. They stepped inside the restaurant and approached the counter where she ordered a meal for herself, with a large coffee, and the same for Cherub, but with an orange juice. Half an hour later, with the food nothing but a memory and a smile on Cherub's face, they left the restaurant and crossed the parking lot in front of the plaza clinic.

They entered and approached the counter, only to be asked for ID, and handed a form on a clipboard to fill in.

Julie's gut tightened.

But Gloria was right again. The woman behind the counter didn't bat an eyelid when Julie informed her that they had no insurance or identification.

"Just fill the form out as best you can. Anything you're uncomfortable with, just leave blank," she said, winking at Cherub, who smiled shyly back at her. "There's no judgment here."

"Thank you." Julie took the form and sat down while Cherub wandered around the lobby, looking at the pictures on the walls, and sitting on different seats until she got bored and wandered back. There was only one other person waiting. An older woman with a bandaged wrist who was soon escorted through a door and into the back of the building by a nurse wearing blue scrubs. They sat and waited for another twenty minutes, during which no one else entered, before the same young woman in scrubs came for them. She took them to a small room and weighed Cherub, then asked a few questions, before leading them to yet another room where they sat and waited for a further fifteen minutes.

After that, the rest of the visit went quickly. A male doctor with graying hair came in and examined Cherub, placing a stethoscope on the little girl's chest and back, which made her wriggle even as she tried to follow his instructions to breathe deeply. Then, after a few minutes, he agreed to write a prescription for the inhaler that she so desperately needed. Even better, he told her it was a generic, and would only cost five dollars. They could pick it up later that day from the pharmacy of their choice.

There was only one problem. Julie had no idea where the closest pharmacy was or how to get there. But when they left the office and returned to the front counter, the receptionist was only too happy to provide directions to a Walmart three blocks behind the Del Ray Inn. It would take a couple of hours to fill the prescription, she told them, which was perfect because Julie and Cherub had a date with three flavors of ice cream in the meantime.

# THIRTY-FOUR

AFTER ARRIVING IN SAN DIEGO, it didn't take Carl long to realize that he had a problem of immense proportions. The city was so large and sprawling that he could look for years and never find Angel and his daughter. He might as well be hunting for a specific drop of water in the Pacific Ocean. The enormity of the task threatened to overwhelm him, and for the first time, it occurred to Carl that threatening Angel, saying that he would kill her family if she ever tried to go back there, might have been a mistake. How much easier would it have been if she had run back to her family in Queens? He could have bided his time, waited for the heat to die down and Angel to become complacent, then killed the father and reclaimed his family. Sure, it would have meant abandoning the farmhouse and his old life, but he would have to do that anyway under the circumstances. And there would have been no need to dash all the way across the country and back, only to end up no closer to finding Angel and Cherub than he had been when he first discovered them missing.

But there were a few factors that would narrow down his search. For a start, Angel would not have checked into any of the swanky hotels frequented by tourists and business travelers in the downtown and waterfront areas. She had stolen money, but nowhere near enough for that. And since she had no credit or debit cards, her choices would be limited to places that accepted cash. In the 21st century, those were few and far between.

Also, she would not have any identification, which would make it harder not only to secure accommodation but also to find work, and without a job, Angel would be broke in no time.

Which meant that she would be forced to mingle with the city's homeless and undocumented population. Not that Carl thought Angel would be living on the streets. He didn't, if only because of their daughter. That meant he could discount the many tent communities that had sprung up around the city over recent years. Likewise, the homeless shelters that cleared everyone out each morning and forced them to brave the elements until their doors opened again in the evening. Which left him with one obvious place to look. Seedy hotels, many of them weekly or monthly rental places, frequented by those with enough money to put a roof over their head but not enough to raise them out of poverty.

It made him angry to think of his family living like that when they could have stayed safe and warm at the farmhouse. Instead, Angel had left his mother on the kitchen floor with scant regard for her dignity, stolen her car, and took off with his daughter. It made no sense. Hadn't he always been good to her? Fed and clothed her? In an ideal world, she would be grateful to him for saving her from the drudgery of everyday life with all its uncertainty and stress. But instead, she had fought him at every turn, especially at the beginning, when she had clawed and punched him, resisted his advances whenever he tried to show her any tenderness, both in and out of the bedroom. She had begged him to let her go, cried herself to sleep every night for the first two years, until she finally accepted the pointlessness of the endeavor. And even after that, when most of the fight had left her, he still saw the simmering hatred in her eyes, and it tore at his heart. Families weren't meant to hate each other. Sure, all couples had an occasional disagreement, but when a person doted on you, gave you the world, you were supposed to be grateful.

Not Angel.

Which was why he had been forced to lock her in that room, brick up the window so she couldn't see the world she so desperately yearned for.

Carl took a deep breath, calming the fresh wave of rage that threatened to swamp him. Everything would be fine, just as soon as he found them. Right now, he needed to focus on the future, and not think about all the ways Angel had disappointed him over the years, or even how she had let his mother die on that cold, hard linoleum. The most important thing was Cherub. He couldn't let her take his little girl away. That was too much.

There was only one problem. Even after narrowing his search parameters down and figuring out the type of places Angel might hide, he still had no idea exactly where or how to begin looking for her. Because something else had occurred to him, a realization that made his heart sink. She would not be using her own name—either the one he had given her when he first took her, or the one she had been given at birth—at least, if she had any sense. And he had no way of knowing what her new name would be.

# THIRTY-FIVE

PATTERSON AND BAUER drove across town to the first of the two clinics that Bauer had identified as most often frequented by the population of homeless people and undocumented immigrants who lived in the southern parts of the city, closest to the border.

The clinic occupied a drab building surrounded by a parking lot with cracked tarmac and weed-filled verges. Its interior was not much better. The small waiting room was painted an off white, but desperately needed a touchup, with scuffs and dirty spots staining the walls, especially behind the rows of chairs that backed up to them. An older model flatscreen TV on the wall above the reception desk was tuned to a Spanish channel. Patients occupied three of the chairs. One of them was a Latino man browsing a cell phone wearing a bright yellow T-shirt with the name of a lawn care company on the left breast. The other two were women who had their eyes glued to the TV. None of the three paid any attention to the FBI agents.

When Bauer approached the desk and flashed his credentials, the woman on the other side eyed him with suspicion. When he explained why they were there, she shook her head.

"I'm sorry," she said in a heavy accent. "But we can't release patient information, not even to the FBI."

Patterson was hardly surprised, but she stepped forward anyway. "Please. We're not here to cause trouble. I'm looking for my sister, Julie. She's been missing for sixteen years, and we think she might be in the area. I understand, don't share medical information, but if I show you a photo, could you at least tell me if you've seen her?"

The woman shook her head again. "I'm sorry for your situation, but the clinic has a policy of not talking to the authorities. I don't want to get fired. I need this job."

"I understand," said Patterson, taking out her phone and bringing up the age enhanced photo of her sister. She held it up for the woman to see. "How about this? A simple yes or no. Do you remember seeing someone who looks like this coming here over the last two or three weeks?"

The woman studied the photo for a few moments before a flash of relief passed across her face. "No. I haven't seen anyone who looks like that."

"How can you be sure?" Bauer asked. "You must get a lot of patients through these doors."

"We do, but your sister isn't the type of person who normally comes in here. This area has a big Latino community, and that's who we mostly serve. I would have remembered someone who looked like that photo. She's so..."

"White?" Bauer said.

"Yes." The woman's attention turned to Patterson. "She looks a lot like you in that photo, but older."

"Yes, she does." Patterson had thought the same thing. It was uncanny how the age progression software had produced an image that could have passed for either sister. She had almost sent a copy of the photo to her father when she first saw it, but held back, because she was worried it would upset him.

"I hope you find her," the woman said, her gaze now shifting toward the door. A clear hint that she wanted them to leave.

Patterson reached into her pocket and produced a business card, which she laid on the counter. "If you change your mind about seeing her, or anyone who looks like this photo comes into the clinic in the future, please call me."

The woman eyed the card but said nothing.

"Thank you for your time," Bauer said after several uncomfortable seconds had passed. He touched Patterson's arm. "Come on. Let's try the next place."

Out in the parking lot, Patterson turned to Bauer, frustrated. "That woman in there wouldn't have told us even if she had seen Julie."

"I know," Bauer replied. "But she didn't show any signs of recognition when you showed her the photo, and there was no hesitation when she answered you, no indication that she was lying. I don't think that your sister was here."

"This is hopeless. I must've visited twenty clinics and walk-in medical centers yesterday, and none of them wanted to cooperate. They were looking at me like I was the enemy."

"To a lot of people around here, you are."

"I'm an FBI agent, not border patrol. I have no interest in arresting people just because they're looking for a better life."

"You're a federal agent, and that's all they see. When people get scared, they don't make a distinction. Authority is authority, regardless of the badge you carry."

"Even if people were willing to talk, it might not make any difference. We don't know if Julie has visited a medical center, or even if she has a daughter. Just because you found some children's clothes and an inhaler—"

"You're right, we don't know for certain, but all the evidence suggests that she bore a child to Bonneville and took that child with her when she fled. And as for the inhaler, it's a long shot, I agree, but it's all that we've got right now." Bauer motioned toward the car. "Shall we move on to the next?"

"Why not?" Patterson said, struggling with the sense of

hopelessness that had enveloped her. "It's not like we have anything better to do."

"That's the spirit." Bauer grinned and nudged her as they approached the car.

Patterson ignored his attempts to cheer her up and climbed behind the wheel.

They drove in silence.

When they reached the next clinic, she climbed out and started across the parking lot toward the door. There was a McDonalds on the corner, and her stomach growled, reminding her that she hadn't had anything to eat yet. It was almost eleven, which meant that breakfast was over, which was a shame. She preferred their breakfast sandwiches, but it was convenient and wouldn't take too long.

She was about to ask Bauer if he wanted to grab quick a burger and fries, when her attention was drawn to something else. A pair of figures standing at a bus stop in front of the restaurant, out on the road. A woman and a young girl, holding hands.

One of the figures glanced around briefly, and in that moment, the breath caught in Patterson's throat. She was overcome by a sudden sense of familiarity. "Oh my God."

"What?" Bauer stopped and glanced at her.

"Over there," Patterson said, pointing across the parking lot even as she changed direction. "That's Julie."

Bauer turned around to look, just as a city bus trundled down the street and pulled up to the stop.

The pair moved toward it.

"Julie!" Patterson called out, even as the woman and child boarded the bus. "Wait."

Patterson broke into a run.

The bus stop was at least a couple of thousand feet away.

She watched as the bus doors whooshed closed before she had even covered half the distance.

Still, the vehicle didn't move.

Five hundred feet.

Patterson willed the bus to stay right where it was.

Two hundred feet.

She was close enough now to see the faint silhouettes of passengers from behind the bus's tinted windows. Most of them were sitting, but two dark shapes moved down the aisle, nothing but indistinct outlines. One tall, the other short.

Thirty feet.

Patterson waved, frantically trying to attract the driver's attention. Then, just as she drew level with the back of the bus, it pulled away from the curb.

"No!" She ran faster, desperate to reach the front before the bus moved too far, but it was useless. The vehicle was picking up speed now. It rolled down the road away from her with a belch of diesel fumes, and then she was standing on the sidewalk, watching helplessly as it carried her sister away.

# THIRTY-SIX

IT WAS HER," Patterson said breathlessly, as the bus moved further away down the road. "My sister. It was her."

"Are you sure?" Bauer had caught up with her.

"She looked right at me. I mean, not *at me* specifically, but I saw her face. She was exactly like the photograph. The one that I age progressed. And now I've lost her all over again."

"Not yet, you haven't." Bauer was already turning back to the parking lot and their car. "Come on. We can catch up with that bus."

"You drive," Patterson said, offering him the keys. "I'll watch the bus."

Bauer nodded and took the keys.

A minute later, they were pulling out of the plaza and onto the street. But now, the bus was nowhere in sight.

"Where is it?" Patterson asked in a panic. "Where did it go?"

"I don't know." Bauer picked up speed. "It must have turned onto a side street."

"We have to find that bus."

"Doing my best." Bauer slowed as they approached the first cross street. "Did you get the number?"

"No." Patterson couldn't believe that she hadn't thought to look. The route number would have been right there, displayed on a screen at the back of the bus. Except that she had been so focused on catching up with Julie, reaching the bus before it moved off, that she hadn't noticed. "I'm so stupid."

"Hey, it's okay. You weren't expecting to see her." Bauer glanced down the side street.

Patterson did the same.

No bus.

She grimaced. "I'm an FBI agent. Noticing things other people miss is kind of in the job description."

"You're being too hard on yourself." Bauer accelerated. "Look on your phone. There must be route maps on the internet. If we know where it was going, we can find it again."

"That's right." Patterson took her phone out and found the public transportation website, then glanced around, looking for a street name to search for. When they approached the next cross street, she typed the intersection in.

Three bus routes came up.

She cursed. "This is ridiculous."

"Calm down."

"We can't catch a break."

"We just did, at least if that really was Julie that you saw. We know that she's still in San Diego, and that she has a daughter, both of which were nothing but speculation until now."

"But we don't know where she was going."

"Not yet." Bauer checked yet another side street, but it was becoming apparent that the bus was gone. They weren't going to find it again without knowing its route. "Look at the schedules for those buses. See if any of them were due to stop at that plaza around eleven o'clock."

"On it." Patterson brought up the schedule for each bus, checking the times they arrived at the bus stop. One stood out. The 704 bus, which stopped at 10.55 A.M., heading west. "Got it."

"Great. Tell me where to go."

"Take a right up ahead, then left at F Street," Patterson said, comparing the route on her phone to the car's GPS. "We might be able to catch up with it."

"Gonna give it my best try." Bauer followed her directions.

The bus was nowhere in sight, but at least they knew where it was heading now, which lifted Patterson's spirits. As they passed each bus stop, she looked around, hoping her sister might have disembarked, but Julie was nowhere in sight. "Can you go any faster?"

"Not in this traffic." Bauer weaved around a slow-moving SUV, approached an intersection, then breezed through a traffic light moments after it turned yellow and turned onto F Street. "See it anywhere?"

"Not yet." Patterson scanned the street ahead, looking over the roofs of the cars in front of them for the bus, but her view was obstructed by a delivery truck sitting in the line of traffic several vehicles away. They were almost at the waterfront now. She saw a strip of shimmering blue ocean beyond the traffic. It glistened in the sunlight. She glanced at the car's GPS and saw that it was San Diego Bay, with the thin ribbon of Silver Strand State Beach beyond, and then the vast expanse of the Pacific. If the bus was still ahead of them, it didn't have far to go before reaching its terminus at the E Street Transit Station.

Then she saw it.

The bus was way down the street, pulling over at a bus stop. Several people got off, and new riders got on, but Patterson couldn't see if any of the passengers who had disembarked were Julie and the little girl.

Without needing to be told, Bauer said, "I see it."

He blew his horn at a taxi that cut him off, then accelerated past it when the cab pushed back into its original lane, doing the same to another motorist who slammed on their brakes and barely avoided a collision.

"Idiot," Bauer mumbled as the taxi made a turn and vanished from sight.

The bus stop was up ahead, the bus still idling at the curb.

"We can catch it," Patterson said, craning her neck.

"That's the plan." Bauer swung the wheel, crossed into the other lane.

The bus was still there, but Patterson sensed that it would move off at any moment. She gripped the side of her seat and watched with a furrowed brow.

They drew level with it.

Passengers were visible above them through the tall vehicle's side windows. But no sign of Julie.

And then the bus inched forward, right-hand turn signal blinking.

"Oh, hell no," Bauer muttered, pressing the accelerator and surging forward. As they passed the bus, he turned the wheel hard and maneuvered in front of it, forcing the driver to slam on his brakes and come to a shuddering stop with a hiss of air brakes.

"Good enough for you?" Bauer asked.

"What do you think?" Patterson was already half out of the car. She sprinted around the vehicle and approached the bus door, then banged on it, pulling her credentials wallet out at the same time and pressing it against the glass. "FBI. Open up."

The door opened with a faint hiss.

Patterson jumped aboard.

"What's going on?" asked the driver, a middle-aged woman with short brown hair and thick-rimmed glasses.

"Nothing to worry about," Patterson told her. "We're looking for someone, that's all."

"Like a criminal?" The woman's face turned white.

"A missing person," said Bauer, climbing aboard the bus.

Patterson turned from the driver and walked down the aisle. Nervous riders looked up at her, some with concern on their faces, others with curiosity. It wasn't every day that federal agents stopped and searched your bus.

A black woman in a bright red top touched her arm as she passed by. "Are you looking for someone in particular?"

"A mother and daughter," Patterson said, looking down the rest of the aisle and realizing that her sister was no longer on the bus. She took out her phone and showed the woman the photo of Julie. "Caucasian. The mother is in her thirties. The daughter is young. Five or six years old."

"There was a woman that looked like that who had a little girl with her," said the woman after studying the photo. "Walked right past me. I think she got off at the last top, or maybe the one before that."

"You're sure?"

"Sure as I can be."

"Thank you." Patterson returned to the front of the bus and held the photo up for the driver. "You remember this woman?"

She shook her head. "Not in particular."

"Please, try to remember. It's important."

The driver huffed, clearly annoyed at the interruption to her route. "Look, I see lots of people, lady. Hundreds of them a day, and I've been doing this job for ten years. After a while, you stop looking at the faces."

"Come on," said Bauer, turning back toward the bus door. "The longer we stay here, the less chance we have of finding Julie."

Patterson cast one last glance back down the bus, as if her sister would magically appear sitting right there on a bench, then she stepped down and returned to the car. After climbing in, she looked at Bauer. "We were so close."

"I know. But don't give up. We'll backtrack. See if we can find her. Julie can't have gone far on foot."

Patterson smiled weakly, thankful for Bauer's optimism, but deep down, she was losing faith. Had it even been Julie that she saw climbing aboard the bus in front of the McDonalds? So many years had passed, and who knew how much her sister would have changed since college? Maybe Patterson had seen what she wanted to see. Or maybe she had been right there, within reach of her sister for the first time in sixteen years, only to lose Julie all over again.

# THIRTY-SEVEN

SENATOR BILL NEWPORT WAS NERVOUS. Actually, he was beyond nervous. Since the previous day, when he had learned of Corbin Pope's daring escape from custody, he had been living in a perpetual state of terror. There was no doubt in the senator's mind that the hitman would come after him. Maybe if he hadn't tried to kill the guy... But there was no point in dwelling on what ifs. The damage was done, and all Newport could do now was deal with the repercussions and do his best to stay alive until Pope was recaptured or killed.

Which was why he had kept the Desert Eagle close at hand since removing it from his safe in the Capitol Building. The gun provided a small measure of comfort, even if he wasn't sure it would do any good against the deadly assassin. The other thing that went a small way to calming Newport's fears was that Pope didn't know about the Austin condo he had purchased several years before so that he wouldn't have to live out of a hotel room every time the Texas Legislature was in session.

Even so, Newport had not slept easily the previous night, despite the gun tucked under his pillow. He had tossed and turned, lying awake until the first rays of sunlight splashed across his bedroom floor. At one point, sometime around 2 A.M., he had heard a sound somewhere else in the building—a door closing with a muffled bang—and for a brief moment he imagined the hitman creeping through the condo with deadly intent, merging with the surrounding darkness like a chameleon. But then he realized that it couldn't be Pope. He wouldn't have heard a sound if the assassin had really found him. It was probably one of his neighbors coming home late and drunk, letting their door slam.

Even so, Newport had locked the bedroom door—even though it was a flimsy privacy lock—and turned the light on after that. Then he had lain under the covers, his hand on the gun and ears straining for any aberrant noise. He even considered getting dressed and fleeing to a hotel but soon thought better of it.

He was safer right where he was.

Pope was not just a skilled killer. He was also a master hacker. If Newport used his credit card to pay for a room, he would locate the senator within hours, maybe even sooner. Going to a hotel would be akin to placing a target on his own back. Better to stay in the condo, which had been purchased through a shell company he had set up years before to keep his real estate investments separate—and shielded—from his political career. And while there was a chance that Pope could track down that company, Newport was sufficiently confident of his skill in nesting LLCs one inside the other like Russian dolls, that he figured the odds were low. After all, his political opponents, many of whom were just as corrupt as him, hadn't managed to pierce the veil of Newport's many dubious business ventures. Neither had the press, nor the Secretary of State, who oversaw elections, and was, ironically, the same entity that handled his registration of the LLCs in question. The more he thought about it, the more that Newport had convinced himself that the condo was his best bet if he wanted to stay alive and out of Pope's way.

Which was why he had called the office that morning and

told them he was otherwise engaged, even though he was supposed to be in a legislative session at 9 A.M., and then had a full slate of afternoon meetings.

Now he was pacing the condo's living room. The TV was tuned to CNN, but he was barely paying attention. He just couldn't stand the silence without it playing. It was noon, but it felt more like late evening thanks to the many hours he had already been awake. Three cups of coffee—the strong Columbian brew that he favored—had done little to perk him up. At one point he had gone into the bedroom and laid back down but had soon given up when sleep remained as elusive as it had the previous night.

What a mess.

Newport went to the window and stared out toward the Capitol Building, the largest and most distinguished capitol in the United States. A fact that filled him with pride whenever he gazed at its grand façade, and the Goddess of Liberty, holding her sword and star, sitting atop the towering dome. Maybe he should have gone to work, after all. It wasn't like Pope would try anything while he was inside the building. Not with all the security measures in place. But that hadn't been what worried him. It was when he inevitably had to leave for the night.

Pope might be surveilling the building, waiting for Newport to show himself, and there were so many ways that an assassin of Pope's caliber could kill him right out on the street, even in broad daylight. He might step in front of a bus or fall through a faulty sewer hole cover. A death that would be labeled a tragic accident, which was Pope's specialty and one of the reasons why Newport had used him so many times in the past.

Or maybe the killer would just follow him, find out where he lived, then sneak back later and stage an accidental electrocution at the hands of the toaster oven sitting on the kitchen counter, or help the senator leave the building via a dive from the tenth-floor condo's balcony.

Newport shuddered. He was best off right where he was, safe

and sound in the one place Pope that wouldn't find him. And he could stay holed up in the condo for as long as it took for the feds to catch up with the hitman and hopefully gun him down, thus removing the threat to Newport, while also silencing the assassin before he could say anything that might incriminate the senator.

That was a plan Newport could get behind. Frustrating as it would be to shack up in the condo long-term, it wouldn't pose much of a hardship. Anything he would need was simply a mouse click away thanks to online retailers like Amazon, and delivery services like Grubhub and DoorDash. They would even bring his toilet paper. The modern world was an agoraphobic's dream, and while Newport hoped that he would not be forced into the life of a hermit for too long, it was better than being dead.

# THIRTY-EIGHT

THE FIRST THING Carl had done after arriving in San Diego was find somewhere to lay his head for the next several days. He found a cheap hotel on the south side of the city and paid in cash, because he didn't think it was safe to use a credit card. Thankfully, they let him check in early, and soon he was in the room and taking a hot shower, washing away the grime and sweat of days in his truck, and put on fresh clothes. He stashed the bag of money he had taken from the farmhouse under the bed and pushed it as far back as it would go—the last thing he wanted was to get robbed and end up penniless on top of everything else—then he went to his truck, climbed in, and got to work.

He spent the next several hours cruising the neighborhoods around the hotel, mostly because it was as good a place as any to start. He went from street to street, studying the faces of everyone he saw, in the vain hope that—by some stroke of luck—he would come across Julie. He hadn't adopted this approach because he thought it was the best use of his time, but rather because he didn't know what else to do. At least until he stopped at a convenience store for a coke and a hotdog, and had an epiphany triggered by a ripped sheet of paper stapled to a power pole in the parking lot.

**LOST CAT**
HERCULES
BLACK AND WHITE
LARGE MALE ADULT
BLUE COLLAR
MISSING FROM ALLEN LANE AND SURREY ROAD.
LAST SEEN ON 6/19

There was also a photo and a phone number.

Carl stared at the flyer, all thought of his lunch now gone. It wasn't that he was an animal lover. Far from it. Carl had never seen the point of having a pet. As far as he was concerned, they were just hungry mouths to feed that didn't contribute to the household in any meaningful way. The flyer had caught his attention for another, more pertinent, reason.

There he was, driving around like a mad person, relying on no one but himself, when he could put the entire city to work looking for Angel and Cherub.

He plucked the flyer from the post, studied it for a few seconds more, then crumpled the ragged sheet of paper and tossed it into a trashcan outside the store. Soon, that power pole, along with many other similar ones scattered throughout the city, would become makeshift billboards, enlisting all who saw them into willing searchers, looking for his Angel.

But there was an obstacle. He had no flyers, nor any way to make them. Then he thought of another, even bigger issue. He didn't have a phone number to put on the flyers anyway, and without that, there was no point. He had ditched his phone days ago after visiting Angel's father and making the dumb mistake of picking up that frame from the mantle. The one with the picture of Angel in it. And he was glad that he had since they had obviously found out about him. The tire tracks and crime scene tape at the farmhouse told him that much. What he didn't know was *how*, although he suspected that it was from his fingerprints. Apparently, that sealed record back when he was seventeen hadn't been sealed enough. Ditching the phone had been smart. It could have been used to track him. Not that he would have put his real phone number on the flyer, anyway. That would be stupid beyond belief.

He returned to his car and sat there for a while before he came up with a solution to the first of his problems. He could visit any print and ship place, like a FedEx Office, that offered the use of computer workstations, make a flyer, and have hundreds of copies printed right there in no time. And he had taken plenty of photos of Angel and his daughter over the years. Photos that had kept him company during the days and weeks he was away from his family, driving his truck. Granted, they had been on the phone that he no longer possessed, but it wasn't a big deal. The store was sure to have internet access, and the photos were backed up on the cloud. He would need to login if he wanted one for the flyer, but it was a slight risk—assuming anyone was even monitoring his cloud account—so long as he didn't hang around for too long after doing so.

And his second problem had a simple solution, too. A prepaid phone. Anonymous and disposable. Sure, there was some risk involved. Once the flyers were up and the phone number was out there, the FBI could track the device using nearby cell towers, even if he deactivated location tracking. Which was why he would be careful and keep the phone turned off most of the time, only powering it up in safe locations for a few minutes to see if anyone had responded. It wasn't convenient, but it might keep him out of prison.

Carl smiled. He felt better now that he had a plan. A task to focus on that might lead him to Angel. And he couldn't wait to implement it. He glanced toward the convenience store, decided that he could do better than a flat coke and a gross hotdog that had probably been sitting on a roller grill for the last several hours. There must be an In-N-Out somewhere close by. The thought of that made his mouth water. Which was why, a couple of minutes later, he was driving again with thoughts of a hamburger and fries on his mind. After that, he would make those flyers, and then Angel would have nowhere left to hide.

# THIRTY-NINE

TWO HOURS after catching up with the bus, Bauer and Patterson had driven the entire route, and checked every stop, all the way back to the plaza where Julie had climbed aboard. Despite their best efforts, searching the surrounding streets, there was no sign of her.

Patterson was disappointed. Her sister had disembarked, along with her daughter, and melted away, vanishing as if she had never been there. Worse, they had been so close. If only Patterson had looked back toward the McDonalds, and the bus stop, a few moments earlier, maybe she could have stopped Julie from climbing aboard. Her search would be over. But that wasn't what had happened, and all she could do now was move forward with the knowledge that her sister was close by.

Bauer must have been thinking the same thing.

"Hey," he said as they pulled back into the plaza where the clinic was located. "At least we know that she's here now. That we're not chasing our tails."

"I guess."

"And we still have the clinic." Bauer climbed out of the car. "Mayde they can tell us something."

"Not if it's anything like the first one," Patterson said as they crossed the parking lot.

"Have some faith." Bauer pulled on the door and held it open for her.

This clinic was nicer than the previous one, with a bright, clean waiting area, comfortable chairs, and the faint scent of jasmine hanging in the air from an air freshener plugged in near the door.

The woman behind the counter greeted them with a friendly smile when they approached. "Can I help you?"

"I hope so," said Bauer, showing her his badge. "We're looking for someone who might've been in here earlier today. A woman and her daughter."

Patterson took her phone out and showed the age progressed photo to the woman. "She looks like this."

There was a moment of hesitation before the woman said, "I would love to help you, but we're not allowed to give out patient information."

"Does that mean you recognize her?" Patterson asked.

"She was here, but that's about as much as I can say."

"We understand," said Bauer. "And we're not looking for medical information. Can you at least tell us the name she provided, and maybe an address?"

"She's a missing person," Patterson added, not mentioning that Julie was her sister. She wanted to keep that piece of information in reserve. "We believe she was abducted and held against her will for sixteen years."

"Oh, my. That's dreadful."

"Which is why we need to locate her," Bauer said. "And quickly. The man who took her might also be in San Diego and means her harm."

"Goodness." A look of shock passed across the woman's face, quickly replaced by one of frustration. "I would love to help you. I really would. But the rules are clear. We're not allowed to share patient information regardless of circumstance. Unless you have a warrant, that is?"

"We don't," Patterson said. "Yet."

"And it will take a while to get one," Bauer said. "Which is why anything you can tell us, no matter how small the detail, will help."

"The missing woman is my older sister," Patterson said, finally playing the last card in her hand. "This isn't just work. It's personal, too."

Bauer placed his hands on the counter and leaned forward. "She's family. Can you release the information now?"

"Not unless she gave us permission on the form she filled out." The woman looked sideways toward a stack of papers. She leafed through them for a moment, then shook her head. "The woman in question didn't list anyone under that section. I'm sorry, but I still can't tell you anything more than I already have."

Bauer straightened up. "We understand."

"I really do wish I could help," the woman said. "Maybe if you get that warrant?"

"We'll be doing that," Patterson replied, glancing toward the stack of paperwork and hoping that her sister's form would be visible. It wasn't. The sheet of paper on top bore a man's name. "And then we'll be back."

Out in the parking lot once more, Patterson turned to Bauer. "Do we even have enough to get a warrant?"

Bauer shrugged. "We can try, but right now, everything is circumstantial. We don't even know if the woman who visited this clinic was really your sister."

"Which is why we need to see that form." Patterson knew there was a high benchmark for obtaining a warrant to access patient information. They would need to provide enough proof to convince a judge that it was more likely than not that Julie had visited the clinic. All they had was a photograph of the postcard, with its San Diego postmark, an asthma inhaler recovered from

Carl Edward Bonneville's farm outside of Flagstaff, and Patterson's conviction that the woman she saw climbing aboard the bus was her sister. What they didn't have was hard evidence that Julie had a daughter beyond some children's clothes recovered at the farmhouse, that the inhaler belonged to that daughter, or that her sister was still in San Diego.

"Under the circumstances, we might need to bring out the big guns," Bauer said. "A warrant application might be received more favorably if it comes from higher up the chain, like, say, the ASAC of the New York field office."

"Jonathan."

"Right. He's your direct supervisor, which means that he's also supervising this case. And it doesn't hurt that he's currently tapped to replace Marilyn Khan as Special Agent in Charge of the Criminal Investigative Division when her promotion comes through."

"It's worth a try." Patterson waited for Bauer to unlock the car and then climbed in. "But it could take days to get that warrant. What do we do in the meantime?"

"What we always do. We keep working the case. Looking for your sister," Bauer replied, slipping behind the wheel and starting the car. "And I've got an idea about where to do that…"

# FORTY

CORBIN POPE WAS RESTLESS. He was anxious to take care of the senator. After getting a few hours of sleep at the hotel—Pope rarely needed more—he had risen and made his way to the building where Newport owned a condo. The senator was still there—a fact Pope had confirmed by calling the Capitol's Media Relations team for a second time under the guise of journalist Harvey Bent. The woman he had spoken with the first time was not there, but another employee, a man this time, told him that Newport was not feeling well and would be out all day, and possibly longer. Next, Pope had crossed the street and went to the building's parking garage, ducked under the barrier, and searched until he found the space reserved for the senator's condo. Newport's Mercedes SUV was parked there, and the engine was cold. Having confirmed his target's location, Pope returned to the front of the building and did a quick turn around the block, noting all the entry ways, exits, and other pertinent details that would help him later, like the cameras at the front entrance, the lack of a doorman, and the swipe card entry system. Then he found a place to watch the main entrance, even though he didn't think Newport would leave any time soon.

The senator, realizing he had doomed himself with the failed shower attack, was probably cowering ten floors above in the mistaken belief that the hitman did not know about the condo. If Newport had been smart, he would have climbed into his car and gotten the hell out of there, putting as much distance between himself and Austin as possible before Pope had even arrived in the city.

Not that it would have mattered. Newport wasn't smart enough to stay so far off the grid that he couldn't be tracked. At least, not by someone with Pope's skills. Even if the senator had fled to the ends of the earth and beyond, he would still have been on borrowed time.

Standing in the shadow of a doorway on the other side of the street and looking up at the condo building, Pope wondered how long Newport could sequester himself before the walls started closing in. The hitman was tempted to find out, just for kicks, and also because prolonging the senator's torment by days or even weeks held a certain appeal. But there was no time for such indulgences. Pope had other matters that needed his attention. Like the FBI agent, Patterson Blake. Which was why he would move quickly. But not too fast. It would be risky to go after the senator in broad daylight. Everyone was paranoid these days. A stranger in the building, no matter how innocuous he looked, might attract curious eyes. Better to wait until those eyes were safely tucked up in bed and closed.

The same went for the senator, although Pope didn't think he would find Newport snug under the covers and sleeping like a lamb. That would be too easy. The senator might not be able to stay awake indefinitely, but he would certainly be restless. Alert for any intrusion into his space. He would also be armed. Pope was sure of that. Not that it mattered. Newport was a soft target compared to many of the people Pope had put in their graves. Men and women who might have been called paranoid if they weren't correct in their assumption that they had made an enemy with deadly intent. Influential targets, both domestic and foreign, who had surrounded themselves with all manner of security and firepower in an attempt to stay alive. It hadn't worked. Every last one of them was now six feet under.

Pope looked around quickly, then stepped out of the doorway and walked in the direction of his car, parked a couple of blocks away. He would come back later and deal with the senator. He was sure the man wasn't going anywhere. In the meantime, there was something else that he needed to do. Secure a fresh identity that would allow him to travel by air unimpeded and unnoticed. Because driving everywhere was a chore and also took much too long. And he figured that even though they had fingerprinted him in Las Vegas, it was still safe to fly domestic. International was another matter. Pope wasn't sure how he would circumvent the biometrics required to board a flight to another country since his prints would now be in databases used by both the TSA and border patrol. At least, not yet. But nothing was impossible, especially for someone with his connections. He would figure it out.

But that could wait. Right now, Pope's main concern, beyond dispatching the senator, was finding Patterson Blake and swiftly getting to wherever she was currently located. Which meant he would need a new identity. His previous alias, the one he had used in Vegas, was burned, and although he had used others over the years, he didn't trust that they hadn't been compromised since his arrest. Apart from that, he didn't have access to them. The passports, driver's licenses, and other artifacts of his false identities were stored inside safe deposit boxes in New York, Miami, and San Francisco. He also had a box in London that contained several foreign identities. But none of these were within easy reach, regardless of his newfound distrust in them.

To that end, Pope had reached out to one of his underworld contacts. A man adept at crafting ironclad legends. He was an even better hacker than Pope, and a master forger, who operated in the gray area between patriot and enemy of the state, having spent much of his career providing services to clandestine agencies such as the CIA. He had crafted identities for operatives buried deep within Russia, China, and the Middle East. Legends that had kept the unsung heroes who protected democracy safe in locations so dangerous that any chink in their credentials or background would get them a life of backbreaking labor in some frozen hell of a Gulag, or more likely, a bullet to the head. Such was his skill—not to mention knowledge that the United States government would rather keep secret—that they turned a blind eye to his less honorable activities, just so long as they didn't endanger national security. Which was why the man—who went only by the codename Phoenix thanks to his ability to resurrect a person from the ashes of their old identity and give them a whole new life—was selective with whom he worked. The pair had become acquainted many years before when Pope had assassinated a high-ranking official in the government of a major adversary. One of many off-book jobs he had performed for the Central Intelligence Agency. Best of all, Phoenix was located less than three hours up the road in Dallas. By the time Pope got there, his new identity would be ready, and then he would drive back to Austin in plenty of time to deal with Senator Newport.

# FORTY-ONE

AFTER THEY LEFT THE CLINIC, Julie fulfilled her promise to take Cherub for ice cream. They took the bus again, disembarking a couple stops before the waterfront and walking three blocks south to an ice cream parlor that Gloria had told her about. Ice creams in hand, they strolled down to the water and a small park that overlooked San Diego Bay, where they sat and ate the creamy cold treats.

It was a glorious day with a deep blue sky that stretched all the way to the horizon, and a cooling breeze that took the edge off of the late summer heat. Seagulls circled and swooped, their cries mixing with the sounds of distant boat engines and the chatter of excited children playing in the park. Cherub watched her peers with a mixture of curiosity and fear. She had never spent any time with other kids. Her entire world until they left the farmhouse had been her mother, Carl, and Ma.

Julie would have loved nothing better than for her daughter to jump up and join in with the fun, but one look at Cherub's face told her it wasn't going to happen. Not yet, anyway. Maybe in the future, when all this was over—if it ever was—her daughter would go to school like a normal child, make friends, and forget the miserable solitude that had marred the first years of her life.

"I like it here," Cherub said finally, licking the last of her ice cream and starting in on the waffle cone. She looked up and Julie smiled, her mouth covered with strawberry, caramel, and chocolate. When Julie, who was still working on her ice cream, offered Cherub a lick of mint chocolate chip, the girl shook her head, even us her gaze returned to the children playing in the park. A shadow fell across her face. "Why aren't I allowed to do that?"

"You are," Julie said, her heart practically breaking at the sad note in her daughter's voice. "If you want to."

"That's not what daddy would say."

"Well, daddy's not around anymore." *And if we're lucky,* thought Julie, *it will stay that way.* She ran a hand through her daughter's hair, smoothing it out. "Your life is going to be different now. Better."

"How?" Cherub crunched the last of the cone and chewed noisily.

"For a start, we never have to go back to the farmhouse. We'll never be locked in that room ever again."

"I don't like where we are now any better," Cherub said. "The hotel room smells funny, and the bed is too hard."

"It's only temporary." Julie couldn't eat any more of her ice cream. She tossed what was left into a trashcan near the bench. "I'll find us somewhere better to live, I promise."

"When will that be?"

"Soon, when it's safe."

Cherub pulled a face.

"Hey, don't be like that." Julie put an arm around her daughter and pulled her close. "You ready to go back?"

"I suppose." Cherub cast a final lingering glance at the other children, clearly too afraid to approach them, but wishing that she could. Then she stood up. "Can we have McDonald's again for lunch?"

"Twice in one day?" Julie replied with a laugh. "I'm not sure that's a good idea."

"But I'm hungry, and I want the chicken nuggets."

"How on earth could you possibly be hungry right now?" Julie asked, staring at her daughter in disbelief. "You ate a breakfast sandwich and hash brown less than three hours ago, and you just wolfed down a huge ice cream cone with three scoops."

"So?"

"Fine, we'll get some lunch on the way back to the hotel. We have to pick up your prescription, anyway. Will that make you happy?"

Angel nodded enthusiastically.

"But not McDonalds."

"What are we going to have, then?"

"I don't know." Since arriving in San Diego, they had lived off a mixture of fast food—mostly Domino's Pizza, because it was within easy walking distance down the block, and Del Taco, which was equally close—and foods purchased from the local convenience store like hot dogs and TV dinners that could be heated in the hotel room's small microwave. It wasn't ideal, but Julie was hardly in a position to do anything else under the circumstances. McDonald's was, apparently, becoming something of an obsession with her daughter. This was probably because it was the first such food she had ever eaten after fleeing Carl's farmhouse, and also because there wasn't one within walking distance of the hotel, so the only other time she had it was this morning when they visited the clinic. "How about we look for somewhere to eat after we pick up your prescription?"

"Okay." Some of the enthusiasm drained from Cherub's voice, but when Julie stood and took her hand, led her from the park, she left willingly.

They rode the bus back to the hotel, then followed the directions to the Walmart provided by the receptionist at the clinic, and collected Cherub's inhaler. After that, Julie relaxed.

The events of the night before had left her shaken, and a nagging fear had remained until she had the medicine in hand. Now there was only one thing left to do. Fulfill her pledge to get lunch.

But there was a problem.

They hadn't passed anywhere while they were walking to the Walmart, and Julie didn't want to stray further from the hotel. The issue of her daughter's asthma might have been settled, but her encounter with the two men in the muscle car was still fresh in her mind. While she didn't think that they would still be around, the incident had dinged her confidence and served as a reminder of the fear that Carl had instilled in her every day for sixteen years. All she wanted to do was hurry back to the hotel, lock the door, and feel safe again. Which was why, when she saw a McDonald's in front of the Walmart, she gave in. Thirty minutes and one happy daughter later, they finally arrived back at the Del Ray, where Gloria was sitting out on the second-floor balcony in her lawn chair, waiting for them.

"I have some news," she said as Julie and Cherub walked toward her. "I spoke to my contact, the guy who can get you a job, and he'd like to see you."

"Really?" A flutter of apprehension mixed with a flash of hope surged through Julie. If she could get a job, she might be able to fulfill another promise. Getting Cherub out of the rundown hotel, and into somewhere better. "When?"

"Tonight. He'll meet you at the bar. Nine o'clock."

"Why so late?" Julie asked. Her stomach clenched at the thought of another trip down the block to the bar in the dark.

"Don't know. Didn't ask. He's a busy man. Take it or leave it."

"I can't," Julie said, looking down at her daughter. "I don't want to leave her alone in the hotel room again."

"You won't have to. Bring the kid along. I'll sit with her while you talk."

"To the bar?" Julie might have been out of touch, but she was sure that bars still didn't allow children.

"You got a better idea?"

"No." Julie thought for a moment. "Won't you get in trouble, having a kid in the bar like that?"

"Nah. I'm sure it'll be fine just so long as you don't dally. Besides, how else am I going to get my 40 percent?"

*Right*, Julie thought. *It's all about the money*. But she didn't say that. Instead, she forced a smile, swallowed her fear, and nodded. "I'll be there."

"Good." Gloria stood up and turned toward her hotel room door. "I'll see you tonight. And don't be late."

# FORTY-TWO

CARL HAD SPENT most of the afternoon in the print and ship store putting together the flyer that he hoped would bring Angel and Cherub back to him. He had figured that it wouldn't take very long, but once he got on the computer, he found the software confusing. Still, by four in the afternoon he was standing at a beast of a laser printer and watching a couple of hundred missing posters slide out of the machine and into the tray.

**MISSING: MOTHER AND DAUGHTER**
DEANA TAYLOR AGE 35
BRITNEY TAYLOR AGE 6
MISSING SINCE JULY 26TH
**$5000 REWARD**
FOR INFORMATION LEADING
TO THEIR SAFE RETURN.
PLEASE, IF YOU HAVE SEEN THEM
OR KNOW WHERE THEY ARE,
BRING MY FAMILY BACK TO ME.

At the bottom of the flyer was the number of a prepaid phone he had purchased specifically for that reason.

He picked up a flyer and studied it, thinking how good it looked, despite his struggles with the computer. The reward was a nice touch. Sure, it would deplete his stash of money a little, but it would also be a powerful incentive to call. He had also dreamed up fake names for his missing family, because he figured it was safer, and it wouldn't matter. The last thing he had done before sending his creation to the printer was to access his cloud account and find a suitable picture of mother and daughter. A photo he had taken a few months before when they were celebrating Cherub's birthday. Not only was it a good likeness of the pair, but it would also tug at the heartstrings. His daughter beaming as she looked at the birthday cake on the table in front of her, and Angel sitting to one side with a slightly less enthusiastic smile.

He put the poster back down and looked at the digital display on the printer. Forty copies to go and then he could get out of there, which was good because he was still nervous that Patterson Blake and her FBI buddies had been monitoring his cloud account, looking for him to access it. A great way to pinpoint his location, much like the prepaid cell phone that was now turned off in his pocket. He had purchased it from a Best Buy on the way to the print and ship store and wasted no time in activating the device, choosing a number with a San Diego area code. People were more likely to respond if they thought they were helping a fellow citizen of the 619.

He walked to a water cooler near the computer stations and poured himself a drink, more as a distraction than because he was thirsty. When he turned back toward the laser printer, he noticed a young woman in her mid-twenties with long brown hair and hazel eyes watching him from behind the counter. She was wearing a store uniform with a tag over her left breast that said her name was Claire. She hadn't been there before. When he entered the store, he had spoken to a man in his forties, paid him cash for use of the computer station and for the prints that he wanted to make. Now the guy was gone, replaced by Claire.

The young woman smiled, and he smiled back, his stomach doing a quick flip. She reminded him of Angel. Not now, but back when he had first met her. Strangely, it wasn't a physical thing so much as the young woman's posture. The way she held herself and how she looked at him with those shy yet inviting eyes. They spoke to him in a way that few others had since that day long ago when he walked into Amy's Roadhouse and met a girl calling herself Stacy, who would later turn into his Angel. He had known from the first time he met Julie Blake that she would be his, and he had that same feeling about this girl.

Claire.

It was a cute name. Simple. Honest. But not one that he would use when she came to live with him in Mexico, or wherever they ended up. He would find her a better name, just like he had with—

The reality of his situation crashed down on Carl. What was he doing, fantasizing about this slip of a girl behind the counter, even if she was cuter than hell? He needed to find Angel and get rid of her permanently before he could even think about replacing her. And he certainly couldn't go back to the farmhouse. The FBI were onto him, so his old homestead was a no-go. It saddened him to think that he would never again see the farmhouse, at least if he wanted to stay a free man. Never get to visit his mother's grave. Although it was probably empty now anyway, his mother gone forever.

Carl lowered his head and returned to the printer in time to see the last sheet come out. He picked up the stack of flyers and put them into the bottle green backpack he had purchased at the same time as the phone. Then he stepped toward the door, resisting the urge to look back toward the counter. Maybe later, when this was all over, he would return and pay another visit to Claire. But until then, the store was out of bounds. He didn't want to show his face in the same location twice, which was why his flyer was saved on a flash drive and snug in his pocket. If he needed more copies, he would find somewhere else to make them. But right now, he wanted to get started distributing the pile he already had. And there was no time like the present.

# FORTY-THREE

BAUER'S IDEA was to search the streets around the bus route again, but this time, they wouldn't be looking for Julie and her daughter. At least, not directly. If they were riding the 704 bus, he speculated, then they must be living somewhere close by. Probably within walking distance of the bus stop. He also theorized that Julie wouldn't have access to credit cards, bank accounts, or any other form of credit, given her circumstances, making it almost impossible to rent an apartment or a house. That left hotels, and specifically those places that still accepted cash.

But Patterson saw a flaw in his logic. Hotel rooms were expensive. Even places that rented by the month, targeting people who couldn't find any other accommodation, were not cheap. "How would Julie get ahold of enough cash to rent a hotel room for that long?"

"I don't know," Bauer admitted. "But it doesn't mean that she didn't. Maybe she found work. Or maybe she stole money from Carl before she fled. We found a bunch of empty cash boxes at the farm. It appears that our man had an aversion to bank accounts. Like, he didn't have one. Neither did his mother. He must have kept a lot of cash stashed around the house."

"I don't know," said Patterson. "It's a lot of speculation without much evidence to back it up."

"Do you have a better idea?" Bauer replied. "Because unless something new comes to light, some piece of evidence that sends us in a different direction, it's all we've got."

"Fine. Even if we assume Julie is renting a room in some dive of a hotel, we're still no closer to finding her. There must be hundreds of hotels in San Diego, and she might have caught a bus from somewhere else before transferring to the 704."

Bauer nodded thoughtfully. "Maybe. But I think it's unlikely. We're pretty sure that she visited the clinic, even if no one there would tell us anything. If she isn't staying locally, why would she take a trip all the way across town when there would be other clinics closer to where she was staying?" He took a breath. "Look, I'm not saying it's a perfect plan, but we don't have anything else. We'll take that photo and show it around. See if anyone recognizes her. We'll start with the hotels closest to where you saw her board the bus and work our way out from there."

Patterson agreed, reluctantly, because Bauer was right. They had no leads, nothing else to pursue. They spent the next several hours driving from one dingy motel to another, asking questions and showing Julie's photo, but no one had seen her. Finally, with the sun slipping below the horizon, and night approaching, they gave up.

"So much for your idea," Patterson said as they walked back to their car after visiting one last hotel.

"We'll pick it up in the morning," Bauer said. "There are plenty more places to visit."

"This is hopeless." Patterson was frustrated. Her sister had been mere feet away at that bus stop. "She was right there, Marcus. If only she had just—"

"Hey. We'll find her." Bauer unlocked the car. "You want to drive?"

Patterson shook her head. "What I want is a stiff drink..."

"That can be arranged."

"But I should probably keep a clear head." She climbed into the passenger seat. "How about something to eat instead?"

"On it, boss." Bauer started the car and pulled out of the parking space. "How about pizza? I know it's your favorite. There's a place downtown that gets awesome reviews."

"I'm not your boss. And pizza is your favorite, not mine."

"Worth a try." Bauer grinned. "But still…"

"Fine. Pizza it is." Patterson laughed despite herself. "How does Phoebe put up with you?"

"That's a good question," Bauer replied, turning out onto the street. "A very good question indeed."

# FORTY-FOUR

CORBIN POPE HAD BURNED ALMOST seven hours on his round trip to Dallas, but it had been productive. His contact, Phoenix, was waiting with a whole new identity for the hitman. Roger Bauman. He wasn't sure if he liked the name, he would have preferred to pick his own, but it was a miracle he could even get a new legend at such short notice, and a testament to Phoenix's skills, so he wasn't going to complain. He had also procured a firearm. A Glock pistol with the serial numbers filed off. It wasn't a weapon he would normally carry, but he had a feeling that it would come in useful later.

Now, as he drove the last few miles back to Austin in the late evening darkness under a rainy sky split by an occasional bolt of lightning, he mulled over his options for the senator.

His original plan had been to wait until the early hours of the morning when everyone would be asleep in their beds to take care of Newport. But then he would be forced to sit around for several more hours, and Pope was itching to move on to his next target, the FBI agent, and close out this deplorable chapter of his career. With Patterson Blake dead, he could fade back into obscurity, maybe take some personal time while the heat died down and reemerge whenever the moment was right. His CIA handlers wouldn't be pushing any jobs his way for the foreseeable future, and after the Newport fiasco, he was done with private contracts.

Or he could retire.

That idea held a certain appeal. Pope had spent a couple of decades doing other people's wet work, and it was about time he thought about himself. He couldn't see himself on a tropical beach with a cocktail, but there were other places he could go. Like a cabin in the wilds of Alaska, where the solitude would wrap around him like an old friend, or maybe Central Europe. He had been to Prague a couple of times, and quite liked the city. Maybe he would settle down there and find some new, less deadly, pursuit to occupy his time. At least once he resolved the small issue of international flying now that he was in the system.

But first... the senator.

By the time he reached the city, Pope had made up his mind. He wasn't going to wait. And he had the perfect plan. Which was why, instead of going to his hotel room, he drove to a business on the outskirts of town that would have what he needed to implement his plan.

Texas Tommy's Fireworks Emporium.

Even though the July 4 holiday was long gone and the next good opportunity to blow shit up wouldn't roll around until New Year's Eve, the store was open. In fact, according to the internet, they never closed. A banner on their website proudly proclaimed that they were open twenty-four hours a day, seven days a week. How the store stayed in business with such ridiculous hours baffled Pope. Who needed fireworks at three o'clock on a Wednesday morning? He couldn't imagine. But it didn't matter. The store had what he wanted, and that was all he cared about.

Pope pulled into the parking lot, then hurried inside and completed his transaction in less than five minutes. He left with a couple of smoke bombs—available in either blue or pink and used mainly for gender reveal parties according to the display—

and two packs of twenty-foot fuse. Then he hopped back in his car and drove straight to the condo building, leaving the vehicle several blocks away and walking the last half-mile.

Now he needed to gain access to the condos without drawing attention to himself. The building had both a keycard entry system and a security camera covering the front entrance. He assumed there would be at least one more camera in the lobby and maybe even some in the corridors. But the cameras were easy to eliminate with nothing more than a hooded rain jacket, which he was already wearing. Sure, the cameras would record his entry and passage through the building, but they wouldn't see his face. And anyway, if his plan worked, nobody would be checking the security footage because they wouldn't know that a crime had taken place.

That left the key card entry system. Given access to his old laptop that was now sitting in an evidence room in Las Vegas, Pope could have cloned a key in minutes, but instead, he would have to go old school. Which was why he lingered on the sidewalk a block from the condo building, watching the door. It was late evening, which meant that plenty of the tower's residents would be coming and going. All he had to do was find one who looked like a suitable mark. And soon, that person left the building and came strolling down the street. A gentleman in his seventies with wispy gray hair combed neatly back over his scalp. He wore spectacles and a tweed jacket that gave him a scholarly appearance. The cane he leaned on, made of polished oak with a gleaming silver handle, only added to the look. He might have been an old college professor—there were certainly enough schools in Austin to support that hypothesis—or maybe a writer of literary works, thought Pope, as the man ambled down the street toward him. Certainly, he was someone with enough money to afford a condo in one of the most expensive buildings in the city. But honestly, it didn't matter how the man had made his money. All that mattered was the small white oblong of plastic that he had just slid into his jacket pocket.

Pope glanced around quickly to make sure that no one was paying him any attention, then walked slowly toward the man, pulling his phone out at the same time and pretending to be distracted by it long enough to bump the gentleman ever so lightly.

"My apologies," he mumbled, stepping aside to let his mark pass.

"You should watch where you're going with that damn thing," the old man grumbled, before continuing on his way.

"I'll take that under advisement, muttered Pope, hurrying away in the other direction, the man's key card now snug in his own pocket.

Moments later, he was walking quickly away in the direction of the condo building. But he didn't go straight to the main entrance. Instead, Pope veered off toward the parking garage where he would implement the first phase of his plan. He had already scoped it out earlier in the day when he was looking for the senator's car and confirmed that the only security cameras were at the entrance and exit. It was easy enough for Pope to skirt their field of vision, which focused primarily upon the roadway, and walk deeper into the garage. As he went, he looked up at the concrete roof above his head until he found what he was looking for. Then, after making sure there was no one around, and checking one last time for cameras, he removed the smoke bombs from his pocket and placed them on the ground between a white Lexus sedan and a Porsche Panamera. Next, he removed the packets of fuse, each one containing twenty feet that would burn at approximately thirty seconds a foot, opened them, and attached one end of each fuse to the pair of smoke bombs. After rolling out the fuses near the garage wall where they would be hidden by parked cars, he removed a lighter from his pocket and lit them.

He waited only long enough to make sure that they were burning, before turning and hurrying from the garage as fast as he dared. He had about ten minutes before the smoke from the bombs, either pink or blue—he hadn't bothered to check the color when he purchased them because he didn't care—activated the smoke detector mounted on the garage ceiling near the Porsche. Just enough time for what he needed.

It took him less than a minute to reach the front steps of the building, with the hood of his raincoat pulled over his head and his gaze cast down to the floor to hide his face. A few seconds after that, he was inside, and ready to implement the next phase of his deadly plan.

Pope crossed through the lobby to the elevators. And rode up to the tenth floor.

He glanced at his phone. Eight minutes had passed. By now, the fuses would be growing short.

There were four condos on the floor, one occupying each corner of the building. Pope had no idea how many of them were currently occupied, except for condo 10C. He looked around for somewhere to conceal himself, but apart from the elevators, there were only five doors. The four condos and the emergency stairs, conveniently right across the hall from 10C.

That was where he would hide. Pope went to the emergency stairs, pulled the door open, and stepped onto the concrete landing beyond. Then he flattened himself against the wall behind the door so that when it next opened, he would be concealed. Not that he thought anyone would be looking for him. They would be more concerned with saving themselves.

Satisfied, Pope glanced at his phone again.

Nine minutes.

Pope reached under his coat, his fingers touching the Glock pistol concealed there.

Ten minutes.

He held his breath and waited.

The muggy, stale air trapped inside the emergency stair shaft shifted around him in silence.

Eleven minutes.

Pope was getting nervous. Had the fuses gone out before

they reached the smoke bombs? If so, then he had a problem. He hadn't purchased extras as a backup, which was unlike him, and if he relit the original fuses, he wouldn't have time to get back to the tenth floor.

Pope cursed under his breath. Maybe the events of the last few weeks had taken a greater toll than he realized.

Twelve minutes.

Pope was sure something had gone wrong with the fuses now. Maybe, if he was lucky, they had fizzled immediately after he lit them. He stepped forward to exit the emergency stairs and take the elevator back down to the lobby.

At that moment, the fire alarm went off in a frantic, high-pitched screech.

# FORTY-FIVE

SENATOR BILL NEWPORT was sitting on the sofa watching TV when the fire alarm went off. More accurately, he wasn't watching TV. He was playing it in the background, still tuned to CNN, and staring at the Desert Eagle laying on the coffee table in front of him next to a box of ammunition that he had taken from a safe hidden under the floor in the bedroom. The safe had been one of many upgrade options offered by the company that built the condo tower, and the previous occupant who purchased it from new had been wise enough to have it installed. It was a perfect place to keep his ammunition, which he shied away from storing alongside the Desert Eagle in his Capitol Building office safe not because it would get him into trouble—Texas was one of a few states where anyone could walk into the Capitol Building with a firearm, and state lawmakers could even bring their guns onto the chamber floor—but more because walking through the halls with that much firepower might raise eyebrows.

Newport looked up, uneasy. The fire alarm had only gone off once before since he owned the condo, and that had turned out to be kids messing around in the lobby who accidentally set it off when their hijinks got out of hand. This time, he wasn't so sure.

It felt like too much of a coincidence that the alarm would go off on the same night that he was sitting in his condo, staring at his gun, and contemplating the trained assassin who he knew was hunting for him.

But at the same time, he didn't want to take any chances. He had read somewhere that fire truck ladders could only reach up about a hundred feet, and although he wasn't sure exactly what floor that would be, he knew it would be lower than the tenth. Even if he went out onto the balcony, the ladder be too far below him to do any good.

Newport stood and went to the window. He couldn't see any sign of a fire. No smoke or gawkers standing in the street looking up. But that didn't mean that there wasn't one. He would have called down to the lobby and asked the doorman, but the condo association that ran the building had gotten rid of that particular perk the previous year, citing the expense of paying an employee to stand in the lobby twenty-four hours a day for no reason other than to greet the tenants when they entered, summon elevators, and carry the occasional grocery bag. Newport thought that for what he had paid for the condo, plus the exorbitant monthly fees the association charged, they should have kept the doorman. Now, he could see even more point to it.

But there was no use in thinking about that now. The doorman was long gone. Newport would have to make up his mind based on the available facts, and quickly. If there really was a fire in the building, then every second would count. The only problem was, he had no facts. Only that there was a fire alarm, which might or might not be a trap. He went to the bedroom and picked up his cell phone from the charger next to the bed, then dialed one of the few other people he was acquainted with in the building. A woman on the fourth floor who he'd met several months earlier while dining at the steakhouse that occupied a corner unit on the ground floor of the building. The two had gotten to chatting at the bar while they waited for their tables, and had ended up eating together, since they were both alone. They had seen each other several times since then when he was in town, but it wasn't a relationship. The woman—her name was Patricia—was a couple of years younger than him, and pretty enough in an austere way, but he wasn't looking for a partner. Sure, they had hooked up a few times, but it was purely casual, at least for him.

He dialed her number and put the phone on speaker, then waited. After a couple of rings, she picked up.

"Bill?" Her voice faded in and out, probably because of the amount of concrete and steel between them. "Where are you?"

"I'm still in my condo. What's going on?"

"You haven't left yet?" There was worry in her voice. "You need to get down here right now. It's not safe."

"That's why I'm calling. I figured it was probably a false alarm and I'm in the middle of cooking dinner," Newport lied. "I don't want it to spoil for no reason."

"It's not a false alarm. There's smoke in the parking garage. Lots of it. For heaven's sake, Bill, get yourself down here right now before it's too late."

A sudden panic overcame Newport. How ironic would it be to stay in the condo hiding from a hitman who hadn't even found him, only to end up dying in an accidental fire, and doing Pope's job for him? He went back into the living room and picked up his jacket from the back of the chair, then pulled it on. "I'm on my way now."

"Thank goodness. Be quick. And don't use the elevators."

I'm not stupid, thought Newport. He had no intention of using the elevators, even though walking down ten flights of stairs held little appeal. Besides, they wouldn't work, since most elevators returned automatically to the ground floor, then shut down if the fire alarm went off. He wedged the phone between his shoulder and chin as he pulled his arm into the jacket. "I'll see you in a few minutes."

Newport didn't wait for her answer before hanging up. He

put the phone in his pocket, and turned toward the door, then stopped. He was almost certain that the emergency was real, but just in case... He backtracked and picked up the Desert Eagle, then took his jacket back off and put on his shoulder holster. After donning the jacket once more, and with the gun now concealed beneath it, he raced from the condo and made for the stairs.

# FORTY-SIX

POPE STOOD BACK against the wall of the emergency staircase. Moments later the door opened, and the first worried residents, a blurry eyed man and woman in their fifties wearing dressing gowns over their nightclothes, even though it wasn't even ten o'clock yet, started down the stairs toward the lobby many floors below. Another couple, this time fully dressed, followed not far behind. None of the terrified residents noticed Pope, or even glanced his way, just as he had hoped.

The door closed when no one else stepped through it.

Pope waited patiently. He figured that the third apartment was probably unoccupied. Maybe the owners were having a late dinner, or they might be out of town. He didn't care. But the owner of 10C, who Pope knew was in residence, had yet to make an appearance, and Sen. Newport vacating his condo, at least temporarily, was key to the hitman's plan.

A minute passed.

Pope wondered if Newport was so afraid that he refused to leave, even when there was an emergency in the building. Had he decided that the fire alarm was a trap, thereby staying one step ahead of the assassin?

But then, just as Pope was wondering what his next move

would be, he heard footsteps. Moments later, Senator Bill Newport pushed the door to the emergency stairs open, hurried through, and started down.

Pope breathed a sigh of relief, even as he slipped out of the stairwell and back onto the tenth-floor lobby just in time to see the Senator's door swinging shut on an automatic door closer of the same kind that hotel rooms had. He had counted on the door being fitted with one of these, given the high-end nature of the condos. No one paid millions to hear doors slam shut in the middle of the night.

He sprinted forward, catching the door moments before it clicked shut, and stepped into the condo. Thanks to his earlier endeavors, Pope already knew the layout of the residence. He was in a short corridor, with doors on both sides, that opened into a large living and dining room combo with panoramic windows that overlooked Congress Avenue below. The door on his right was the bathroom. The door on his left was a coat closet. He moved into the main living space, to find a comfortable living room that flowed into a dining area dominated by a dark oak table, beyond which was a central island and a kitchen that even to Pope's untrained culinary eye looked top-of-the-line, with double ovens, two huge built-in refrigerators, and a huge wine fridge that must have held a couple of hundred bottles. Recessed ceiling lights positioned to eliminate shadows illuminated everything in a soft glow.

But he wasn't there to admire the opulence.

Pope turned away from the kitchen and one last door on the opposite wall that was standing open. The bedroom. He poked his head inside. The king-size bed was unmade, the sheets twisted in knots. Pope smiled, imagining the senator tossing and turning as he lay awake the previous night, wondering when the hitman would come for him.

From somewhere outside came the wail of sirens, drifting up from the street below. Fire trucks responding to the smoke bombs that Pope had set off in the parking garage. They would find the source of the alarm in no time and quickly declare the building safe. Pope didn't have long before the senator would return.

He stepped away from the door, moved back into the living room. That was when he noticed the box of ammo sitting on the coffee table. And not just any ammunition. This was .50 Action Express large caliber ammo, one of the most powerful pistol cartridges in the world. Powerful enough, in fact, to bring down a bear. It appeared the senator was armed, and that his choice of gun was formidable. It would make the Glock Pope had obtained earlier that day look like a toy in comparison. That was worrying. Even more worrying was the thought that Newport might actually know how to use the weapon. And since Pope didn't see a handgun anywhere near the ammunition, he felt it wise to assume that the senator was carrying the pistol about his person, probably under his jacket in a shoulder holster, when he had left the condo.

Pope grimaced. He had trained himself to expect the unexpected. Even a heavily armed senator who looked soft enough, by outward appearance at least, that he would flinch from a BB gun. It changed nothing, except that it was now more vital than ever that his plan went off without a hitch, because he had no intention of giving the senator any opportunity to use that gun.

Pope tore his gaze away from the ammunition.

At that moment, the fire alarm fell silent.

He went to the panoramic window, pulled back a slider, stepped out onto the balcony and peered down at the street below. Two firetrucks were sitting at the curb. There was probably at least one more on the other side of the building, near the parking garage. A pair of firefighters exited the lobby and climbed into the cab of one truck. More firefighters were leaving now, too. There was no urgency to their gait, suggesting that they had deemed there to be no danger to the building or its occupants.

In a few minutes, the senator would be back.

It was now or never. Pope had already figured out where he was going to hide. The closet on the right-hand side of the door was large and deep. Big enough to walk into, with racks on both sides for coats and shoes. The senator had been wearing a suit jacket when he left, but he wouldn't hang that up in the coat closet. That was where Pope would conceal himself.

He retreated inside and closed the slider, then crossed to the closet, opened it, and stepped inside. Sure enough, there were coats on hangers lining the closet walls. Many of them were expensive. Pope recognized the labels. Not the sort of outerwear that a public servant should be sporting. Unless that public servant was bringing in a hefty amount of cash by other means. Pope didn't care where Newport was getting his money, although he suspected that most of it was ill-gotten. He turned and pushed the closet door mostly closed, leaving it ajar by the tiniest crack, so he could still see it.

Less than a minute later, the condo door swung open, and Bill Newport entered.

Pope tensed.

This was the most dangerous part of his plan.

He took the Glock out, waited for the senator to pass by the closet, then moved into the corridor behind him, quiet as could be.

Newport, already on high alert, must have sensed Pope behind him. Maybe it was a faint stirring of the air, or a subtle movement of the shadows, but it didn't matter. He had barely begun to turn when Pope placed a hand over his mouth and the muzzle of the Glock to his neck.

"Good evening, Senator Newport," Pope said softly. "I've been thinking about you."

# FORTY-SEVEN

CARL HAD SPENT the rest of the afternoon since making the flyers driving around and stapling them to lampposts, utility poles, and anywhere else that he could find. Now it was getting dark, and he was getting tired and hungry. He was three blocks from his car and stapling a flyer to one last utility pole when he saw a bar across the street. The Barrel Room. He didn't know if it served food, but it would certainly have ice-cold beer, and a frosty one sounded pretty good right then.

Carl stapled the flyer to the post, then crossed the road and entered the bar. A skinny woman, with limp blonde hair that fell below her shoulders and a red blotchy face, watched him approach the counter.

"What'll it be?" she asked when he reached the counter.

"Light beer." Carl dropped his backpack on the counter and unzipped it. He put the stapler inside, next to the remaining flyers. He had done well, posting at least a quarter of them, and maybe more, even if his wrist was sore from pushing staples into so many posts. Tomorrow, he would move to a different area of town, maybe down by the water, and start all over again. The phone in his pocket pressed against his leg. He took it out and turned it on. He'd read somewhere that the cops needed a couple of minutes to trace a call, and even though this wasn't the same thing—he was worried that the FBI would use the phone to track him if they got ahold of the number—he figured it was safe to keep it on for short periods.

No one had called and left a message, which was disappointing. But it had only been a few hours. What had he been expecting?

Carl shut the phone back off and returned it to his pocket just as his beer arrived.

"That'll be four bucks even," said the server. "Want to open a tab?"

"Nah." Carl reached into his pocket and pulled out a slim wad of ten-dollar bills held together by a rubber band. He peeled one off and slipped it across the counter. When the server came back with his change, he left a one on the bar top and put the five back in his pocket along with the rest of his cash. He looked around at the dimly lit room. There was a pool table at the back, and a couple of old pinball machines full of flashing lights. The floor was covered with a worn carpet that was sticky underfoot. An odor of stale beer hung in the air. Even though it was a Friday, there were only a few other patrons. "Nice place you have here."

"Thanks." The server smiled wryly, obviously picking up on his sarcasm. "I'm Gloria. What's your name?"

Carl picked up his beer. Gloria was watching him with hazel eyes, expecting an answer. "Franklin," he said, saying the first name that came into his head and immediately regretting using Angel's father. But then he relaxed. It wasn't like this woman would know Angel, and anyway, there were a lot of Franklin's in the world. It wasn't a big deal.

"Franklin." Gloria leaned on the bar, her cleavage visible, breasts pressing together. "I like that."

"Thanks." Carl wanted to look away but couldn't help himself. Gloria was hardly beautiful. Far from it. She looked used up and sickly. He suspected she was a former drug user.

But those breasts. He could see the barest hint of a lacy red bra that came further into view when she leaned even lower. He cleared his throat and finally forced his gaze up. "You live around here?"

"Not far." Gloria was still studying him with those hazel eyes. "Why? You looking to come home with me?"

"No," Carl sputtered. "I mean... I was just making conversation... It's a thing people ask."

"It is?"

"I guess." Carl's face was burning. He wondered if it was red. Picking up his beer, he mostly drained it, gulping the amber liquid down partly because he was thirsty, and also because he felt stupid.

"You want another one?" Gloria asked, watching him with a bemused expression.

"Sure." Carl drained the last of the beer and set the glass down.

He was relieved when she took the glass and turned away, placing it under the counter and grabbing a clean one before pouring a fresh beer. When she turned back toward him, he already had the five-dollar bill, the change from his last drink, in his hand. He swapped it for the beer. "I'm sorry if I offended you."

Gloria observed him for a moment. "You didn't. Guys have said a whole lot worse to me in this place. I can assure you of that."

"Good." Carl picked up his beer. "I mean, not good that men said things to you. Not that. I meant that I'm glad I didn't offend you."

"I know what you meant." Gloria glanced sideways as another customer entered and approached the bar. "You good here?"

Carl nodded.

Gloria turned and walked away. Before long, she was pouring a beer and in conversation with the newcomer. Twenty minutes later, after finishing his second beer, he motioned for a third, doing his best not to engage the waif-like bartender in conversation again. Thankfully, the bar was busier now, so she didn't try to flirt with him again, assuming that had been what she was doing. She had probably just wanted a bigger tip.

When she walked away, Carl slumped with relief.

He hated how tongue-tied he always got around women, even unattractive ones like Gloria. All except Angel. He was never tongue tied around her. For a split second, he forgot what she had done, how she had left him, and he smiled, but then he looked at the backpack containing the flyers, and the blissful moment shattered. He took another swig of his beer, then stared sullenly into the amber brew. A week ago, everything was great. Now his life had turned into a living hell. Angel was gone, his mother was dead, and the feds were looking for him. His thoughts turned to the girl in the print shop, Claire, and his heart skipped a beat. Soon, once he found Cherub, he would go get her, and then it would all be different.

But right now, he needed to pee.

Carl downed the last of his beer and slid off his stool. He picked up his backpack, then made his way to the back of the room, weaving around a pair of guys who were heading for the pool table and talking loudly. It was almost nine o'clock, and he was tired. He entered the restroom and relieved himself, watching his beer vanish into the urinal, and as he did so, he took the phone back out and checked it again. Still no messages. Disappointed but hardly surprised, he turned it back off and put it away. It wouldn't be long, he told himself, before someone saw Angel and called. Maybe not tonight, or even tomorrow. But soon. She was out there somewhere, right under his nose, and sooner or later her luck would run out. Then he would teach her a lesson she wouldn't forget, at least for the short time she had left to live.

# FORTY-EIGHT

JULIE HAD BEEN nervous since she spoke to Gloria earlier that day. And it wasn't just because another walk down the block to the bar in the dark made her stomach churn, especially with Cherub in tow. It was also that she had never held a real, full-time job. Carl might have wanted her to contribute to the household, doing all the dirty work Ma wasn't inclined to do, but she had never actually worked for anyone and earned money to support herself. Just thinking about meeting Gloria's contact made her weak at the knees, especially since she had no idea what kind of work he would require of her or how long she would be away from Cherub each day.

Now, as she walked the short distance to The Barrel Room from the hotel, holding Cherub's hand tightly and keeping watch for any signs of trouble, like that muscle car from the previous night, she almost turned back.

But even as she contemplated doing so, she realized that fleeing back to the safety of the hotel room was not an option. Without work, she and her daughter would be homeless within weeks, and then what would they do? Go live in a tent on the sidewalk, or worse, sleep under a bridge? She might have resorted to that as a last resort for herself, but never for her daughter. Which was why she kept going, even though her stomach was in knots. Her only comfort was the pistol pushed into the waistband of her jeans and concealed beneath her shirt. It was the same gun she had found in the cashbox before fleeing the farmhouse. Until now, she had kept it out of Cherub's reach in a high cupboard above the sink in the hotel room's small kitchenette—unloaded of course—because she was too afraid to handle the weapon. But after what had happened the previous night, she had retrieved it, loaded the weapon, and took it with her, even though she had no idea how to use it.

When they reached the bar, Julie stopped and kneeled in the parking lot to talk to her daughter. "When we go inside, you need to stay quiet and do what Gloria tells you. Understand?"

Cherub nodded. She had been silent ever since they left the hotel, perhaps picking up on Julie's unease.

"Good girl." Julie straightened up, and they entered the building. It was busier than the previous evening, and the pall of cigarette smoke hanging in the air was thicker.

Julie ushered Cherub toward the bar, where Gloria was waiting for them. She glanced around, nervous, even though she knew that the two thugs from the previous night were not there. Gloria had made it clear that they were not welcome in The Barrel Room, and even if they eventually returned to try their luck again, it wouldn't be so soon. But what she did see almost sent her scurrying back out into the parking lot. A man was walking away from her toward the restrooms, and for a brief moment, she was overcome by the certainty that it was Carl. He had the same build and gait. She came to a halt and watched for a few seconds, unable to tear her eyes away. Part of her wished he would look around so she could see his face and know once and for all that it wasn't the man who had kept her locked in a dark bedroom for sixteen years and abused her both mentally and physically. But he didn't, and soon vanished into the restroom.

"Pull yourself together," she muttered under her breath. "It's not him. It can't be him."

And she believed that, because she couldn't see any way that Carl could have tracked her to San Diego, let alone a specific dive bar at a specific time on a specific night. He might be evil, but he hadn't cut a deal with the devil.

She forced herself to calm down and continued toward the bar, where Gloria greeted Cherub with a glass of soda and a bag of potato chips.

"You're a few minutes early. Marco isn't here yet."

"Better than being a few minutes late," Julie replied with a weak smile. She lifted Cherub onto a stool, then glanced around, but there was no sign of the man who looked like Carl. She assumed he was still in the bathroom.

"It's not him," she muttered again.

"What?" Gloria looked at her with narrowed eyes. "You okay?"

"I'm fine. Just nervous, I guess."

"There's no need to be nervous. Marco's a good man. He'll treat you right."

"It's not just—" Julie started to say, then stopped herself. She hadn't told Gloria about Carl, and why she had fled to San Diego. At least, not the truth. All she had said was that she was running from a bad relationship. A man who beat her and abused her. She never mentioned that he had also kept her captive for a decade and a half, raped her repeatedly, impregnated her, and threatened to kill her family if she ever escaped. Saying any of that, good as it might feel to unburden herself, could only lead to trouble. Either Gloria would pull away and not want to get involved, or she would insist that Julie went to the police. Knowing her neighbor, it would probably be the former. She suspected Gloria was as averse to authority as she was, but probably for different reasons.

"Not just what?"

"Never mind." Julie looked down at the floor. When she

looked back up, Gloria was watching her with a puzzled expression, as if she sensed Julie was holding back. "I'm fine. Really."

"If you say so." Gloria folded her arms. "You want something to drink while you wait? A beer, or maybe something stronger?"

"I don't think that would be a good idea. I'm here to get a job, remember?"

"For heaven's sake, lighten up." Gloria shook her head. "You're not interviewing for a spot on the Supreme Court. You'll be scrubbing toilets and emptying trash cans. I can't imagine that Marco cares if you have a beer or two. Might even help you relax. You've been acting weird ever since you stepped into the bar."

Julie wanted to contradict her, but she knew it was true. Instead, she glanced down at her daughter, who was ignoring the conversation and happily sipping her drink through a straw, then said, "I'll have a Coke."

# FORTY-NINE

CORBIN POPE SAT opposite Senator Bill Newport in the expansive living room of the lawmaker's Austin condo. The fire trucks summoned by the hitman's smoke bombs had long since departed, having established that there was no real threat to the building, and the residents had returned to their accommodations, blissfully unaware of the dire situation one of their neighbors now found himself in.

"I thought we were friends," said Pope, looking relaxed in an easy chair across the coffee table from Newport, who was perched on the sofa with his hands in his lap and a hangdog expression on his face. In truth, the assassin was like a coiled spring, ready to pounce at the slightest provocation. Not that he thought the senator would try anything. After ambushing him in the hallway, Pope had quickly relieved Newport of the Desert Eagle hiding under his jacket. A gun that now lay in Pope's lap, the hitman's gloved hand resting upon it. The Glock, less powerful but equally capable of putting the senator in his grave, was now in Pope's pocket. "Then you tried to kill me for no reason."

Newport glowered at Pope. "You got yourself caught. You were a liability. You'd have done the same in my position."

"That's true," Pope conceded. "But the difference is that I wouldn't have failed. Perhaps you should have trusted me."

Newport never responded.

Pope cleared his throat. "Question is, what happens next?"

"If you've got any sense, you'll walk out of here right now before this goes any further. I'm a sitting member of the Texas Senate. You won't get away with killing me."

"On that point, we'll agree to disagree." Pope leaned forward. "Let me clarify. I need information that I believe you can provide. Get me that information, and I'll consider it just recompense for your misguided attempt on my life."

"We'll be even?" The senator asked, hopefully.

Pope nodded. "We shall be even."

"And you won't kill me for... well, you know..."

"I will not kill you for sending those two inept thugs after me." Pope placed a hand on his chest. "Cross my heart. Like I said, we'll be even."

Newport observed Pope for a short while, perhaps gauging his sincerity. "What do you want to know?"

"Special Agent Patterson Blake. The woman you sent me to eliminate. Where is she?"

"That's it?" Newport stared at the hitman in disbelief. "You want to finish the job?"

Pope nodded silently.

"Why? I figured that after what happened... I mean, it's not like I expect you to fulfill your contract under the circumstances."

"Don't flatter yourself, Senator Newport. This has nothing to do with you or our previous arrangement. It's purely a matter of pride. I've never failed to eliminate a target, and I don't intend to start now."

"And also, she outsmarted you," Newport said, clearly regretting the words as soon as they tumbled from his mouth. He shrank back, his gaze dropping to the Desert Eagle. "I'm sorry. I didn't mean—"

"Yes, you did. Don't be so spineless." Pope tapped a finger against the muzzle of the Desert Eagle. "And you're right, she outsmarted me, much as I'm pained to admit it. Again, it's a matter of pride. Now, perhaps you would be good enough to tell me where she is."

"I don't know where she is."

"But you can find out."

"I don't know. Well, I guess so. I have to be careful after what happened in Amarillo. I could've ended up in prison if I hadn't called in a mountain of favors."

"And yet, after all that, you thought it was a good idea to send a contract killer after the person you tried to frame for murder. A federal agent, no less."

"You didn't have to take the job."

Pope shrugged. "It's not my place to be your conscience, or to save you from yourself. Can you find her for me, or not?"

"I'd have to make some calls."

"What kind of calls?"

"I know some people who would know, or at least, could find out quick enough."

"What sort of people? Like in the FBI?" Pope asked. "I need this to be done discretely. Blake can't find out that I'm coming for her. Not again."

"No." Newport shook his head. "Not the FBI. The United States Justice Department. I'm vice chair of the Senate Criminal Justice Committee. I can say it's a matter of state security."

"How ironic." Pope couldn't help but smile. The same man who had tried to have a land surveyor sent to prison for a rape he didn't commit, had killed at least two people in that same scheme, attempted to frame an FBI agent for murder when she got too close, then put a contract out on her when he failed, was second in command of a committee on criminal justice. "Your contact in the Justice Department… they won't alert Blake of your inquiry?"

"No. I'll tell them it's classified. Need to know only."

"And they won't be suspicious, given your history?"

"Even if they are, it doesn't matter. I'm a free man, aren't I?"

"Fair enough." Pope had reservations about handing a phone to the senator, but he didn't have much choice. Not if he wanted Patterson Blake's current location. He took the senator's phone from his pocket, the same phone he had confiscated after Newport returned to the condo. He held it out. "Make your call."

"Right now?"

"Unless you prefer the alternative." Pope tapped a finger against the Desert Eagle again. A subtle message, but one the senator received loud and clear.

"Okay. Fine. It's not that late on the east coast. He probably isn't in bed yet."

When Newport reached for the phone, Pope drew it back. "No tricks. You say anything out of place, and…"

"Yeah. I understand. I'm not stupid."

"Very well." Pope extended the phone again and let the senator take it this time. Then he sat quietly, hand still resting on the gun, while Newport made his call.

Fifteen minutes later, the senator hung up and handed the phone back. "All done. It will take him a while to get the information you want. A couple of hours, at least. He'll call when he has it."

"Excellent." Pope smiled and returned the phone to his pocket. "Now there's nothing to do but wait and hope for your sake that he comes through…"

# FIFTY

CARL WASHED HIS HANDS, then stepped out of the restroom and started back across the bar toward the front door. He resisted the urge to look back toward the counter, and Gloria, even as an image of her cleavage and that hint of lacy bra flashed through his head. She wasn't his type, wasn't even attractive, and it went a long way to showing his state of mind that he was even thinking about her.

Once outside, he hurried across the road, past the utility pole and the flyer he had put there only an hour before, then made his way back to the truck. But as he rounded the last corner, he came to a halt. There was a police car parked behind his truck, lights flashing, and two cops in black uniforms inspecting it.

He stood there for a moment, shocked into inaction, then turned and hurried away in the other direction before they saw him.

# FIFTY-ONE

JULIE WAS SITTING at the bar with Cherub, who was chatting happily with Gloria and sipping on her second soda, when Marco arrived. He was a stocky man with a dark tan, and jet-black curly hair. A heavy gold chain hung around his neck, visible past the V of his partly open shirt. He strolled in as if he owned the place. He was also fifteen minutes late.

After Gloria introduced them, Marco ordered a Jack and Coke, then motioned for her to follow him. He led her to a booth near the back of the bar, not far from the toilets. A faint smell of urine hung in the air. It was also the darkest part of the room, and Julie wondered if Marco didn't want to be seen.

Once they were settled, he got right to business. "Gloria tells me you're looking for work. A job that pays cash, no questions asked."

Julie nodded.

"You got any experience?"

"I've cleaned. Mopped floors. Done laundry." Julie squirmed in her seat. The answer sounded lame, even to her. "Beyond that, not much."

Marco snorted. "Fantastic. We'll find you work as a housewife."

"I'm sure that's not all I can do," Julie said, taken aback by his abrasive attitude. "I'm hard-working, and I learn quickly."

"Yeah. Everyone says that." He studied her face. "What's the deal, anyway?"

"I don't understand."

"You're not exactly my normal clientele." Marco gripped his drink in one hand as if he were afraid someone would steal it. "I doubt you're undocumented, with that fair complexion and homespun accent. What gives?"

"I just need to work, that's all."

"You a cop?" Marco finally took a sip of his drink. "Or maybe homeland security? Because if you are, you have to tell me, otherwise it's entrapment."

"Do I look like a cop?" Julie asked, confused.

"How would I know?" He cast a glance toward the bar, where Gloria was still entertaining Cherub. "Nah. I think I'm good. Cops don't bring kids into bars, and Gloria would never set me up. That ain't her."

"Does that mean you can get me a job?"

"Sure. Why not? I just need your resume and a couple of references."

"What? That's not... I don't..." Julie went to stand up. "This isn't going to work out."

Marco chuckled and nodded toward the chair. "Sit back down. I was just screwing with you. I can get you a job. In fact, I have one in mind, since you're so good at the custodial arts."

"Really? Where?"

"Hotel downtown. I know the executive housekeeper. Fancy place, but they're not averse to saving a little money and helping the less fortunate at the same time. You'll be cleaning rooms and washing sheets. Scrubbing shit stains off toilets. Think you can handle that?"

"Sure." Julie was far from sure, since she had never held a real, full-time job before, but she figured that it couldn't be worse than doing chores for Ma back at the farmhouse. Nothing could be that bad. "When do I start, and how much does it pay?"

"Whoa. Easy there, sweetie. I appreciate the enthusiasm, but I'll need to make a call before we nail down the specifics. But since you asked, I guess we can clear up the matter of pay right now. It ain't gonna be a whole lot, given the circumstances. Hiring workers like you comes with a not insubstantial risk, so there has to be a decent reward. I figure you'll get about eight bucks an hour."

Julie did some quick math in her head. Even if she worked full time, that would only come to $320 a week. After Gloria's cut, she would walk away with less than two hundred. It wasn't much to live on. In fact, it wouldn't even cover the hotel room. "I can't survive on that. Do you have anything that pays more?"

"You kidding me? I don't even know if you're a good worker. You show me you're reliable, that you can hold a job, and we'll talk about finding you something that pays a little better. In the meantime, this is it."

"Please," Julie begged. "Even if it's just a dollar or two more. I'm desperate."

Marco shook his head. "Best I can do."

"Okay." Julie had no choice, and a trickle of rain was better than a drought.

"Is that a yes?"

Julie nodded.

"Good. Here's the deal. You work for the hotel, but I collect your wages and pay you in cash, minus my 15 percent fee."

"Wait. No one mentioned anything about a fee."

"What, you think I do this for fun? I find you work, I get paid. Think of me like an employment agency, only I don't care about your background, and there ain't no forms to fill out."

"Gloria's already taking forty percent. If you take another fifteen, I'll be working for practically nothing."

"Whew. Forty percent. I should up my fees. I'll say this for Gloria, she's a better negotiator than I'll ever be."

"It's not a fee. She's going to look after my daughter while I'm working."

"Ah. Daycare."

"Something like that."

"I sympathize with your situation, but it's not my problem. Whatever deal you have with Gloria is between the two of you. My finder's fee is nonnegotiable." Marco paused, a lopsided smile lifting the corner of his mouth. His hand dropped beneath the table, touched her knee. "Unless, of course, you'd like to work out a different arrangement."

Julie tensed, even as Marco's fingers inched higher up her thigh. She slid back on the bench, trying to wriggle free of his touch. "What are you doing?"

"Making you an alternative offer." He glanced toward Cherub, then back to Julie. "You're an attractive woman, considering. Play nice, and I'll waive my fee. I might even pay an extra buck an hour. Keep me happy, and who knows what might happen." His hand curled around her thigh and squeezed, just a little too close to her crotch for comfort. "What do you say?"

"No!" A sudden swell of panic overcame Julie. She jumped up, hitting the table and almost knocking Marco's drink into his lap. "I don't want your stupid job, and I don't want you anywhere near me."

Marco sat still for a moment, then he lifted his drink and swallowed it before slamming the glass back down on the table. He stood up. "You'll change your mind. Your type always does."

He pushed past her and stormed toward the exit. On the way out, he turned to Gloria. "You should tell your friend that she ain't all that." Then he kept going, slamming the door behind him.

Julie watched him go, then turned to Gloria, who was staring at her, openmouthed. Next thing she knew, the tears were flowing.

# FIFTY-TWO

THE PIZZA WAS GOOD, but not *Queens* good. Patterson washed it down with an ice-cold beer, while Bauer stuck to Coke. When they left, he insisted on driving, then headed north, toward downtown.

"Where are you going?" Patterson asked. "I'm in the other direction."

"Not tonight." Bauer kept his eyes on the road ahead, possibly because he didn't want to see her reaction when he said: "I booked you a room at the Garden Inn where I'm staying. Well, not me exactly. It was your boyfriend's idea."

"What? Why?" Patterson had enjoyed dinner. It had been a pleasant distraction to do something other than dwell on Julie's case. Now her recently found good humor vanished in an instant.

"Because there's a hitman out there who might want to clean up loose ends." Bauer still didn't look at her. "I can't protect you if you're all the way over on the other side of town in your van."

"I don't need your protection," Patterson shot back, a little too sharply despite her annoyance. "I can take care of myself."

"Okay. Bad turn of phrase. What I meant was that we need to stick close, watch each other's backs, and that van isn't big enough for the both of us. At least, not unless you're down with sharing a bed."

"You could have told me earlier," Patterson said. "Or better yet, how about you and Jonathan discuss it with me before deciding where I should be sleeping."

"Hey, it was nothing to do with ne. The Bureau booked my room, and yours came along with it. I figured you knew. You want to blame someone, talk to your ASAC."

"Obviously I didn't, otherwise I would have packed a bag. You think I'm going to sleep in the buff, not bother to clean my teeth, and wear today's undies again tomorrow?"

"Ah. Good point. Never thought of that."

"That's because you're a man."

"Ouch. I never pegged you for a sexist." Bauer slowed and turned into the parking lot of a grocery store to turn around and head back in the other direction.

"Really? How about we call Phoebe and see if she agrees with me?"

"Alright. Enough. I surrender." Now Bauer looked at her, a grin spreading across his face. "We'll go get your bag. Happy?"

"No." Patterson folded her arms and refused to meet his gaze. "I would have been fine in the van. It has wheels. I can park it anywhere. Hide in plain sight. Much safer than a hotel room."

"Jonathan Grant didn't agree. He sent me here to keep you safe, and that's what I intend to do. Hotels have cameras in the public areas. Doors with security locks. Staff at the front desk twenty-four hours a day."

"None of that helped in Vegas."

"Granted. But we're ready for him this time. And he doesn't have his toys anymore. That fancy laptop of his, and the tech he used to clone room keys, is in the LVPD evidence locker."

"Doesn't mean he can't replace it."

"Look, short of making you sleep in the field office, you're not going to get much safer."

Even though she didn't like it, Patterson knew that Bauer was right. The van was convenient, but hardly Fort Knox. The door catch was flimsy, it could be immobilized easily enough, and the thin bodywork wouldn't stop a bullet. Or a barrage of them. She could end up shot to death in her sleep. She took a calming breath. "I prefer my own space, but I guess the hotel makes sense."

"Then you won't give me any more trouble?"

"Trouble?" Patterson snorted. "You realize that I'm the senior agent here, right?"

"A fact you haven't let me forget since we first met in Dallas." Bauer joined the interstate, heading east toward the RV park on the outskirts of the city. "I offer my humblest apologies for getting above my station, oh great one."

"See, that's what I'm talking about." Patterson shook her head and fought a grin. "The sarcasm."

"It's my best feature."

"Again, I think Phoebe would disagree."

"Then it's a good thing she's not here," Bauer said, a second before his phone rang.

He answered, lifting it to his ear with one hand and keeping the other on the wheel. When he hung up, he glanced at Patterson. "That was San Diego PD. After we raided the farmhouse, I pulled the Arizona Motor Vehicle Department records for Carl Edward Bonneville to find out what, if anything, is registered to that address. There are three vehicles. A dark blue 2001 Ford F-150 pickup truck registered to Bonneville, a 2010 Freightliner tractor truck he uses for work, and an equally old Sebring registered to his mother. Then I had SDPD put a BOLO out on all three vehicles, figuring that San Diego is the most likely place he'll show up since he took the postcard Julie sent and must have seen the postmark."

"And we got a hit?"

"Yup. The pickup." Bauer changed lanes ahead of an upcoming off ramp. "PD found it parked on a backstreet in

# I WILL FIND HER

Chula Vista, on the south side of town. No sign of Bonneville. They're waiting for us to get there before they do anything else."

"You think he knows we're onto him?"

"He's in San Diego, so maybe not. If he knew that we'd pulled his prints and got a match from that picture frame, that we raided the farmhouse, he might run instead."

"Unless he *really* wants to get Julie back," Patterson said. "Or more likely, his child."

"Right. But either way, he'll know soon enough when he finds his truck has been towed." Bauer took the offramp and pulled into the parking lot of a nearby business, then entered the location given to him by San Diego PD into the car's GPS.

"Or we let the truck sit right where it is and see if he returns."

"It's worth a try." Bauer pulled back out onto the street. "I'd love to spend a few hours in an interrogation room with that man."

"You're not the only one," Patterson said through clenched teeth. "Just don't leave me alone with him!"

# FIFTY-THREE

CARL COULDN'T BELIEVE his bad luck. The cops had found his truck, which meant they had been looking for him in San Diego, and they now had confirmation that he was there. He should have realized that the FBI would ask the local police to be on the lookout for him after they raided the farm—because Carl was sure it was the feds who had been there. Who else could have found out about him from those fingerprints on the picture frame since his juvenile record was supposed to be sealed?

Still, he'd had a lucky escape. If it wasn't for that third beer, and needing to pee, he would probably be in custody right now. It made him question the wisdom of staying and looking for Angel and his daughter. If he had any sense, he would head to Mexico right now. Get across the border before it was too late, assuming it wasn't already. But he couldn't bring himself to leave Cherub behind. She was his offspring. She *belonged* to him, and there was no way he was going to abandon her to Angel's care.

And anyway, he had no wheels. How would he even get across the border? Find a hole in a fence somewhere and run across on foot? Not likely. Then he'd be stuck on the other side with no means of transportation and a bag full of cash. He'd be easy pickings for every lowlife in Tijuana. He probably wouldn't last through the first night. Hell, he didn't even know if there *was* a fence. It might be a wall too high to scale, or a barren strip of no-man's-land with Border Patrol watching it like hawks.

Carl swore.

It would be a long walk back to the hotel—which thankfully he'd paid for in cash under an assumed name—and every cop in the city would have his description, because if they knew the truck was his, they could only have gotten that information from the Arizona Motor Vehicle Department. The same department that had also issued his driver's license, which included details like his height, eye color, and a photograph.

He wished he still had the baseball cap that was currently behind the driver's seat of the pickup truck. It would offer at least a modicum of anonymity. But at least he still had the USB drive, which was in his pocket, and the flyers that were safely tucked into his backpack. It would have been a disaster to lose those. Not that he was sure if it would be safe to continue posting them. And even if he wanted to, there was still the not insignificant matter of transportation. Without the truck, he would be forced to walk everywhere, or ride the bus.

Neither option was safe or convenient.

Which left him at an impasse. He didn't dare stay in San Diego much longer with every cop in the city looking for him, and he had no way to wrap up his business there and flee.

Carl swore again.

How quickly things had gone south... which was, funnily enough, where he should have gone the moment he'd realized the farmhouse was compromised.

He lowered his head and kept on walking at a brisk pace, scanning the street ahead for threats. After a while, when he didn't hear a screech of tires to his rear, see blue and red lights bouncing off the nearby buildings, even as a commanding voice boomed out for him to get on the ground and stay there, he relaxed. The cloak of darkness helped, and also that he stuck to residential side streets, skirting the primary thoroughfares.

But then, when he was only halfway back to the hotel, a black and white sedan with a light bar on top turned from an intersection up ahead. A SDPD patrol car.

Carl's heart skipped a beat.

The vehicle was a good thousand feet away but heading toward him. Another minute and it would be on top of him.

He looked around, trying to remain calm. The cops were more likely to notice him if he panicked. Most of the houses on the street had cars in their driveways and lights on, but there was a small concrete block house up ahead that looked dark and empty.

Carl picked up the pace and hurried toward it, then turned quickly into the driveway and walked past the front door.

A motion activated floodlight snapped on, momentarily bathing him in bright white light until he moved past it and down the side of the house. He worried there would be another light, because the patrol car must be getting close, and security lights coming on like that were just the sort of thing they might stop and investigate, but he was soon enveloped in welcome darkness.

Deciding it was safe enough, he stopped and turned around, pressing himself against a tall fence that ran along the property line. The branches of a eucalyptus tree overhung the pathway, providing even more cover. There were similar such trees in Arizona. Carl had read somewhere that they were known as the world's tallest weed because of their hardiness and growth rate.

He pushed the errant thought from his mind. Here he was, hiding from the police, and musing about foliage—probably a subconscious defense mechanism to stop him from freaking out and doing something stupid, like turn and run, which would almost certainly get him noticed.

The cop car was almost upon him now. Its headlights splashed across the road, growing brighter as it drew closer.

Carl shrank back further into the shadows and held his breath.

The cruiser came into view, moving at a snail's pace. Were they looking for him? Scouring the streets near where they had found his truck? If so, they hadn't seen him, because they soon moved on past the house without slowing further.

Carl released the pent-up air in his lungs.

His heart was hammering.

He could feel the adrenalin racing through his veins.

He remained where he was for a minute or two, giving the cruiser time to move away, then he returned to the street and continued on. But he was more careful now, because that cop car had been searching for him. He was sure of it. And it wouldn't be the only one.

# FIFTY-FOUR

CORBIN POPE WAS FEELING RESTLESS. It had been several hours since Senator Newport had placed a call to his contact in the Justice Department, and there was still no answer regarding Patterson Blake's whereabouts.

"How much longer is this going to take?" he asked, shifting in his seat. The Desert Eagle was still on his lap, and it was getting heavy, but he wasn't willing to let it stray from his person. The last thing he wanted was for Newport to find his moxie and somehow get the drop on him. Getting shot with a smaller caliber handgun of the type he would have expected Newport to carry might be survivable, but not the high-powered Desert Eagle, and especially not at such close range. He couldn't afford to let his guard down, even for a moment.

"I told him it was an urgent matter that needed his immediate attention," Newport said, eyeing the gun with the look of a man who understood the futility of his situation. "He said he'd get back to me as soon as he could, but it's late. If he can't get hold of anyone with knowledge of Patterson Blake's whereabouts, he might not call back until tomorrow."

"He'd better not take that long, for your sake." After so many hours sitting across from the senator, watching him fidget and listening to his labored breathing, Pope was tempted to just kill him and get the hell out of there. He didn't like the time it was taking to get the information he needed, or how long he'd been forced to stay at the scene of what would soon become another deadly notch on his belt.

"We're still good, though," Newport said. "I mean, with our agreement?"

"Sure." Pope was fine with telling the senator that finding the FBI agent's location made them even. It didn't make any difference to what would happen once the information was in the hitman's possession. Before that, there was one other matter that Pope wanted to clear up, mostly because they had the time, and he couldn't see the point of wasting an opportunity. Also, because it was hard to negotiate with a dead man. "Speaking of which… You owe me some money."

"What?" Newport looked puzzled.

"I know you're not deaf." Pope leaned forward, ever so slightly, his hand resting on the gun. "So listen carefully. You owe me fifty grand for killing the FBI agent."

"Huh? I already paid you fifty thousand plus another ten for expenses. We're good."

"No. You paid the deposit. The agreement was that I'll kill the FBI agent for a hundred thousand. You owe me the balance."

"But you haven't finished the job yet."

"I'm aware of that," Pope replied. "But you're not considering the extraneous circumstances. I'll take care of Patterson Blake. You have my word. And I don't make promises like that when I don't intend to keep them. But once I leave here tonight, we won't ever see each other again. I think it will be better that way. Which is why I need the rest of my payment upfront." Pope tapped the barrel of the Desert Eagle with his index finger. "Unless, of course, you'd prefer to renegotiate."

"Oh. Well, I guess that's reasonable," Newport said, although the look on his face told Pope that he thought it was anything but. "I'll need my phone back."

"Naturally." Pope took the Senator's phone from his pocket and handed it across the coffee table. "Same rules apply. No funny business, or our deal is off in a way that you will find distinctly unpleasant."

Newport took the phone. "Same account as usual?"

Pope nodded. He was the owner of several offshore bank accounts, and not just in Switzerland. He also held accounts in Hong Kong, Belize, and the Cayman Islands. None of them had been compromised by his arrest in Las Vegas, because the authorities had never learned his true identity.

The Swiss account Newport knew about was more of a clearinghouse than anywhere he would actually store his money long-term. Once the cash hit that account, it would be immediately transferred to a secondary account, and from there to one of his safe harbor accounts in the aforementioned countries. None of this would create a paper trail that could be followed thanks to the strict Swiss banking regulations that valued privacy over accountability, and similar regulations in the other countries where he kept money.

Newport was busy tapping away on his phone screen. After a few minutes, he looked up. "All done. I've transferred the cash."

"Excellent." Pope reached out to take the phone back, but at that moment, it rang.

"It's him," Newport said. "My contact at the Justice Department."

"What impeccable timing he has," Pope replied with a faint smile.

Newport hesitated a moment, then answered.

Pope listened to the conversation with interest, and also with a wary ear, in case the senator tried to alert the person on the other end of the phone to his current predicament.

After the call was over, Pope took the phone back. "Well?"

"We're good once I give you this information, right?" Newport asked, clearly distrustful of the hitman.

"I shall consider us even," Pope said. "As I have most laboriously promised twice already."

"My contact in the Justice Department spoke to the assistant director of the FBI, who I presume sent the request down the chain of command until it reached someone with knowledge of Blake's current whereabouts. Discreetly, of course. She won't be aware of the inquiry, and neither will her direct superiors at the New York field office. Blake's in San Diego, following a lead on her missing sister. She's been living out of a van, but right now she's in a hotel under the protection of another FBI agent named Marcus Bauer from the Dallas field office. Apparently, there's some concern regarding her safety because of… well… to put it bluntly… you."

"Ah." That was good to know. Blake would be on her guard, which complicated matters, although it was not unexpected. "Please, do continue."

"She'll be there for at least the next several days, and possibly longer. I have the name of the hotel, and even the room numbers of both agents."

Pope raised an eyebrow, waiting for the senator to impart this last nugget of information.

Newport hesitated, perhaps realizing that very little now stood between him and the hitman's wrath. Then, obviously deciding he had no choice but to put his faith in Pope's promised forgiveness, he said, "They're staying at the Garden Inn downtown. Bauer is in room 402, and Blake is in 404."

Pope was silent for a moment, absorbing this information and storing it away in the memory palace he had constructed in his mind for the contract. It was a technique he had discovered many years before to recall information with near perfect precision. He had created a similar palace for every job he'd taken, and could still access all of them, regardless of how much time had passed. Then he nodded. "It would appear that our business is concluded."

That statement did nothing to relax the senator. He stared at Pope, wide eyed, a mixture of hope and despair flashing across his face. "Then we're done?"

"Yes. I believe we are."

# FIFTY-FIVE

JULIE SAT in the darkness and watched Cherub sleep. The little girl was tuckered after the excitement of a trip to the bar so late at night. She had nodded off soon after they returned to the hotel. Julie, not so much.

The meeting with Marco had ended in disaster, leaving her no better off than she had been before. Afterward, Gloria had admonished her despite Julie's tears, telling her not to be so sensitive. Maybe she should go after him, agree to his terms, she had said. Unless, of course, she wanted to end up on the streets.

That was the last thing Julie wanted, but she couldn't bring herself to sleep with Marco. Let that man put his hands all over her to save a measly few bucks. And the notion that an extra dollar an hour in pay would sway her... it was disgusting.

*He* was disgusting.

Which meant that she had blown her only chance to earn money, and probably lost a friend in the process. Assuming that Gloria was ever her friend, which she was starting to doubt. The hopelessness of her situation pressed down upon her like a lead weight. In a few weeks, she would be out of money. Then she would also be out of a place to stay.

Julie touched Cherub's forehead, moved a strand of hair

away from her eyes. The little girl didn't stir. And in that moment, Julie realized something. It didn't matter if she wanted to sleep with Marco, because it wasn't about her. The streets were no place for a six-year-old child. Julie knew that much, even if she was woefully unqualified to hold even the most menial of jobs. Eventually, she would have to give in to Marco's demands. Or if not him, then some other sleazeball with a carrot to dangle and an urge to be satisfied. Maybe she should just go to Gloria, tell her to set up another meeting, and let Marco have his way. Then everyone would get what they wanted. At least, mostly.

But no matter how she reasoned with herself, there was one sticking point. Money. Even if she traded the 15 percent fee for her body—a ridiculously low amount for such a demeaning act—there wouldn't be enough cash left over to keep a roof over their heads, anyway. She was sure that Marco would be taking a slice off the top even before he paid her wages. He would probably charge his friend at the hotel ten bucks an hour for her services, or maybe more. After all, he'd offered to increase her pay pretty quickly when she hesitated to take him up on his offer. But even if she negotiated her way up to ten or eleven bucks an hour, the same still applied. She would need twice that to survive, and no one was going to pay a wage that high under the table.

Julie slumped back on the bed.

It was no wonder so many down-and-out women turned to selling themselves. When it was either that, or starve, what choice did they have? The cruelty of it all sickened her. But at the same time, Julie wondered if she would eventually end up under the thumb of someone much worse than Marco, forced back into a life of depravation no better than the one Carl had subjected her to.

But not right now.

She still had time to find work, and when she did, Gloria

would happily take her cut of the money to look after Cherub, despite what the woman currently thought of her.

She glanced at the digital clock on the nightstand. It read 2 AM, but she still wasn't tired. She turned on the TV and watched a show with the sound turned down. She flicked through the channels and eventually settled on a documentary on penguins. It was that or a shopping channel hawking colorized state quarters that would, apparently, be treasured as valuable heirlooms one day. They were the sort of useless crap that Ma would have purchased if she hadn't already been dead.

That brought a smile to Julie's face for the first time since she went to the bar. Not the thought of Ma buying those schlocky painted coins for dollars more than they would ever be worth, but the thought of her lying lifeless and cold on that linoleum in the kitchen. And of Carl coming home and finding her rotting corpse.

Julie didn't know what the future might hold, or if she would one day be forced to earn a living doing things that sent a shudder up her spine, but at least she would always have that.

# FIFTY-SIX

POPE LIFTED the Desert Eagle from his lap with one hand and rose to his feet. He went to an antique pedestal desk placed against the living room wall near the bedroom door. Upon it was a laptop computer, a Tiffany style lily lamp with three opaque glass shades that might be the real deal, and a penholder containing three exquisite writing instruments. Two Montblanc fountain pens and a Cartier. Pope took a moment to admire them, then selected a Montblanc. He opened the desk drawers, searching them until he found a notepad, then returned to Newport, who was still sitting on the sofa, watching him warily.

"I would like you to write a few words for me."

"Huh?" Newport looked up at him, confused. "You want me to write something?"

"I do. A simple phrase that I shall dictate." Pope placed the pad down on the coffee table in front of the senator and offered him the pen. "If you would be so kind?"

Newport took the pen, a slight tremble touching his hand. "What do you want me to write?"

"Three small words." Pope took a step back, gun hand at his side, and seemingly relaxed. Only the barely perceptible tension in his arm gave away that he could bring the gun up in a split second should Newport become combative. "Mea maxima culpa."

"I don't understand."

"It's Latin," Pope said, without bothering to explain that it meant *through my most grievous fault*. "I assume by your blank expression that you were not raised Catholic."

"My mother's side of the family was Methodist. My father's beliefs didn't expand much beyond the bottom of a liquor bottle," Newport replied, as if it was the most normal thing in the world to be discussing family history while being held captive by a deadly assassin. "I never went to church."

"For which I applaud you. I have never found much proof of a divine entity, and plenty of evidence against, including myself. If there was a supreme being, they would never permit a person such as me to roam the earth. I also commend you for not following in your father's footsteps," Pope said, then nodded toward the writing pad. "If you wouldn't mind?"

Newport hesitated.

"Would you like me to spell it for you?"

"No. I think I can manage." the senator put pen to paper and wrote the words, then looked back up. "Satisfied?"

"Immensely." Pope glanced around. "I assume that you have liquor somewhere around despite your father's proclivity for booze." he asked. "If only for guests?"

"Over there," Newport said, pointing toward a cherry wood cabinet against the wall near the dining area.

Pope went to the cabinet and opened it to find an array of bottles, mostly whisky. He picked one up. A Macallan single malt in a custom cut-glass decanter that must have cost a thousand dollars or more. "For someone whose father was so enamored with the hard stuff, you have fine taste."

"A man can appreciate good Scotch without being an alcoholic."

"So true." Pope placed the bottle on the coffee table, then took a crystal tumbler from the cabinet, set it down, and poured a large dram. "Before we part ways, I feel that a toast is in order."

Newport reached for the glass, then paused. "You're not having one?"

Pope shook his head. "Unlike you, my own demons are not so easily kept at bay." He looked at the glass of whisky. "Please, humor me."

"Very well." Newport picked up the glass. "What are we toasting?"

"The end of a long and productive relationship."

"I'll drink to that," Newport said, probably comforted by the thought that the hitman would soon be out of his life forever. He lifted the glass. "To the end of an era."

He downed the amber liquid.

"Another." Pope poured a second, even larger measure, almost filling the glass this time.

"Are you serious?" the senator looked down at the drink with dismay. "That's an awful lot of whisky."

"Again, humor me." Pope raised the gun, his finger sliding to the trigger.

Newport took the glass and lifted it to his lips.

Pope watched while the senator forced the whisky down, pausing a couple of times to take a breath. When the glass was empty, he motioned for Newport to stand up. "Now, come with me."

"Where are we going?" The senator's eyes had taken on a glassy sheen. Apparently, he wasn't used to imbibing such a large amount of alcohol so quickly.

"The bedroom." Pope motioned for Newport to lead the way.

"Why?"

"It's late and you look tired."

"I'm not—"

"Just move."

Newport delayed a moment longer, perhaps suspecting that Pope was not truly concerned with making sure he got enough sleep, then he stumbled forward when it became obvious that he had no choice. Reaching the bedroom door, he steadied himself against the doorframe, then continued toward the bed.

"Lay down," Pope told him.

"I don't want to." Newport shook his head. "You can go now. I'll be fine."

"I don't think so." Pope's voice turned hard. "Lay on the bed."

Newport sat on the edge of the bed and swung his legs up but didn't recline.

"This would be easier if you just did as you're told." Pope reached down and pushed him back roughly until his head hit the pillows. "Lift your hands to your chest."

Newport complied slowly.

Pope lowered the Desert Eagle and forced it into the senator's grip. He kept his own hands on it, too, and applied downward pressure to keep the weapon in place. The last thing he wanted was for Newport to point it in the wrong direction and shoot him. Satisfied, he maneuvered the gun and pressed the end of the barrel under the senator's chin. "Finger on the trigger, if you please."

"What are you doing?" Terror pulsed in Newport's eyes. He shook his head and pushed back against Pope, but the hitman was too strong. "I thought you said we were even if I found out about the FBI agent?"

"I did, and we are. This isn't about you trying to kill me," Pope lied, then added the reason that he would have killed the senator, regardless. "It's about you being a loose end."

Newport tried to sit up and push the gun away from his chin. He twisted and thrashed in a blind panic, making small guttural noises. Pope pressed down even harder. Lifting one of his hands away from the gun, he took the senator's hand and pressed it against the weapon, forcing his finger over the trigger, then curled his own finger atop the senator's.

"Please, you don't have to do this." Newport's voice cracked.

He kicked and twisted, trying to dislodge Pope, but it was no use. "I'm begging you. I don't want to die."

"No one does." Pope flexed his index finger, a small movement, but it was enough to push Newport's digit down and onto the trigger. There was a brief moment of resistance, then the gun went off.

The top of Newport's skull exploded against the headboard in a spray of blood, bone, and brains. Pope turned his head at the last second, lest any gore splatter on him, but thanks to the angle of the gun, and the path of the bullet, which had exited Newport's skull, punched through the headboard, and buried itself in the wall behind, he remained mostly clean save for a few spots of blood that had rebounded.

Pope released the senator's now limp hand.

There wasn't much time. Someone would have heard the gunshot. He took the gun and moved it, placing the weapon on the floor next to the bed where the recoil would have flung it if Pope's hand had not prevented it. Then he turned and hurried from the room, crossed to the front door of the condo, and stepped out into the hallway after checking that the coast was clear. He closed to the door and removed a set of lock picks from his pocket. It only took him a few seconds to engage the deadbolt, which was crucial if Newport's death was to appear self-inflicted. That done, he hurried to the emergency stairs—the elevator was too risky—and slipped out onto the landing, even as the first confused residents stumbled from their condos, groggy with sleep, to investigate the gunshot.

# FIFTY-SEVEN

FIVE HOURS after they arrived at the pickup truck registered to Carl Edward Bonneville, Patterson had come to a frustrating conclusion. It was after 2 AM, and there had been no sign of the man who had abducted her sister all those years ago. The only nearby bar, several blocks away, was now closed, and the pickup was parked on a residential street far enough from the closest hotels to make it unlikely that Bonneville had intended to leave the truck there overnight.

"He isn't coming back," Patterson said, finally. They were sitting down the street in their car with the lights off, far enough away to be innocuous, but close enough to move quickly and cut him off should Bonneville return. Two unmarked SDPD cruisers were also parked nearby, ready to pounce.

"It would appear that way," Bauer said. "Maybe he returned while San Diego PD was still on scene, and they spooked him."

"Maybe. I think we should call it and search the vehicle. With any luck, we'll come across something to tell us where he's been staying."

"I like your optimism." Bauer yawned. "Let's go see what we can find."

He started the car and rolled down the street toward the

truck while Patterson notified the San Diego PD units that they had called off the stakeout.

Patterson was eager to see what evidence the truck contained, but they waited for the SDPD units before proceeding.

Both doors were locked, but it only took one of the police officers a few minutes to gain access, after which he stepped aside for Patterson and Bauer to conduct a search.

In most other circumstances, they would have needed to go before a judge and obtain a warrant, but in the case of a vehicle suspected of being used in a crime, there was an exemption because it could be driven away, and any incriminating evidence removed by a suspect, long before a warrant could be secured.

Patterson leaned into the drivers-side door, while Bauer searched the bed of the pickup, which contained a rusty toolbox, a bunch of empty water bottles and soda cans that Bonneville must've thrown back there because he was too lazy to find a trashcan, and some short pieces of weathered 2 x 4.

Bauer struck out, and soon returned to the front of the truck. Patterson, after searching the glove box, center console, and behind the seats, was about to do the same, but then she noticed a piece of paper wedged in the gap between the passenger seat and the console. She pulled it out with gloved hands and stared in disbelief at what she had found.

It was a missing persons flyer. But not for some random person she didn't recognize. Julie's face stared back at her, along with that of a young girl who was obviously her daughter. She read the flyer with a growing sense of horror, noting the large cash reward offered for information leading to Julie's return. Bonneville hadn't used her real name, probably because he didn't want anyone connecting her to the missing persons case that he knew would have been open, if not active, for the past sixteen years. There was a telephone number at the bottom of the flyer.

Patterson stared at the photo, noting just how close to reality the digitally aged version she had made on her phone had come. It was uncanny. It really was her sister, and she was alive after all these years. Emotion took over, and Patterson's eyes grew moist.

"Hey, you alright over there?" asked Bauer, leaning into the cab from the passenger side of the truck.

"Look at this." Patterson held the flyer out. "The bastard must've been posting these around town."

"And he's offering a reward," Bauer said. "Trying to turn the entire city into extra pairs of eyes and ears."

"And whoever responds would be handing Julie right back to the maniac who abducted and imprisoned her without even realizing it." It made Patterson sick to think that people would call that number on the flyer, trying to do the right thing, moved to action by the photo of a missing mother and daughter, and end up condemning her sister to the same living hell that she had just escaped, possibly for the rest of her life.

"It's not all bad," said Bauer. "The number on that flyer is undoubtedly a burner phone, but it doesn't matter. We have the number, which means we can use the cell towers to triangulate his position and find him."

"Assuming that he keeps it turned on long enough," Patterson said.

"Even if he doesn't, we can still track him. He'll have to turn it on at some point to see if anyone has responded to the flyers, and when he does, he'll put a pin on the map."

"And he'll be long gone by the time we get there."

"Maybe. But every time he powers up the phone, he gives us another data point. With enough of those, we can start to close in. And if we're really lucky, he'll turn it on wherever he's hiding, and we can just swoop in and take him off the streets."

"I wouldn't hold your breath on that." The flyer proved that Bonneville was cunning. That he wasn't just acting on instinct. He was a smart predator who wouldn't make it that easy for them. "But we can use the flyer another way."

"You mean to set a trap?"

"Exactly." Patterson was looking at the phone number with rising excitement. "All we have to do is call and say that we know where Julie is—or Deana Taylor as he's calling her—and he'll come to us."

"Or he'll figure out that it's a trap and won't respond. He didn't show up at the truck tonight, which means he might know that it's been found. He'll be on his guard."

"Maybe. But I bet he doesn't know that we have one of his flyers. And even if he's suspicious, he won't be able to tell the difference between us and a genuine respondent. His need to find Julie will force him to show up. We just need to be smart and not give the game away until we're sure that we have him trapped."

"It might work," Bauer said, nodding thoughtfully. "But not right now. It's too soon. If he came back and saw the police at his truck, which I'm guessing that he did, then he probably freaked out. We'll wait a while. Let him calm down, think he got away."

"What if someone else calls in the meantime?" Patterson asked. Every minute that they delayed was more chance that some well-meaning resident of San Diego would turn her sister in. The reward didn't help. An amount that large would sway even the most hesitant caller.

"It's a chance we have to take," Bauer said. "He's less likely to believe us so soon after his truck was found. We don't want to blow this opportunity because we moved too fast. It might be our only chance to catch him."

Patterson knew that Bauer was right, even if she didn't like it. "I'll give it twelve hours, but not a moment longer."

# FIFTY-EIGHT

POPE WAS AT THE AIRPORT. It was 5 AM local time, and 3 AM at his destination of San Diego. After sending the senator into the great beyond, he had wasted no time in exiting the building, and descending to the ground floor via the stairs where it was unlikely he would encounter anyone else.

Before he stepped into the lobby, he had peeled off his hoodie and turned it inside out, then put it back on. The hoodie was reversible, and he had worn it for that reason. One side was dark blue, the other light blue. He figured the cameras covering the lobby would record in color—it was a modern building after all—and so it would look like one person had entered the night before, and another had left. Maybe if someone looked too closely… but that probably wouldn't happen, and Pope had made sure to conceal his face, keeping the hood up.

After leaving the condo tower behind, even as the first police sirens wailed in the distance, no doubt responding to reports of a gunshot, he had sat in his car and used his phone to check early flights. Ten minutes later, he had booked a 6 AM direct to San Diego, using his newly minted identity. Then he had swung by the hotel, grabbed his meagre belongings, and set off for the airport.

The only problem was the Glock pistol. If he'd had the correct, lockable container, he could have checked the gun, but he didn't, and he was also wary of attracting undue attention. It didn't help that the serial numbers were filed off, which would have raised all sorts of red flags if the TSA had inspected the weapon, which he thought was likely. In the end, he drove downtown to the park that fronted the Colorado River, waited for an opportune time when no one was around—easy because of the early hour—and tossed the gun and ammo into the water. It would be easy enough to pick up a replacement on the streets when he got to San Diego, probably another Glock.

Now, as he sat in the departures lounge, he reflected on the events of the past few days. He was pleased with himself for making the senator pay him the other half of his fee before killing the man. There was no point in leaving the money in Newport's possession, since he would have no further need for it. And he had found Patterson Blake's location with very little fuss, which was also a bonus. But the thing that pleased him the most was being able to ruin the senator's legacy. Newport had wriggled out of accountability for the land sale scheme, using his high-powered associates to dodge all consequences. But now, having seemingly taken his own life in remorse—the Latin phrase Pope had forced Newport to write down was a succinct suicide note that would surely make headlines—the man would forever be linked with his crimes, even if he had evaded justice in life. The ancient Egyptians had believed that your soul only died if no one remembered you. If they were right, then Newport's soul would live on in perpetual torment, forever aware of what those he had left behind thought, and how history would paint him.

His thoughts turning from the senator, he pondered the next step of his plan. Killing Patterson Blake. He knew where she was staying, but he had no intention of going after her there. It would be too risky given the events in Las Vegas. Plus, he didn't have his NSA grade laptop anymore, or any of his other high-tech gadgets. In time, he could replace them, but not at such short notice. Which left him with a problem. She was on her guard. And it wasn't just her. There was the other FBI agent, Marcus Bauer. He had also been in Vegas and had played a not insignificant role in thwarting Pope's original plan and putting him behind bars, albeit temporarily. While Pope didn't know how he was going to proceed, he thought it would be nice if he could eliminate Bauer, too, just as a bonus. How any of that would happen was not presently clear. But Pope wasn't worried. An opportunity would present itself. All he had to do was follow his instincts and not get sloppy, like the last time.

An announcement rose over the chatter of passengers waiting in the departures lounge. The boarding process had begun. Passengers with disabilities, followed by those seated in the aircraft's small premium cabin at the front of the plane, were invited to board. Pope stood up. He had booked two seats in the front row of premium, thus guaranteeing that no one would be sitting next to him, and also that he would be one of the first to disembark at the other end. It was expensive, but why not? The credit card he had used, in the name of his new alias, had a huge limit, and would never get paid off, making it free money. Once his business in San Diego was completed, he would abandon the false identity and adopt a new, deeper legend, tailored just for him, which his contact in Dallas was already working on.

He approached the gate and scanned the digital ticket on his phone, then made his way down the jet bridge to the aircraft. Once he was seated, Pope settled back and closed his eyes, arms folded across his chest, ignoring the flight attendant as she went through the safety briefing. Soon after, as the plane rose through the clouds on the way to its cruising altitude, he slept and dreamed of a life in retirement that didn't require him to kill people for a living. Just him, a cabin, and the endless wilderness of Alaska's far north, where he could sit on his porch and watch ribbons of light shimmer across the sky in a dazzling celestial display that might, perhaps, convince him there was a God after all… but probably not.

# FIFTY-NINE

GLORIA SAT on the bed in her room at the Del Ray and stared at the sheet of paper she was holding. The woman she knew as Anna stared back at her, except the name on the flyer was Deana.

She'd found the flyer attached to a pole near the bar after she had left work for the night. Gloria recognized her neighbor immediately. Now, she pondered what to do, mostly because of the reward that was being offered for the woman's safe return. And the kid, too.

Gloria wondered what had happened to make Anna, or Deana, or whatever her name was, run away and hide in the melting pot that was San Diego. She wasn't naïve enough to think that her neighbor had simply up and left, taking the child for no good reason other than to deprive the father of access to his kid. While that was a possibility, it was more likely that she was running from a bad situation. Gloria had met a lot of abused women, both physically and mentally, during her time living with what the well-heeled elite and local politicians considered the dregs of society, and she knew there was always a story, often filled with rampant misogynism and violence.

Gloria herself had escaped a drug dealer boyfriend who had eventually suggested that she earn some money for him *the old-*

*fashioned way*, meaning with her body. That was after he got her hooked first on heroin, and then on fentanyl. And for a while, she had complied, until a john pressed a knife to her throat and whispered that he wanted to know what it was like to kill a person. Watch them bleed out. Thankfully, he had not followed through on the urge—she still wasn't sure why—but it was enough to wake her up to the path she was treading, which only led in one direction. The next time her boyfriend left her alone, she had fled, which was how she had come to be hiding in a grubby hotel and slinging beers for drunks and lowlifes in a filthy dive bar.

In truth, it was a miracle she had survived, let alone gotten clean. She had often wondered why a man who professed to love her would have done such a thing, even if he did make a living preying on the weakness of others.

Which left her in a predicament. Anna had agreed to hand over half her earnings if Marco found her employment, but after the disastrous meeting earlier that night, it was looking like a bust. If only he'd kept his hands to himself, or Anna had been a little less uptight. But there was no use in worrying about that now. It was done. But even if Marco did calm down and find Anna a job, the pay would be miniscule. At least, compared to the reward offered on the flyer for her 'safe' return.

Five grand.

It was a huge amount of money to Gloria. More than she had ever possessed at any time in her life. Her money was usually spent before she even got it. The bar, with its miserly customers, was hardly a source of unlimited wealth.

What to do?

Wait and see if Marco came though, then collect a hundred bucks a week if she was lucky, and Anna didn't somehow shaft her… or take a quick payday?

The answer was obvious, even if Gloria hated herself for considering it. But not that much. It was everyone for themselves on the streets. And if she didn't make the call, then someone else would. Maybe the weasel of a desk clerk who worked the overnight shift in the hotel's front office, or even Marco himself. He would be no less averse to a quick payday than her.

But despite it all, she hesitated. She liked Anna and didn't want to see her come to harm.

Crap.

Gloria sighed and placed the flyer on the nightstand, then she rose and undressed, before climbing between the sheets and shutting off the light. She would sleep on it, and maybe tomorrow, in the cold light of day, the answer would be clearer.

# SIXTY

PATTERSON LAY IN BED. Not the one she wished she was in, back at her van, but a hotel bed that she found a little too hard. But it wasn't the firmness of the mattress that was keeping her awake. It was Carl Edward Bonneville, or more accurately, the flyer she had found in his truck.

Up until San Diego PD had come across the pickup truck parked on that side street, there was no concrete evidence he was in town and looking for Julie, or that the woman he had held in captivity was absolutely her sister, but now they knew for sure. She couldn't get the flyer out of her mind. Bauer had said they should wait when she suggested they call the number and draw him out, and he was right. If he knew that his truck had been found, which she suspected that he did, Bonneville would be spooked. They had to give him time to calm down.

But the wait was excruciating.

After they left the truck in the hands of SDPD, who were waiting on a tow truck to take it to their impound lot, Patterson had insisted they take a tour of the neighborhood, even though she was exhausted. And it had paid off. They had found four more flyers pinned to poles. There were almost certainly more. Which meant that someone could call about Julie and beat them to it, especially with that reward. But as Bauer had pointed out, it was late, and therefore unlikely anyone would see the flyers before morning. Even so, Patterson had torn down all those they found. She would have kept going, searching further afield for more flyers, but Bauer had insisted they go back to the hotel and get some rest.

So here she was, wide awake and thinking of all the things that could go wrong before they put their plan into action. And it wasn't just another tipster that bothered Patterson. Bonneville might have decided it was too dangerous in the city now that his truck had been discovered. He could be making a break for the border even as she lay there, crossing over into Mexico and vanishing. But if he was, she reasoned, then calling that number would do no good, anyway.

Unable to stand it any longer, she rose and opened the bottle of complimentary water the hotel had left in the room, then went to the window and stared out through a gap in the curtains as she drank. If she had been on a higher floor, she might have been looking at a skyline view of the city, but as it was, all she could see was the façade of another hotel on the opposite side of the road. Lights burned behind a couple of the windows, proving that she wasn't the only night owl whiling away the small hours, although she suspected that whatever was keeping the occupants of those other rooms up, was nothing compared to the dire thoughts that rattled through *her* mind.

Finishing the bottle of water, she closed the curtains and turned away from the window. The room was bathed in darkness, save for a glimmer of light coming from the bathroom. She had left the light on in there because even though Bauer's room was right next to hers, and the connecting door was unlocked, she didn't feel safe in complete darkness. Not when the hitman who had almost ended her life in Las Vegas was still out there and might be coming for her once again.

Dropping the empty bottle into a trash can under the desk, she returned to the bed and climbed back in, pushing her hands under the pillows and touching the Glock pistol concealed there. Feeling about as secure as she could under the circumstances, Patterson closed her eyes and let her mind wander. Tomorrow, she would call that number, and lure out the man who had abducted her sister all those years ago, and then, if she was lucky, there would be one less depraved asshole on the streets. But in the meantime, she needed sleep. If only it were that easy.

# SIXTY-ONE

DESPITE HERSELF, Patterson finally fell asleep. She awoke the next morning with a light headache and eyes that were stuck together until she splashed cold water on her face.

She felt far from rested.

When she went down to the hotel lobby, Bauer was already there, partaking of the free breakfast. She toasted a bagel, poured a cup of coffee, and joined him.

"You look like hell," he said between mouthfuls of scrambled egg.

"Thanks," she replied, looking at his plate, which was loaded with eggs, bacon, hashbrowns, and sausage patties. "Phoebe lets you eat stuff like that in the morning?"

"Phoebe's not here." Bauer forked a sausage and bit into it with a grin. "And we're not married. I get to eat what I want, when I want."

"Sure. I believe you." Patterson lifted her coffee cup and took the first glorious sip of the day. She could almost feel the caffeine hitting her system before she even swallowed. "I want to call the number on that flyer before we do anything else. The longer we wait, the more chance that a real tipster will call. We can't let him get his hands on Julie again."

"He might not even be looking anymore. Not after his car got towed. He must know we're looking for him. Mexico is right down the road."

"Except that he has a daughter. He might just as easily want to get ahold of her, first, even if he doesn't care about Julie."

"You're right." Bauer nodded and picked up an overcooked piece of bacon, then crunched it with a satisfied look in his eyes. "But we should call from a local number. He'll know for sure that it's a trap if we use either of our phones. New York and Texas area codes."

"Which is why our first stop, once you finish stuffing your face, is the San Diego field office. We'll need backup once we lure him out anyway."

"A good breakfast provides a solid foundation for the day ahead, as my Grammy used to say."

"You call that a good breakfast?" Patterson shook her head. "With all the pizza and fried food that you eat, it's a miracle you keep so trim."

Bauer shrugged. "Good genes, I guess. And hitting the weights every day helps, too. I already worked out in the hotel gym this morning before I came down here."

"Now I feel like a slacker." Patterson liked to work out, but not every day, and certainly not since she had started searching for Julie.

"Okay. I'm done." Bauer set his fork down and stood up. "You ready to catch Bonneville?"

"More than ready." Patterson downed the last of her coffee, set the empty cup down, and pushed her chair back. "Let's go!"

# SIXTY-TWO

THREE HOURS after he settled into his premium seat at the front of the plane and went to sleep, Corbin Pope was on the ground in San Diego, California. He picked up his rental car, an inconspicuous Toyota Corolla, then hopped on the interstate, heading out of the city, because there was a task he needed to take care of before he went after Patterson Blake.

After driving for forty-five minutes in ridiculous traffic, he exited the interstate and drove south for another ten miles until he came to a run-down bar sitting beside the road in a sparsely populated area on the outskirts of town. Later in the day there would be rows of motorcycles lined up in the dusty dirt parking lot fronting the bar, but right now, his was the only vehicle there.

He parked and climbed out, then circled to the back of the building, going to a metal door with a PRIVATE-KEEP OUT sign posted on it.

He banged on the door with a clenched fist.

When he got no response, he hammered again.

"What?" hollered a gruff voice from somewhere behind the door. "Who is it?"

"Let me in."

"Bar opens at noon. Come back then."

"Open the damn door, Lawrence," Pope said, raising his voice enough to be heard on the other side. "It's me."

There was a pause, then the sound of bolts being drawn back. The door opened a crack, and an eye peered through, groggy with sleep, before door swung wide to reveal a man in a sweat stained tee and boxer shorts. "Bailey?"

"I don't go by that name anymore." Pope pushed past the man and into the building. "I need a gun."

"Good morning to you, too." Lawrence raised an eyebrow. "How long has it been, Bai... whatever you want to be called now? Three years? Five?"

"Does it matter?" Pope glanced around the room. It was dimly lit by a weak shaft of sunlight filtering through a grimy window covered by a plastic louvre blind. He could make out aluminum beer kegs stacked against one wall, crates with bottles in them, and a desk piled high with paperwork. A set of stairs rose into darkness. Above them, Pope knew, was a small apartment where Lawrence had probably been sleeping until he showed up and roused him.

"I guess not." Lawrence ambled further into the room. "You looking for a gun?"

Pope nodded. He thought back to Newport's Desert Eagle. A fine weapon, but too hard to conceal. "Something untraceable and unassuming."

"All my guns are untraceable," Lawrence replied. "That's why people come to me. You have a preference? Glock, SIG? I have a nice Beretta."

"Don't care as long as it works and can't be linked to a previous crime."

"Now you're hurting my feelings." Lawrence pulled a face. "I don't deal junk."

"Never said you did." Pope was growing tired of the conversation. He wanted to get back to the city and track down Patterson Blake. "Just doing my due diligence. Like you said, it's been a while. Things change."

"Not around here, they don't."

"My humble apologies."

"That's better." Lawrence walked to a bookcase standing against the wall near the desk, its shelves laden with assorted bar room paraphernalia covered in an unhealthy layer of dust. The one thing it lacked was books. He reached to the side of the bookcase, flipped a concealed latch, then slid the whole unit sideways on hidden rails. Behind it was a metal door, which he unlocked with a key he pulled from his pocket. Beyond the door was a staircase that led down into gloom.

Lawrence flipped a switch on the wall and an overhead light came on, bathing the secret space in cool white light. He started down the stairs. "Please, walk into my parlor."

"Said the spider to the fly," Pope replied under his breath.

"What?"

"Nothing." Pope followed Lawrence down into the bowels of the building, wondering if Lawrence was familiar with Mary Howitt's poem, or if he had merely heard the oft-used phrase somewhere. The fact that he didn't misquote it as *step into my parlor* made Pope think that the sweaty bar owner was better read than his outward appearance and the lack of volumes on his bookshelf would indicate.

They reached the bottom of the staircase and Pope found himself in a large room that had obviously been an unassuming basement until Lawrence converted it into something more akin to a bunker. There was a cot against one wall, a toilet against another, and shelves laden with canned goods and MRE ration packs. A wall mounted TV displayed feeds from several surveillance cameras both in the bar and outside the building. Pope could see his car in one of them, parked in the dusty lot out front. The space had been nothing but an empty basement the last time he was here.

"Expecting the apocalypse?" Pope asked, bemused.

"Set this up a couple of years ago in case the ATF or some other unfriendly visitors come a-calling. Can't be too careful."

Pope glanced over his shoulder towards the stairs. "Hope you have another way out, or this might become your tomb."

"Always, my man. Always." Lawrence winked and went to another door at the back of the bunker. He opened it to reveal a second room. This one looked more like an armory. There were racks of weapons on the walls. Shotguns and semi-automatic rifles. Pope guessed that at least a few of the guns were full auto and highly illegal.

Lawrence went to a cabinet and opened it, then turned around with a Sig Sauer P320 pistol. "This should fit the bill. Clean gun. No serial numbers. Nice and small."

Pope took the weapon and weighed it in his hand. "It'll do."

"Your enthusiasm is infectious," Lawrence said. "You'll need ammunition, I assume?"

"What do you think?"

"Right." Lawrence went to another cabinet and brought out a box of 9x19mm Parabellum. He held it out to Pope. "One enough, or are you starting a war?"

"Funny."

"Not really. I know you. Matamoros a couple of years ago. The shootout that almost wiped the Devorador de Pecados Cartel off the map. I mean, sure, it looked like a turf war, but… that was your handiwork. Am I right?"

Pope didn't answer him. "I'll need a suppressor, too."

"Naturally."

"What's the damage?"

"Fifteen hundred, even."

"Your prices have gone up." Pope furrowed his brow.

"Inflation, my man. You want the gun or not?"

Pope took his phone out. "Just tell me where to send the money. I've got better places to be."

# SIXTY-THREE

WHEN PATTERSON and Bauer arrived at the FBI building, Special Agent Holmes was waiting for them.

"We're going to catch him," he said as if Patterson needed reassuring. "Bonneville."

"That's the plan," Patterson replied.

"Just as soon as you let us use a phone," Bauer said, skewering the junior agent with an icy stare.

"Oh. Right." Holmes turned on his heel and led them from the lobby to a conference room on the third floor, where several other agents waited. Patterson recognized them as the same ones who had helped canvass the walk-in clinics and pharmacies a couple of days before. But there was one face she didn't recognize.

Holmes closed the door, then introduced them. "This is Assistant Special Agent in Charge Robert Gibbs."

"I thought it might be prudent to sit in, given the high-profile nature of the case," Gibbs said. "The sister of an FBI agent who has been missing for sixteen years, and her abductor caught right here in our jurisdiction."

"We haven't caught him yet, sir," Patterson replied.

"But we will," Gibbs replied. He glanced toward one of the other agents. "Are we ready?"

"Yes, sir." The agent stepped forward with a phone in his hand. He offered it to Patterson. He had a notepad in his other hand, which he held up so that she could see the phone number written on it. "Local number with no association to the FBI. We'll be tracing the call. If we're lucky, Bonneville will give himself away and we won't need to set up a meet."

"I wouldn't count on it," Bauer said. "He'll know we're looking for him."

"Maybe," Gibbs said. "But that doesn't mean he'll be smart."

"He was smart enough to keep my sister captive for sixteen years," Patterson said, unable to keep the edge from her voice. "We shouldn't underestimate him."

"We're not," Gibbs replied. "You want to make the call?"

"What do you think?"

"You know what you're going to say?" Gibbs asked.

Patterson nodded, glancing around at the row of expectant faces. She saw determination, hope, and expectation reflected back at her. Even if they didn't have a personal stake in the outcome of what was about to happen, every person in that room wanted a piece of Carl Edward Bonneville, and to bring Julie home safe and sound. "I'll need a place to meet him. Somewhere public that we can surveil easily without making him suspicious."

"Bayside Park," said Holmes. "Near the pier. It's flat with great sightlines and isn't usually too busy. It also has water on one side, which will help to keep him contained if he runs."

Patterson looked at the ASAC for confirmation.

He nodded.

"Bayside Park it is." She dropped her gaze to the flyer in her hand, the one she had found the previous night in the pickup truck, and dialed the number.

After two rings, it went to voicemail.

Either Bonneville was screening his calls, or the phone was

turned off. One glance toward the agent responsible for tracing the call, a man with graying hair and glasses who sat at the conference room desk hunched in front of a laptop computer, told her which it was when he shook his head wordlessly.

Patterson waited. At first, she had wondered if she was going to hear the voice of the monster who had taken her sister, steeled herself for that eventuality, but instead, the default greeting played. When it was finished, she left her message after the beep. During the ride over to the field office, she had come up with a script in her head, had run through it what felt like a hundred times. Now that it was time to perform, her throat was dry as sandpaper.

"Hi. My name's Eileen Feldman," she said into the phone. "I know where Deana and Britney are. I work the front desk at a local motel, and there's a woman and her daughter staying here, and I'm sure it's them. It just breaks my heart to think of that woman taking your kid like that. You must be beside yourself. Please, call me back, okay? I want to help bring your family home."

Then Patterson read off the number on the notepad before hanging up. It sickened her to feed into Bonneville's lie on the flyer, to pretend that she wanted to hand Julie back to the man who took her like that, but the more sympathetic she sounded, the more she appealed to his warped sense of injustice, the more likely he was to fall for her trap.

She clutched the phone, staring at the screen for a moment, before looking up. "Good enough?"

Bauer nodded. "And now we wait."

# SIXTY-FOUR

CORBIN POPE DROVE BACK to the city and went straight to the hotel where Patterson was staying. He didn't expect her to be there, since it was after eleven, but he wanted to see the place for himself. As he drove, he had mulled over several ideas for getting rid of the troublesome FBI agent, but he didn't like any of them. Now, as he pulled into the parking lot and found a space at the side of the building, he knew one thing. He wasn't going to move against her while she was at the hotel. That hadn't worked so well last time, and he didn't like that her partner was in the room next door. Dealing with two targets at the same time complicated matters, and Pope hated complicated.

He exited the rental car and watched a guest cross the parking lot toward a side door that led into the building. He waited for them to step inside, then hurried to the door, noting that there were no security cameras mounted anywhere nearby. A sign on the glass informed him that the door could only be unlocked with a key card after 9 PM, but right now, it opened easily, allowing him access. Apparently, security was only a concern after dark.

He went to the elevators and rode to the fourth floor. The rooms occupied by the FBI agents were close by. The door to

## I WILL FIND HER

Patterson Blake's room stood open. There was a cart laden with towels and cleaning materials standing outside. Through the open door, he could see a woman in a light blue housekeeping uniform making the bed.

Pope moved on down the corridor, passing a family of four who were heading in the other direction. The kids, a boy and a girl who looked no older than ten, chatted excitedly. The parents, burdened with a cooler and a couple of large bags, looked anything but. The man nodded slightly as they crossed in opposite directions. A moment later, they stepped into the wide hallway where the elevators were located and disappeared from view.

Pope continued to the end corridor, then stopped at the window and gazed out, his eyes dropping to the parking lot that surrounded the building. After a few moments, when he could no longer hear the two kids talking, he turned and went back in the other direction, casting another quick glance into Patterson Blake's room as he passed. The maid was out of sight now, but the bathroom door stood open, and he could hear running water.

Pope went back to the elevators, descended to the ground floor, and exited the hotel via the same door he had used a few minutes earlier. He returned to his car and climbed in, then sat looking up at the building and the rows of windows reflecting the late morning sunlight. His stomach growled, reminding him he hadn't eaten since boarding the flight to San Diego many hours earlier. There was a restaurant across the parking lot. One of those breakfast places that offered huge piles of pancakes and waffles drenched in maple syrup. Its location in front of the hotel offered as good a view as the car but was much less conspicuous. He pulled out of the parking space and drove to the restaurant. There was a newspaper stand by the door. He purchased a paper, then asked for a table next to a window.

A short while later, he was sipping a mug of steaming coffee —no sugar or cream—and surreptitiously watching the comings and goings in the hotel parking lot while pretending to read the newspaper that was spread out on the table in front of him. He figured the restaurant was suitable for at least a couple hours of surveillance, and he liked pancakes well enough. Which was good, because he wanted to get eyes on the FBI agent and her partner, even though he didn't yet know how to proceed. But Pope had learned over the years that opportunity often presented itself in the most unexpected ways, and if that happened, he would be ready.

# SIXTY-FIVE

CARL WAS STILL on edge after the events of the previous night. He had spent the hours since dawn sitting in the hotel room and afraid to leave. It didn't help that his truck was gone. Even if he'd wanted to flee, he was stuck in the city, and with every cop within a hundred-mile radius looking for him, just walking across the street to get a sandwich at the Burger King in the plaza opposite was a risk.

He would need a new set of wheels. That much was obvious. He had already looked through yesterday's newspaper, which another guest had left for the maid to remove from their room and Carl had snagged off her cart when she wasn't looking. He had identified a few private sellers with inexpensive used cars that might fit the bill. If he'd been willing to consider used car lots, he would have had a greater selection. There were full-page advertisements touting clean, gently used vehicles—low money down and credit on the spot—that looked nothing of the sort. But he didn't dare buy from a lot, because they would insist that he fill out the registration paperwork and provide proof of insurance before they would let him drive the car away, and that was a no go. With a private seller, he could just hand them the money along with a promise to visit the DMV, and he was good.

By the time anyone realized that he'd never transferred the title into his name, he would be long gone and sitting on a beach somewhere in Mexico.

Luckily, he had more than enough cash, and one of the cars was close by. Or at least, close enough to minimize his risk of exposure. But he hadn't gotten up the courage to call and inquire about the vehicle yet. Just like he hadn't mustered the courage to venture away from the hotel and check the messages on his burner phone. For all he knew, Angel and Cherub were just a voicemail away. And once he took care of Angel and reacquired his daughter, there would be no reason to stay in the city.

Which was why he eventually concluded he had no choice but to set out on foot, find somewhere safe to turn the phone on, and see if anyone had responded to his flyers. He certainly didn't want to check his voicemail right there in the hotel room, for fear that the FBI somehow knew the number and could pinpoint his location the moment he turned the phone on. He'd seen TV cops do that, and while he didn't buy into the fictional worlds that played out on the idiot box, he figured the writers of those shows must have done their research.

The hotel that Carl had chosen as his base of operations was close to the interstate on the edge of an industrial area. There were large warehouses behind the building, and what looked like an enormous, yet anonymous, distribution center with at least fifty truck bays. The road out front was a mix of fast-food restaurants and small businesses, mostly auto body shops, car mechanics, and appliance repair. There were also several bail bond places, which only served to remind Carl of all he had to lose if he wasn't careful.

He decided that his best bet was to head behind the hotel, where a maze of small access roads ran between the warehouses and distribution centers, mostly used by tractor-trailers loaded with goods. He had seen the trucks coming and going all morning. Carl couldn't be sure, but the industrial landscape looked familiar, and he wondered if he had driven his truck there at some point over the years to pick up or drop off a load. It was certainly possible, and even likely, given the location.

He was sitting on the bed with pillows propped behind his back and the newspaper spread across the comforter to his left, because it was the only comfortable spot in the room. The inactive burner phone was next to him on the nightstand. He swung his legs off the bed, scooped up the phone and his room key, and slipped his shoes on before walking to the door. Then he hesitated, hand on the latch. There was no way the police knew where he was staying, but what if there was a cop over at the Burger King getting lunch, or a patrol car driving by just as he stepped out the door?

Carl went to the window and pulled the curtain back, then looked out. He didn't see any cops. Satisfied, Carl went back to the door and opened it, and stepped out onto the second-floor walkway running along the front of the hotel. He hurried to the stairs and descended, then walked around the building and across the back parking lot. After stepping over a dusty strip between the hotel and the neighboring warehouse, littered with old soda cans and fast-food containers, he followed the road for close to a mile, until the industrial units gave way to sprawling sub-developments, each house looking much the same as the next. He wandered through the maze of curvy streets until he came to a house with a FOR SALE sign out front, then stepped into the back yard where he could make his call without being seen.

He took out the phone and activated it. At first, he thought there was no service, but then it climbed up to three bars. Even better, there was a message.

Carl followed the instructions and listened as the voicemail played. When it finished, he smiled. Perhaps he wouldn't be stuck in San Diego for that much longer, after all. He listened to the voicemail again, paying particular attention to the callback number. Then, after looking around to make sure that he was still alone, he dialed and waited for an answer.

## SIXTY-SIX

PATTERSON WAS SITTING in the conference room on the third floor of the San Diego field office and staring at the phone in front of her on the table. It was early afternoon, and the frustration was rising within her like a black tide. With nothing better to do while they waited for Bonneville to call back, she had wanted to continue her search for Julie, visiting hotels close to the bus route her sister had taken to see if anyone recognized the photo of her, but ASAC Gibbs had nixed the idea.

"That's a no go," he said. "We need you here. If he calls back, you're the only one who can speak to him, since you left the message. If you're running around all over town, you might miss the call. We can't risk that. It might be our only opportunity."

"And don't forget, we can trace the call," Bauer added. "With any luck, he'll give his location away."

And so here they were, several hours later, staring at the walls and waiting for the phone to ring while somewhere close by, in another room, an equally bored agent sat in front of a laptop waiting to trace the call and hoping that Bonneville would make it easy for them.

Bauer sat leaning back with his hands behind his head and

his legs up on the table. He looked at Patterson. "Have you spoken to your father recently?"

Patterson nodded. "I checked in with him last night."

"And?"

"He's doing good. Still mad that he let Bonneville into the house without asking to see some ID. Blames himself for losing the postcard. Said he should have known better as the father of an FBI agent."

"He shouldn't be so hard on himself. He was already expecting a visit from the FBI. Who would have thought Bonneville would be so bold?"

"That's what I told him. I also pointed out that if he'd confronted Bonneville, asked him to prove his identity, things might have turned out differently. The man could have turned violent. Dad might have ended up hurt, or even dead."

"Let me guess, that didn't make him feel any better."

"Not in the least. He stood face to face with the man who abducted his daughter and never even knew it. At least, not at the time. I think there's more going on than just self-recrimination."

"Understandable." Bauer shifted in his seat. "How did he handle the news that you saw Julie here in San Diego? That she has a daughter?"

Patterson said nothing. She cast her gaze downward.

"You didn't tell him."

Now Patterson looked up. "What was I supposed to say? That I was mere feet from his daughter—from my sister—and I failed to bring her home? That she vanished out of our lives yet again and that her abductor is in San Diego, searching for her thanks to that postcard he let walk out the door?"

"How about you don't phrase it like that. Give the man some hope. Tell him that Julie's alive and that he has a granddaughter."

"All he's had is hope for the last sixteen years, even while he told himself that Julie was probably dead. The last thing I want to do is raise his expectations until I know that Julie is safe, because if the worst happens and Bonneville finds her before we do, if he loses her all over again in the worst possible way, I think it will be the end of him."

Bauer absorbed this, then nodded. "Fair enough, although he might not look at it that way when he eventually finds out."

"It's my call to make."

"Never said that it wasn't." Bauer dropped his arms and folded them. "And your mother?"

"What about her?"

"Does she even know that you're searching for Julie?"

"I have no idea. Maybe dad told her. I don't know."

"You don't think she deserves to be told, under the circumstances?"

"I doubt that she'd care."

Bauer frowned. "That's harsh."

"You don't know her. After Julie disappeared, she was barely there. I still needed a mother, and she'd checked out. Then she left. Just walked away like it was nothing. Broke dad's heart all over again."

"Maybe it was the only way she knew how to cope."

"Don't you dare to defend her. She's had plenty of time to come to terms with what happened, reach out to the daughter she still has, but she's never bothered."

"All I'm saying is that with you so close to bringing Julie home, you might want to take the high road. Try to understand her point of view, even if you don't agree with it, because if you find Julie—*when* you find Julie—she'll need her family. All three of you."

"I'll think about it," said Patterson, grudgingly.

Bauer nodded.

And then the phone rang.

# SIXTY-SEVEN

PATTERSON LOOKED DOWN at the phone. "It's him."

"Keep calm and let him lead the conversation. Remember, you're a nervous hotel desk clerk wondering if she's doing the right thing," said Bauer, before picking up his own phone and sending a quick text message to the agent in charge of tracing the call, just to make sure the man hadn't nodded off while they were waiting.

"More like I'm a hotel clerk without a conscience wanting to get my hands on a quick five grand," Patterson shot back, wondering if anyone had called and left a legitimate message. There was only one way to find out. She picked up the phone, took a deep breath, and answered.

"Hello?"

"Eileen Feldman?" said a man's voice on the other end of the line.

"Yes." Patterson marveled at how normal his voice was. Was this really what evil sounded like? Sadly, she knew the answer to that already. Most of the monsters she had put away during her time with the FBI, serial murderers like the one she had caught in Oklahoma City, a man whom the press had dubbed the Bracken Island Killer, were more remarkable for how outwardly normal they were, than for any easily identifiable streak of evil. That was how they could move freely in society, choosing victims who never realized the danger until it was too late. "I'm Eileen Feldman. Who's this?"

"You saw my flyer and left a message," Bonneville replied. "Said you know where my wife and daughter are."

"That's right." It took all of Patterson's resolve to keep her voice calm and even. "Deana and Britney. They're staying at the hotel where I work."

"You're sure it's them?"

"Yes. I saw them again after I called you this morning. Deana came into the office looking to extend their stay for a couple more days. Paid in cash. We're not exactly a high-end place. Cater to a lot of people who want to remain anonymous for one reason or another, so we don't press for ID, but I'm sure it's your wife and daughter."

"What's the name of the hotel?"

"Hey. Not so fast," Patterson said, doing her best to stay in character. "You offered a reward, remember? Five grand. You get the hotel name and room number once I get paid."

There was a small sound on the other end of the line, a brief exhalation as if Bonneville were sighing in exasperation. "Fine. I'll leave the money somewhere. You tell me what I want to know, and I'll tell you where it is."

"I don't think so. How do I know the money will actually be there after you get what you want?" Bauer had advised Patterson to let Bonneville lead the conversation, but it was clear he didn't want to meet in person. It was time to take it up a notch and hope that she didn't blow it. "Let's meet up. You bring the money, and I'll bring the information you need. Unless, of course, you're not really looking for your wife and daughter, something else is going on, because if that's the case, I want nothing to do with it."

Patterson could feel Bauer's gaze upon her. When she looked

at him, he was frowning. He mouthed three words. *Don't blow this.*

She had no intention of blowing it, but if they didn't draw Bonneville out, get him somewhere where they could take him down, it would all be for nothing.

There was a heavy silence on the other end of the phone. For a moment, Patterson thought he might hang up, but then he spoke again.

"Look, I just want my wife and daughter back. That's all. I'll bring you the money at the hotel."

"No offence, but I don't know or trust you, and I certainly don't want you coming to the hotel with the money. We'll meet in public. Bayside Park," she said, using the location they had all agreed upon earlier. "J Street Pier."

There was another hesitation, before Bonneville asked, "what time?"

It was already 2 PM, and Patterson was tired of waiting. She would have loved to say right now, but if they were going to do this, it had to be done properly. They would need a couple of hours to plan the takedown and get everyone in place. "I finish work at four, and it will take me a while to get there. How about five o'clock?"

"How will I recognize you?" Bonneville said, apparently agreeing to the time and place.

"I'll be wearing blue jeans, a pale-yellow polo, and a brown Padres baseball cap," she said, trying to come up with something that would be easily recognizable. "Your turn."

"Since we're going with a sports theme, I'll put on my Arizona Diamondbacks T-shirt. Shouldn't be too many people in the park wearing one of those."

"Sounds good," Patterson said. "Keep your phone on. If we somehow miss each other, I'll call you."

"Sounds good. See you there." Bonneville hung up without waiting for a reply.

Patterson was shaking. She had just spent the last couple of minutes talking with the man who took her sister. It made her feel dirty, as if a small part of his vile nature had somehow rubbed off on her. She looked over at Bauer. "Did they trace the call?"

Bauer shook his head. "Not long enough. They triangulated his location using cell towers to a three-square mile area around I-805 in the south of the city, but I'm guessing he was smart enough not to call from wherever he's staying. Not that it matters. With the population density in that area, we'll never find him before your five o'clock meeting, if at all."

"Then I have a date with a monster," Patterson said. "All I need now is a Padres cap and enough willpower not to shoot him on sight."

# SIXTY-EIGHT

PATTERSON WASN'T herself for the rest of the afternoon. Everything felt slightly off kilter, as if she were living in some almost perfect, yet slightly different, alternate reality. She sat in the briefing organized by ASAC Gibbs and listened as plans were made to place agents around the park ready to close in the moment Bonneville showed up with a detachment noticeable enough that Bauer nudged her at one point to bring her back to the present.

After the briefing ended, they left and drove the short distance to the hotel so Patterson could change into the outfit she had told Bonneville she would be wearing. On the way, they stopped at a sporting goods store and picked up the necessary baseball cap. By the time they arrived at the hotel, it was 3:30 PM, and Patterson's stomach was in knots.

"You alright there, partner?" Bauer asked as they climbed out of the car and made their way into the hotel lobby.

"What do you think?" Despite the strange mood that had settled upon her, she was looking forward to taking Bonneville down, but it didn't get her any closer to finding Julie, and she said as much.

"Hey, I get it," Bauer said. "But we take Bonneville off the streets and it's one less thing to worry about. We won't have to worry about him finding her first."

"I know," Patterson said. "And I want to see that bastard behind bars. I really do. But my sister is out there somewhere, and she must be terrified. We have no way of telling her it's safe to come home, that she doesn't have to worry about that man anymore, and it's eating me up inside."

"We'll bring her home." Bauer pressed the elevator button and let her step in first when the doors opened. "First thing tomorrow morning we'll hit the streets again, visit the rest of the hotels along that bus route. Someone will recognize her. I'm sure of it."

Patterson forced a weak smile. She appreciated Bauer's attempt to lift her spirits, but she wasn't so sure. Just because Julie had ridden that bus didn't mean she was staying within walking distance of the bus route. She might've transferred from another bus, which meant that she could be anywhere in the city. When they arrived at their rooms, she told Bauer to meet her in the lobby fifteen minutes later, then stepped inside and closed the door.

She undressed and took one of the quickest showers of her life, as if the steaming hot water could wash away the memory of Bonneville's voice, and how scarily normal he sounded. Then she got dressed, cut the tag off the baseball cap and put it on, then stood in front of the mirror and stared at her own reflection. Did she look like a woman who worked the front desk at a seedy motel? Patterson couldn't tell. All she saw was a stressed-out federal agent with bags under her eyes and a baseball cap that looked a little too new.

She took the cap back off and returned to the bathroom, then rummaged in her makeup case for a foundation stick. She dabbed a little on her finger, then smeared it around the rim of the baseball cap, blending the lighter brown with the darker color so that it looked faded. Next, she took a pair of nail clippers and pulled at the embroidered logo until some of the cotton strands frayed. When she was done, she studied her handiwork. It wasn't perfect, and certainly wouldn't stand up to close scrutiny, but it would work well enough to fool Bonneville.

Satisfied, she put the cap back on her head, checked herself one more time in the mirror, and left the room.

# SIXTY-NINE

CORBIN POPE BEEN WATCHING the hotel for several hours when he finally saw Patterson Blake and Marcus Bauer pull into the parking lot, exit their vehicle, and headed inside. He had left the pancake restaurant after his third mug of coffee, then found a place to park on the road in front of the hotel for a while and was now sitting in his car at the far end of the lot where he wouldn't be noticed, in the shade of a large oak tree.

He made no attempt to follow the two FBI agents into the building. He wasn't yet sure how to deal with Patterson Blake, but he knew one thing. The hotel was off limits. He wasn't going to make the same mistake twice. That presented him with a problem. Pope had always prided himself on creating a narrative of accidental death around his targets. This was partly why he was in such high demand by both private clients and clandestine organizations such as the CIA. Sure, a sniper rifle from 800 meters, or roughly half a mile away, might get the job done, but it would scream assassination and create a vacuum into which all manner of accusations and conspiracy theories could be poured. It would also attract unwanted scrutiny upon anyone with a vested interest in killing the victim of the sniper's bullet. But an accident provided plausible deniability and relegated conspiracy theories to the far fringes of the internet. Especially if that accident was not a cliché, like being encouraged to fall from a hotel room window fifteen stories above the ground or developing a mysterious case of food poisoning after a seemingly innocuous dinner.

But Pope was worn out. Something had changed after his arrest in Las Vegas. The close call had given him a fresh perspective on his chosen career, and highlighted the fact that he wasn't getting any younger. Eventually, if he kept going, he would make another mistake, if only because the passing years had blunted his mental acuity. And next time, his pals at the CIA might not come to his rescue. They could decide to silence him permanently instead, much as Senator Newport had attempted to do. Except that, unlike Newport, the CIA would not fail.

Once again, Pope's mind turned to the subject of retirement. Over the last couple of hours, as he had sat in the car and pondered the best way to deal with Patterson Blake, he hadn't experienced the usual thrill of anticipation. He had always promised himself that when the job became mundane, when he no longer cared about his craft, that he would call it quits. That time might have come. And it wasn't like he needed to work. Pope had amassed a small fortune over the years—more than he would need in ten lifetimes—and it would be of little use if he was sitting on death row.

In that moment, Pope made up his mind.

But not until he finished the job the late Senator Newport had hired him for. Then he could retire with a perfect record and sleep easy, knowing that the source of his only failure had paid the price.

Pope sat up and stretched, working a kink out of his back. Another reminder that he wasn't getting any younger. He picked up a bottle of aspirin from the center console, shook two tablets from the bottle, and swallowed them before taking a swig from a bottle of water to wash them down. When he turned his attention back to the hotel, Blake and Bauer were coming back out.

He snapped to attention.

There was something different about Patterson Blake. She wasn't wearing her usual bland business attire. Instead, she wore a pair of blue jeans, a polo shirt, and a brown baseball cap with a logo that he couldn't make out.

They walked to a dark-colored sedan that just screamed *feds* and climbed in. A few seconds later, the car pulled out of the parking space and headed toward the exit.

Pope waited a moment to make sure they wouldn't notice him, then rolled out from under the shade of the tree, drove slowly through the parking lot, and followed behind.

# SEVENTY

CARL HAD no idea where Bayside Park was, but of course he hadn't been able to say that since he was pretending to be a local.

After hanging up, he had looked on the phone's map app and discovered that it was next to San Diego Bay and too far away to reach on foot. That meant he would have to take a taxi, which was a slight risk, but not that big a deal. Besides, it was probably safer to meet the desk clerk somewhere far away from his accommodation, he thought as he had walked back to the hotel. If she ended up speaking to the authorities later on—like when they found Angel's body—they would look for him in the wrong place.

Not that he intended to stick around once he had found his *family*. First, he would meet the desk clerk and get the information he needed, then he would purchase a new set of wheels before going after Angel. He had already narrowed it down to a couple of options from private sellers advertising in the newspaper. Cheap vehicles that could get him out of the city and to the remote town of Jacumba Hot Springs in the Sonoran Desert an hour to the east. Once there, he would drive over the border unnoticed and with no need for the driver's license or passport that would be required at the official border crossing between San Diego and Tijuana. He knew about the illegal crossing point thanks to his days driving a truck. He had been offered quick money more than once to pick up migrants, hide them in his trailer, and drive them to points far away. Carl had always refused—the last thing he had wanted was extra scrutiny given his home situation—but now those offers had provided him with the information he needed to escape the country.

Now, as he climbed out of the taxi with a backpack full of cash in his hand, he was overcome by a rush of anticipation, and a not insignificant measure of relief. He had been worried that it might take days for someone who knew Angel's whereabouts to see one of his flyers and call. Time that he could ill afford since he was a wanted man. He was eager to get the meeting over with, deal with Angel, and get the hell out of there. But that didn't mean he was going to rush in without exercising at least a modicum of caution. With that in mind, he had asked the taxi driver to wait until he returned, offering a sufficiently tempting bonus of an extra hundred bucks if he would do so. The driver had grudgingly accepted, saying he would wait for twenty minutes and not a moment longer.

That was good enough for Carl. He figured it wouldn't take him anywhere near that long, and even if it did, he doubted the driver would leave and forfeit such a large amount simply for enjoying the view.

But making sure he could affect a quick escape was not the only precaution Carl had taken. He was wearing the Diamondbacks T-shirt, just as he'd promised, but it was underneath a black sweater. That way, he could assess the situation before revealing himself. The only drawback was that he looked a little overdressed for a late summer afternoon in San Diego. But there was nothing he could do about that. He had tried a polo shirt first, but it didn't sufficiently conceal the garment beneath, so he was forced to go with long sleeves. And the only such piece of clothing he had brought with him was the black sweater.

As he stepped into the park, he looked around. It was mostly filled with families enjoying a lazy Saturday. Parents who had brought their kids out to enjoy an afternoon kicking a soccer ball or throwing a frisbee. A few people were walking dogs. An older couple sat on a bench eating ice cream. He didn't see anyone in a yellow shirt and wearing a brown baseball cap.

He moved further into the park, following the path past a building that housed public toilets, and toward the J Street Pier, which stuck out into the bay next to a Marina crowded with expensive-looking boats. He marveled at the amount of money there must be in the city for so many people to own a vessel that served no practical purpose beyond a pleasurable day out on the water.

Tearing his eyes away from the marina and its obscene display of unbridled wealth, he scanned the landscape ahead. And that was when he saw her. The woman with the brown baseball cap and the yellow polo shirt. She was standing close to the water near the entrance to the pier, with her hands pushed into her pockets.

At first, he quickened his pace and was about to peel off the black sweater to reveal the Diamondbacks shirt beneath. But then, as he drew closer, he came to a halt.

Because he recognized her.

This was no desk clerk from a seedy motel. It was the same woman he'd met in the bar of the Welcome Inn back in Oklahoma City. A woman he knew all too well because he'd been keeping tabs on her for years. And if Patterson Blake was waiting for him in the park, she wouldn't be alone. There would be other FBI agents circling nearby, ready to pounce the moment he made his presence known.

He glanced around nervously, trying to discern which of the seemingly innocuous park goers were actually federal agents. He could discount the families because he didn't believe for one second the FBI used children for their undercover operations, but that still left an awful lot of people. Because what had seemed like a fairly empty park just moments ago now appeared to be teeming with potential feds. If he hadn't been so concerned about escaping, Carl might have pondered how a slight shift in circumstance could so quickly alter perception.

He glanced back over his shoulder. The taxi was still there, waiting as promised. He pulled the sweater down, tugging at the hem to make sure it fully covered the T-shirt beneath, then turned and hurried back the way he had come.

# SEVENTY-ONE

CORBIN POPE HAD FOLLOWED Patterson Blake and her partner to a park near the water and watched as they exited their vehicle and split up. Marcus Bauer was dressed in a pair of shorts and a tight T-shirt. He wore sunglasses and sneakers. As soon as they entered the park, he peeled off and started jogging, following a path near the water's edge. Patterson strolled to the end of a peer next to a marina full of glistening yachts and other pleasure craft, came to a halt, and stood with her hands in her pockets, as if she were simply enjoying the view.

Pope didn't believe the two FBI agents had driven to the thin sliver of greenery next to San Diego Bay because they wanted to take some time out and enjoy the city's amenities. He suspected that there was a deeper purpose to their destination. This was confirmed when he studied the rest of the park's occupants and noticed several suspicious characters. A couple walking hand-in-hand who held each other just a little too stiffly. Two grown men throwing a frisbee without much glee. A woman sitting on a bench reading a book. Or at least, pretending to, because her eyes kept lifting over the top of the volume and watching the park beyond. These were, Pope suspected, FBI agents doing their best to blend into the scenery. And to a casual observer, they were doing an adequate job. But to Pope, a man who had spent years honing his sense of observation to a fine point, they stuck out like sore thumbs. It was a trap, and Patterson Blake was the bait. But, Pope wondered, who was the target?

Sitting behind the wheel of his rental car, parked in a bay close to the spot where the two FBI agents had entered the park, he glanced around again, but saw no one who looked like they might be the subject of a sting operation. At least, until he spotted a man climbing out of a nearby taxi.

The newcomer looked harmless enough—a middle-aged office worker looking to make use of his days off, perhaps, who had taken a cab to the park for a relaxing weekend stroll—except that he was hardly dressed for the weather. It was in the high seventies, yet he was wearing a black sweater over what looked like a T-shirt. Either the man was used to a much hotter climate, perhaps Miami or the Florida Keys, or he didn't want anyone to see what he was wearing beneath. This was confirmed when he glanced down and tugged at the hem of his sweater, making sure that it didn't reveal even a hint of the T-shirt. And if the unusual choice of clothing wasn't a big enough giveaway, there was the backpack, which he gripped tightly in one hand, when he could easily have slung it over his shoulder. He was clearly protecting whatever was inside. Lastly, there was the taxi. It wasn't driving away even as the man walked into the park toward the marina and the pier. It was waiting for him to come back. An unwitting getaway vehicle.

Pope leaned forward. He was sure that the man in the black sweater was the target of the FBI's sting. But so far, none of those he had identified as federal agents had made a move, or even appeared to have noticed their quarry.

The man was walking toward Patterson Blake, proceeding slowly and looking around once in a while. He was clearly on edge, and with good reason, considering the number of potential FBI agents whom Pope suspected were waiting for his arrival.

But when the man spotted Patterson Blake, he sped up. At least, until he came to a sudden halt.

He stood for a moment, staring at the FBI agent, then he turned and hurried back in the other direction, trying to make his retreat look casual. But Pope wasn't fooled. He watched with growing curiosity as the man arrived back at the taxi. He looked back over his shoulder one more time, then climbed inside and slammed the door. A moment later, the vehicle pulled away from the curb.

Pope cast a quick glance toward Patterson Blake, who was still standing near the pier. None of the other FBI agents were on the move, either. Their quarry had walked into the park, realized it was a trap, and quietly made his escape without anyone noticing.

Except for Pope, that was.

And now he saw an opportunity. Patterson Blake was interested in the man wearing the black sweater. That much was obvious. And since Blake's sole purpose in the city was to find her sister, he must be connected to the case. That was something Pope could use, even if he wasn't quite sure how. At least, not yet. But the opportunity would slip away if he didn't act fast.

With that in mind, Pope put the car into reverse, backed out of the space, and followed the taxi.

## SEVENTY-TWO

HE WASN'T COMING. The realization hit Patterson at about the same time that she saw Bauer jogging toward her with an expression on his face that told her he'd come to the same conclusion. It was five thirty, a full half hour after Bonneville should have shown up, and even though she was tempted to give it another fifteen minutes, tell Bauer to take another turn around the park, she knew it was pointless. Either Bonneville had gotten cold feet, or he'd somehow known she was FBI.

"Where the hell is he?" Bauer said, coming to a stop and leaning forward with his hands on his knees to catch his breath. "He should have been here by now."

"Ya think?" Patterson retorted, then winced. "Sorry."

"Don't worry about it. I'm frustrated too." Bauer wiped his brow. "Want to call it a day?"

"Not really." Patterson let her gaze wander across the park one last time, but she saw no one wearing a Diamondbacks shirt. If Bonneville had been there, he wasn't anymore. "But I guess it's pointless to keep going. I blew it."

"You didn't blow it. This was a team effort. For all we know, he spotted one of the undercover agents and it spooked him."

"Or he recognized me," Patterson said, suddenly realizing

what she should have thought of before. "He kept my sister hostage for sixteen years. I bet he's been keeping tabs on us."

"You think?"

"Yeah, I think. He knew my father's name and where we lived. Was bold enough to go there and steal the postcard. He knows that I'm a fed, too. After all, he impersonated an FBI agent. Told my father that he was a colleague of mine at the Bureau."

"There's no way he could've known about the postcard," Bauer said.

"That much I agree with. My guess is that he went to Queens because he thought Julie might try to contact us, or even go back there, and he just got lucky." Patterson swore under her breath. "I'm so stupid. There's no way he didn't know what I look like. We should have used another female agent as bait. Someone he wouldn't recognize. If only I hadn't been so hell-bent on catching him myself, he might be in custody right now. This is all on me."

"Don't be so hard on yourself. You did your best."

"And it wasn't good enough." Patterson took the baseball cap off. She tossed it on the ground, then pushed past Bauer and started toward the parking lot. As she went, she called over her shoulder. "You might as well call it. Tell the others that we're done. That I screwed up and Bonneville got away."

"And where do you think you're going?" Bauer called after her.

"Where do you think? To the car." Patterson replied without looking back. "And after that, the closest bar to drown my sorrows."

# SEVENTY-THREE

POPE FOLLOWED the taxi for several miles through the crawling San Diego weekend traffic until they came to a rundown motel near the interstate. He pulled in behind the taxi, but continued on when it came to a stop and circled slowly back around before finding a space and parking.

By the time the man in the black sweater had climbed out of the cab, Pope was already approaching him on foot. He drew close as the man reached the stairs and followed him up until they emerged onto the second-floor balcony.

The man cast a nervous glance over his shoulder, perhaps wondering if Pope was an FBI agent who had followed him from the park. The hitman merely smiled and offered an amiable good evening before quickening his pace, stepping past him, and continuing on down the walkway as if he was returning to his room. But he didn't move too fast, because he was watching the man in the black sweater from the corner of his eye. And when he stopped at a room and pulled out his key card, Pope was ready.

He whirled around just as the man opened the door, closed the gap between them in a heartbeat, and pushed him through the door and into the room before he even knew what was happening.

Kicking the door closed with his heel, he spun the man around, grabbed him by the hair, and slammed his head down onto the desk underneath the wall-mounted TV so fast that he didn't even utter an exclamation of surprise.

Pope repeated the maneuver twice more, eliciting a pained grunt each time, until the man went limp.

Pulling the desk chair out, Pope maneuvered his unconscious prey onto it. Then he set about finding something to tie him up with.

# SEVENTY-FOUR

AFTER LEAVING THE PARK, Bauer drove downtown and parked outside of a fancy-looking brewpub called the Cask and Barrel. When Patterson queried why they were there, he shrugged.

"You wanted a drink. Let's go get one." He turned the engine off and opened his door. "I looked this place up last night. They have the best chicken wings on the West Coast, apparently. Figured we could get some grub while we're at it."

"I appreciate the gesture, but I was just blowing off steam. We should probably go back to the field office and face the music."

"That can wait until tomorrow." Bauer climbed out of the car and waited for Patterson to do the same. "Right now, you need a distraction, and maybe a couple pints of good old-fashioned IPA."

Patterson shrugged. After such a crappy day, a cold beer did sound appealing. "You buying?"

Bauer tapped his back pocket where his wallet lived. "Figured I'd expensive it."

"Putting alcohol through on your per diem. That's living dangerously."

Bauer grinned. "What's the worst that can happen? Another couple weeks of desk duty?"

"You've been climbing the walls. How about we go Dutch, instead?"

"I'm buying, and that's all there is to it," Bauer said, stepping toward the door and holding it open for her to enter. "Anyway, your highflying boyfriend is the one who wanted me to come here. I doubt he's going to let me get a reprimand for protecting you."

"Is that what this is?" Patterson asked.

"Sure. The way you looked after Bonneville didn't show up, I'm protecting you from yourself."

"Fair enough." Patterson approached the bar and perused the day's beer menu written on a chalkboard hanging from the back wall. She ordered a beer that went by the playful name of Salty Sailor Haze, then waited for Bauer to choose his libation before they weaved to through the crush of Saturday evening revelers until they found a table at the back of the room.

Patterson sipped her beer with relish, then pulled the phone she had used to call Bonneville from her pocket. She placed it on the table and stared at it for a while as she drank. "I've been thinking. Maybe I should just call him back and ask why he didn't show," she said eventually.

"You kidding?"

"No." Patterson shook her head. "Maybe he didn't know the park was a trap. Maybe something happened, and he got held up."

"If that were the case, he would have called you."

"You don't know that."

"No. But I can hazard a guess. He's desperate to find Julie and the kid. That's why he had flyers made up. San Diego PD has found a bunch of them stapled to utility poles and fences. And don't forget the reward. Five grand." Bauer shook his head. "I'm sorry, Patterson, but there's only one reason that he didn't show up, whether you want to admit it or not."

"You might be right," Patterson admitted. "In fact, you probably are. But if I call him back, then at least I'll know if it was my mistake or not."

"He probably won't answer."

"Which is an answer in itself." Patterson took another swig of beer, draining the glass.

"How about you think on it a while," Bauer said. "ASAC Gibbs has already applied for a warrant to use location tracking on Bonneville's phone. No more vague cell tower triangulation. He's pulled some strings to get it before a judge ASAP. We could get it back as early as tomorrow."

"Or we might not."

"Granted. But we might have gotten ourselves into this mess by rushing in. Let's not make the same mistake twice."

"I don't see what harm it can do at this point." Patterson put the empty glass down. She glanced toward the bar. "I need another drink."

"Allow me." Bauer drained the last of his beer and grabbed their glasses, then stood up. He started toward the bar, then turned back around, his gaze settling on the phone sitting in front of Patterson on the table. "And don't do anything rash while I'm gone."

"You realize that I'm the senior agent, right?" Patterson raised her eyebrows. "The one with all the experience. I'm supposed to be giving the orders."

"I might be a newbie, at least in the FBI, but we're not in Dallas and I'm not officially shadowing you anymore. We're equals."

"I was just saying—"

"And as for experience… I did my time up the road in LA solving homicides before I ever stepped foot in Quantico. Not that any of it has a thing to do with you making a phone call that might just make the situation worse."

"I really don't see how," Patterson said. "You going to get me that drink or not?"

Bauer rolled his eyes. "BRB, as the kids say."

Patterson laughed. "Do they, though?"

"Beats me." Bauer turned and disappeared into the crowd on his way to the bar.

Patterson stared down at the phone, then she reached out and picked it up. Her fingers hovered over the screen as she was caught in a moment of indecision. Bauer might be right. Calling Bonneville again could cause more problems than it solved, even if she couldn't see how. But on the other hand, letting it slide was guaranteed to waste the only opportunity they had to lure him out. She glanced around, the fingers of her free hand absently drumming on the table, looking for Bauer to return with their drinks. There was no sign of him. He was probably still waiting to get served at the bar.

She put the phone down, picked it up again, stared at the screen and the call log that contained only one number.

Then she made up her mind.

# SEVENTY-FIVE

CARL AWOKE to a throbbing headache and a sharp pain in his left temple. At first, when he opened his eyes, all he saw was darkness. But then the hotel room swam into view, blurry at first, before clicking into sharper focus.

He was sitting in the desk chair. The room around him was mired in a gloomy half-darkness. The curtains were drawn, and he could see no chink of daylight around the edges, meaning it was probably night outside. The only illumination came from the bathroom, where a sliver of weak light spilled through a crack in the mostly closed door and cast the man sitting on the edge of the bed opposite him in an unnerving chiaroscuro, with one side lit by the glow of the bathroom wall sconce, and the other in deep shadow.

Carl tried to lift his hand to his forehead, only to discover that he couldn't move. When he looked down, he saw that his hands were bound by strips of linen torn into ribbons from his bed sheet. Several loops of sheet tied to the chair's legs similarly restrained his ankles. Another piece of cloth was stuffed into his mouth and held in place by another ribbon of cloth wrapped around his head.

"Welcome back, sunshine," the man said in a voice soft

enough that he might have been talking to a beloved child who had just woken up from a deep slumber, but which still filled Carl with dread.

"I'm going to remove the gag now," the man continued in an equally quiet voice. "If you call for help or scream—if you do anything to attract attention to your plight—it will end badly for you. Understand?"

Carl stared at the man.

"I need an honest answer. Do you understand?"

Carl nodded.

"Excellent." The man leaned forward and loosened the gag, pulled it down and removed the cloth from Carl's mouth.

Carl licked his lips, noting the coppery taste of blood from what he assumed was a gash on his forehead that had bled down his cheek to his chin and soaked into the gag.

"Who are you?" Carl asked, discovering that it hurt more when he talked. "What do you want with me?"

"I think the real question is, who are *you*?" the man replied, leaning forward and resting his elbows on his knees.

Carl said nothing, sensing that the longer he stayed silent, the better off he would be. Maybe it was one predator recognizing another, but when he looked into the man's eyes, he saw his own indifference to the suffering of others reflected back at him.

The man stayed silent for a short while, then he nodded and picked up an object from the bed with gloved hands, which Carl recognized as his wallet. He opened it and studied the driver's license contained within. "Carl Edward Bonneville. 42 years of age. Resident of Arizona."

Still, Carl said nothing.

"You're a good way from home, Mr. Bonneville. I wonder what would bring you all the way out to San Diego?" The man closed the wallet and dropped it back onto the bed. "Better yet, why are the FBI so interested in catching you, and particularly Patterson Blake?"

Carl didn't move, tried not to react, but despite his best

efforts, a twitch pulsed at the corner of his eye. He looked down at the floor.

"Ah. The name is familiar to you. I thought so. Let me guess… You're the person responsible for Julie Blake's disappearance and you're here for the same reason as the FBI agent."

"You don't know what you're talking about," Carl said, deciding that his best bet was to feign ignorance. "I've never heard of Patterson or Julie Blake."

"Really?" The man reached down onto the bed again and this time he came back up with a sheet of paper. One of the flyers from Carl's backpack, which was sitting on the floor near the hotel room door. He held it toward Carl so that Angel's face was staring at him from the photograph. "Deana Taylor sure looks a lot like Patterson Blake. Almost as if she were her sister."

"I don't know anything about that," Carl said. "Deana is my wife. We've been having some marital problems. She took my kid and ran. I've been looking for her, that's all."

"Bullshit." The man released the flyer and let it flutter to the floor. "Here's what I think. You're a loser with low self-confidence, and you always have been. You're also a sexual predator, because it's the only way that you can get a woman. You took Julie Blake sixteen years ago and you've been keeping her captive ever since. At least, until she escaped along with the daughter conceived through your forced attentions. You tracked her to San Diego using the same information as the FBI agent. Then you had these flyers made up because it was the only way you could think of to find her. Am I getting warm?"

"I told you, she's my—"

"Please don't insult my intelligence. You were out cold for a while, which gave me an opportunity to go through your possessions. I found the postcard. I also found a considerable sum of money, both in the bag you were carrying at the park, and an even larger stash hidden under the bed. I haven't counted it, but I'm guessing the cash in that bag you were carrying would come to an even five grand. Same amount as the reward you're offering."

Carl broke out in a clammy sweat. He swallowed hard and met the man's gaze, even as a realization occurred to him. One that he could use to extricate himself from the situation. "Let me guess. You're some kind of a private investigator hired by Franklin Blake to track me down. Did he tell you to assault me and tie me up? I bet he didn't, because that would look real bad for his little federal agent daughter. Might even interfere with her investigation. So, what, you just decided to go off the rails? Have a bit of fun?" A swell of confidence surged within Carl. "So, here's the deal. You untie me right now, let me go, and I'll keep quiet about this little incident. Otherwise, I'll shout it from the rooftops the moment you turn me in. Kidnapping. False imprisonment. Hell, maybe it's even attempted murder, given how hard you smacked my head."

The man sat with his hands held in his lap, looking at his captive with a placid expression on his face. Or was it bemusement? It was hard to tell in the gloomy half-light.

Carl licked his lips and kept going, pressing his perceived advantage. "The five grand in that bag. I bet it's more than Franklin Blake offered to pay you. You can take it. Every last dime. It's yours just for walking away."

"Kidnapping and false imprisonment?" the man said in that quiet voice of his.

Carl nodded.

"That's kind of rich, don't you think, given your own proclivities?"

"This isn't about me."

"I beg to differ. And I'll take you up on the offer of that cash, because there's no point in leaving it behind. Any of it. But I'm not untying you and I'm not letting you go."

"What? Are you stupid? The minute you turn me in, they'll arrest you, too."

"What makes you think I'm going to turn you in?" the man

countered evenly. "You're the only one who said that I work for Franklin Blake."

A cold dread enveloped Carl. If his captor had not been sent by the old man, then who the hell was he? "Look, I don't care who you work for. I won't say anything, I promise. The money is all yours. Just take it and leave. Please, just don't hurt me, okay? It's not worth it."

"I'll decide what is and isn't worth it." The man folded his arms. "Now, do you have anything to add regarding my theory of your identity and past transgressions, or is this conversation over?"

Carl didn't like the way his captor said that last bit. The words were loaded with lethal subtext. Unless he came up with a way out of this predicament, and fast, it wouldn't end well for him, he was sure. But he was hardly in a position to negotiate. Unless... He took a deep breath, and played the last card in his hand, weak as it might be. "Look, the money in this room. That's not all of it. I don't trust banks. There's a lot more hidden back at my farmhouse in Arizona that I didn't have time to recover. Let me go, and I'll tell you where it is. All of it."

The man observed him for a long minute, then stood up. "I don't believe you, and more importantly, I don't care." He reached inside his jacket and pulled out a pistol with a suppressor attached.

"Shit. Fuck. Come on dude, you don't need to do this." Carl twisted and bucked in the chair, tugging at his bindings.

The man watched him cooly; the gun held at his side, then he reached down and pushed the ball of cloth back into Carl's mouth and pulled the gag back up, cutting off his frantic protestations.

Carl closed his eyes and waited for the inevitable.

At that moment, a phone on the nightstand rang.

# SEVENTY-SIX

GLORIA HAD SPENT most of the day holed up in her hotel room hiding from her neighbor and trying to distract herself from thinking about that flyer and the $5000 reward.

It was an obscene amount of money to earn for simply making a phone call. Much more than she would ever get by looking after Anna's kid, even if the woman did somehow find a job without Marco's help. But she still hesitated to call, because Anna had to be running from something more than a run-of-the-mill breakup. You didn't change your name and live in a squalid motel room with your kid in tow just to avoid a heartbroken ex.

She was now at work but remained equally distracted. It was Saturday night, and the bar was standing room only. She had already messed up three orders, and was working on screwing up a fourth, when the other bartender, a woman in her late twenties named Jill, with ample, firm breasts and a *barely there* top that guaranteed her twice the tips Gloria could ever hope to make, pointed out the error.

"Your customer ordered two Manhattans and a dirty martini," Jill shouted over the thrum of heavy rock blasting from the bar's speakers and the hubbub of barroom chatter. "You're making whisky sours."

"Crap." Gloria pushed the tumblers aside and grabbed a couple more martini glasses, then went about making the correct drinks. After she finished serving the customer, Jill pulled her to one side.

"What's going on with you tonight?" she asked. "It's like you're on autopilot or something."

"Sorry. Got stuff on my mind."

"Man stuff, or money stuff?" Jill asked. "Because there ain't much else."

"Money. Kind of." Gloria glanced around.

Three customers were waiting to be served. One of them held an empty glass up. "Hey, sweet cheeks, cut the yacking and get over here, we're thirsty!"

"I'll be with you in a moment," Gloria said.

The man grinned. "Not you, honey. The cute one with the tits."

The two men next to him, presumably his buddies, cracked up laughing.

"Nice," Gloria said, turning back to Jill. "I think they want *you* to serve them."

"Grit your teeth and think of payday," Jill said, turning back to the bar.

Gloria had thought about nothing else since she saw that flyer. A big fat $5000 payday. And watching those men ogle her coworker as she poured a round of beers, their tongues practically hanging out, she made up her mind.

"Hey," she said, sidling close to Jill so she could be heard over the din. "I need some fresh air. Mind if I take a five-minute break?"

"Go for it." Jill placed the beers on the bar and took the man's credit card. As she turned to enter it into the POS system, she leaned in and whispered into Gloria's ear. "Maybe I'm a little distracted tonight, too. This asshole's gonna find one hell of an overcharge on his next statement, and my guess is he's too drunk right now to know if he really spent that much."

"You're evil." Gloria said, starting toward the stockroom, and the door beyond that led outside to a small, fenced area at the rear of the building stacked high with empty kegs. Once outside, she took her phone out, then removed the folded flyer from her back pocket.

She stood there awhile, staring at the picture of Anna and her daughter and wondering what was going through their minds at the moment the photo had been taken. Were they happy in their life back then, or was her room neighbor's smile just for show? It certainly didn't look wholehearted. For a second, she wavered, overcome by the same sense of betrayal that had bothered her all day. But then she shook off the emotion and dialed the number before she could once again change her mind, lifted the phone to her ear, and waited for the source of her friend's plight to answer.

## SEVENTY-SEVEN

THE PHONE'S shrill ring hit pause on Pope's decision to wrap up his business in the hotel room and get out of there. He slipped the gun back under his jacket, then walked to the nightstand and picked it up, noting that the incoming call did not match the only other number in the phone's memory, which he already knew had been placed by Special Agent Patterson Blake in her attempt to smoke Bonneville out.

He knew this because, after rendering the man unconscious, he had found the phone in Bonneville's pocket and listened to the voice message from Blake. He had also noted the outgoing call Bonneville had placed responding to that same message a little while later. When he had discovered the phone, it was turned off, no doubt in an attempt by Bonneville to elude the authorities by making sure they could not track him back to his accommodation. This was, Pope knew, a waste of time. While the FBI could use cell towers to triangulate a rough position, it wouldn't pinpoint Bonneville's location with enough accuracy to find him. For that, they would need to go through the service provider, and get them to turn location tracking back on remotely. All well and good, except that it required a warrant, which would take a while to obtain, even if they could convince the judge that there was sufficient evidence for one to be issued. The phone was new. Purchased only a couple of days before according to the receipt Pope had found on the desk. There was no way the FBI would have a search warrant in hand that quickly, which meant it was safe to leave the phone on and see what transpired, at least for the short time that Pope intended to be Bonneville's unwelcome guest.

Now, he was glad for his forethought. There was a small chance it was Patterson Blake calling again from a different number. Maybe she had coerced another agent, someone Bonneville would not recognize, into trying again. But Pope didn't think so. She wouldn't risk a second attempt so close on the heels of her first failed takedown. The call was probably genuine.

He answered.

"Um, hello," said a hesitant female, so unsure of herself that Pope knew for certain he wasn't talking to an FBI agent. Feds were not *that* good at acting. "I'm calling about the flyer. Deana and her daughter. Did I call the... am I talking to the right person?"

"You are," Pope replied.

"Oh, good." The woman hesitated, possibly unsure of her motivations. "I know where they are."

If she were smart, Pope thought, she would listen to her conscience, hang up, and walk away. An oft used cautionary phrase rattled through his mind. *No good deed goes unpunished.* If the caller continued along her current trajectory, she might soon discover how accurate the saying was. "Please, do go on."

"Is the reward still available?" the woman asked, cutting to the heart of her dilemma.

"Five thousand dollars. Just waiting for the right person to claim it," Pope replied. Up until this moment, he hadn't been sure exactly how to deal with the FBI agent and her partner, but now a plan was forming in his mind. A way to end this debacle quickly and move on to the next phase of his life, enjoying a peaceful, and anonymous, retirement. Because if the woman on the other end of the line really knew where Julie Blake was, could deliver her to him, he would hold the advantage. "If you tell me where Deana and her daughter are currently located, and if your information is accurate, I shall make sure you receive it posthaste."

"Not so fast. You get the information when I get the money."

"Fair enough." Pope hadn't expected his hesitant caller to blurt out the location of Patterson Blake's sister over the phone, but it had been worth a try. He had learned over the years never to underestimate a person's intelligence... or their stupidity. "I can meet with you tonight and bring the reward. Just tell me where and when."

"There's a bar in Chula Vista. The Barrel Room. Do you know it?"

"I don't, but I'm sure I can find it."

"Okay. Good. We can meet there. I'm working a shift tonight."

Pope was already on his own phone looking up the bar on the internet. It was close enough that he could be there in less than twenty minutes, but that wouldn't work. Apart from the obvious disadvantage of exchanging a large amount of cash in what was sure to be a crowded tavern, he didn't want the witnesses. "What time does your shift end? We can meet then."

"I'm not sure that would be a good idea," said the woman, clearly wary of meeting a stranger without the protection of those same witnesses.

But Pope was ready for her reaction. "You really want to conduct our business in front of a bar full of people? I'm not sure that would be wise."

"We're not doing anything illegal, are we?" the woman asked, a note of caution edging into her voice. "I thought you were just looking for your family."

"I am, and we're not." After discovering the bar's location, Pope had gone straight to Yelp, where he noted such words as *seedy*, *gross*, and *dive* in the few reviews the establishment had garnered. "Forgive me for saying this, but I'm guessing that your establishment hardly attracts the most upstanding of clientele. I would hate for you to be parted from your money so soon after receiving it, perhaps in a violent fashion."

This must have struck a chord. Pope heard a brief inhalation of breath on the other end of the line. "Okay, fine. We can meet after my shift ends. But you have to promise me you're not some weirdo."

"I promise," Pope replied, deciding that his informant fell on the stupid end of the spectrum. "The bar closes at 2 AM. Let's give it thirty minutes for your patrons and coworkers to clear out before we conduct our business."

The woman hesitated, took another trembling breath. "That works for me," she said, her desperation apparently overcoming her misgivings. "I usually take care of the cash for the night safe and lock up, anyway, so it won't seem unusual that I'm staying behind."

"Wonderful." Pope had a feeling this was going to turn out well. Very well, indeed. "There's just one more thing... Your name?"

"Oh, right. How silly of me. It's Gloria," the woman said, without bothering to ask for Pope's name in return.

"A pleasure talking to you, Gloria. And I look forward to meeting you later this evening." Pope ended the call and put the phone in his pocket, then did the same with his own phone.

His captive, still tied to the chair, was watching him with wide eyes. When Pope took the gun back out, they grew even wider. He shook his head vigorously and mumbled something behind the gag that Pope couldn't make out. Not that it mattered. He had no further need for Carl Edward Bonneville.

The gun, as a method of execution detached from any larger narrative, felt strange in Pope's hand. Up until now, he had prided himself on making every death look like an accident. It was his signature and had brought in more work than he ever could have dreamed of when he started his career. It had also allowed him to amass a small fortune scattered over several offshore bank accounts. Now, though, he was tired of the grind. The thought of conceiving and implementing a clever accidental death for his captive felt like too much work. It wasn't like he needed the accolades at this point, and Bonneville was too insignificant to be associated with him, anyway. Even if he was, Pope didn't care. After disposing of the FBI agent and making sure that his record was a perfect hundred percent, he was done with the contract killing business. The wilds of Alaska were calling, and Pope intended to answer in the form of a gentler identity, a log cabin, and all the solitude he could soak up.

Stepping forward, he raised the gun.

Bonneville's muffled pleas became frenetic. He tried to stand and only succeeded in almost toppling the chair.

"Take solace, my friend," Pope said in an almost reverent voice, "for as Bram Stoker once wrote, *death be all that we can rightly depend on.*"

Then he pulled the trigger.

# SEVENTY-EIGHT

BY ELEVEN O'CLOCK, with three beers and more chicken wings than she should probably have eaten in her belly, Patterson was back in the hotel room. She took her jacket off, unclipped the holster containing her gun and set it down, then took two phones out of her pocket. One of them was hers. The other was the phone with the local number provided by the San Diego field office. The same phone she had almost used to call Bonneville back from the bar earlier that evening.

But Bauer had been right. It was foolish to rush in. Better to wait and plan their next step with care. Which was why she had reluctantly returned the phone to her pocket, ignoring the voice inside her head that worried the opportunity to nab Bonneville and find her sister was slipping away. She would have pressed the matter, but another, equally loud voice, told her that Bonneville had made them in the park. That he knew what Patterson looked like before he even showed up and had recognized her.

"Tomorrow we'll get a different phone and try again," Bauer had said. "Have another agent call. Someone he won't recognize this time."

Patterson had been skeptical. "You really think he'll fall for the same trick twice?" she had asked, digging into her first chicken wing.

"I don't see why not. He still wants to find Julie and his daughter. We just have to make it convincing enough and sufficiently different to this evening's debacle that he won't be able to resist."

And that was how they had left the matter.

Patterson went to the bathroom and turned on the shower, then undressed. She stood under the scalding water for fifteen minutes, letting the spray rinse away the tension in her neck and shoulders. After drying herself and cleaning her teeth, she put on her nightclothes and climbed into bed.

She took comfort in Bauer's closeness. He was only feet away behind the unlocked connecting door that separated their rooms. At the first sign of trouble, he would be there, gun at the ready.

But Patterson didn't think the hitman who had tried to kill her in Las Vegas would make a second attempt inside the hotel. That strategy had failed him miserably the first time, and there was no reason to believe that he would rely upon it again. Rather, any attack from an unexpected quarter. Assuming, of course, that he hadn't decided to cut his losses, happy to have escaped accountability against the odds.

She reached up and touched the wall, wondering what Bauer was doing on the other side. Her mind drifted to another time and place, and the moment of ill-advised passion they had shared in another hotel room before realizing their mistake. It had been nothing but a brief kiss that could have led to so much more, and wrecked both their relationships. Since then, their interactions had been purely platonic, but she couldn't deny a faint undercurrent of attraction that still lingered, highlighting the path not taken. In different circumstances, a wall might not separate them at that moment.

The thought jolted Patterson back to reality, riding a wave of guilt that her mind had even gone there. She rolled over and picked up her phone. Typed out a quick text message.

*Thinking of you.*

She hit the send icon, put the phone back down, and settled back into bed. It was the early hours of the morning on the East Coast, so she didn't expect Jonathan Grant to respond, but the sentiment eased her guilt.

Apparently not enough.

She grabbed the phone again and typed another brief message.

*Love you.*

It went off with a whoosh.

She put the phone down for a second time, plumped the pillows under her head, pulled the covers over her shoulders, and closed her eyes. Then she waited for sleep to come.

# SEVENTY-NINE

POPE DIDN'T WAIT until 2:30 AM to check out the situation in The Barrel Room. He didn't believe for one moment that the call was a setup, or that Gloria was an FBI agent. But he never made assumptions, which was why he arrived at the bar a couple of hours early, parking his car down the block on the street rather than using the small parking lot at the side of the building.

Even if he was wrong and it was a setup, he was probably safe, because the FBI would be expecting Bonneville to show up, not him. His concerns were allayed almost immediately after walking through the door. The place was busy, but not packed, which was understandable since it was now after midnight. The casual drinkers had all left for their respective homes and better halves, leaving only the *party hardy* to carry the torch.

Pope approached the bar and slid onto a stool. As he did so, he looked around for security cameras, which were so inexpensive now that even the lowliest of establishments could afford them. He expected there to at least be a camera behind the bar streaming a live feed to the cloud, but the owners of The Barrel Room were either too cheap, or too tech-averse to bother.

He had already checked the parking lot and the bar's entrance on his way inside, and saw no cameras there, either.

Satisfied that he wouldn't be under electronic observation when he returned later, Pope shifted his attention to the staff.

There were two bartenders, separated in age by at least a decade and maybe more. The younger of the pair had clearly figured out where her talents lay, and they were firmly around chest height. She jiggled up to customers, exclusively men, and leaned on the bar so that her already ample assets were hard to miss.

When she spotted Pope, she made a beeline for him and went through the same routine he had watched her perform for the previous customers, leaning forward on the bar and pressing her arms to her sides so that her cleavage bulged.

"What can I get for you, hon?" she asked in a syrupy voice, even as she chewed a piece of gum.

Pope waited a moment before replying, his eyes sliding from her face down to her chest and the expanse of taut flesh on display. But not because he couldn't help himself, but rather because she wore a name badge pinned to her black tube top.

Jill.

That meant the older bartender must be Gloria.

This was confirmed when she pushed past Jill toward the other end of the bar, carrying a couple glasses of beer that sloshed over the rims as she went.

He shifted his gaze from Gloria back to Jill. "Bourbon. Neat. No ice. Something good. Not the well stuff."

"Coming right up." Gloria turned to the back of the bar and reached for a bottle on a high shelf. As she did so, her skirt slid up and he saw a wedge of pink fabric before she pulled the bottle down and it vanished.

She poured the drink and handed it to him.

Pope pushed a twenty-dollar bill across the bar and told her to keep the change, then lifted the drink to his lips and silently toasted the recently departed Carl, who had footed the bill, even though he would never know it. Aside from the moderate amount of cash that Pope had brought into the bar, the rest of Carl's loot now rested in the trunk of his rental car. Both the bag containing the $5000 reward, and the larger duffel that held considerably more. It wasn't often that someone unwittingly paid him for their own execution, so Pope felt he deserved the toast.

Jill had moved on to another easy mark and started her routine all over again. Pope wondered how much she took home in tips every night. He guessed it was a lot more than Gloria, who possessed considerably less panache—not to mention bare flesh—than her coworker. Maybe that was why she was so eager to get her hands on the reward for Patterson Blake's sister.

Not that Pope gave a crap about her motivations.

She wasn't an FBI agent laying a trap. That was all he cared about.

He lifted his glass and sank the whiskey in one gulp, relishing the burn as it went down. Wiping his mouth, he slid off the stool and made his way to the exit. Once outside, he walked to the car, hands pushed deep into his pockets, and climbed in. Then he settled down to wait for the bar to close, and his early morning date with Gloria.

# EIGHTY

GLORIA HAD BARELY BEEN able to focus on anything else since her phone call earlier that night. In a little over thirty minutes, she would be rich. Well, maybe not rich, but certainly better off than she had been at any other point in her life.

Five grand.

She had hardly ever seen that much money in one place in her life, except on a few rare occasions at The Barrel Room, like on New Year's Eve, when cash flowed across the bar like water. But that didn't count, because it wasn't *her* money. And also, because she didn't *really* see it. At least, not all at once. When the register was full, probably around fifteen hundred bucks at most, one of the bartenders would empty it, put the cash into a deposit bag, and stash it in the night safe located in the stockroom. The only people who had a key to that safe were the bar owner and her daughter, who would collect the previous night's take the following morning to deposit in the bank.

Five thousand dollars.

The words rolled through her mind on an endless loop, now completely disassociated with the unpleasant task by which she would soon come into the money. Selling out Anna, or Deana, or whatever the hell her real name was. But even then, she couldn't help a flicker of apprehension. Because the more she thought about it, the more Gloria had become convinced that the man on the other end of the line had not been honest with her. There was something about his voice. Hard edged and emotionless. For a guy about to be reunited with his family, he didn't sound very excited. She had briefly considered calling the police and letting them deal with him, but soon rejected the idea. For a start, she had no idea what he looked like, and hadn't even bothered to ask his name, which was stupid in hindsight. But the main reason she hadn't done so was the reward. The cops were hardly likely to let her collect the money before they swooped in and arrested him. Assuming that they even took her seriously.

So she had pushed her suspicions aside and focused on what she was going to do with the money instead. Like take a few weeks off and go on vacation. Maybe even take a longer sabbatical—could you even call it that when you worked in a bar?—and travel the world. Visit such exotic locales as the Grand Canyon, Niagara Falls, and that place in Kansas that had the world's largest ball of twine. The furthest she had ever ventured was Barstow, which was hardly a must-see destination.

She looked up at the clock mounted above the bar.

Last call had come and gone almost fifteen minutes before. Now, she watched the second hand tick around the clock face until it reached its apex and started around again.

They were now officially closed.

She cast her gaze downward to the dimly lit room beyond the bar. Earlier in the evening, when she had stepped outside to make her call, the bar had been a sweaty crush of bodies desperate to make something of their Saturday night. Now, only a few stragglers remained, the rest having either gone home, hooked up and went home with someone else, or left in search of somewhere that stayed open even later than The Barrel Room.

She busied herself collecting glasses, emptying beer trays, and wiping down the bar, until she and Jill were the only two left. When she looked at the clock again, she saw that it was now 2:15 AM.

"I can cash out and lock up," Gloria said.

"You sure?" Jill asked.

Gloria nodded. "You worked hard tonight. You look tired. Go home and get some rest. I've got this."

Jill didn't need telling twice. She hurried to the stockroom and grabbed her bag and car keys from her locker, then scurried out the front door before Gloria could change her mind.

The bar was a different animal once the customers had left, and the music was turned off. The only sounds were a soft purr from the glass-fronted coolers behind the bar, and a faint hum from the air conditioning vents set into the ceiling. With the lights up, Gloria could see every stain in the carpet and ding on the walls. If The Barrell Room was a dive when it was open, it looked like a complete shithole after hours.

Any other night, Gloria would have locked the front door before turning her attention to the cash register. It wasn't the best neighborhood, and the last thing she wanted was a gun in her face. Now, though, she ignored the register and hurried to the door, pulling it open a crack and peering out into the dark parking lot beyond. She took her phone out and checked the time. It was 2:30 AM. There were no cars left, and for a moment, Gloria wondered if she had been stood up, but then a figure separated itself from the darkness on the other side of the parking lot.

Gloria took a step back on instinct, almost slammed the door and locked it despite herself, but then she pulled herself together. There was a lot of money on the line, and she had no intention of losing out.

The figure walked forward, stepping into the weak pool of illumination cast by the light fixture above the door, and Gloria got her first look at him.

He wore black trousers, a dark shirt, and a leather jacket. He also wore gloves, which was odd, thought Gloria, because it wasn't particularly cold.

A baseball cap was pulled low on his head, partially obscuring his face. He carried a bulging backpack in one hand.

"Are you alone like we agreed?" he asked, pausing several feet from Gloria.

Her voice momentarily failed her, so she nodded.

"Excellent." He started forward again, stepping inside even as Gloria back peddled. The man turned, closed and locked the door. When he saw the look on her face, he lifted the bag and said, "Can't be too careful with this much money around. Wouldn't want to get robbed."

"Oh. Right." Gloria wondered if she had made a mistake letting this black-clad stranger into the bar.

"Don't worry," the man said, as if reading her thoughts. "I'm harmless."

Gloria wanted to believe him, because, well, all that money right there in his hand. "You promise?"

"I do." He crossed to the bar and placed the bag on the floor. "We should have a drink together to break the ice. I'll take a bourbon, neat. Old Rip Van Winkle, if you have it, otherwise a comparable substitution. Then we shall get down to business."

# EIGHTY-ONE

POPE STEPPED into the bar and looked around, taking in his decrepit surroundings. It looked worse when it was empty with the lights up, and he wondered if the owner ever spent any money on upkeep.

Gloria looked nervous, but her eyes kept shifting to the bag in his hand, telling him that her desperation for money would overcome her unease. He walked to the bar and placed the bag down on the floor next to a stool with a ripped seat, then told her to pour them both a drink.

She put a bourbon down in front of him and poured one for herself. Pope lifted the glass and sipped in silence, waiting for Gloria to finish her drink.

When the glasses were empty, he continued.

"I believe you have information for me."

Gloria was standing behind the bar, which created a barrier that Pope suspected made her feel safer. It didn't.

She cleared her throat. "Money first."

"Don't trust me, huh?"

"I don't trust anyone."

"Touché." Pope reached down and lifted the bag, placing it

on the counter and unzipping it. He turned it around to show her. "Satisfied?"

Gloria eyed the cash with a quickening breath. "Do I need to count it?"

Pope shrugged. "Be my guest. But don't take too long."

Gloria studied him for a moment, then grabbed the bag. "If it was short, you wouldn't be so indifferent about me counting it, so I'll just assume it's all there." She zipped up the bag and placed it behind the bar.

"Now, your end of the bargain."

Gloria bit her lip. "You're not going to hurt her or the kid, right?"

"You have my word," Pope said, transforming his face into a picture of longing. "I just want my family back."

Gloria hesitated a moment longer, then took a deep breath. "She's staying at a hotel a couple of blocks down the street. Place called the Del Ray. She's staying in the room next to mine."

Pope waited for her to divulge the room number. When she didn't, he gave her a gentle prod. "And?"

Gloria was still tugging at her lip with her teeth. With a tell like that, Pope thought, she wouldn't last long in a poker game.

He let a few more seconds tick by before nudging her again, harder this time. "If you're having second thoughts, I can always take the money back and leave."

"No. I'm good. She's on the second floor. Room 208."

Pope repeated the information back to her, just to make sure. When Gloria confirmed it, he smiled. "Thank you for bringing my family back to me."

"Thank *you* for the money," Gloria replied. She glanced toward the door. "I guess we're done here."

"Just one more thing," Pope said. "Deana. She won't answer the door if she knows it's me. We had a fight and I'm sure she's still mad at me. I mean, she booked a crappy hotel room and has been living there for weeks just to avoid me… no offence. I wasn't disparaging your lodgings on purpose."

"It's fine. You're right. The place is a shithole. I wouldn't live there if I had any other choice." Gloria picked up the empty glasses and put them beneath the bar. "But as for Anna, I mean Deana, I'm not sure what I can do."

"Maybe you could call her, tell her you need to come over. That way, when I knock, she'll answer the door thinking it's you."

"It's almost three o'clock in the morning. Why would she do that?"

"Because she thinks you're her friend." Which this woman most certainly was not, Pope thought. "Just tell her you have an emergency. Say that you're upset, perhaps?"

Gloria shook her head. "I don't know. This isn't part of our deal."

Pope expected this. He reached inside his jacket and pulled out a ward of fifty-dollar bills secured with a rubber band. Money taken from the larger of Carl's two bags of cash. He dropped the money on the counter in front of her. "Another thousand dollars. Will that take care of it?"

Gloria stared at the money. He could practically see the conflicting thoughts churning through her mind as she debated the wisdom of selling her neighbor out even further. Then she nodded and picked up the cash. "I guess we've come this far."

"You've earned my everlasting gratitude," Pope said. "Now, perhaps you could make that call?"

"I'll do my best. I don't think she has a phone, and even if she does, I don't know the number. But I can call her room at the hotel. Hopefully she'll pick up."

"Let's keep our fingers crossed," Pope said.

Gloria looked like she was going to say something else, but then she took a cell phone out of her pocket and made the call. When connected, she tapped away on the screen, obviously navigating the hotel's automated system. Then she put the phone to her ear and waited.

After a while, she ended the call and looked at Pope. "She's not answering."

"Try again."

"She might be asleep," Gloria said, as if that would give Pope pause.

"Please, try one more time." Julie might ignore the call once, but probably not twice.

Gloria nodded and placed the call.

This time, the FBI agent's sister answered.

"Hey, it's me," Gloria said, her voice suddenly full of angst. "I'm so sorry for calling this late at night, but I didn't know where else to turn." She sniffed, as if she were crying. "I'm so afraid. A guy that hangs with my ex-boyfriend came into the bar tonight. I'm sure he recognized me. He'll run right back to Jayden and tell him. I can't let that man find me again. He'll force me to work the streets just like before. Get me hooked on drugs again. That's if he doesn't kill me."

Gloria paused. Pope couldn't hear what Julie Blake was saying, but he didn't need to.

Gloria feigned another sniff. "Can I come over? I don't want to be alone right now."

Another pause.

"You're a lifesaver. I still have to cash out and lock up at work. I'll be there in thirty, okay?"

A pause.

"Great. See you then." Gloria ended the call and pushed the phone back into her pocket, then turned her attention to Pope. "How was that?"

"A masterful performance," Pope said. "You should have been an actress."

"I played Frenchie in my high school production of Grease," Gloria said. "But that was a long time ago."

"Talent never fades."

"I guess not. She's expecting you—well, me really—in thirty minutes." Gloria folded her arms. "Are we done now?"

"I suppose we are." Pope stepped away from the bar. "Care to see me out?"

"Sure." Gloria sounded relieved. She was, no doubt, anxious to get rid of him, because even if she had ignored her misgivings, Pope suspected that deep down, she knew it had been foolish to let him into the bar alone with her.

And she was right.

Pope followed her to the door, waited until she was reaching for the latch, then he stepped close and reached for her neck.

# EIGHTY-TWO

GLORIA COULD HAVE FAINTED with relief when the man on the other side of the bar agreed to leave. For a while there, she had wondered if it had been a mistake to let him inside, even with five grand on the line. There was something about him. An air of menace that led her to believe that Anna wouldn't be too pleased to see him.

She had almost refused to tell him where his wife was—assuming he was even being truthful about that—despite the reward. But she could really use that money, and anyway, he was already inside with her. If she went back on the deal now, who knew what he would do?

But now, her ordeal was almost over. The money was safely behind the bar, and she'd even made an extra thousand. A couple more minutes, and the man would be gone. Even so, she had decided to stay a while in the bar, just to make sure he wasn't loitering outside, waiting to snatch the money back.

But she didn't think he would do that, mostly because he would lose his opportunity with Anna, who was expecting Gloria to show up just as soon as she locked up the bar and walked the two blocks back to the hotel. And anyway, she had no intention of taking the money back with her at such a late hour. She figured it would be safe enough in her locker until the next morning, when she could come back and retrieve it during the light of day.

She arrived at the door, was about to unlock the deadbolt and let her guest out, when she sensed movement to her rear. A faint stirring of air. She half turned, realized the man was much too close, tried to step away, even as his hands found her neck.

She wanted to scream, but nothing came out.

The pressure on her neck increased.

She lifted her hands, clawed at her attacker, pulled to free herself, but it was no use. He was too strong.

Her ears were ringing now.

A strange sensation pulsed behind her eyeballs, as if they were being pushed from their sockets.

The world around her shifted from sharp focus to a blurry haze.

She tried to speak, beg him to stop, but all she managed was a vague croak.

An unbridled thought flashed through her mind, of the money in that backpack behind the bar, and what she would do with it... like visit the Grand Canyon, Niagara Falls, and that enormous ball of twine in the middle of Kansas. It would be so nice, she mused, to get away, even as the world around her shrank to a vague point of light at the end of a long, dark tunnel. And after that, there was nothing at all.

# EIGHTY-THREE

POPE WATCHED the light fade from Gloria's eyes, then he dragged her back, away from the door, and lowered her gently to the floor. He went behind the bar and picked up the backpack stuffed with cash, then retrieved the extra thousand he had paid her to call Julie Blake. Opening the cash register, he scooped out the night's takings and stuffed that into the backpack, too, taking only the paper money and ignoring the coinage. All except a couple of ten-dollar bills he had let fall to the floor behind the bar. A nice touch that would lead investigators to think they had been dropped by the nonexistent thieves who had killed Gloria and robbed the bar in their haste to escape.

He almost felt bad for her. She had died solely because she befriended the wrong person. But then he reminded himself that her demise was self-inflicted. If she hadn't been so keen to betray her friend for a quick payday, she would still be alive.

He checked his watch. Fifteen minutes had passed since gloria had called Patterson Blake's sister. He slung the backpack full of cash over his shoulder, stepped out from behind the bar, and made his way to the door. A couple of minutes later, he was crossing the parking lot and heading down the block toward his car. In the morning, whoever turned up to open the bar would find a grisly surprise waiting for them, but by then, Pope and his captives would be far away from the city. After that, the final showdown with Patterson Blake would commence before he retreated quietly into obscurity to enjoy his well-earned retirement.

# EIGHTY-FOUR

JULIE WAS CONCERNED. She had been sleeping when the hotel room phone on the nightstand rang, curled up next to Cherub with one arm draped over her daughter's shoulder. At first, she had ignored it. There was no reason for anyone to be calling her. They had probably just dialed the wrong room number.

The phone had fallen silent, and Julie closed her eyes again. Until it rang a second time.

Cherub, lying in the bed next to her, mumbled something incoherent. Another few seconds, and the ringing phone would wake the child up. Julie had cursed under her breath, then rolled over and snatched the handset from its cradle.

That was almost thirty minutes ago, and now she was waiting for Gloria to show up.

As if on cue, there was a light knock at the hotel room door.

Cherub stirred again, shifting in bed.

Julie rushed to the door and pulled back the security bar, then twisted the deadbolt, worried that another knock would disturb the child and prevent her from falling back to sleep.

She opened the door, was about to usher Gloria inside, but then she froze. Because it wasn't her neighbor standing out there. It was a man she didn't recognize, and he was carrying a pistol, which he wasted no time in pointing at her, even as he stepped inside, closed the door, and locked it behind him. He forced her back to the bed, motioned for her to sit down. Then, finally, he spoke in a soft yet menacing voice.

"Julie Blake," he said at length, his pale blue eyes, cold as steel, boring into her. "It's a pleasure to meet you."

# EIGHTY-FIVE

THE FIRST RAYS of morning sun were poking over the distant mountains that dotted the eastern horizon. Corbin Pope was seventy miles east of the city and driving through the rugged desert landscape toward the western shore of the Salton Sea. The large lake had become a popular tourist destination during the middle years of the twentieth century before a series of man-made and natural disasters, including severe floods and agricultural pollution, had left the area's resort towns like Bombay Beach on the lake's eastern shore practically uninhabitable. Tourism had dwindled, and the once prosperous communities around the lake had withered and died.

But that wasn't Pope's destination. When he came to a dusty trail twenty miles east of the lake, he turned off the road and pointed his car toward the ironically named ghost town of Hopefulness, California, a mining community that had prospered for a few brief years in the 1890s before the promise of riches from beneath the ground faded and the inhabitants departed. Now, it was nothing but a few disintegrating buildings that lay mostly forgotten among the scrub at the end of a winding trail through a narrow canyon.

Along the way, he had discarded the Sig and its suppressor,

with which he had dispatched Carl Edward Bonneville, burying them in the desert where he was sure they would never be found. He would now have been short a weapon, but by a stroke of luck he had discovered a Glock pistol and a box of ammunition hidden in the kitchenette of Julie Blake's hotel room, stashed in a cupboard out of her daughter's reach. But that still left him lacking the weapon he needed if his plan to kill Patterson Blake, which had coalesced in his mind the previous evening after his conversation with Carl, was to be successful.

This was why, with his two captives in tow, he had paid another early morning visit to Lawrence, rousing the man from his slumber for the second time in as many days. To describe the bar owner come arms dealer as annoyed at Pope's reappearance would have been an understatement, at least until he heard what the hitman wanted, and how much money he would make from its sale.

Less than a quarter of an hour after he pulled into the biker bar's empty parking lot, Pope had resumed his journey to the town of hopefulness, with Julie Blake and her daughter restrained in the backseat of his rental car, and his new purchase safely stashed in the trunk.

The town of Hopefulness had once boasted a population of over a thousand people. Now, most of the buildings were long gone, with only a few concrete foundations and some rotting planks of wood to bear witness that they had ever been there. But surprisingly, a couple of structures endured. The shell of the old two-story jailhouse, built of stone blocks, and missing its windows, roof, and all internal structure, stood like a skeletal sentinel on the southern end of what had been Main Street. Further along the drag, separated by an empty expanse that had been quickly reclaimed by the desert, was an almost intact wooden building that had once gone by the name of Cobbett's General Store. Now, it was nothing more than an empty husk, devoid of any clue to its former existence, except for the faded sign that still hung above the door on rusty chains.

It was to this structure that Pope made his way, parking next to the sagging boardwalk that ran along the front of the building before disappearing under drifts of sandy earth on each side.

After checking out the building's interior and determining that it would be suitable for his needs, Pope wasted no time in ushering Julie and her daughter from the car, after untying their legs but leaving their hands bound behind their backs with strips of fabric cut from a pair of Julie's jeans that he had found in the hotel room and leading them inside.

There were a few sticks of furniture left in the building. Part of the store's original counter, which had mostly collapsed upon itself, a few shelves clinging tenaciously to the back wall behind the counter even though the wares they had once held were long gone, and three wooden hoop-back chairs, one of which was missing a leg and leaned precariously. But Pope only needed two of them.

He led Julie and her daughter to the middle of the room, where a corroded metal post supported a thick beam that bore the weight of the floor above, even though many of the floorboards were missing and Pope could see all the way through in places. With the gun he had found back at the hotel in his hand, he ordered them to stand still, then dragged the two good chairs to the middle of the room and set them back-to-back against the metal post. He instructed Julie and Cherub to sit down, then retied their ankles, binding them to the chair's legs. He untied their hands, forced their arms through the slats in the back of the chairs and around the metal post, before retying their wrists so tightly that Cherub cried out. Finally, he ran longer strips of fabric around their chests, under their arms, and behind the pole, before cinching them so tightly that it was hard for Julie to breathe.

She glared up at her captor and repeated the same question she had asked several times since they left the hotel room. "Why are you doing this to us?"

As before, Pope didn't answer. He had finally silenced her

earlier inquiries by pulling over to the side of the road, taking the gun from his jacket, and pushing it in her face. Pressing the barrel against her temple, he had told her to remain quiet for the rest of the journey, then reiterated his warning about trying to attract help. The same warning he had issued back at the hotel room. Do anything to attract attention, scream for help or try to run, and I'll put a bullet in your daughter's head. He had issued a similar warning to Cherub, who had turned pale and hadn't uttered a single word since. Now, apparently, Julie had decided that she wasn't going to survive this encounter either way and thus resumed asking questions.

"Did Carl send you?" she asked, meeting his gaze with a defiant stare.

"Carl's dead," Pope answered, deciding that his reply might shock her back into silence, because the truth was that he really didn't want to kill her or the child. They had been through enough already at the hands of the man he had dispatched the previous night. Just so long as they served their purpose and brought Patterson Blake to him, he couldn't see the point of snuffing out innocent lives. "He won't ever bother you again. I put a bullet in his head."

There was a moment of silence while Julie absorbed this information, then she nodded, showing neither gratitude nor sorrow. "That still doesn't answer my question. Who are you, and what do you want with us?"

"Who I am is unimportant," Pope replied. "And as for my motives—you're the bait I need to kill your sister."

# EIGHTY-SIX

JULIE STARED at the man in disbelief. All this time, she had thought that he was an associate of Carl's, sent to bring her back to the farmhouse north of Flagstaff. When he had driven out of the city heading east, her belief had only solidified.

The only thing that had confused her was his detour to the bar out in the middle of nowhere, surrounded by desert. He had left her tied up and locked in the car and taken Cherub with him inside the building, after issuing a threat that any attempt to escape or summon the help of a passing car would result in her daughter's instant death. He had come back out of the building a while later, pushing Cherub ahead of him with one hand and holding the biggest gun she had ever seen in the other. After putting the gun in the trunk, he had returned Cherub to the back of the car and retied her ankles. Then they had set off again, driving for another hour and a half through increasingly desolate terrain until they finally arrived at the ghost town in which she now found herself.

She reeled, trying to absorb the man's answer. Carl was dead, shot in the head by the same person who now held her and Cherub captive. A man who wanted to kill Patterson and use them to accomplish the task. Which was crazy. She could think of no earthly reason anyone would want to harm her little sister. Of course, she knew nothing about her sister. The last time she had seen Patterson, the girl was barely a teenager and obsessed with boy bands, the latest fashions, and not getting braces because she thought no one would date her. And now, here she was, tied to a pole in a California ghost town, as bate to lure Patterson to her death, no doubt using the gun her captor had loaded into the trunk earlier that morning. She would have asked more questions, pressed the man to explain why he wanted to end her sister's life, but she never got the opportunity.

After announcing his plans for Patterson, he produced more strips of cloth cut from the pair of jeans she had found in a Goodwill a couple of weeks before and gagged her. He did the same to Cherub, stifling the girl's terrified whimpers.

Then he took a phone from his pocket, turned it on, and made a call.

# EIGHTY-SEVEN

PATTERSON WAS in bed sleeping when the phone rang. At first, the noise wove itself into her dream, where she was chasing her sister through the darkness in a strange city and calling out her name, even as Julie led her through endless alleyways and back streets, oblivious to her cries. It was raining, a deluge that soaked through her clothes and stung her face. At first, her slumbering mind interpreted the ringing as the plaintive wail of a distant police siren. Then the nightmare faded, jolting her back to reality.

She rolled over, noticing how the sheets had bunched up around her sweat-drenched body, and fumbled for her phone. But when she picked it up, the screen was blank, even though the incessant ring continued. Then she realized. It wasn't *her* phone that was ringing. It was the one given to her by the FBI the day before. The same one she had used to call Bonneville.

She put her phone down and grabbed the other one, her heart rate quickening when she saw it was Bonneville's number.

But when she answered, the voice on the other end was not that of Julie's abductor.

"Patterson Blake?" The man said before she even had time to speak.

"Yes." Patterson held her breath, wondering what this new development meant.

"Are you alone?"

"Yes."

"Good. Listen carefully and don't interrupt. I have your sister, Julie, and her daughter. If you want to get them back alive, you will do exactly what I tell you. Do not report this conversation to your colleagues or superiors. Do not tell anyone. It stays between us, and us alone. On this first point, do you understand?"

Patterson hesitated, then she said, "Yes. I understand."

"Excellent. There is an abandoned mining town about hundred and ten miles east of San Diego. It goes by the rather optimistic name of Hopefulness. There are only two buildings left standing. The old jail, and a general store. I will be waiting with your sister in the general store. The drive takes a little under two hours. Allowing for traffic in the city, I will give you three hours to get here from the moment this call ends, which is more than enough time, considering that it's Sunday morning. Are you still with me?"

"Yes," Patterson replied, wishing that Bauer was there to listen in on the call despite the caller's warning. She almost went to the connecting door and summoned him but was afraid that the man on the other end of the line would hear and hang up, then follow through on his threat to kill her sister.

"Repeat the name of the town back to me."

"Hopefulness," Patterson said.

"Good. Don't forget it. Come alone and unarmed. If I suspect you have brought anyone with you, or that you have backup, your sister dies. If I see anyone but you approach the town, she dies. If a drone flies over, she dies. Likewise, a helicopter or any other aircraft. If I see any vehicle except yours, she dies. Tell me you understand."

"I understand."

"Call me when you arrive. I don't want any surprises. Understand?"

"Yes."

"Good. I'm going to hang up now, and your three hours will begin."

"Wait," Patterson said quickly. "You can't expect me to just show up on my own and unarmed without knowing why."

"I already told you why. If you don't show up, Julie and her daughter die."

"No. Not the consequence. The reason."

"You really can't figure it out?" The man gave a soft laugh. "I thought you were the hotshot FBI agent who outwits serial killers."

"You're the man who tried to kill me in Las Vegas."

"See, that wasn't so hard to figure out."

"Which means you'll kill me the minute I show up there."

"The way I see it, you don't have a choice unless you want to find Julie's corpse rotting in the desert sun, along with that of her daughter. What would your father think of you then? After all this time, you end up being the reason she's dead. And you could have saved her by following a few simple instructions."

"I'm not stupid. If you kill me, you'll kill them, too."

"You have my word that if you follow my directions, neither of them will be harmed. Your sister has spent the last sixteen years in captivity, being abused by an absolute monster of a human being. I despise men like that, and I have dispatched with him. Your sister been through enough, as has her daughter. This is between you and me. It has nothing to do with either of them. Once I get what I want, they will walk free. After I've made my escape, I'll call your partner at the FBI and tell him where they are. He'll find them safe and sound. They can go back to Queens and your father. Live happily ever after. That *is* what you want, isn't it?"

"You're a killer. Why should I trust you at your word?"

"Because you have no choice."

"How do I know that you even have Julie? You could be lying about everything."

Patterson heard a brief exhalation on the other end of the line. There was a faint rustling, then a female voice filled her ear. "Patterson?"

She recognized it instantly. "Julie?"

"Oh my God, I can't believe it's really you. I didn't think I'd ever hear your voice again."

"Me either." Patterson blinked away a sudden well of tears. "Are you okay?"

"I'm fine, for now. He hasn't hurt us. But you can't come here, Sis. He'll kill you. Don't trade your life for—"

Her sister's warning was quickly cut off. "That's enough with the family reunion. You have your proof. I'll see you in three hours. Don't be late and don't be stupid."

The call abruptly ended, leaving Patterson staring at the phone in disbelief. She wiped the tears from her eyes and sat down on the bed. When she looked up, the connecting door between their rooms was open, and Marcus Bauer was standing there watching her with narrowed eyes.

# EIGHTY-EIGHT

AFTER POPE ENDED the call with Patterson Blake, he turned his attention to Julie. "I hope you enjoyed that little reunion with your sister, because the next time you see her, she'll be dead."

"Why are you doing this?" She looked up at him with tears in her eyes.

"Because I don't have any choice."

"You always have a choice." Julie met his gaze with an unwavering stare. "For instance, you could release us now and get out of here before she arrives. You don't want to be on the bad side of my sister, trust me."

Pope chuckled. "I think it's a little late for that. Besides, you know nothing about your sister. You haven't even seen her in sixteen years. I bet you weren't even aware that she's an FBI agent."

"It doesn't matter if I've seen her. I know Patterson. It doesn't surprise me that she joined the FBI. It's just like her to do something like that. She's tough. Tenacious. When she gets an idea in her head... Well, you'll find out soon enough. She won't let you kill her."

"You don't know what you're talking about." Pope took a

step forward and shoved the ball of fabric back into Julie's mouth, then lifted the gag back into place and pulled it tight. "By the time your sister realizes what's happening, it will be too late."

Julie mumbled something behind the gag, even as her eyes widened.

Pope didn't have a clue what she was trying to say, and he didn't care. He reached out and stroked her chin, sensing the tension when he touched her. "Don't worry, I'll keep my end of the bargain. If she shows up on time and doesn't try to trick me, you and your daughter will get to walk out of here unharmed. You have my word. Of course, the same won't be true for your sister, but at least you'll know that she loved you. Giving up her life like that to save you."

Julie's eyes flew even wider. Her mumbles became frantic. From the other chair, he heard another sound. Cherub was crying, her heaving sobs muffled by her gag. If he were wired differently, Pope might have felt sorry for her, but he wasn't capable of such emotional depth. Even when it came to Julie's abductor, or Senator Newport, there wasn't any genuine emotion. On a rudimentary level, he despised the likes of Carl. Men who abused women for their own base gratification. But even then, it wasn't so much an emotional reaction as an intellectual one. He saw their proclivities, their inability to control their vile urges, as a sign of weakness. And as for the senator... his revenge was borne from a need to protect himself more than anything else. If people thought they could go around trying to kill him without repercussion, more of his old clients might get the same idea. And some of them might not be so inept. Like his handlers at the CIA. They had saved his butt this time, but if he got into another jam, they might decide he was a liability and go the other route.

Pope ignored the girl's sobs and looked around the building. The only other chair was missing a leg, but there was an old wooden crate standing against the far wall. He walked over and dragged it back toward his captives. It would be at least a couple of hours before Patterson Blake showed up and there were preparations to be made before she arrived, but not quite yet. He didn't want to leave Julie and her daughter alone for that long. If her sister displayed even half of Patterson's tenaciousness and wits, that would not be smart. He figured it would take him about an hour to get in position and get set up, which left him with at least that long again to wait.

He sat down on the crate, cradling the gun he had found in Julie's hotel room in one hand, and Bonneville's cell phone, which he hadn't bothered to turn off, in the other. He watched the pair with a beady eye, but they weren't the only reason he felt it prudent to delay his preparations a while longer. If the FBI agent did something stupid, if she betrayed him and sent a helicopter full of feds or a surveillance drone in his direction, he didn't want to be caught unawares and out in the open. And not just because of his promise to kill the older Blake sister and her daughter if Patterson didn't stick to her promise, although that was a consideration. It was also because he would be too easy a target. Better to wait a while and make sure she was sticking to her end of the bargain before committing to his plan. If a helicopter with an FBI SWAT team hadn't shown up within the next hour, give or take, he figured he was safe, and he would still have plenty of time to make his preparations since it would take Blake at least a couple of hours to reach the ghost town by car, even if traffic cooperated and she floored it. In the meantime, he would keep his captives company. He smiled at Julie, ignoring the glare he received in return. "Looks like we have some time to kill."

# EIGHTY-NINE

HOW MUCH DID YOU HEAR?"

"Most of it." Bauer stepped into the room. "You can't do this, Patterson."

"He has Julie."

Bauer took his phone out. "I'll inform the San Diego Field Office. Tell them what's going on. Get a team out there."

"No. You can't do that. He'll kill Julie and the kid."

"And if you go to that ghost town alone, he'll kill *you*."

"That's a chance I'm willing to take."

"But I'm not." Bauer's finger hovered over the phone screen.

"It's the only way to save Julie."

Bauer shook his head. "The man's a hardened killer. He's not going to leave a witness alive, no matter what he says."

"I believe him."

"And I think he's lying."

"Please, Marcus. Listen to me. He doesn't care about Julie and her daughter. He wants me. If I give him that, they get to live. Go home to Dad."

"You're fooling yourself." Bauer's finger dropped to the screen. He lifted the phone to his ear.

"No!" Patterson jumped to her feet. "Just hear me out. Please?"

"It won't change my mind," Bauer said, but even so, he lowered the phone and ended the call. "You have one minute."

"Thank you." Relief flooded over Patterson. "If you bring in the troops, he'll panic. The man won't have any qualms about putting a bullet in Julie's head. Or the kid, for that matter. He's probably done worse. If I go in alone, there's a chance they live, even if I die. It's a trade I'm willing to make if it comes to that, because we don't have any other choice. He's holding all the cards, Marcus, and I'm not going to risk losing Julie again."

"This is nuts. Are you even listening to yourself?"

"Yes, and I know what I'm doing. If Gibbs sends a team in there, guns blazing, Julie and her daughter don't stand a chance. He'll kill them before anyone can get to him. You know how these things end."

"Patterson…"

"He holds the high ground. He selected that location for a reason. He'll see that team coming a mile off… literally."

"It's a classic hostage situation. We'll get a negotiator in. Deal with him that way."

"Because that always ends so well."

"This isn't Waco, Patterson. He's just one man, and he wants to live."

"He's an assassin."

"Which is why you can't deal with this yourself."

"Look, I've spent my whole life since I was a teenager wondering what happened to my sister, thinking she was dead. I watched my family fall apart because of it. My mother abandoned us because she couldn't handle Julie's disappearance. My father spent years mourning her loss. He's never gotten over what happened. I joined the FBI because of Julie. How can I go to him and say that she was right there, just a short drive away—that I could have brought her home to him alive and well—and I let her die?"

"Trading your life for theirs isn't the answer, even if he lets them live, which I don't believe he will. Your father wouldn't want that, either."

"I don't have a choice." Patterson was desperate. Apart from anything else, the clock was ticking. She didn't have time to argue. "Besides, who said I'm going to die?"

"He did. And like you said, he's a trained assassin."

"And I'm a trained FBI agent. I know it's a trap, and I'm going to do everything in my power to stay alive and take him down."

"He has the upper hand."

"And I have determination."

"That isn't enough."

"We've faced worse." Patterson went to the room safe, unlocked it, and took out her gun.

"I thought he told you to come unarmed."

"He did, but he knows I won't. I'm not *that* stupid." She put on her shoulder holster and slipped the gun into it, then grabbed her jacket.

"Even more reason not to go. He isn't stupid, either."

"If you want to make that call, go ahead." Patterson went to step around Bauer. "But I'm going regardless, and you can't stop me."

"Okay. Fine." Bauer held up his hands. "But at least let's do this thing smart."

"Then you'll back down?"

"For now. But look, you're not going in alone. I'm coming with you, and if I think it's too dangerous, if it goes south, then we do it my way. Call in a team. Is that fair?"

"He told me not to bring anyone."

"Which is why we'll make sure he doesn't see me."

"How?"

"We'll figure that out on the way. He gave you three hours. We'd better get going if you don't want to be late."

"No. I go alone. It's too risky."

"This isn't up for discussion. We do this my way, or not at all."

"Marcus…"

"I mean it."

"Fine. Just don't get in my way." Patterson started toward the door. When Bauer didn't move, she turned around. "You coming?"

"Hold on a moment. I just need to make a call."

"I thought you agreed not to call this in."

"I did, but I'm not going out there unprepared. If you want to take him down and get your sister and her daughter out alive, you'll have to trust me."

"Guess I don't have a choice."

"No, you don't." Bauer dialed and lifted the phone to his ear again. After a brief conversation, of which Patterson could only hear one side, he hung up. "All done. We'll have to stop by the field office on our way out of town."

"I thought you said…"

"Hey, relax. I'm not going back on my word, but we need to collect something… to even the playing field."

"Like what?"

"You'll see." Bauer turned toward the connecting door. "Give me one minute, and I'll be with you."

Patterson nodded and watched him vanish into the room next door. When he returned, he was pushing his gun into its holster. His backup weapon was strapped to his ankle. He readjusted his trouser leg to cover it, put his jacket on, then stepped toward the door. "What are we waiting for? Let's go."

# NINETY

PATTERSON WAITED in the parking lot of the FBI's San Diego Field Office and stared out the car window, looking for Bauer to return. She glanced at her watch. He had been gone for fifteen minutes, and she was getting nervous that they wouldn't have time to reach the ghost town before the hitman's deadline expired.

Then, thankfully, he reappeared carrying what looked like a compact laptop.

When he climbed back in, she looked down at the device. "We stopped for *that*? What are you planning to do, check your email and pay a few bills on the way out there?"

"Funny. This isn't a laptop. It's a Stingray IMSI-catcher."

"A what?"

"A portable cellular transceiver system. It mimics a cell tower and forces phones to connect to it."

"And that helps us how?"

"Because the judge got back to us with that emergency warrant. We can trace Bonneville's phone, which the hitman used to call you. This device will find the phone, connect to it, and tell us where he is."

"We already know where he is. A ghost town out in the desert."

"No. We know *approximately* where he is. This will pinpoint his specific location within the ghost town."

"Which means we'll know if he's in that building with Julie or holed up somewhere else."

"Exactly. It minimizes your risk."

"If the phone is turned on."

"That doesn't matter. The phone will still connect to the nearest tower even if the unit is powered down, because it's never really fully disabled if the battery still has a charge, which we know it does."

"That doesn't mean he'll have the phone in his possession. He might have left it somewhere, like in his vehicle."

"Except he told you to call him when you arrive. If he answers, we'll know he's with the phone."

"Then what are we waiting for?" Patterson started the car. "Let's get my sister back."

"Not yet. There's one more thing we have to do, first." Bauer placed the cellular tracking device on the floor and climbed back out. "Come on."

Patterson exited the vehicle and followed him to the trunk. Ten minutes later, their task completed, she slammed the lid and climbed back behind the wheel.

After joining her, Bauer placed a hand on her arm. "You sure about this? It's an awful big risk you're taking."

"I don't have a choice." Patterson pulled out of the parking space and started toward the exit. "One way or another, I'm bringing Julie home... alive."

# NINETY-ONE

NINETY MINUTES after he spoke to Patterson Blake, Corbin Pope left Julie and her daughter tied up and gagged in the general store and went to his car, which he had parked further down the canyon beyond the boundaries of the old ghost town where it wouldn't be seen by anyone approaching from the highway several miles distant.

He opened the trunk and removed the gun he had purchased from Lawrence earlier that morning. An M110 SASS .308 semiautomatic sniper rifle fitted with a 3.5-10x scope and a bipod. He grabbed the accompanying box of ammo and closed the trunk. Then he set out to a point of high ground he had identified on his approach to the town. A steep rise covered with creosote bushes and burro-weed that overlooked what had once been Main Street and its two surviving buildings while providing the cover he needed to conceal himself.

He found an area of flat ground with good sightlines and put the gun down, then set about preparing his nest. After loading the weapon, he peered through the scope, making sure that his view of the street was unobstructed. After that, he checked and double checked the equipment, so that nothing would be left to chance.

Satisfied, he reached into his pocket and removed his cell phone. The other phone, the one he had taken from Carl before he killed him, was no longer in his possession. It was still in the general store. He had concealed it behind the rotting sales counter, making sure that Julie and her daughter didn't see him put it there.

Carl's phone was still on, although he had silenced the ringer and set it to forward calls to his own phone. This was important. Patterson Blake wasn't stupid, even if her devotion to her sister was blinding her objectivity. The FBI would have applied for a warrant to track Carl Bonneville's phone the moment he had called to set up the aborted meeting in the park. Pope was sure of that. If they were smart, they would have fast-tracked the warrant, citing the urgency of the situation. And with modern technology, the phone's location could be pinpointed with a device no bigger than a notebook computer. There was no way the FBI agent would walk into such a deadly situation blind. She would confirm that Pope was in that building with Julie and her daughter.

Except he wouldn't be.

When she called, he would be on the ridge, ready to take the kill shot. All he needed was for her to exit her vehicle and walk toward the general store believing he was inside waiting for her. And if she was tracking Bonneville's phone, which was stashed behind the counter, she would have no reason to think he was anywhere else.

The trap was set, and she would walk right into it.

Just get her into his sights, and boom, one dead FBI agent.

It wouldn't be his best work, but it would let him round out his career with a perfect kill ratio, a feat few other people in his profession could boast, if any. After that, it was adios. Sayonara. Ciao. He would craft a new ironclad identity and vanish, leaving others to whisper about the hitman who never failed. His myth would grow, embellished with each retelling, until he was more urban legend than man. And all the while, he would be far away, enjoying the fruits of his past labors in well-earned retirement.

Pope settled in, lying flat to the ground and ready to put his eye to the scope the moment Patterson Blake showed up. He checked his watch, figured he still had at least thirty minutes.

Then he waited.

# NINETY-TWO

PATTERSON HAD BEEN DRIVING for two hours when she reached the turnoff and the dusty road leading to the town of Hopefulness, California. After that, she drove for another twenty minutes through rugged desert terrain bordered by low scrub until the land around them rose on both sides as they entered a wide canyon. It was then, as they navigated a narrow pass, that Bauer told her to stop. She pulled over and came to a halt under the shade of a catclaw tree that was clinging to the top of a steep rise, its branches overhanging the trail.

"What are we doing?" she asked, glancing at Bauer.

"You have a phone call to make."

"He said to call when I arrive. We're not there, yet."

"It's close enough," Bauer said, picking up the device that looked like a laptop and setting it on his knees before opening it. "Because this is where I get out. We're half a mile from the town, and if the guy who has your sister sees me in the car, he might follow through with his threat to kill her and the kid. We can't risk that. But first, we need to confirm his location. You need to make that call."

Patterson nodded and pulled the phone provided by the FBI from her pocket. She glanced at Bauer, who was hunched over the cellular transceiver system, his fingers flying over the keyboard. "You ready?"

"Ready."

Patterson made the call.

It was answered on the first ring. "I told you to call when you arrived. I don't see you."

"I'm right outside of town," Patterson said, thinking fast. "But I need to know that Julie and her daughter are unharmed before I show myself."

"They're fine." There was a note of displeasure in the man's voice. "But if you keep disobeying me, they won't be."

"I didn't disobey you. I'm here just like you told me to be." Patterson glanced at Bauer, who was still tapping away on the keyboard and studying the device's screen. His face was a picture of concentration. "Put Julie on, let me talk to her, and then I'll continue into town."

"Come to me and you can see her for yourself. The general store. Far end of the street. Don't park too close. I want to make sure you're alone and unarmed before I let you into the building. You have ten minutes, or they die, starting with the kid."

The line went dead before Patterson could reply.

"Shit." Patterson pounded the steering will with her fist. "Please tell me you got his location."

"Sure did. I pinpointed him to within ten feet. He's in the general store, just like he said."

"That's all I need to know."

Bauer closed the transceiver and pushed it under his seat, then he opened the car door and unclipped his seatbelt. "I'll keep out of sight and walk from here. Don't be too hasty once you get there. Buy me some time to catch up."

"I'll do my best," said Patterson, as Bauer climbed from the car.

He leaned back in. "Good luck, and don't do anything rash. I'll do my best to back you up, but we have no idea what you're walking into."

"When have I ever done anything rash?" Patterson asked.

Bauer raised an eyebrow. "Just be careful." He tapped the roof of the car twice with the palm of his hand. "You'd better get moving. If he's watching the road and you're out of sight for too long, he'll get suspicious."

Bauer closed the door softly and waved for her to continue on. She started along the trail again, leaving her partner to walk through the cloud of dust kicked up by her tires. She could see him in her rearview mirror, hurrying along behind her and using the escarpments and scree covered slopes that rose from the canyon floor for cover. With any luck, Julie's captor would be so focused on her and the car that he wouldn't be looking for anyone following behind on foot.

She drove for another couple of minutes before the canyon widened and she saw the crumbling shell of an old stone building rising from the surrounding landscape. Beyond this was a dusty unpaved thoroughfare with the foundations of other buildings visible on each side, the structures they supported now nothing more than a scattering of bleached dry planks baking under the brutal desert sun. All except for one wooden building at the other end of the street that had somehow escaped the ravages of time mostly intact. Even if there had been any other similar structures left standing, the sign that still hung above the door provided ample clue that she had reached her destination.

Patterson slowed the car and crawled past the stone building toward the general store. Somewhere behind her, now out of sight and proceeding on foot, was Bauer. She wasn't sure how much use he would be, but she was glad he was there. If the worst happened and she didn't survive this encounter, he might still get the drop on her killer, then rescue Julie and the kid. Because she didn't trust the hitman's word that he would let them live, despite his assurances. Not for one moment.

When she was about fifty feet from the building, she stopped the car. After studying her surroundings for a moment, she pushed the car door open and climbed out. Julie's captor had told her to come unarmed. Reaching under her jacket, she removed the pistol from her shoulder holster, held the gun up for the hitman to see, then placed it on the driver's seat, before closing the car door. A second, smaller weapon, the Glock 27 Sub-Compact that Bauer had given her back in Dallas, was nestled in the small of her back, held in place by her belt, and concealed under her shirt. Normally, her backup weapon would be in an ankle holster, but she knew that would have been too obvious. She had agreed to come unarmed, but there was no way she was walking into that building with no means of defending herself, because despite the hitman's assurances, she suspected that the only way Julie and her daughter would walk out alive, was if she killed their captor. The only problem was, she had no idea how to accomplish that without getting herself killed, too.

# NINETY-THREE

AFTER HER CAPTOR LEFT, Julie sat for a while, wondering if he would return. Her daughter, tied to another chair on the other side of the post, was still sobbing quietly behind her gag. Julie wished she could comfort the young girl, but her own gag allowed nothing but muffled grunts, and she soon gave up in frustration. And as the minutes ticked by and stretched to what felt like hours, even though she suspected that nowhere near that much time had passed, her thoughts turned to her sister.

Patterson was driving through the desert on her way to the ghost town at that very moment in a futile quest that Julie feared would end with her sister's death. And it would be because of her.

For the first time since escaping Carl's farmhouse back in Arizona, Julie was certain that running had been a mistake. Not because it would have resulted in any better situation for herself and Cherub, but because then, at least, the other members of her family would still be safe.

If it weren't for the gag, she would have howled with frustration. If she hadn't opened her hotel room door the night before, none of this would be happening. But she had thought it was Gloria knocking. After all, the woman had phoned from the bar less than thirty minutes earlier, and she was so upset. How could Julie have refused her request to come over and talk, despite the late hour?

Now, though, Julie wondered if everything Gloria had told her about a friend of her ex showing up at the bar—that her ex-boyfriend would find out she was there and come looking for her—was even true. Which led Julie to an even darker thought. What had happened to Gloria after the phone call? The man who'd shown up at her door was clearly not averse to violence, at least if the gun he loaded into the trunk of his car, and his conversation with her sister, were anything to go by. Not to mention the pistol he had pushed into her face after she answered the door, expecting Gloria to be on the other side. Even though she didn't want to acknowledge it, Julie thought there was a good chance her captor had murdered Gloria before he knocked on her hotel room door in the middle of the night. His demeanor and previous actions indicated he wasn't someone who left witnesses alive. Which meant that regardless of what he promised, she and Cherub were in mortal danger and her sister was driving toward certain death.

Julie had long ago abandoned any hope of salvation for herself. Carl had made sure of that. Even after she escaped his clutches, she saw no future for herself beyond ensuring Cherub's safety. Now, not only was her daughter's life in danger, but that of her sister. If she just sat there and waited for events to play out, they would all end up buried in a remote desert grave come evening. She couldn't allow that. But her captor knew what he was doing. There was no give in the strips of cloth he had tied her up with. No matter how much she struggled and pulled on her bindings, she could not get loose.

That left the gag.

If she couldn't escape, then at least she could warn her sister that she was walking into a trap. Because she recognized the rifle her captor had picked up at the biker bar, if not by make and model, then by design. Carl had been as fascinated with military documentaries as his mother was with chat shows and shopping channels. On the evenings she had ended up in his bed for what he called her *nightly duties*—after he had pawed and abused her, put his hands all over her naked body—he would often turn the TV on and make her sit with him like they were a happily married couple instead of abuser and abused, while he watched shows about Navy SEALs or the Marines… or snipers.

Which was why she recognized that gun.

Her captor wasn't coming back. At least, not while Patterson was alive. He was out there somewhere with that gun, waiting for her sister to show up so that he could shoot her dead.

There was only one thing Julie could think of to do. Decades of exposure to the harsh desert environment had corroded the metal post behind her. It had probably been smooth once and painted a bright color, but was now pockmarked and scarred, with only the barest traces of paint remaining and a surface more akin to sandpaper. There were sharp edges in places where oxidation had eaten deep pits into the metal. Eventually, in several more decades, the decaying pole might fail entirely and allow the general store's second floor and roof to crash down with nothing left to support them. But right now, it was just about corroded enough for Julie's purposes.

She pressed her head against the post, trapping the fabric of the gag between the back of her skull and the rough metal. Then she started to grind her head against the metal, moving up and down in a sawing motion that she hoped would fray the fabric. If she had been able to move more freely, if her bindings had not been so tight, she might have gained enough leverage to slide the gag up and off her head. But as it was, she could only manage a few inches of vertical movement, even when she pressed her back against the post and tried to lift the chair.

It was slow going, and she had no idea if her efforts were

achieving anything except scraping the hair and skin from the back of her head and leaving her scalp bloodied and raw. But she persisted, clenching her jaw against the pain and ignoring the tears that flowed over her cheeks, even as she pressed harder still. Because if she didn't get that gag off before her sister arrived, Patterson wouldn't stand a chance.

# NINETY-FOUR

POPE WATCHED the car approaching from his vantage point on the ridge above town, kicking up a plume of dust on the winding trail into town as it went. The vehicle vanished from sight behind a rise, reappeared again, then disappeared as the land rose higher once more. But this time, it didn't come back into view.

He tensed, wondering if the FBI agent was up to something. But then his phone rang. He answered. It was Patterson Blake. He suspected she had stopped where she did because the escarpment shielded her from view. Right now, she was probably pinpointing his position, or rather the location of Carl's phone, even as she talked to him.

He hung up, satisfied that the FBI agent believed he was there, along with Julie and the kid, waiting for her in the general store. She was probably hoping to take him out somehow, save her family, and walk away alive. Well, she had a surprise coming. Not that she would have long to think about it, Pope mused, as her black sedan reappeared and proceeded slowly into town. The moment she stepped from the car and started toward the building he would put a bullet through her, a center mass kill shot that would end her ability to think about anything ever again.

The vehicle was rolling past the old jail now. Blake was taking it steady, no doubt wary of a trap, as she should be. It continued up Main Street and stopped a distance away from the general store, just as he had instructed. The driver's side door opened. She stepped from the car and pulled her service weapon out, holding it up. She placed it on the front seat and closed the door, no doubt in an attempt to convince him that she was now unarmed. But Pope wasn't that stupid. There was no way Patterson Blake would walk into a situation that dangerous, willingly offering herself up, without a way to kill him if the opportunity arose. But it didn't matter, because Pope held the high ground, and the advantage. An ambush she would never expect.

He settled down behind the gun and waited for the FBI agent to move toward the building. But he didn't shoot. Not yet. The gun was capable of eliminating a target at a range of over half a mile. This shot was nowhere near that long, but he still had to take wind speed and gravity into account, even in the millpond air of the Anza Borrego desert. Pope made some quick mental calculations, worked out his lead time, which amounted to how long the bullet would be in the air and the forward speed of his target. Once that was done, he set his lead ahead of the FBI agent, took aim, and waited as she walked toward the building and into his point of impact. Then he cleared his lungs, held his breath, and took the shot.

# NINETY-FIVE

THE BACK of Julie's head felt like it was on fire. Blood weaved down the back of her neck and wormed under her collar as she scraped her head against the pole, grinding away at the gag, and rubbing the skin of her scalp raw in the process.

Cherub's sobs had diminished to occasional whimpers, either because she had calmed down after their captor left, or she was too exhausted to keep crying.

From somewhere beyond the building, she heard the faint purr of a car engine growing steadily louder. Her chest tightened. It was Patterson. There was no one else it could be, and she was driving into a deadly trap. The man with the gun was out there somewhere, waiting for her to show up.

Julie sawed harder, pressing the back of her head against the post's rough surface with so much force that sharp needles of pain erupted with each new pass.

The car was closer now. It sounded like it was right outside. She heard a crunch of tires, then the engine noise ceased.

The slam of a car door.

Her sister was out in the open now and easy pickings.

Julie intensified her efforts, ignoring the searing agony that flared from her scalp down through the back of her neck. The blood was flowing freely. Much more of this, and she wouldn't have any skin left back there.

She tensed, expecting to hear the crack of a rifle at any moment.

Then, with one last, almost unbearable effort, the gag loosened, dropped away, and fell into her lap.

But she wasn't done yet. There was still the tight ball of fabric in her mouth.

She pushed at it with her tongue, working the obstruction forward with what felt like excruciating slowness. But just when she thought her efforts were succeeding, the balled-up wad of denim caught behind her teeth.

She forced her jaw open wider. Pushed with renewed vigor.

The fabric remained stubbornly caught.

There was a moment when she thought it was useless, that she didn't have enough strength to expel the wadded denim with only her tongue. If her hands had been free… but they were bound behind her back. Her sister was going to die, and all because she was too weak to spit out a stupid piece of denim.

But then, suddenly, the ball of denim shifted, slid past her teeth, and tumbled over her lips. It bounced off her leg and dropped out of sight onto the floor.

Julie sucked in a gasping breath, filled her lungs, and screamed a frantic warning at the top of her voice, even as the crack of a rifle split the air.

# NINETY-SIX

PATTERSON WAS WALKING toward the building, taking it slow and watching for any sign of movement from behind the empty glassless windows, when a frantic cry rang out from somewhere inside the old general store.

"It's a trap. Don't come any—"

The end of her sister's warning was drowned out by a sudden blast from somewhere high above her. Patterson was already turning to dive behind the car in a frantic attempt to reach cover. She felt a rush of air as the bullet flew past, dangerously close.

A second shot rang out.

This time the bullet found its mark, slamming into her chest with a force that sent her spinning out of control even as she launched herself toward the vehicle.

Her feet left the ground.

There was a momentary sensation of weightlessness before a wave of pressure like nothing she had ever experienced before spread across her chest, forcing the air from her lungs so fast she was sure they must have burst.

She impacted the hood of her car, bounced, and rolled off.

The world spun around like an out-of-control carousel as she tumbled toward the ground. The feeling of weightlessness returned, if only for an instant. After that, a merciful darkness descended and then there was nothing.

# NINETY-SEVEN

CORBIN POPE TOOK the shot at the same moment that Julie's frantic cry sent Patterson scrambling to find cover. The bullet missed its target and whistled through empty air inches away from where she should have been. He jerked the gun, trying to compensate for her sudden backpedal, and fired again. With no time to recalculate, he was gratified to see the FBI agent spin in the air and tumble sideways when he scored a hit to her torso, anyway.

She flipped over, landed on the hood of her car, and vanished behind it, leaving only her legs visible.

Pope waited for her to move.

When she didn't, he rose to his feet. Leaving the sniper rifle in place, he pulled the pistol he had found in Julie's hotel room from the waistband of his pants and retraced his steps from the top of the range back down to Main Street. It was tough going, and he slipped at one point as a loose rock gave way under his foot. He almost fell, but managed to regain his balance at the last moment even as a small avalanche of scree went tumbling away down the slope.

Reaching flat ground, he approached Patterson Blake's car

and the prone agent. He kept the gun raised, ready to put another bullet in her if the FBI agent so much as twitched.

He rounded the vehicle to find her sprawled on the ground, face down. She still wasn't moving. His shot should have punched right through her, but he saw no obvious exit wound, even though she appeared to be dead. With no time to adjust his aim after Blake scrambled for cover, he had squeezed off a frantic Hail Mary and scored a lucky hit. He knew that much by the way she jerked with the impact. The bullet could have entered at an angle, with the exit wound concealed by the way she was laying. Or the bullet might have glanced off a rib, changed direction, and buried itself somewhere deep inside her body. There was no way to tell.

Not that he cared. She was down, and that was all that mattered. Even if the FBI agent had somehow survived the last bullet, the one he was about to put in her head would seal the deal. Pope had never cared much for guns, at least when it came to his work. They were crude and messy. They lacked panache. It was also hard to disguise the end result as an accident, and Pope had found that it was easier to get away with murder when no one suspected. But that didn't mean he wasn't well versed in how to commit an execution, and the so-called *Failure Drill*, where the shooter followed a double tap to the torso that might otherwise leave the target alive, with a third shot to the head, just to make sure.

Pope's original intention had been a single, center mass kill shot, sniper style. With the high velocity rifle and such a short range, he didn't need a double tap, because it was unlikely anyone could survive a direct hit. The *Failure Drill* was more often employed with less powerful weapons in close quarters combat. But even if he hadn't strictly followed the *two to the body, one to the head* technique, he knew one thing. A bullet through the skull meant you weren't getting up again, and Pope was taking no chances.

He stepped close to the FBI agent's prone body, drew in a deep, cleansing breath, released it slowly, and took aim.

# NINETY-EIGHT

BAUER WAS ALMOST at the ghost town, staying low to the ground and using the rugged, uneven terrain for cover, when he heard the shots. He drew his gun and broke into a sprint, all thought of concealment now abandoned. The shots had come from somewhere above him and out in the open, and not from inside the general store located at the other end of town. They also hadn't originated from either of Patterson's Glocks. The twin reports sounded more like a high velocity rifle. That could only mean one thing. Patterson had walked into an ambush.

He rounded a curve and saw the town ahead of him, or at least what remained of it. Patterson's car was parked toward the far end of what had once been Main Street, near the dilapidated wooden structure where the hitman had claimed to be waiting for her with Julie and the kid. He could see the general store sign hanging above the door. But it was the other thing he saw that made his blood run cold.

Patterson was down. She lay on the ground next to the car, and she wasn't moving. At least one of the shots he'd heard must had found its mark. And standing over her, with his pistol pointed at Patterson's head, was the hitman. He was facing away from Bauer and hadn't yet noticed the FBI agent's approach, but there was no doubt it was the same person they had apprehended in Las Vegas. Bauer recognized his wide shoulders, lean physique, and dark hair. But it was more than that. The way he carried himself, his confident stance and cool demeanor, only added to Bauer's certainty.

Bauer couldn't tell if Patterson was alive or dead, but in another few seconds it wouldn't matter. The hitman was about to put a bullet in her brain and end all uncertainty.

He hurried forward, raised his gun, and issued a loud command. "FBI. Drop the gun, put your hands in the air, and turn around."

For a moment, the hitman didn't move, then he turned slowly, but he didn't discard the weapon. Instead, Bauer found himself staring down the weapon's barrel.

"What a surprise," said the hitman, one side of his mouth curling up into a half smile. "Special Agent Marcus Bauer. I told your partner to come alone."

"Yeah, she's not very good at listening." Bauer continued forward until the two men were separated by no more than twenty feet. "Do as I said and put the gun down, nice and slow, then step away with your hands in the air."

"Or what?" The hitman was about as cool and collected as Bauer had ever seen for someone with a loaded pistol pointed at them. "Strikes me that we're at something of an impasse. Either one of us twitch, we end up shooting each other. I can't attest to your accuracy, but I guarantee my shot will have its intended effect, and you will be dead before you hit the ground."

"You're very confident for a man who isn't sure whether he scored a kill shot," Bauer said, his gaze shifting momentarily to Patterson's inert form, before he looked back at the hitman. "Maybe you're not quite as good as you think."

"Oh, I'm pretty sure she's dead, despite her sister's unfortunate warning that almost ruined my plans. But on one point, I will concede. My gag tying skills could use a little work."

"Then why were you standing with a gun pointed at her head?"

"It never hurts to seal the deal." The hitman wet his lips. "The way I see it, Agent Bauer, we're in a standoff. Neither of us dare make a move against the other for fear of getting shot themselves. Therefore, I have a proposal. You let me climb into my car and drive out of here unimpeded, and both of us live. Moreover, you can try to save your partner if she isn't already dead, which she probably is. Either way, you get to rescue Julie and the kid. Bring them home alive. What do you think?"

"I think you're full of shit. Now do what I told you."

"Not going to happen." The hitman's finger tensed on the trigger.

Bauer realized the assassin was going to shoot a hair's breadth before the shot rang out. He tensed, even as he squeezed off a round of his own in return, then waited for the hitman's bullet to slam into him and end his life. And in that last moment, an image of Pheobe's face flashed through his mind, accompanied by a pang of bitter sorrow, because he would never get to see her again, or tell her how much he loved her.

# NINETY-NINE

IT HURT TO BREATHE. Patterson forced her eyes open, and for a moment she couldn't figure out where she was. She saw dust and rocks. A black shape curving away from her. Then, in an instant, it all came flooding back. She was lying on the ground near her car and staring at the sidewall of her tire. And she had been shot.

There were voices. Two of them. The first was Marcus Bauer. The other was the hitman. She recognized him from their phone conversation.

She shifted, praying that whatever injuries she had sustained were not too bad. That she wasn't bleeding out. When she looked down, she saw no blood, even though pain wracked her chest. When she and Bauer had stopped at the field office on their way out of San Diego, they had put on ballistic vests. The bullet must have impacted her body armor. Even so, Patterson worried she had been shot. The hitman had made a sniper's nest on the rise overlooking town. She had only realized her mistake when Julie shouted out a warning of the trap she had walked into. Turning, she threw herself back toward the car for cover, but there was no time. She heard the crack of a rifle, felt the bullet whizz past her, then a second shot rang out in quick succession, before her world shattered into a cacophony of pain. The last thing she remembered was tumbling across the car's hood and slamming into the ground. After that, everything was a blank until now. She must have passed out.

Patterson wondered how she was still alive. The hitman was clearly using a high-powered rifle, probably a sniper weapon. At such close range, her FBI standard issue ballistic vest wouldn't stop a weapon like that. Maybe if she had been wearing special threat armor, but she wasn't. The bullet should have punched right through the vest and into her body.

Deciding she wasn't mortally wounded Patterson turned her attention to the hitman. He was standing several feet away with his back turned. Further away still was Marcus Bauer, gun raised. They appeared to be in a standoff.

The conversation was nearing a climax. Neither man was going to back down. It could only end one way.

Then she remembered her backup weapon pushed into her belt in the small of her back. She moved ever so slightly, pulled her arm out from beneath her body with great effort, and reached back to it.

The pain in her chest reached a level eight. The bullet might not have punched through her vest, but there was no way it hadn't broken a couple of ribs. She prayed that was the only damage.

Gritting her teeth, Patterson reached further back. She fumbled for a moment before her hand brushed the grip of her Glock 27 Sub-Compact. She closed her fingers over it and slipped the weapon free.

The hitman was about to shoot. She could see it in the way he tensed his legs and shoulders. Another couple of seconds, and Bauer would be dead, because this time the assassin wouldn't bother going for the torso. He was close enough to go for a headshot.

She couldn't let that happen.

Mustering all her strength, Patterson rolled over onto her

back and swung the gun up, clenching her jaw against the fresh wave of pain that almost caused her to pass out all over again.

Unlike herself and Bauer, the hitman wasn't wearing a ballistic vest. She could tell by the way his shirt fell over his body. She aimed for a point between the assassin's shoulder blades, where she had the greatest chance of scoring a hit in her weakened state.

Then she pulled the trigger.

# ONE HUNDRED

BAUER LOWERED HIS GUN. Somehow, against the odds, he was alive and unscathed.

The same could not be said for the hitman. He stumbled forward, a look of utter surprise transforming his face. He stayed upright for a few seconds more, the fabric of his shirt turning a deep crimson, before his jaw went slack and he pitched forward. And there, behind him, lying on her back with her gun raised, was Patterson Blake.

He could hardly believe it. She was alive.

Then he realized something else. It wasn't the hitman who had fired. It was Patterson. She had taken her shot a fraction of a second before the assassin could do the same, hitting him in the back. Bauer's retaliatory shot had slammed into the man's chest a split-second later, all but sealing his fate.

Bauer rushed forward, kicked the assassin's gun away even though he could tell that the hitman was already dead. Just to be sure, he bent down and checked for a pulse. Nothing.

He went to Patterson and kneeled next to her.

"Are you alright?"

She grimaced. "I've been better. Feels like I got thumped in the chest by a baseball bat."

Bauer studied her for a moment. "No blood. I don't see any injuries. Your vest must have stopped the bullet."

"Gun like that, it should have killed me." Patterson struggled to sit up.

"Bullet must have hit at an oblique angle and deflected." Bauer took her hand and helped her. "You're going to be black and blue, though."

Patterson winced. "At the very least. Probably cracked a few ribs."

"Better than the alternative."

Patterson nodded, then she glanced toward the general store. "Julie."

Patterson's sister had slipped Bauer's mind in the heat of the moment. He stood and pulled his partner up. She leaned on him for a few seconds, her face crunched with pain, then she took a stumbling step forward.

They made their way toward the old general store, with Bauer supporting Patterson, a hand around her waist, as she leaned on him.

They saw Julie the moment they entered the building.

"Oh my God." Patterson pulled away from Bauer and rushed forward, her injuries momentarily forgotten. "I can't believe it's really you."

Julie's eyes flew wide. "Me either."

Patterson reached the chair and began tugging at the knots that held Julie in place.

Bauer stepped forward and went to the little girl to do the same. The first thing he did was pull the gag off and throw it aside. "We're going to get you guys out of here, okay?"

"What about that guy?" Julie said, ripping the restraints off her wrists and chest the moment Patterson untied the knots. "He might still be out there. It's not safe."

"He's dead," Bauer said, freeing the little girl and helping her up. "He won't be bothering anyone, ever again."

Patterson was kneeling now and working on Julie's ankles.

The bindings fell away, and Julie sprang to her feet, then helped Patterson up before throwing her arms around her in a tight hug.

"Ouch." Patterson grimaced.

"Sorry. You're hurt?" Julie loosened her grip.

"Just a bit. I'll be fine." Tears were streaming down Patterson's face. But for once, they weren't tears of sorrow. "Jelly. I never thought I'd see you again." She almost added, *not alive, anyway*, but she didn't.

"You should know better than to give up on your big sister." Julie released her sister and turned as the little girl came up beside them and pressed shyly against her mother. "Patterson, I want you to meet your niece."

"Hello," Patterson said, looking down at the girl. "What's your name?"

"Cherub," the girl replied, meeting Patterson's gaze for a moment before dropping her eyes.

"That was *his* name for her," Julie said, a note of venom in her voice. "We're going to fix that." She glanced down at her daughter. "We'll find you a better name. Something that won't remind us of him."

"Can I choose my own name?" the girl asked eagerly.

"We'll see." Julie put an arm around her daughter. "But not right now."

Bauer was standing to one side, his arms folded. Now he stepped forward. "I hate to break up the family reunion, but we need to call this in." He looked at Patterson. "And you need a hospital."

"Sure. Go ahead. Make the call," Patterson said. She took her phone from her pocket. Her *real* phone, not the one she had used to call Bonneville and the hitman. "I have a call of my own to make."

She unlocked the phone and dialed. A moment later, her father answered. "Peanut?"

"Dad." Patterson swallowed a sob. "I have someone here who wants to say hello."

"You okay?" her father asked. "You sound strange."

"I'm fine." Patterson held the phone out to Julie. "Here."

Her sister stared at it for a long moment, then reached out with a trembling hand. She put the phone to her ear. Her bottom lip trembled. She remained silent.

"Go ahead," Patterson urged.

Julie looked at Patterson, and their eyes locked for a moment, then she nodded. "Dad? Hi, it's me... Julie!"

# ONE HUNDRED ONE

**TWO MONTHS LATER**

PARK PIZZA NEVER CHANGED, thought Patterson as she glanced around the institution that had occupied the same red brick building in Queens for as long as she could remember. But some things did change, even when you had given up hope.

She looked across the table at her sister and resisted the urge to cry for joy. It had been eight weeks since the events at the ghost town in California, and she was mostly healed. The hitman's bullet had cracked three ribs and left her so bruised that for a month afterward her chest had resembled a brown and yellow map of some strange continent.

She had been lucky. If the bullet hadn't hit the way it did, slamming into her at an oblique angle and deflecting off her vest, she wouldn't now be sitting opposite her sister, marveling that Julie was back with them after so long.

"I still can't believe this," said her father, looking around the table at his two daughters, and the grandchild who had spent the last two months following him around with gleeful excitement and calling him Grampy. "My family is back together after all these years."

*Not quite back together*, Patterson thought.

The moment she found out that her daughter was alive, their mother had booked a last-minute flight to LaGuardia from Colorado, where she was living with her latest boyfriend, a man named Tim who Patterson had never met and wasn't inclined to. Their mother had stayed for two weeks, saying all the right things and doling out plenty of hugs, at least to her daughters and newly discovered grandchild. But beneath the joy, she was distant, as if Julie's reappearance had forced her to confront the bad decisions she had made in the months and years following her elder daughter's disappearance.

When she had declared her intention to leave and fly back to Colorado, Patterson was almost relieved. The recombined family unit felt nothing like the one shattered by her sister's disappearance and her mother's subsequent actions years before. There was an underlying tension that weaved itself throughout all their interactions, and in the end, Patterson wondered if her mother had departed not so much because she was desperate to get back to Colorado and Tim, but because she didn't want to be reminded of all she had lost when she walked away. But if Patterson had expected an apology from her mother, an admission of her negligence, it never came. In the end, all she got was a mumbled *I love you*, before she climbed into the taxi waiting to take her back to the airport.

If Julie had been disappointed at her mother's indifference, she had showed it only once, later that night when she sat down on the sofa next to her sister and said, "Mom isn't like I remember."

"No, she's not," Patterson had replied.

Julie had taken her sister's hand and squeezed it. "But that's okay, because you're exactly like I remember."

And that was the last they spoke on the subject.

In the weeks since, the four of them had grown steadily closer, finding their way through a vast sea of conflicting emotions that had left them lurching from bitterness at the years they had lost, to overwhelming happiness at those they would now be able to share.

Julie's daughter was the one who best navigated this ocean, taking the world in her stride and finding joy everywhere. She had swiftly discarded the name forced upon her by Carl Edward Bonneville and adopted a new one after Julie had climbed into the attic and found her old copy of Black Beauty—the book she herself had loved more than any other as a child—and read it to her daughter. She had chosen the name Anna, in honor of the book's author, and also because it was the name her mother had chosen to live under in San Diego.

"Peanut?" Her father's voice cut through Patterson's thoughts.

"Sorry." Patterson snapped back to the present, realized everyone was looking at her. "I was miles away."

Her father tapped the menu. "Let's order. I'm hungry. You know what you want on the pizza? I'm good with anything except those fancy toppings."

Anna looked up from the paper placemat she was coloring with a pack of crayons. "What are fancy toppings?"

The two sisters exchanged a look and spoke in unison. "Anything but pepperoni." Then they collapsed into fits of laughter.

Franklin Blake glanced between his daughters. "I'm glad the pair of you agree. Two large pepperoni pizzas it is."

---

An hour later, out on the sidewalk, before heading to the subway and the train that would take her across town to her apartment, Patterson hugged her sister. "I know I keep saying this, but I love you."

"Love you, too." Her sister said as they broke the hug. She lifted her hand, her index finger crooked. "PB…"

"And J," Patterson replied, lifting her own finger and looping it around her sister's. "Forever inseparable."

Julie laughed. "Amen to that."

Anna looked at them with a confused frown. "What are you talking about?"

Patterson looked down at her. "It's a sister thing."

"I don't get it."

"Don't worry," said Julie, putting an arm around her daughter. "I'll tell you all about it, I promise. But right now, it's past your bedtime."

"But I'm not tired," Anna said, even as she suppressed a yawn. "Can I stay with Aunt Patterson tonight?"

"Not tonight," Julie said. "It's only Tuesday, and you have school tomorrow."

"I don't like school." Anna scrunched her face up.

Patterson laughed and looked down at her niece. "I'll let you in on a secret. Neither did your mother."

"That's not true," Julie said. "I loved school."

"Funny," Franklin said, shaking his head. "I don't remember it that way."

"Hey," Julie glared at her sister and father. "I'm trying to set a good example here. The least you two could do is back me up."

"Sorry." Patterson kneeled and took Anna's hand. "Tell you what, if you're good for the rest of the week, and you do all your homework, you can come stay with me at the weekend. We'll go to Coney Island for hotdogs and ice cream, and anything else you want."

The little girl's face lit up. "I'll be good, I promise."

"I know you will." Patterson stood and gave her sister another tight hug, then threw her arms around her father in a quick embrace. She watched the three of them as they walked down the block toward the Ozone Park home that she and Julie had grown up in. Then she made her way to the subway. Fifteen minutes later, she was riding the train to her apartment, where she hoped the other important person in her life would be waiting.

# ONE HUNDRED TWO

WHEN PATTERSON ARRIVED BACK at her apartment, she found it silent and empty. Disappointed, she made her way to the bathroom and ran a shower. She had hoped that Jonathan Grant would be there, waiting for her, but since accepting a promotion to Special Agent in Charge of the Criminal Division at the New York field office, his workload had only increased, and they had seen less of each other than she would have liked.

It didn't help that she hadn't been in the office. After four weeks of medical leave, she had taken another month of personal time while she sorted out her feelings and readjusted to life with her sister back. Now, that time was coming to an end, and she would have to decide. Return to the FBI or make her personal leave permanent and look for something else to do with the rest of her life.

She undressed and stepped into the shower, closing her eyes and relishing the hot stream of water that played over her body. She stayed that way for a while, unwilling to swap the warm water for the chilly bathroom air. Then, just when she was mustering the courage to step out, the curtain pushed aside, and Jonathan Grant stepped in.

He wrapped his arms around her and held Patterson tight. "Sorry I wasn't here when you got home."

"That's okay. You're here now." Patterson pushed against him and rested her head on his shoulder. When she had first returned from California, Patterson had wondered if their relationship would survive all that had happened. She had sensed him growing distant during the time she was searching for Julie and didn't know whether it was because of his imminent promotion, her absence from New York, or a combination of both. But in the weeks since, things had improved. His promotion had come through, which meant he was working longer hours than ever, but they still found time to spend with each other, even if it was stolen moments at the end of the day, and the occasional lazy Sunday morning.

She had no idea where the relationship was going, or where they would be a year, five years, or even ten years from now. But at that moment, they were good. They'd even talked about moving in together, although the matter was far from settled. Neither of their apartments were big enough for a couple, and there was also Julie to consider. Right now, she and Anna were living with their father, but the arrangement was far from ideal. What had seemed like a large house when they were children now felt cramped with the three of them in it. Yet Patterson wasn't sure that Julie was ready to strike out on her own. She was doing well, but Carl Edward Bonneville was never far away, even in death. He haunted her dreams, and even though she was seeing a therapist, Patterson wondered how long the emotional scars would take to heal. Perhaps they never would. Which was why Patterson suspected that eventually her sister and niece would need somewhere else to go, somewhere they could feel safe, but take a small step toward independence. And where better than the home of an FBI agent?

"Hey," Grant said, wiping a strand of wet hair from Patterson's face. "You look like you're miles away."

"Sorry. Just thinking about Julie. She's doing better, but..."

"Give her time. What she went through… you can't expect her go get over it in a couple of months."

"I know."

"And the money will help."

"I hope so," Patterson said. They had found a duffle bag full of cash in the hitman's car back in California when they searched it. Almost fifty grand. And along with the money was a small stack of the flyers Bonneville had printed up, and also his wallet. After forensics examined the bag and cash, they had quickly determined that it must have belonged to Bonneville, because his fingerprints were all over it, and the only way that could have happened was if the hitman had taken it from his hotel room after he killed him. Since Anna was Bonneville's only surviving heir, it would go to her, with Julie acting as custodian. And even if there was any doubt regarding the money's origin, no one was willing to do much about it under the circumstances. Julie and her daughter had gone through a living hell, and it just felt right that the money should go to them. "It won't undo the past, and all they went through, but it *will* give them the chance of a better future. For that, I'm grateful."

"Speaking of which, have you given any thought to your own future, and coming back to the Bureau?"

"I have," said Patterson. "And I'm no closer to an answer than I was before."

Grant was silent for a moment. He looked into her eyes, as if he would find an answer there that she wasn't otherwise able to give him. Eventually, he spoke. "I'm putting together a new task force, and I need someone to lead it. I can't think of a better person than you."

"Me?" Patterson was bewildered. "Less than four months ago, I was suspended for losing my shit in the field. Marilyn Khan would happily have left me sidelined for the rest of my career, except that my search for Julie was useful to her. I'm hotheaded, impetuous, and I have a problem towing the line. What on earth makes you think I'm leadership material?"

"You're also tenacious, loyal, and have a knack for thinking outside the box. Those are attributes I can use. Besides, it's not up to Marilyn Khan anymore. She's happily on the next rung of the ladder and only looking further up. I'm in charge now."

"I still think you're nuts. There must be other people with more experience."

"I'm not so sure about that. You've caught more serial killers and murderers in the past four months than most federal agents manage in a lifetime. And the job comes with a promotion. Supervisory Special Agent. What do you say?"

Patterson wasn't sure how to respond. She had been considering whether to even stay with the Bureau, and now she was being asked to come back in the most unusual manner ever. "You're seriously asking me this right now? I must be the first FBI agent ever to have been offered a promotion while standing naked in the shower with her supervisor."

"It is a little unorthodox, I'll admit," grant said with a grin, "and a first for me, too."

"I'm relieved to hear *that*," Patterson shot back. "Otherwise, we might be having a whole different conversation."

"So, do I get an answer? Because the shower's getting cold, and I can think of better things we could be doing."

"You haven't told me what this task force is about yet," Patterson said.

"Missing persons. Specifically cold cases like your sister's. People who might have fallen prey to monsters like Carl Edward Bonneville. You brought Julie home, but there are a lot more victims out there who need your help. And if you still need convincing, there will be a familiar face on the task force along with you."

"Please tell me it's not you," Patterson said. "The last thing I need is my boss breathing down my neck twenty-four hours a day."

Grant chuckled. "Relax. It's not me. I spoke to the Dallas field office last week, and they've agreed to transfer Special Agent

Bauer to New York. Since the two of you work together so well, I figured it was a no brainer."

"Marcus?" Patterson could hardly believe what she was hearing. "I can't imagine Phoebe's happy about that."

"Actually, she's transferring right alongside him. You'll need a research assistant on the task force. Someone detail oriented and focused. She's perfect for the job. They're arriving in New York next week, which is why I need an answer."

"That's a lot to drop on me out of the blue. Can I think about it?" Patterson asked, pushing the shower curtain back and stepping out before grabbing a towel.

"Sure." Grant turned the water off and joined her. "But don't take too long, okay? I can't hold the position open forever."

"Just a few days, I promise." Patterson dried herself, then took Grant's hand and led him into the bedroom. Tonight, she was happy to spend time with the man she loved. That was enough. But deep down, she already knew what her answer would be, because Grant was right. There were other victims out there who needed her help, people just like Julie still waiting to be found, and she had no intention of turning her back on them. And with Marcus and Phoebe on the team, they would be unstoppable.

# ABOUT THE AUTHORS

A. M. Strong is the pen name of supernatural action and adventure fiction author Anthony M. Strong.

Sonya Sargent grew up in Vermont and is an avid reader when she isn't working on books of her own. They divide their time between Florida's sunny Space Coast and a tranquil island in Maine.

Find out more about the authors at
AMStrongAuthor.com

Made in United States
North Haven, CT
29 August 2024